Praise for  and the Wi

"Erica Ridley is a delight!"

—Julia Quinn, *New York Times* bestselling
author of *Bridgerton*

"Erica Ridley's love stories are warm, witty and irresistible. I want to be a Wynchester!"

—Eloisa James, *New York Times* bestselling
author of *My Last Duchess*

"Ridley's motley crew of Wynchester siblings is as charming as it is unforgettable."

—BookPage

The Duke Heist

"This entrancing Regency . . . is a knockout."

—*Publishers Weekly*, starred review

"Schemes, heists, and forgeries abound in this charming series starter. This unconventional and quirky Regency will have readers falling for the plucky family."

—*Library Journal*

The Perks of Loving a Wallflower

"A plot full of mystery, high jinks, and tender personal revelations."

—*New York Times*

"The holy grail for Regency fans: like Georgette Heyer, but with sex ... a feminist fairy tale readers will rejoice in."

—Publishers Weekly, starred review

"Completely enchanting."

—Kirkus, starred review

"[An] exquisitely written, utterly transcendent romance that perfectly captures the joy of being loved for who you truly are ... pure reading bliss."

—Booklist, starred review

"This clever novel will delight readers."

—Library Journal, starred review

"A sapphic Regency romp that radiates all the good, fuzzy feelings readers want in a romance."

—BookPage

Nobody's Princess

"Ridley hits the sweet spot of tickling readers' funny bones and pulling on their heartstrings in equal measure. This is a joy."

—Publishers Weekly, starred review

"Writing with plenty of panache, a flair for thoughtful characterization, and an exhilarating sense of humor, Ridley deftly delivers another marvelously imaginative addition to her Wild Wynchesters series that proves to be another perfect dose of reading joy."

—Booklist, starred review

my
Rogue
to
Ruin

BOOKS BY ERICA RIDLEY

The Wild Wynchesters

The Duke Heist
The Perks of Loving a Wallflower
Nobody's Princess
My Rogue to Ruin

The Dukes of War

The Viscount's Tempting Minx
The Earl's Defiant Wallflower
The Captain's Bluestocking Mistress
The Major's Faux Fiancée
The Brigadier's Runaway Bride
The Pirate's Tempting Stowaway
The Duke's Accidental Wife
A Match, Unmasked

Rogues to Riches

Lord of Chance
Lord of Pleasure
Lord of Night
Lord of Temptation
Lord of Secrets
Lord of Vice
Lord of the Masquerade

Magic & Mayhem

Kissed by Magic
Must Love Magic
Smitten by Magic

Heist Club

The Rake Mistake
The Modiste Mishap

The 12 Dukes of Christmas

Once Upon a Duke
Kiss of a Duke

Wish Upon a Duke
Never Say Duke
Dukes, Actually
The Duke's Bride
The Duke's Embrace
The Duke's Desire
Dawn with a Duke
One Night with a Duke
Ten Days with a Duke
Forever Your Duke
Making Merry

Gothic Love Stories

Too Wicked to Kiss
Too Sinful to Deny
Too Tempting to Resist
Too Wanton to Wed
Too Brazen to Bite

Lords in Love

Beguiling the Duke
Taming the Rake
Romancing the Heiress
Defying the Earl
Matching the Marquess
Chasing the Bride
Undressing the Duke

The Siren's Retreat

A Tryst by the Sea
An Affair by the Sea
A Spinster by the Sea
Love Letters by the Sea

my Rogue to Ruin

ERICA RIDLEY

FOREVER
New York Boston

Copyright © 2023 by Erica Ridley

Cover design and illustration by Caitlin Sacks.
Cover copyright © 2023 by Hachette Book Group, Inc.

Forever
Hachette Book Group
1290 Avenue of the Americas, New York, NY 10104
read-forever.com
twitter.com/readforeverpub

First Edition: September 2023

Forever is an imprint of Grand Central Publishing. The Forever name and logo are trademarks of Hachette Book Group, Inc.

The publisher is not responsible for websites (or their content) that are not owned by the publisher.

The Hachette Speakers Bureau provides a wide range of authors for speaking events. To find out more, go to hachettespeakersbureau.com or email HachetteSpeakers@hbgusa.com.

Forever books may be purchased in bulk for business, educational, or promotional use. For information, please contact your local bookseller or the Hachette Book Group Special Markets Department at special.markets@hbgusa.com.

Library of Congress Cataloging-in-Publication Data

Names: Ridley, Erica, author.
Title: My rogue to ruin / Erica Ridley.
Description: First edition. | New York : Forever, 2023. | Series: The wild Wynchesters ; 4
Identifiers: LCCN 2023012572 | ISBN 9781538726112 (trade paperback) | ISBN 9781538726129 (ebook)
Subjects: LCSH: Art--Forgeries--Investigation--Fiction. | Extortion--Fiction. | Aristocracy (Social class)--England--Fiction. | London (England)--Social life and customs--19th century--Fiction. | LCGFT: Romance fiction. | Novels of manners. | Novels.
Classification: LCC PS3618.I392255 M9 2023 | DDC 813/.6--dc23/eng/20230327
LC record available at https://lccn.loc.gov/2023012572

ISBNs: 9781538726112 (trade paperback), 9781538726129 (ebook)

Printed in the United States of America

LSC-C

Printing 1, 2023

To anyone who has ever wondered if you were enough:
You are.

And to Roy, for everything.

my
Rogue
to
Ruin

1

✿

*I*t was a glorious morning for a robbery.

The warm sunlight felt like splashes of pink and green against Marjorie Wynchester's upturned face. Her bonnet slid from her head with a whoosh of yellow, rescued by a white ribbon at her throat. The sky above the museum was uncommonly blue today, and speckled with fluffy clouds. The aquamarine breeze, constant enough to keep the air fresh but not so strong as to give a chill. Even the taste in the air was less like hot summer tinged with coal, and more like bouncing spirals of orange and gold.

She would have thrown her arms in the air and twirled through the garden in delight were it not for two important considerations.

First, her joy would not be understood. No other person of her acquaintance could feel and smell and taste colors the way she could. Marjorie had asked every artist and aspiring artist she'd come across in academies and societies all across London. They looked at her not as though she were mad, but rather with envy, as though she had a special power they would do anything to possess.

The manager of the art studio where Marjorie volunteered suggested with some awe that it might be her body's method to compensate for partial deafness. It was not. The extra colors and smells and sensations in her life predated the bout of smallpox that had stolen her birth family and half of her hearing. They had helped her get through all the darkest periods in her life.

"Is this the place?" piped up a tentative voice. "The British Museum?"

Ah, yes. The second reason Marjorie could not fling her arms wide and spin through the wide green garden like a wood sprite.

It was not yet time for the robbery.

First came art. She had her newest gaggle of nine- and ten-year-old little girls eager to prove themselves in their first expedition as a group. Most hoped art would become part of their profession one day.

"This is the place," Marjorie confirmed, smiling at her charges.

Although her words often sounded muffled to her ears, she had been told—with varying degrees of kindness, or lack thereof—that her voice could be loud and atonal to others.

The little girls didn't mind. They thought Marjorie was a goddess. Almost all professional art instruction and organizations were by and for men, and certainly not accessible to wide-eyed girls with not-yet-stained pinafores protecting their dresses. They clutched their precious wooden boxes of paints and brushes to their chests.

No matter what else happened in the museum today, she would give them a Saturday to remember.

Marjorie glanced over her shoulder at her brothers. The bright white of their footmen's wigs covered up the black of their hair, and set off the rich brown of Jacob's skin and the smooth caramel of Graham's. In any costume, her roguish brothers were striking and dapper.

Real footmen could have handled this step, of course, but playing as servants gave them an additional reason for visiting the museum, and an ostensible explanation for any abnormal activity observed.

"Ready?" she asked them.

Her brothers grinned at her. Each lugged half a dozen oak easels in his strong arms. "Ready."

"Then follow me."

With a pile of protective canvas tarpaulins folded over one arm, Marjorie led the group through the main doors. The attendant greeted her by name and with a smile. Marjorie did the same. She was as familiar a sight within these walls as the frames about the paintings or the shelves beneath the curiosities. Often she gave her artistic re-creations to the staff so that they could take home a little bit of the beauty that surrounded them every day.

The museum had just opened, making Marjorie and her group among the first through its doors. The empty halls made this a splendid opportunity for young artists to have the museum mostly to themselves for the morning.

Briskly, she led her pupils away from the oils and watercolors and past the reading room for scholars, which was bustling with two dozen eager-eyed young ladies. Nothing like the dour-faced, serious gentlemen who usually haunted those walls. These women belonged to a ladies' reading circle run by Marjorie's sister-in-law Philippa. They met in a private library at the Wynchester residence on Thursdays, but had reconvened for a second appearance this week in order to—

Blond, lace-wrapped Philippa winked heartily at Marjorie as she led her students through the connected rooms.

Marjorie tried to send back a quelling glare. *Winking* before committing a burglary was hardly innocent behavior. But who could blame any of the Wynchester crew for their buoyant moods? Their latest client was hours away from seeing a cherished heirloom returned to her hands where it belonged. Nothing in this world was half as satisfying as putting wrongs to right. The air fairly sparkled with fireworks of pink and turquoise.

She herded her lambs toward the natural history galleries and began setting up easels on protective tarpaulin sheets all around the woodland creatures salon. The stuffed beasts were preserved in various poses under glass, making them the perfect models for young artists just learning to paint living things.

Less perfect had been her brother Jacob's overly optimistic attempts to bring a selection of his live animals to the studio where Marjorie normally taught. The girls spent more time petting puppies and cooing over kittens than they did attending to their palettes and paint. The baby hedgehogs had been pandemonium.

Even worse were the occasions when big, strong Elizabeth attempted to model for the group. Marjorie's sister was rarely without a sword or two and hated holding still for more than a second at a time. Each of the girls' canvases looked as though she'd been invited to sketch a tornado. If they managed to draw anything at all! Elizabeth's mouth moved as often as her body, and she could not stop herself from throwing her voice to poke fun at every person and object in the room. Most of Marjorie's poor pupils could not stop giggling long enough to make a straight line.

This salon was much better. The animals were life-like but stationary, making them ideal models. They also weren't currently speaking, which meant Elizabeth was somewhere else in the museum causing mayhem. Marjorie had begged her siblings to allow the girls to complete a painting or two before the excitement began.

Her brothers helped set up the easels, and the girls started to paint.

She strolled past each student's canvas. "Lovely work. That's it. Your shading is much improved. Look at those colors!"

At the studio in Charlotte Street, there was exactly one table in an out-of-the-way corner, with a large jug of water for rinsing off brushes without fear of splatter or other disasters. Today Marjorie set out multiple smaller pitchers at each girl's feet, right in the center of their tarpaulins on either side of their easels. A convenient and irresponsibly dangerous location to place light, round-bottomed containers brimming with water.

Exactly according to plan.

Her brothers disappeared. At this hour, the museum employed one guard on each of its primary floors. The one assigned to this level poked his head through the doorway at reliable intervals, checking every half hour to ensure that the paints and the little girls remained a safe distance from the stuffed beasts on display, before hurrying off to inspect the other chambers.

Movement in the open archway separating the rooms caught Marjorie's eye.

There at the threshold stood the most exquisitely handsome ton gentleman she had ever seen.

Black boots shined to perfection. Muscular legs encased in butter-soft buckskins. A moss-colored coat that set off perfectly the darker emerald of his waistcoat and the fluffy white cloud of his cravat. Bronze hair casually tumbled to perfection. A full, lush mouth over a strong jaw. Cheekbones that could cut diamonds. Heavy-lidded bright green eyes that watched her watching *him* with obvious interest. Even the air glowed with pinks and turquoise, and she caught the scent of spun sugar.

Marjorie was too startled by his direct gaze to blush. She did not attend balls or rub shoulders with aristocrats at vaunted venues such as Almack's and Vauxhall. She was a wallflower. Because of the working nature of her visit, she wore an old gray gown. The stained muslin shimmered like oily pigeon feathers from past encounters with paint.

"Good morning," she stammered.

"It *is* a good morning, now that I've had the good fortune to lay my eyes on *you*." His voice was a rich chocolatey brown, rumbling over her skin with hints of green and blue and nutmeg. "What luck to stumble across the most beautiful woman in London."

The dapper gentleman was bamming her. He had to be. A man

such as this could have any woman he wished. He wouldn't waste time on wallflowers. He wouldn't even notice—

Except he *had* noticed her, hadn't he? Was still gazing at her. Drinking her in as though he'd been praying for just this moment and had come to despair of ever finding her.

Being the object of such direct focus was a heady sensation. Her feet longed to step toward him, to let him look as close and as long as he pleased, provided he allowed her the luxury to do the same.

"I'm surprised you're up at this hour," she managed.

Not particularly flirtatious, but true. The people of the beau monde were infamous for allowing the sun to reach its zenith before squinting their eyes and rising from bed. Marjorie hadn't expected to find *any* other guests at the museum this early in the morning. Much less one who looked as though his morning toilette could rival Brummell's.

The gentleman smiled. Marjorie's insides melted like caramel in a crumb cake. Good Lord, was such a face even legal? How was she supposed to keep two thoughts in her head with a slow, sensual smile like that pointed in her direction?

"Have I shocked you with my country hours, little lamb? How I wish I had time to treat you to countless more surprises." He glanced at a carved wooden wall clock and made an expression of poignant disappointment at the position of the hands. "How long will you and your cadre be enjoying the museum this fine morning?"

"Two hours," piped up one of Marjorie's pinafored girls.

Doubtful. They might have an hour, if her students were fortunate. Marjorie's siblings wouldn't take long to assume their places and put today's caper into motion.

"Then I shall endeavor to return quickly," replied the gentleman, his voice still a rich chocolatey brown. His green eyes never left Marjorie's own.

This time, she did manage to blush. There was no misconstruing his interest... or her own. She could not recall the last time she'd been this flustered by a man. It would certainly be no hardship to see this gentleman again, for a second time in one day.

He bowed deeply, then spoiled the formal effect by tossing her a cheeky wink before striding away down the marble hall.

She stared at the empty spot where he had been for some seconds in stupefaction, still unable to credit that a man so fine would have interrupted his busy day specifically to flirt with *her*.

Fortunately, she had twelve little girls with wet palettes and a hundred questions to pull her back to the present moment.

To Marjorie's surprise and gratitude, her charges were able to complete more than the two watercolors she had promised them. They were each on painting three or four when Philippa's reading circle spilled into the room, indicating that mischief was finally afoot.

Marjorie lifted an especially fragile jug of water and hurried to her tarpaulin in the center of the room.

The toes of her half boots had barely touched the fabric when woodland beasts sprang to life all around them.

Oh, not the animals under glass. The stuffed models were the only creatures in the salon to hold their positions. Wild animals streamed from every other nook and cranny. Weasels, squirrels, cats, foxes.

A river of fur and clacking claws carpeted the room, creatures darting between legs and easels, barreling into one another, and sending the paint-muddied water bowls spinning across the floor.

The ladies' reading circle screamed in unison, rushing about the room with their hands waving wildly. They swooned into each other's arms, only to spring up with a howl and start dashing about all over again.

The first guard skidded into the salon with an expression of such shock, it took him a full minute to shout an alarm.

Marjorie chose that precise moment to lose her grip on the delicate pitcher of water.

The guard looked in her direction just in time to see a formidable splash. Large pieces of clay shot across the room as droplets of water rained down around her.

The clatter sent the animals swirling anew. Kittens and squirrels climbed over the stuffed beasts and across the guard's shoes.

A second guard ran into the room, followed quickly by the third and final guard. They tried in vain to round up the wild creatures, succeeding only in chasing them from one side of the salon to the other, overturning more bowls of paint-water in the process.

Elizabeth threw her voice into every corner, using her skill of mimicry to make it sound as though the confused guards were barking incoherent orders at each other from opposite directions of the chamber.

The ladies' reading circle continued to shriek and run amok, the spark in their eyes the only hint that they were not quite as panicked as they pretended.

A few of Marjorie's students stood stock-still in wonder. They surveyed the circus with delight, their hands gripping their easels to protect their paintings from falling. The rest took advantage of the mêlée, either dashing their wet brushes against their canvases in a frantic attempt to capture the chaos of the moment, or dropping to their knees on the wet tarpaulins in the hope of petting a passing squirrel.

Marjorie's sister Chloe was somewhere overhead performing the exchange. The tiara would then be passed to their brother Graham, who had a knack for disappearing out windows and up walls and across roofs.

The poor guards were still fruitlessly chasing the weasels and the foxes. They didn't notice that the seemingly savage beasts were conveniently confining themselves to a single chamber while performing a carefully choreographed routine.

Marjorie could not see her brother Jacob, but he must have given some sort of signal. All of the animals slid to a stop at once, then scampered away in all directions, escaping in flying streams of fur. They vanished even faster than they had appeared.

The wide-eyed, out-of-breath guards scrambled to their feet in astonishment.

"See here," barked Marjorie's sibling Tommy, in costume as a belligerent old lady. "What kind of establishment are you people running?"

"I..." stammered the guards, exchanging flabbergasted looks. "I never..."

Marjorie's soon-to-be sister-in-law Kuni strode toward the students, looking regal as ever in a flowing gown of bright, eye-searing pink. "Oh dear, just look at those tarpaulins!"

The ladies' reading circle spontaneously recovered from their shrieking and swooning, and sprang into action at once. "We'll help! You girls stand still. We'll have you put to rights in no time."

In moments, Marjorie's pupils, the reading circle, and the entire Wynchester clan were out the door, bursting into the sunlight with their canvases and easels and smiles bright enough to fill the sky with rainbows.

"That...was...*marvelous*!" All twelve damp-kneed, paint-splattered little girls danced around Marjorie, tugging her hands and clothes in glee. "Can we do it again next week?"

2

One more time."

Lord Adrian Webb sent his hackney driver on another jaunt through Mayfair. What difference did a few more minutes make? Seven years had passed since Adrian was last on English soil. Seven years since he'd flirted with a pretty English rose, like the one he'd met this morning.

Had they been long years? Short years? A little of both, he supposed. Years ago, his puritanical father and conniving brother had done their best to ensure there would be no pesky homesickness to deal with, but there was no accounting for the tiny little things one became maudlin for after years of drought.

Gray skies, sooty with coal. The terrible, insipid tea at Almack's. Rain, every bloody day for months on end. Burning the roof of one's mouth after biting into a pie too soon after it left the oven. Staying out all night at Vauxhall to watch the fireworks and dance till dawn, despite the crush of people and stench of sweaty bodies.

Adrian missed London despite himself, blast it all. He hadn't meant to, or wanted to. He'd been all over the Continent. To places that welcomed him, in contrast with the frigid reception that awaited him here.

If indeed *any* reception awaited him here.

"Stop."

The carriage was already halting. After five circuitous trips through the same cobbled streets, the driver had no trouble anticipating his passenger's commands.

The crescent Adrian was keeping under surveillance was his own.

Well, not *his* own. It belonged to Adrian's father, the Marquess of Meadowbrook, and would pass to Adrian's elder brother Herbert, the earl. But it was the same town house they'd lived in the first half of every year throughout his childhood.

The London social season roughly matched the parliamentary sessions. This year had ended early, in June, but the family tended not to remove to their country estate until mid-July. Which gave him at least another fortnight.

At least, such had *been* their custom. He hadn't spoken with any of them in seven years. Hadn't exchanged a single letter. Who knew how his family might have changed in his absence?

Especially Iris. She was the real reason Adrian was here. Not his father, who had sworn never to speak to him again. Or his brother Herbert, who had stopped speaking to Adrian as well, albeit with less cause.

His sister Iris had been thirteen the spring Adrian had been banished. Young enough to still belong in the schoolroom and old enough for him to catch glimpses of the woman she would one day become.

One day was here. One day had come and gone. She was grown now, and he had missed it. He had missed *her*. Adrian was starved for any contact with the one family member who might still love him. If the others hadn't poisoned her against him by now.

According to *Debrett's Peerage*, Iris was still unmarried, so at least he hadn't missed that. Not that he'd be invited to the wedding. He wasn't even certain she would allow him through the door.

Adrian *was* certain his sister was at home.

Father had left for his club in the coach-and-four. Herbert was off at his residence with his countess. Iris, as far as Adrian could tell, was home alone. This was the moment to pay an unexpected, clandestine call.

"Nothing ventured, nothing gained," he muttered.

Adrian gave the driver an extra coin for his troubles, then hopped out of the hackney and onto the street. The cobblestones felt strange against the soles of his boots. Strange and familiar and uneven.

He strode up to the front door with the confidence of a man who usually got his way... and who had a calling card bearing a false name in his pocket just in case.

He needn't have bothered with subterfuge. Except for a few laugh lines and the lone silver hair peeking among his curly brown locks, Adrian looked much the same now as he had the day he left.

The butler recognized him at once. "What a pleasant surprise, my lord!"

"McPherson, looking handsome as always. How have you been?" Adrian injected his tone with a jolly note, as if he could break through the invisible wall keeping him out with the force of his charm alone.

"It is good to see you. But I'm afraid..." McPherson winced and shifted his weight. "I was told to summon your father if you were ever to appear."

"Who is it, McPherson? I'm accepting calls," came a woman's voice.

A woman. Not a girl. And yet the voice was close enough to Adrian's memories, he knew it must be his sister.

"Iris," he called impulsively. "It's me, your long-lost brother!"

There was a pause. An uncomfortably long pause that stretched on for so many minutes, Adrian had plenty of time to wonder whether she would refuse to see him. Or if she'd forgotten who he was altogether.

Then: "Adrian?"

Bright brown eyes appeared behind McPherson's shoulder. Dark brown hair, not spilling haphazardly from messy plaits, but piled atop her head in artful curls. Instead of pinafores, a sprigged muslin day dress.

"I knew I missed you," he blurted out, "but I did not know the half of it."

"McPherson." Iris turned to the butler. "Weren't you busy polishing the silver when you heard the knock? I believe I called out that I would answer the door. I fear you had no idea who had come to call until much too late to have prevented it."

The butler looked from Iris to Adrian and back again, clearly weighing the wrath of his employer against the wants of the siblings.

"Indeed," McPherson said at last. "The silver is *such* a task. So time-consuming. I shouldn't be surprised to discover I missed glimpsing your caller altogether."

"Thank you," Adrian murmured.

McPherson inclined his head and hurried away to make good on his alibi.

Adrian quickly stepped over the threshold and shut the door. Luckily, the terrace faced a large garden, rather than another row of houses right across the street. Nonetheless, neighbors were neighbors, and it would not be long before the marquess learned his black sheep had come bleating home.

"Can it really be you?" Iris asked in wonder. "Come to the green parlor."

Adrian would have said he knew the way to the green parlor in his sleep, but after so many years of absence, his father's town house was as strange as it was familiar.

Had there always been a slight creak in the floor when exiting the entranceway? Were the wall coverings no longer the same brilliant blue, or had Adrian's imagination made his childhood home brighter than it actually had been?

Yet for all its muted hues and jarring creaks, the town house would always feel like home. A place he had once belonged. Inhabited by a family that had once been his. It was not the moldings and the ormolu he'd missed, but the good moments with his father and his siblings.

Especially Iris, with whom he had never exchanged a cross word. Of course, she'd been young then, and Adrian still perched on his pedestal. There were no longer stars in her eyes when she looked at him. He was just a man. Not even a particularly good one. As strange to her as the creak in the floor had been to Adrian.

Iris preceded him into the parlor. "I'll ring for tea."

"I don't want to cause you any trouble," he said hastily.

"I'm not *making* the tea. I'm just ringing—oh. You mean Father." Iris's brown eyes sparkled with the mischievousness he remembered from her youth. "I'll tell him I didn't remember that I wasn't to let you in."

"He doesn't remind you regularly what a disappointment I am? A blight and shame on the entire family?"

"He doesn't mention you at all. Neither does Herbert. I've not heard your name in... how many years has it been?"

"Seven," Adrian said hoarsely.

Iris took a seat in a beryl armchair and gestured for him to do the same. "Not once in seven years."

Well. That was a twist, wasn't it.

Adrian supposed he should be happy that his fears of his relatives poisoning Iris against him amounted to naught. His dream of rebuilding their once-strong relationship now seemed to have a chance. Iris was six years younger than him, but they had been thick as thieves. He had always loved her more than anything.

But the thought of his name never even having come *up* in his absence... it hurt. He could not deny it.

"Father warned me," he said lightly, trying to make a jest of the awkwardness. Playing the role he had been assigned. "'No son of mine,' 'dead to me forevermore,' et cetera, et cetera. I see he remains a man of his word."

She made a sympathetic face. "If it makes you feel better, he's cross with me, as well."

"Is he?" Outrage shot through Adrian's veins. "For what?"

"Failing to marry the doddering old earl he picked out for me." Iris mimed a shiver. "Even if his aging lordship were young and dashing, I wouldn't have wed him."

"Why not?"

"I want to be like you. Go on a holiday and never come back. Maybe we could have run into each other, if I had started sooner," she added wistfully.

His stomach twisted in sympathy. "Oh, pet, I missed you so much. If I had any notion of Father *allowing* you on a tour of any sort, I would have done everything in my power to be present for it."

"Oh, he shan't *allow* it," Iris said sourly. "As soon as he realized that was what I was saving my pin money for, he stopped giving it to me altogether. But let's not talk about Father. Unless you wish to, of course. Are you going to tell him you're in town?"

"I probably won't have to. I assume he's as well connected as ever. And from the sound of it, as stubborn. He wouldn't talk to me if we were locked in a trunk together."

"And you? Are you still as impulsive and impetuous as they say? Or did you settle down somewhere to build a career as a renowned artist, as you always threatened Father you would?"

Adrian sighed at the ghosts of old arguments. "Father always said nothing would be more scandalous to the family name than a son with a *career*."

True? False? Many younger sons had careers as vicars and soldiers. Father wasn't upholding the capricious whims of polite society. He was rejecting *Adrian*.

As a rebellious youth, Adrian had made it his mission to test his boundaries. It turned out, there were plenty of ways to be scandalous without lowering oneself to gainful employment. So many, in fact, that it surprised no one when, at the tender age of nineteen, the old man exiled him to the Continent and cut him off without a farthing.

"I'm a black sheep of the first order," he promised.

Iris's brows rose skeptically. "You cannot possibly be as bad as they say."

"A no-good, roguish, rakish scoundrel. Ask anyone," he added wryly. Adrian had been living up to the gossips' low regard for so long, he'd forgotten any other way to be. "And you? Have you engaged in dastardly exploits lo these many turbulent years between us?"

"Indeed I have," she answered primly. "Not that it's any of your business."

"I'm your brother," he protested. "*Everything* you don't want me to know is my business."

"I wouldn't mind learning how to generate funds quickly," she admitted. "My dreams of a Grand Tour may be dashed, but the loss of my pin money is more provoking than you can imagine."

"That's easy enough. I'm solvent now," he said cheerfully. "How much do you need? Say the number and it's yours."

She looked startled, then buoyant. "Really?"

"Really." Adrian fished out his pocketbook at once. It had been too long since he was the one Iris came to with her troubles. He was thrilled to be her protective big brother once again. "Most of my funds are still in Paris, but I brought a few bills to change when I arrived. Would five pounds do? Ten?"

Iris blinked at him slowly, as if such sums were beneath her. He frowned. How much pin money could the imperious marquess have parted with?

Many young ladies could outfit themselves for the entire season for a hundred pounds. Iris appeared to possess a fashionable wardrobe. What could she possibly need that their father wouldn't buy her?

Adrian peered into his pocketbook again. "Fifteen pounds for me, and twenty for you. It'll have to do for now, because it's all I have."

It was also more than enough funds to rent a modest room and employ a maid-of-all-work for the rest of the year, if what his sister really wanted was a holiday from their stiff, insufferably correct father.

Iris slumped back in her chair. "Never mind. It's all right. I'll come up with my own solution."

"*How?*" Without pin money or employment income, Iris was about as independent as the bark on a tree. There was no chance she could survive on her own.

Rather than confide in him as she once would have done, Iris pressed her lips together and shook her head, as though she'd already said more than she meant to. Evidently, he would not coax her secrets from her today.

"How long are you in town?" she asked instead.

"I hadn't decided yet. I wasn't sure . . . I'm renting rooms at Grenier's. For now."

She winced. "Father will never let you stay *here*. He converted your old bedchamber into a billiards room the day after you left."

Adrian ignored the icy stab in his heart at the news.

"Private rooms are better for a bachelor upon the prowl anyway," he said blithely. "You know what 'they' say: Lord Adrian's happiest when out debauching virgins and destroying lives. Ah, well, what's a rogue to do? I've mastered the art of scandal, and it would be a shame not to live up to my reputation."

His sister rolled her eyes. "You really haven't changed, have you."

He gave her a sad, crooked smile. "No one ever does."

3

❧

*A*fter leaving his sister's house, Adrian stopped by his rented rooms to retrieve a large wooden box. Instead of making his scheduled delivery, he wished he could return to the British Museum in search of the beautiful artist he'd seen earlier. He'd been away from his studio for weeks. The sight of so many easels had filled his chest with yearning to join in. And the sight of such an intriguing woman at the center of it all . . . Adrian was still kicking himself for not at least asking her name.

With luck, she would still be at the museum when he returned. But before he could turn his attentions to pleasure, there was one last business matter to clear up first.

As the horses clopped along the cobblestone streets, Adrian leaned back on the carriage squab to reread the summons that had prompted his return from the Continent. It wasn't from his father—no one in his family had written while Adrian was abroad—but from Snowley, an unscrupulous moneylender to the desperate, and a broker of not-always-legally-acquired objets d'art for the rich. He was known as the Grandfather of St. Giles, but might more accurately be termed its puppet master.

Was Snowley the crook's surname? His nickname? Who knew? Other than a brief encounter hours before Adrian had boarded a ship to the Continent, his dealings with Snowley had easily been accomplished through intermediaries. Snowley had men lurking in every shadowy corner of London and beyond.

Until recently, Adrian supposed he had been one of those men. Not the dangerous, burly sort that went about threatening and enacting revenge. The gentlemanly sort who acquired valuable trinkets on an extended, years-long holiday, despite the borders being closed during the war.

On the hackney seat beside him was a box containing the last Greek antiquities Adrian intended to sell. Whatever else Snowley had summoned him for, Adrian was no longer interested. This would be the final transaction. From then on, Adrian would find other ways to earn money.

The war had ended and the borders had reopened. Adrian's new objective was to restore his relationship with Iris to its previous closeness. He'd missed his little sister. Now that the prospect of recovering their lost bond seemed possible, Adrian would let nothing stand in his way. Including himself.

No more legally questionable activities. The only way to convince his sister to give him another chance was to *deserve* one.

Which meant cutting ties with Snowley.

This box would be their final transaction. It would be wise to let Snowley down easy. No need to tempt the Grandfather of St. Giles's vengeful nature. Adrian could say he was taking a respite and wouldn't be able to pick up any more artifacts until he traveled again. Which, if all went well, would be never. After wandering the Continent for so long, he was ready to put down roots. To have a home again. To belong.

Maybe even to be forgiven.

Was it overly optimistic to hope that if he regained his sister's trust, he might earn his father's forgiveness as well? That the marquess might one day welcome the prodigal son back home? That all Adrian had to do was…be *good* for a change? That a better, brighter future might be as simple as playing a new role?

The carriage wheels crunched to a stop on dirty, broken stones.

"You sure you want to be let out here, m'lord?" asked the hackney driver doubtfully.

Adrian hefted the wooden box. "I won't be more than ten minutes. Wait here for me."

"I ain't waiting ten seconds." Eyes alarmed, the driver dropped his voice to a whisper. "This is Snowley territory."

Adrian handed him a silver coin. "Drive around in a circle if you must. There'll be another shilling for each minute you wait."

"Give me five up front, and I'll be back in ten minutes," countered the driver. "But I won't wait a second more."

Could Adrian conclude his business in ten minutes? He didn't even know why he had been summoned. Other than for the same old purchase of exotic artifacts, which they'd always handled by post until now. Maybe he wouldn't even need ten minutes.

Our business is over shouldn't take too long to say. *Thank you for seven years. Goodbye.*

It wasn't just that he had to *behave* well from now on to win his sister's love and acceptance. He'd only be deemed worthy if she actually *believed* he was good. Faith was a far higher bar to clear than mere facts.

But he could do it. He *would* do it. He'd prove that bad pennies could bring good fortune. That rogues could be redeemed.

His brother had managed it, hadn't he?

Adrian gave the hackney driver a winning smile. "Five shillings now, if you wait a full quarter hour. Then ten more in your future."

The driver glanced up and down the street, weighing his options.

Adrian could not help but wonder if his own brother had given half as much thought before the events that changed both of their lives.

Of course, no one knew Herbert wasn't as innocent as he appeared. The earl was the angel, and Adrian the scapegrace. No one had ever paused to question whether Adrian was truly always to blame. When he'd tried to defend himself, his own father had assumed Adrian was lying. He was the bad son. Herbert, the good son.

And the earl had said nothing. Not during the row, not when Adrian was banished, and apparently not in the many years thereafter.

Adrian was through letting sleeping dogs lie. He might never earn back his rightful place in society, but if he was good enough, perfect enough, he might earn his sister's trust and affection. If he at least gained a small place in Iris's life, that would have to be enough.

The hackney driver held out his palm toward Adrian. "Fifteen minutes and I'm gone."

"I'll return in a blink," Adrian promised him. "Then we'll both be gone for good."

He strode up to an enormous, scarred wooden door and searched for a knocker.

A small panel slid open in the door.

"Name and business?" came a fatigued female voice. A lady butler?

"Lord Adrian Webb." He shifted his box of antiquities. "I've a summons here from Snowley—"

The door swung open. An aproned woman stepped aside.

A chill ruffled the back of Adrian's neck as he stepped across the threshold and into Snowley's fortress. No one entered or left without Snowley's knowledge and permission.

This was not a cozy residence for social calls. This was a place of last resort.

"Follow me," growled an unreasonably burly guard.

Another, equally over-muscled guard glared at Adrian in silent warning.

Adrian flashed them both a jaunty smile and fell into step beside

Burly Number One. After all, Adrian wasn't concerned for his safety. Even a soulless crook like Snowley knew better than to harm the son of a powerful marquess.

Then again, Adrian's father had a long history of not caring about his second-born son. Adrian was the *spare*. A living, breathing last resort, if you will. Important only if some tragedy were to befall Adrian's healthy, wealthy elder brother Herbert, the virile and respected heir.

In other words, Adrian's existence was irrelevant.

Lest one feel sorry, he quite liked spares. One might say...he'd made a hobby of them. After all, when penniless in Rome, what's a disgraced gentleman to do but dabble in some light forgery?

"This way." His Burliness lumbered up a dark, narrow staircase.

Adrian hefted his wooden box of Greek antiquities and followed.

All right, so they weren't *technically* Greek antiquities. Not that status-hungry aristocrats could tell the difference. Adrian had devoted his adult life to art. His specialties were pottery and sculpture. To be even more precise, he had an uncanny knack for replicating the masters.

Adrian didn't *swindle* his peers so much as...generate spare copies of otherwise accurate antiquities. This predilection wasn't his fault. It was in his blood. The ton *adored* producing spares. Every self-respecting lord had one! If they had no scruple against stocking their nurseries with spare children, surely a spare copy of a previously unique vase must be unobjectionable.

Even better: unlike younger sons, Adrian's duplicate objets d'art were things lords like his father actually *cared* about. What could be more virtuous than that?

"Wait in here," growled the guard.

"Here" was a small but surprisingly pretty parlor. At least it seemed as though it would be pretty, if there were any windows to let in sunlight. Sconces were lit on every wall, ostensibly to brighten the room. Instead the flickering candles seemed to sprinkle amorphous shadows over every surface.

"Charming," Adrian said. "If you could just ring for tea. Tell the kitchen I prefer my cakes—"

The guard shut the door in his face. Enacting the role of "insufferable aristocrat" was always an efficient way to gain privacy.

Adrian set the antiquities box on the floor beside a round rosewood table and flopped into each of the floral armchairs in turn until he found the most comfortable fit. He prayed this last sale wouldn't take terribly long. The hackney driver *might* wait as long as twenty minutes.

To save time, he opened the wooden box to expose the treasures inside. His chest filled with pride at the sight of his handiwork.

Last year, on his twenty-eighth birthday, Adrian realized he was no longer hurting for money. He could have ceased the forgeries if he wished to. But by then, he was good at it, and much in demand. Possibly because...

All right, yes. Snowley—just like everyone else—had no clue that these *were* forgeries. He believed Adrian one of the many self-indulgent lordlings who used their Grand Tour to divest other countries of their *actual* cultural artifacts. Whereas Adrian left every priceless item exactly where he found it. Who was the real villain here?

Lords and ladies who knew absolutely nothing about art—or the people whose treasures they sacked—only wished to brag about the spoils they could put on display. To have what no one else owned. Adrian could give them all the pretty things they desired, without taking them from anyone else.

One might say he was...the protector of other cultures' heritage.

The dragon at the mouth of the cave. Instead of breathing fire, he lived and breathed art. And then sold it. For a hefty profit. To people who wouldn't know an obelisk from an ostrich. By means of an unscrupulous flash-cove called Snowley. *Et voilà*, everyone wins. Adrian smiled with pride.

The door swung open.

Snowley stepped inside, flanked by two different—and even burlier—guardsmen. Adrian hadn't set eyes on the man since the night before he'd left for the Continent, but Snowley had not changed in all the years since.

He looked like a parson. Harmless. No hulking muscles, no ominous scars, no pistols at the ready. He was short and slender with thinning white hair and perpetually rosy cheeks. Even his pink skin smelled like roses. He looked like the sort of grandfather who would bounce his granddaughter on his knee and spoil her with all the dolls and candied fruit money could buy.

Adrian was not fooled by appearances. He'd made his fortune creating things that were not what they seemed. Snowley did the same. Bow Street didn't buy Snowley's kindly persona, but nor had they been able to catch him in the act of anything nefarious.

Which was good for Adrian's pocketbook. Snowley was his best client.

Adrian sprang to his feet.

Snowley's guardsmen—who indeed possessed hulking muscles, ominous scars, and pistols at the ready—tensed in alarm.

"Relax." The barest flex of Snowley's fingers sent the pair of guards skulking back into the shadows. "We're just going to have a little chat, aren't we, Webb?"

"And perhaps a transaction." Adrian made an exaggerated gesture toward the open box beside the table. "I come bearing gifts."

"Yes," said Snowley. "Let's chat about your gifts. Sit down, Webb."

Adrian sat. In the comfortable chair. He hadn't tested all those cushions for nothing.

Snowley did not sit. The diminutive older man stood beside the table and peered inside the wooden box. "These are the Greek artifacts I requested?"

"Yes. But before you give me a new target, I must advise you that I no longer intend to—"

"Let me stop you there." Snowley lifted a delicate vase out of the box and held it up to the dim light. "I will ask you one more time. Think carefully before you respond. *Are* these the actual, original, one-of-a-kind Greek artifacts I requested?"

Shite.

Snowley hurled the vase at the stone fireplace.

The painstakingly re-created amphora exploded against the stone wall with a shower of red and black shards, dissolving the intricate design and classical figures into dust.

"I can explain," Adrian said hastily.

It was the second time in his life that someone had destroyed a piece of art Adrian loved. And the second time he had begged for the desecration to cease with a stammered, "I can explain."

"Good." Snowley lifted another vase from the box. "I should very much like to hear the reason why, after I'd sold a breathtakingly expensive, one-of-a-kind artifact to a grateful duke, his son later went on Grand Tour and came across *the allegedly unique item in question* still standing in its original location, despite also residing in the duke's front parlor?"

"There's an obvious explanation. The lad went on Grand Tour because the bloody war is over. If Napoleon would have kept on escaping and conquering, there wouldn't *be* any tourists, and your duke and his son wouldn't have the least idea—"

"Enough!" Another exquisite creation shattered against the stone.

"I see how this situation could be awkward for your client," Adrian allowed.

Though not nearly as awkward as it was for Adrian at the moment. Now that the war had ended, indolent sons everywhere had resumed the long-delayed practice of Grand Tours on the Continent. This unfortunate discovery would be the first of many.

Snowley drummed the tips of his fingers on the rosewood table. "I suspect that *nothing* you have sold me over the many years we've worked together is actually the treasure you claimed it to be."

"Well…" Adrian began.

Snowley waited.

"Er," Adrian added eloquently.

Snowley cracked his knuckles. "Do you know what happens to fools who dare to think they can steal from me?"

"I never robbed anyone!" Adrian protested. "You can accuse me of whatever you like, but not theft. You're vexed at me because I *didn't* steal those artifacts. I would never. I'm an un-thief. I'm an *artist*, and you're… you're destroying my art."

Snowley's flat gaze was unmoved. "You swindled me, Webb. Plain and simple."

"Did I? Your clients paid every penny you were hoping for and more. Over the past seven years, I've significantly increased your wealth. I hardly think—"

"Clearly," said Snowley. "Clearly, you hardly think. So allow me to spell it out for you. I own you now, Lord Adrian Webb. No one can save you. Not Bow Street. Not your daddy."

Adrian swallowed hard at the mention of his family. Iris's face flashed before him.

He'd been *so close* to leaving his past behind and becoming part of his sister's life again.

"What do you propose?" he asked carefully.

Snowley smiled. "One option is to do my duty to my countrymen. Forgery is illegal, *my lord*. Oh dear, you're not a real lord, are you? That's just a courtesy title. There'll be no claiming 'right of privilege' to weasel out of a public trial. The scandal of the century, I'm sure."

Adrian's comfortable armchair began to feel like an iron torture chair.

If Iris had been understandably hesitant to welcome him back into her life before, due to a years-old crime...she would bar the house to him herself if his current role as rackety forger became known.

Presuming he was let out of prison long enough to knock on her door.

"I'm not in love with that option," Adrian admitted. "What's the alternative?"

"As I said. You belong to me. You're now my exclusive property and personal forger. I've tallied up every farthing I've paid you. You must work off every penny. Plus a healthy inconvenience tax for being such a pain in my arse."

"As it happens," Adrian said, "I came here today to tell you I'm finished with this business. I'm turning over a new leaf. No fraud, no forgery, no becoming the personal property of a notorious criminal. A renaissance, if you will. A phoenix, reborn."

"You'd better hope you can rise from the ashes. Because option three is that my men here begin breaking every bone in your body, starting with the smallest. Until you either agree to my terms...or are rendered permanently incapable of lifting a finger."

Well, that path did not sound better.

Snowley eased into the second-most-comfortable floral chair. "You see, Webb, one way or another, I will have my revenge. You can volunteer to do your part and walk out of here one day...or you can never walk again. The choice is yours."

"I'm thinking it over," Adrian muttered. "One mustn't rush into deals with the devil."

"Shall my men give you a taste of option three?" Snowley inquired politely.

Both guards took a menacing step forward.

"Oh, very well, I 'volunteer.' There's no choice here, and you know it." Adrian cast his gaze at the jagged edges of his hard work littering the fireplace. "Why destroy my vases if you want to keep selling forgeries?"

"I'm finished with art. My reputation as a broker to the ton is now in peril, due to your tricks. But this little misunderstanding gave rise to an epiphany." Snowley's eyes glittered. "Why waste time moving products when one can simply mint money?"

Adrian blinked. "What?"

Snowley waved a careless hand. "We can skip the arduous middle step of uniting objects with buyers. What I want you to forge is currency."

"Currency," Adrian repeated. "That's…high treason. A crime against the Crown. Convicted counterfeiters are led to the gallows and hanged."

Snowley shuddered delicately. "Then it is a good thing *I* am not the one doing the counterfeiting. I *am* the one, however, with convenient means to disburse the false funds. Desperate people visit me all the time hoping to unload this or that trinket in exchange for a few quid."

Adrian had been one of those desperate people, once. That was how he and Snowley had begun. He would not wish such dire straits on anyone.

Snowley steepled his fingers. "Thanks to you, I can no longer target aristocrats. But no matter. The working class may have fewer funds, but there are many, many more of them. Better yet, I don't have to hunt them. They come to *me* with their sad tales of woe. They'll be so grateful for any alms I give them, they won't look too closely. And I'll have an unlimited supply of material to make more coins."

Adrian's stomach sank. "Instead of defrauding those who can afford to lose a few pounds, you intend to send the destitute home with worthless bills, pocket the difference—and their valuable trinkets—and profit from their misery?"

"Exactly." Snowley smiled. "And you're going to help."

4

A week later, the grand Wynchester residence in Islington overflowed with strangers.

Er, *merrymakers*. A wedding breakfast was under way for Marjorie's brother Graham and his new wife, Kuni, whom Marjorie adored
as if they'd been siblings all their lives. This was a celebration!

There were just . . . *so many people.*

Kuni and Graham, of course. Sweet, sensitive Jacob, not even trying to hide the baby hedgehog poking up from his pocket. Chameleon
Chloe and her husband, the Duke of Faircliffe.

Tommy, who had eschewed costumes today and come to the rev-
elry as herself, in breeches and a fresh rakish cut to her short brown
hair. The love of Tommy's life, bookish Philippa, dressed in clouds
of lace and accompanied by all two dozen members of her reading
circle.

Fierce and loyal Elizabeth, swinging a new sword given to her
moments ago by the bride's bosom friend, Princess Mechtilda of
Balcovia. And then the princess's entire retinue: half a dozen lady
companions along with so many uniformed guards, they could put on
their own parade.

Plus all of the Wynchester family's other friends.

Servants were everywhere, rushing hither and yon on silent feet to
restock trays of food and refill glasses of champagne.

At least Marjorie assumed they did so silently. She certainly couldn't hear them. In a crowd such as this, her ability to pick out individual voices diminished considerably.

Those who didn't know her outside of similar social functions assumed she was shy, but the truth was more complicated. It was difficult to join in a conversation you couldn't follow. Much easier to fade back and pretend you were a spectator at a play.

Her siblings had the flashy personalities. Kuni, with her throwing knives beneath her wedding dress. Kindhearted Philippa, who had read every book under the sun. Brilliant and talented Elizabeth, who could throw her voice to sound like anyone. Jacob, the animal trainer. Graham, the acrobatic spy. Tommy, the master of disguise. Chloe, the political force.

And then... Marjorie. The quiet one.

Wallflower had been her lot for so long, sometimes she forgot it was due to circumstance, not choice. She was *used* to standing back, to watching silently. It wasn't until her beloved siblings had begun pairing off with equally impressive partners that Marjorie had become restless to be larger-than-life, too.

Or perhaps being charmed by the attractive gentleman at the museum made her yearn to deserve a second glance.

"What's this?" Tommy grabbed Marjorie's empty hands. "No plate of pies? Come quick, before Kuni's brothers eat them all."

Tommy was a rainbow of color. Oh, not literally. Today's ensemble was monochromatic shades of blue. But she emanated the full spectrum of color just by walking into a room. Every prospect shone brighter with Tommy as coconspirator.

"All right," Marjorie said, laughing at her sister's wide-eyed concern. "You've convinced me. It's been at least five minutes since my last serving."

Her siblings were wonderful at making certain they looked straight at her when they spoke. With them, she was never lost. It was crowds that intimidated her.

And unfamiliar locations. Marjorie knew every inch of their home. Vauxhall was chaos. Even navigating markets or crossing streets could be tricky, with everyone shouting at one another all at the same time.

It was easier to stay home.

Stay safe.

Shortly after raiding the tray of pies, Tommy was lured away by Philippa and the ladies of her reading circle.

Before Marjorie could melt into the closest wainscoting, Kuni appeared before her in her gorgeous Balcovian wedding gown, with flowing pinkish purple amaranth skirts and a scooped white bodice trimmed below with teardrop pearls that set off Kuni's rich dark brown skin to perfection.

"Congratulations again," Marjorie said. "I am honored to count you as a Wynchester. And you look radiant."

Kuni's obsidian eyes sparkled as she tossed her loops of long black braids. "Radiant enough for . . . an *After* portrait?"

"*Shh.*" Marjorie darted her gaze about the bustling salon. "No one else knows what I'm working on."

Kuni winked. "I can't wait for you to visit Balcovia," she gushed. "You are going to love my country as much as your own."

Marjorie smiled weakly. She wasn't even ready to *think* about the planned family holiday. Christmastide was months away. There was plenty of time to pluck up her courage.

Or lock herself inside her studio.

"Apologies." Graham cut in with a grin. "I need to borrow my wife to resolve an emergency situation."

"Are you suffering from lack of kisses?" Kuni teased.

He pulled her into his arms. "Not for long."

As they danced off, Marjorie debated slipping upstairs to her third-floor art studio. Her siblings would notice her absence, but would not judge her if she needed a moment of calm.

For the longest time, art was the only source of joy in Marjorie's life. Art was her solace when smallpox stole her family and part of her hearing. Art was her refuge again when smallpox returned for her *new* family and took her father figure, Baron Vanderbean, with it.

No matter how ugly or overwhelming the world around her, Marjorie could always pick up her palette and create something beautiful.

Her current project was a duet of oil paintings for each of the original Wynchester siblings. *Before*—a portrait of how Marjorie remembered them, that magical summer twenty years ago when six skeptical orphans came together to form a family.

And *After*, which so far included a painting of Chloe and Faircliffe, another of Tommy and Philippa, and yes, next on the list were the newlywed Kuni and Graham.

As for her own *After* portrait... well. What was there to paint? Marjorie might indulge the occasional flirtation, but she did not intend to wed. She liked her life exactly as it was. She knew how to navigate it this way. Staying single was simple.

Safe.

Mr. Randall, the Wynchesters' butler, appeared in the doorway to the salon. Marjorie concentrated on his lips. "Pardon the interruption. You have a visitor."

A visitor? Who hadn't been invited to the wedding breakfast? This must be a new case!

Marjorie abandoned her plate and hurried out of the salon along with the rest of her siblings. She skidded into the corridor in time to see Graham counting a stack of guineas.

"Is it not enough coin?" he asked the butler.

Something wasn't right.

Marjorie took the coins from his hands and held one of the guineas to the light. Ha! "They're *not* proper coins. These are *forgeries.*"

"Bloody good ones." Jacob took them from her and let out a slow whistle. "As good as you could've done."

"Take that back," she demanded hotly. "If *I'd* done it, I wouldn't have been caught."

"Neither has the forger, I'm afraid," said Mr. Randall. "That is why Mrs. Lachlan is here. She has no usable funds, and will soon be evicted from her home. Her landlord has granted her one month's amnesty. She is hoping—"

"Accepted." Marjorie closed her fist about a false coin. "Art is meant to improve lives, not ruin them. This swindle is insult on top of injury. When I find who did this..."

5

⚜

*A*drian exchanged his coat for a leather apron and glanced long-ingly toward the locked sash windows. The second floor of Snowley's den towered over this section of the Seven Dials rookery. From this angle, the view was primarily of dirty brick walls, sooty gray skies, and patched roofs in dire need of repair.

It was the opposite of his father's grand town house in aristo-cratic Mayfair. Notably, Adrian wasn't allowed inside his father's residence...or *out*side of Snowley's. The workroom and the minus-cule linen closet of a bedchamber across the corridor were to be Adrian's home—his prison—until he repaid his debt to Snowley's satisfaction.

He could not help but think longingly of his brief visit to the British Museum, and the woman he'd hoped to return in time to see again. He should never have come to Snowley's. Turning over a new leaf did not start with one last forgery. He'd learned the lesson a little too late.

Footsteps sounded out in the corridor.

Adrian looked over his shoulder at the open door just in time to glimpse one of the guards stroll past with a loaded pistol at his side. Pleasant sight, that. Uplifting. Cheerful.

He crossed the room and shut the door to the studio. There, that was a little better. Artist on one side, guards with guns on the other.

Not that he could lock the door for any semblance of safety.

Snowley hadn't entrusted him with a key. Presumably, the puppet master was trying to impress upon Adrian that here there would be no privacy, no secrets. Snowley and his men could enter any room at any time. Let that be a warning against any ill-advised high jinks.

Adrian *adored* ill-advised high jinks.

One could argue that his entire life had been an unceasing series of rash decision after foolish mistake. As far as he was concerned, it was all part of the adventure.

Admittedly, his current lodgings did not compare to the artists' community where he'd spent a glorious autumn that year in Bordeaux. But were good times really ever good without a few less favorable times here and there to contrast against?

Adrian's bad reputation had afforded him the freedom to go anywhere, say anything, do whatever he wished. The cost of that freedom rarely crossed his mind...

Until Iris had welcomed him home.

She hadn't confided her troubles in Adrian—but nor had she rejected him outright. He trudged toward the worktable. If she could see him now, she would rightfully refuse to speak to him again. Much less forgive him. His chest ached at the lost opportunity.

Would Iris even wonder what had happened to her brother? There one day, gone the next? Or would she assume that his desire to reconnect had never been sincere? By the time Adrian repaid Snowley and escaped this infernal rookery, would it be too late to try again?

More footsteps sounded in the corridor. Softer ones.

The door opened.

"Well?" Snowley leaned one narrow shoulder against the wooden frame, arms crossed. "Am I rich yet?"

"You were rich before I met you," Adrian pointed out. "And you've grown wealthier every day since."

"I'm good at it," Snowley agreed. "But until now, riches have required work. Just think how much easier it will be if the only thing standing between me and a pot of coins is... you." He stepped into the room. "Is the next batch ready?"

"Almost." Adrian flicked one of the newest shillings toward him.

Snowley caught it with one hand and held it up to the light of the locked window.

Adrian would have held his breath were there any point to the effort.

For one, the air in this neighborhood was not of a quality that would inspire anyone to hold on to it any longer than necessary.

For two, the grimy window and even smudgier gray sky were unlikely to illuminate the aspects of the design Adrian intended to keep secret. In short: that he was doing a dreadful job on purpose.

Oh, these molds were close enough to fool the unobservant. But each coin was carefully imperfect in an improbable way.

Adrian's initial aim had been "good enough to trick Snowley and bad enough to cause suspicion." If the Grandfather of St. Giles gained a reputation for attempting to pass off false coins, his vast influence would shrivel.

Snowley flipped the coin high into the air, caught it, and tucked it into a breast pocket. "I need more. Work faster."

"If you try to hurry the cooling process, it will ruin the texture," Adrian reminded him. "This is painstaking, exacting work."

None of that was true. He'd made his first set of molds before he'd learned his multiplication tables. Granted, at the time he'd been trying to copy his father's pipe, not commit treason against the Crown.

Not that the marquess had appreciated his son's restraint—or his ingenuity.

Thinking of his father reminded Adrian of Iris. And thinking of his sister made his heart thump painfully all over again. He missed the winter evenings they'd played draughts together, or the sultry summer afternoons riding horses in the park, after which he'd have to replait her hair lest their father realize Adrian had let her gallop all she pleased. He missed her hand in his at church on Sundays, and her head on his chest when she fell asleep during bedtime stories.

More than anything, he wanted her to believe the best of him. But Adrian had spent so long living down to expectations, there might no longer be a way to restore his reputation. Thanks to this devil's agreement with Snowley, Adrian had become exactly the sort of base criminal the world had always presumed he was destined to be.

Snowley scooped the small pile of finished shillings from the worktable to count them. "Let's see, after I include today's riches in the tally . . . you've worked off precisely two percent of what you owe."

The crook meant this pronouncement to be soul-crushing. Adrian gave him a sunny smile. Two percent after a fortnight of effort wasn't *lightning*-fast, but the plodding pace was a mirage. Adrian was dilly-dallying in the hope Snowley would get caught. And to minimize the damage to victims powerless to fight back.

If this plan failed, Adrian wouldn't be free for well over a year. But at any moment, he could experience a "breakthrough" in his process and whip out the rest in less than a month.

If he had enough raw materials, that was. Adrian's mouth tightened. He needed Snowley to provide gold and silver to work with . . . which required taking it from someone else.

Adrian hated that part of the process. Rings, bracelets, lockets. If he could work even slower, that would give enough sharp-eyed shopkeepers time to notice Snowley's funds were false before too much damage had been done. The entire operation of trading fake coins for real goods would come to a screeching—

Loud, grating laughter rang in the corridor. Two of Snowley's henchmen stumbled in through the open door, wiping tears of mirth from their eyes.

"There you are, m'lord," rumbled the hulking one called Grinders. A silver hatpin protruded from the corner of his mouth.

He gave no acknowledgment to Adrian at all. Rude.

Adrian clucked his tongue. "Such poor manners, and no grasp of the nuance of nobility. I'll have your Almack's vouchers revoked posthaste."

The excitable one called Joey Box o' Crumpets snorted. "You ain't allowed in yerself."

Adrian clutched his chest. "That's hurtful. And true. I shall be forced to execute my contingency plan of pushing you out of the window to fall to your doom."

"Locked," Joey said smugly.

"Latched on the *inside*." Adrian fluttered his eyelashes. "Come take a close look at it with me and we'll see what happens."

"We'll see that we've got pistols and all you've got is a fast mouth," said Grinders.

"Lads, lads." Snowley sounded bored. "I'll throw the lot of you off the roof myself if you don't come to the point. I heard a commotion. I presume you dealt with it?"

"Oh, yes, m'lord," Grinders assured him. "The wailin' and carryin' on was a vexed customer in the pawnshop."

Joey grinned. "One of our special customers came crawling back, all sobbing and frantic-like. Widow said she'd needed those funds to stay in her house, only for her landlord to claim her coins are forgeries."

Adrian glanced up from his mold with interest. Was this it? The moment he'd been waiting for? When Snowley's precious reputation would come crumbling down around him, rendering the entire operation obsolete—and preventing any more victims from falling prey to Snowley's machinations?

"I trust my staff to deal with disturbances," Snowley said.

Joey's smirk didn't falter. "Aye, it's handled."

"Said she wanted her trinket returned or real money." Grinders rolled his eyes hard.

Snowley lifted his brows. "And you gave her..."

"Thirty seconds to get off the property before we told her landlord *she* was the one passing false coins. Prison's got free room and board, don't it? That'll solve her little housing problem. Widow left with her tail between her legs and no more talk of trinkets!"

Joey and Grinders elbowed each other and guffawed.

Adrian's stomach churned with acid. That poor widow. Adrian's grand plan of taking Snowley down with subpar coins had made life worse for the victims instead. A blameless woman had lost her possessions and her home, with no gain to show for it—and no recourse against someone as powerful as Snowley. No one to champion her and the other swindled customers...except Adrian.

"That does it." He dropped the empty mold he'd been holding. It clattered to the floor. A piece chipped off and shot across the dirty floor, ricocheting off Snowley's left boot. "This ends now. I'm an artist, not a ruiner of lives."

"You're both, from what I hear," Snowley drawled. "Wasn't that why you were shipped off to France, *mon artiste*? Something to do with despoiling innocent young ladies?"

Adrian's face flushed. "You've no idea what you're talking about. And I won't stand for—"

"You won't stand at all, if it comes to that." Snowley plucked a pistol from Joey Box o' Crumpets and aimed the barrel at Adrian's kneecaps. "Whether you *ever* walk out of here is up to you. I'm happy to cut off your favorite body parts, one by one. To keep forging, all you need are working fingers. And if that's not enough incentive...I have other ideas."

"The sister?" Grinders smacked his lips.

Joey grinned. "Webb shouldn't be the only one having all the fun despoiling innocents. We enjoy playing that game, too."

"If you go near her," Adrian growled, "you *will* have to chop me into bite-sized pieces to keep me from tearing you apart." Adrian spun to face Snowley. "Stay away from my sister."

"Well now, that's not up to me, is it? It sure would be a shame if any tragedy were to befall Lady Iris. But don't worry. My men will be right there, watching."

"I'm warning you," Adrian said through gritted teeth.

Snowley arched his white brows and smiled his kindly grandfather smile. "Warning me? What are *you* going to do? You're here, and she's there. You can run to her with my blessing after you've paid off the rest of your debt."

The sooner Adrian canceled the other ninety-eight percent of his debt, the faster he could remove Iris from Snowley's sights. He sent up a silent apology to whoever had owned the items melting in the crucible.

"Do we understand each other?" Snowley asked, his soft voice a lazy drawl.

Adrian nodded. "Yes, your evil highness. One storybook elf, at your service. Come back in an hour for more magic coins." He leapt into the air with a click of his heels, then swept into a bow fit for a king. "Fatal curse included for free."

Snowley smirked. "You would not be the first to curse me, nor shall you be the last. Make all the jests you like, so long as you keep filling my coffers."

6

Put a little more on your brush," Marjorie said. "Don't be afraid of the paint."

She and the Duke of Faircliffe were upstairs in the guest studio next to hers for his twice-weekly art lesson. Neither of them had their full concentration on the fruit-and-pottery still life before them. As soon as Marjorie's sister Chloe arrived, they would adjourn to the Planning Parlor to discuss their next steps on the counterfeiting case.

Before she'd married Faircliffe, Chloe had been an early riser. It was unlike her not to be one of the first Wynchester siblings in the Planning Parlor, ready to plot stratagems. Yet she had been late to every session all week.

"You're certain she isn't feeling poorly?" Marjorie could not help asking for the third time. A suspicion had been growing...

"Just a little tired," Faircliffe assured her. "It's been a busy few days."

This was true. They'd immediately jumped on their new case. Poor Mrs. Lachlan was understandably distraught at the impending loss of her home *and* her husband's wedding ring, her sole connection to her late husband. The widow deserved the money she was owed, or her valuables returned. Better yet: both.

Worse, Mrs. Lachlan wasn't the only one Snowley had hoodwinked.

The Wynchesters had uncovered several other victims of his fraud. Snowley and his so-called artist were out there blithely pawning off forged coins on innocent men and women who had lost all support and all hope. People who could not raise funds any other way but to sell the last small treasures they still possessed. And now that avenue was gone, too.

Graham cast out his net of informants and confirmed that the false coins originated from an unprincipled criminal called Snowley. This Snowley was not known to possess any particular artistic tendencies, which meant the forger was someone in his employ.

Marjorie slashed paint at her own canvas. As an artist—and a human with a heart—she was furious that some scurrilous miscreant had decided to use his exceptional talent to destroy lives, rather than better them.

"How did you…" Faircliffe stepped back from his easel to gawp at Marjorie's canvas. "I've barely sketched in the outlines, and you've re-created the entire still life already. How is that possible, in so few strokes?"

Marjorie shrugged. "It's simple, because I'm not re-creating anything. I just capture its essence to convey the *idea* of what it is."

"Oh, sure," the duke said dryly. "What could be simpler than capturing something's essence?"

Something niggled at the back of Marjorie's mind. Something about the case. Before she could puzzle it out, the duke faced her and spoke again.

"Do you still volunteer your time at that studio?"

Marjorie nodded as she cleaned her brushes. "Every Saturday."

"Those girls don't know how lucky they are. You could charge a fortune for your tutoring."

"There's no need. I enjoy helping those without a fortune to spend."

Like the penniless orphan Marjorie had once been.

As she rubbed her paint-stained fingers with a damp rag, she cast her gaze over the series of covered canvases facing the far wall. Her Then-and-Now portraits.

Marjorie's *Before* had been straightforward enough, but try as she might, she could not yet visualize an *After* for herself.

Life was nothing but change, yet she did not feel any different. Had she reached the end of her personal journey? Or was there more to come? How would she know? Would she take the step if it appeared before her?

Faircliffe's head jerked toward the window.

Marjorie's gaze followed. "What do you hear?"

"Carriage wheels." His eyes softened. "Chloe's here."

"Clean the palettes and brushes. I'll meet you in the Planning Parlor."

"But we still have ten more min—"

Marjorie did not wait. She flew down three flights of stairs, reaching the bottom just as her sister stepped into view.

Chloe's body seemed to shimmer bright marigold, with rays of gold and orange. She smelled like sunshine and soft pastels of green and pink and blue. The reason was obvious.

Marjorie bounced on her toes. "I can't believe it! We're to have a new Wyn—"

"*Shh.*" Chloe looped her arm through her sister's. "I won't even ask how you know. I only fathomed it out this week myself. Don't tell anyone. Including Lawrence."

"Don't tell *Faircliffe*? But he's the fath—"

Chloe clapped her hand over Marjorie's mouth. "I'm serious. Not yet."

"But when? Why?"

"He will be over the moon and utterly terrified. He knows from his childhood that not all..." She touched her abdomen meaningfully.

"...survive, and remembers how that loss destroyed his family. I want to be one hundred percent certain before I share any news."

Marjorie was one thousand percent certain that this wrinkle terrified the stuffing out of them both, but she nodded her acquiescence.

Yet another reason to stay a spinster. If even *good* things were potentially bad, she wanted nothing of it. Being Marjorie was a full enough life, without adding complications like "wife" and "mother" to the mix.

Chloe smiled. "Come on, then."

When Marjorie and Chloe entered the Planning Parlor, Graham and Kuni were nestled hip-to-hip on one of the sofas, facing an equally cozy Tommy and Philippa on the sofa opposite.

The pang in Marjorie's chest was due to happiness, not envy. After all, her family was getting bigger, not smaller.

Once upon a time, when all the siblings had was Bean and each other, they'd arranged themselves in a comfortably predictable pattern every time. Over the past few years, they'd lost Bean, gained Philippa and Kuni, and only saw Chloe and Faircliffe on occasion. The pattern was constantly disrupted, their form unpredictable instead of permanent. Yet as much as Marjorie's orderly soul rebelled against the ever-changing picture, she could not deny that her siblings were positively radiant with marital bliss.

Marjorie might be a twenty-nine-year-old spinster, but she certainly wasn't lonely. She had her family, and she'd had flirtations. She wasn't even against taking a lover. But she would never give her home or her family up for any reason. Especially not a man.

The door opened, and Jacob and Elizabeth walked in, arguing. Elizabeth tapped her sword stick to the slate floor to make some sort of point, startling a pair of kittens trailing Jacob like ducklings after their mother.

"Utter rubbish." Jacob scooped up the kittens. "Never mention his name to me again."

"I don't think it *is* his name," Elizabeth shot back. "And if his poetry was such offal, the volume wouldn't be on its third printing in as many months, now, would it?"

"No one said the ton had taste," Jacob said flatly. "I might have thought you were different."

"I'm just saying, Sir Gareth is an experienced, published poet," Elizabeth insisted.

Marjorie hid a smile. Her sister would go to her grave rather than admit outside these walls that she was anything more than a bloodthirsty misanthrope. Only the family knew her for the softhearted, poetry-reading, bunny-snuggling crispy crumpet with a sweet tooth and a fondness for picking spring flowers.

"Be reasonable," Elizabeth told Jacob. "I don't see why your group of *aspiring* poets would not wish to invite him to one of the meetings in order to learn firsthand from a master of his craft—"

"You *wouldn't* see," Jacob said. "And I'm through discussing the matter."

Ah. There was the sore spot. Jacob never let *any* sibling attend the weekly poetry circles on the nights when he shared his work. None of the Wynchesters had heard or glimpsed so much as a single syllable of his poems.

It might have been better for Jacob if the others had no inkling of his ambition. Elizabeth had the bedside manner of a wild bull, but she was staunchly supportive of her siblings. She would hawk copies of Jacob's poetry door-to-door all over England if he hinted that her help would be welcome.

Faircliffe dashed through the door of the Planning Parlor. "What did I miss?"

"Nothing," Chloe and Jacob answered in unison.

The duke drew his wife—and his unborn baby, though he didn't know it yet—over to a chaise longue.

Marjorie settled in an armchair between Elizabeth and Jacob. He offered one of his kittens, which Marjorie accepted gladly. Her hearing might not be in optimal condition, but her sense of touch was fine-tuned. There was nothing like the sensation of a purr vibrating the exposed belly of a newborn kitten while one stroked its soft fur.

"Graham," said Chloe, "take us through what your informants have gathered thus far."

"Snowley lives in a heavily fortified brick structure in a section of the St. Giles rookery known as Seven Dials," Graham began. "The upper floor is residential and who-knows-what-else, whilst the ground floor hosts a handful of Snowley's public-facing commercial operations, such as posing as a pawnbroker to disguise the fact that he fences stolen goods."

"'Who-knows-what-else'?" Philippa teased. "I thought you always knew. Nothing in London occurs without the great Graham Wynchester's knowledge."

"I have no permanent spies stationed within Snowley's ranks... *yet*," he admitted, disgruntled by this setback. "Snowley is shrewd and runs a very tight ship."

"We're running out of time," Elizabeth reminded them. "We've used six of Mrs. Lachlan's thirty days already."

"We could pay her next month's rent—" Kuni began.

"—but we promised to collect her money," Jacob said pointedly. "As well as her ring. The landlord might have given Mrs. Lachlan a month's grace, but we've no such assurances that her wedding ring will remain in Snowley's possession for that long."

"What do we know about the grounds?" Chloe asked.

Tommy began to pass around detailed sketches of the exterior. "As Graham mentioned, we have not yet breached Snowley's security, but we will. These markings show the entrances and exits, including every window and coal chute. The timetable on the back indicates the changing of the guards along the periphery, which occurs with remarkable precision. And on this sheet..."

Marjorie watched in silence as each of her siblings explained their contributions to the case.

While they were out mapping and surveilling and interviewing, she had been...behind a canvas. Not always the same one, mind. There was her portrait project, yes, but she also had her tutoring. Faircliffe, the girls at the art studio...there was rarely an idle moment.

Marjorie's efforts just weren't relevant to the cause.

She wanted to take an active part. Or at least she *wanted* to want to. But "extremely adept at watercolors" wasn't one of the services required when questioning enemy foot soldiers.

If lieutenants mumbled trade secrets beneath their breath, she couldn't hear their answers, but her ears were her least important asset. Marjorie was the sibling the others came to when they needed a document forged or a painting duplicated or the like. But her bit was always safe and subtle. Performed upstairs in the comfort of her own home.

Technically, her presence here in the Planning Parlor was unnecessary. Her siblings never needed her to leave her studio.

This was how she liked it. Or at least, how it had always been.

The rest of the Wynchesters took turns being the star of the show, while Marjorie remained a spectator to their greatness. Silent, awkward, hesitant. Unsure about anything that didn't fit on canvases and palettes.

She shifted in the needlepoint chair. Her comfortable life had never bothered her before. But now that all of her other siblings were taking on new roles—wife, husband, mother, leader—she could not help but fear they might change too much and leave her behind.

The thought of putting herself forth in any capacity other than cloistered artist was terrifying. But for the first time, the thought of *not* branching out, of not being *important* in some way, was significantly worse.

"What do we know about the forger?" Faircliffe asked.

"That he's irredeemable," Marjorie replied at once.

Forging was not the problem. Defrauding the innocent was.

This blackguard was using art—the one consistent source of happiness in Marjorie's life—to bring misery to everyone else's. He targeted vulnerable people in wretched straits, like the despairing young girl Marjorie herself had once been. She touched her fingertips to the item hanging on a chain beneath her bodice.

"He needs to be found and stopped." Marjorie took a deep breath. "I will help."

Half of her siblings furrowed their brows slightly at this pronouncement, as if flummoxed what on earth a wallflower like Marjorie meant to do. The other half didn't even change expression, assuming she'd meant nothing more than to voice her intent to cheer silently from the wings while the rest of them worked their magic.

Her throat tightened. What if *she* was the one who didn't fit into her family anymore? Was that what they thought? Were they right?

Marjorie would have to do more than prove herself to *herself.* Before anyone could believe her a plausible threat, she'd have to prove herself to everyone in this room. Not as their pet, no more terrifying than the kitten purring harmlessly in her lap. But as an equal, credible, capable Wynchester.

Then there could be no doubt that the siblings still belonged together. No matter what other changes the family weathered. *Marjorie* would still belong.

"My sources were able to ascertain the forger's name," Graham was saying.

Everyone leaned forward eagerly.

"Lord...Adrian...Webb," he pronounced with satisfaction.

The siblings blinked and exchanged blank looks.

"The Marquess of Meadowbrook's son?" Faircliffe asked in confusion.

"Younger son," offered Philippa. "I believe there's an elder brother."

"Yes. At least *some* of you recall your *Peerage*." Graham passed around a pair of battered copies.

Each sibling handed the volume of *Debrett's Peerage* to the next person without a glance at its pages.

"Just tell us," Tommy said. "Who is this villain?"

"Maybe he's not a villain," Jacob chided her. "He could be a poverty-stricken lord in penurious straits of his own."

"He's the son of a rich marquess," Philippa said. "Mother would've betrothed me to him sight unseen if he'd come home from the Continent long enough for her to sink her claws into him."

"Villain," Marjorie muttered. Born into a charmed life, and yet *chose* to make other people's lives harder.

Graham clarified, "Before coming into his fortune, Lord Adrian got into a bad scrape. He was cut off and banished at the age of nineteen."

Marjorie narrowed her eyes. "What kind of scrape?"

Her brother winced. "He seduced an innocent and left her with child."

"Left her, like . . . left her behind?" Marjorie asked, appalled.

Graham nodded. "Rumor has it that Webb running off rather than marry and own up to his deed is what caused him to be disinherited."

She shot up straight. "That's not a 'scrape.' That's evil."

7

*M*arjorie's lip curled. *Lord Adrian Webb.* Apt. The man was a spider, drawing in innocent victims like Mrs. Lachlan, only to drain them of what they valued most and leave them hanging with no recourse.

Someone had to put a stop to it.

She touched the tips of two blue-streaked fingers to the neck of her bodice. Hanging on a slender gold chain beneath protective layers of linen and muslin where it would not be damaged or flecked with paints was a pocket watch older than she was.

It had belonged to Baron Vanderbean. For Marjorie, Bean had been more than an adoptive father. He had been her salvation. Her biggest champion. The first person who looked at her and saw a powerful force, not an object of pity.

She'd carried the pocket watch with her since Bean's death, twenty-five months ago.

Marjorie ran a finger over the embossed exterior. Inside the lid was a mortifyingly terrible miniature she had painted of them, back when she was nine years old and a newly minted Wynchester. The portrait was barely recognizable as being of human subjects, much less representative of her and Bean in particular.

Yet he had seen her potential. When Bean professed to admire her artwork, Marjorie had flushed at the attention and attempted to give the portrait to him as a gift.

That was one of the few occasions in which Bean had spoken to her sharply.

"You have created something from nothing," he said. "It is a talent, and if you work hard, it will become a skill. I will purchase this from you for a crown. On one condition:

"Never undervalue yourself again."

She'd never held a crown before. A crown was worth *five shillings.* A scullery maid would be lucky to earn that in six months. And Marjorie had received it all at once, in exchange for something she had done! The thought was dizzying.

At the time, she hadn't believed her art deserved such riches, but she was determined to become worthy. Bean was right. With diligent practice, even the rawest talent could become formidable skill.

Back then, he had meant practicing her art. But didn't his advice apply to everything? Including cases like this?

"Now," said Chloe. "Shall we assign tasks?"

Marjorie leaned forward. No one looked in her direction as they set out their plans.

"All right," said Graham after a few moments. "That's all sorted. But who do we send to infiltrate Snowley's lair?"

Marjorie cleared her throat. "I—"

"Someone who can blend," said Chloe. "I'll go."

Marjorie looked at her sharply.

"You don't blend anymore," Faircliffe reminded her. "You're a duchess now."

Marjorie lifted a finger.

"I'll go in disguise," Tommy offered. "Should be easy enough to sneak in a footman or maid."

"One of the other servants is bound to notice a stranger," Elizabeth objected. "Kuni and I—"

This was what always happened. The more her talented siblings argued among themselves, the worse and less adequate Marjorie felt. Were they right to discard her as a choice? She couldn't blend, couldn't fight, couldn't mimic voices, couldn't sew disguises, couldn't do acrobatics, couldn't train animals, had no network of spies or reading circle of spinsters, couldn't *hear* as well as the others.

Her siblings were trying to protect her. They always did. They loved her. But Marjorie was fed up with being the sibling in need of protection.

Ignorant onlookers felt sorry for Marjorie for losing her hearing. She felt sorry for *them*, for having little grasp of the senses they claimed to master. What average people saw, they forgot immediately. What they smelled and touched, they didn't even notice.

Marjorie noticed it all. She reveled in sensation. She experienced the world more vividly than anyone else she'd ever met.

"*It's an art crime!*" she burst out, her voice echoing through the parlor loud enough to rattle the windows.

At her shout, all the siblings turned to her at once with matching expressions of astonishment.

"It's an art crime," Marjorie repeated. Her voice trembled. She ignored it and forced herself to push on. "*I know art.* None of the rest of you do. It has to be me."

"But Marjorie," Tommy said gently. "You can't..."

Marjorie glared at her.

Tommy closed her mouth, the tips of her ears flushing pink.

"You've all spent the past quarter hour listing the things that I *can't*," Marjorie ground out, her face hot with embarrassment. "Let me tell you what I *can*."

Her wide-eyed siblings gave her their full attention.

"I rarely go far from home," she acknowledged, "for many reasons. The logistics of crowds and new environments are a challenge, yes. But once I've *been*, once I've *seen*—"

"You remember," Chloe breathed, her eyes sparkling. "That's true. Marjorie doesn't need to take notes. She glimpses a thing and can recall every aspect of it, days or weeks later."

Marjorie nodded. "I can close my eyes and relive any stroll I've ever taken. Any spring morning, any winter frost. We don't know what weakness we're looking for behind enemy lines." She pointed at her face. "*These* are the eyes that will find it."

"And if the clue is spoken?" Graham asked.

She tapped next to her eye again. "I don't have to hear. I have to see. They can whisper amongst themselves well out of earshot of any of you, and as long as I am watching, *I* am the sibling most likely to grasp the secrets being divulged."

Her family stared at each other, considering her words with wonder.

"This case is bigger than our client," Graham said slowly. "Countless others are relying on the Wynchester family for justice. We need to take down Snowley and his entire operation."

Marjorie nodded. "Which is why I shall infiltrate this forgery ring and dismantle it from the inside out."

8

*O*ther than the two guards stationed on opposite ends of this floor, Adrian was alone. He could only hear signs of life when the door to the workroom was open, and even then, only if one of the guards walked directly past the open doorway, which rarely occurred.

In the beginning, they peered in at him more often. Adrian played the role of melodramatic *artiste* at once, claiming supervision stifled his muse. Hurry? An unskilled assistant would be counterproductive. He could not work if watched, and refused to try. If a guard peeked into the room, Adrian would immediately cease production and make a nuisance of himself until they fled back to their posts.

Fortunately, the guards had begrudgingly grown fond of him over the past weeks. They left him in peace more often than not, and the intermittent pat-downs occurred less and less. A foppish prisoner with no escape and no visitors did not appear to pose much of a risk.

They'd been right. That was one of the reasons Adrian insisted on working alone. It had thus far proved impossible to save himself.

Joey Box o' Crumpets stepped through the open door, noisily taking a bite out of a small green apple. "How goes the counterfeiting?"

"That's my business. How about you give me one of those apples?"

"I guess they're *my* business."

"If you're not going to share," said Adrian, "may I remind you that no one is to enter this workroom without my express—"

Grinders crowded the doorway and both guards stepped inside, followed by Snowley.

Joey pulled a second apple from his pocket and held it out toward Grinders. "Apple?"

Grinders pointed at the hatpin protruding from his lips and shook his head.

Joey shrugged. "Suit yourself."

Loud footsteps clattered out in the corridor.

Joey shoved both apples into his pockets and placed his hand above his pistol. "What the deuce is that?"

"A herd of elephants?" guessed Grinders, his fingers also going to his pistol.

"Good afternoon," bellowed an extraordinarily loud voice from a tiny wisp of a woman.

The guards whirled toward the open door.

A petite blonde with large blue eyes and an almost imperceptible smear of something green on her left cheek stood blinking angelically back at them. The *same* bonny young woman Adrian had seen at the British Museum two weeks ago. Teaching students, like Adrian had once dreamed of doing.

What would *she* be doing here?

Her eyes widened briefly in recognition. Followed not by flirtatious interest . . . but obvious distaste.

"Who the devil are *you*?" Snowley roared at the new arrival.

Adrian's mood brightened. This was interesting. Snowley was rarely caught unawares. Whoever this peculiar woman was, Adrian liked her already.

"I'm . . . Mary," she said, as if that explained anything.

Adrian hid his grin. Whoever she was, she probably wasn't Mary. He rested a hip on his worktable and settled in to watch the fireworks.

"*You* and *you*," Snowley snarled at his lapdogs. "You should not have left your posts. Have *all* the guards abandoned their stations?"

"Oh no," Mary assured him. "I noted at least five other armed ruffians still at their posts. There's two flanking the primary door, then two guarding the front and rear stairwells, and the one you've got hidden behind the chimney on the roof. It's rather terrifying."

Snowley had an armed guard on the roof? And in each stairwell? If Adrian had still been hoping to make a run to escape, this would be good intelligence to have.

"If they're all still at their posts," Snowley said with exaggerated patience, "then how the devil did you—"

"I'm here to help with your forgery problem," Mary went on, as if the criminal underworld's most ruthless mastermind hadn't been speaking.

All four men straightened. Snowley and his henchmen in suspicion, Adrian with hope. Was this tiny pip of a woman somehow here to save him?

"I'm afraid I don't presently *have* a 'forgery problem,'" Snowley bit out.

Mary blinked at him innocently. "If you believe *that*, then you've an even bigger problem. Might I summarize the situation?"

Amused, Snowley crossed his arms and leaned back. "I find I am all ears."

Her gaze was earnest. "Your counterfeit coins are poor imitations of the real thing. A child could—"

"Now, see here," Adrian blurted out, the words tripping over each other. It was one thing to do a purposefully imperfect job to try to snare Snowley. It was quite another to—

"Lord Adrian Webb, I presume?" Mary did not curtsey. She sneered instead. "You've been on the Continent for far too long if you think that *this*—" She held up what was presumably one of Adrian's shillings. "—would fool anyone with substance between his ears."

"Looks like a shilling to me," said Joey.

Mary gave an oblivious shrug. "Like I said."

"Did you materialize out of thin air just to insult my men?" Snowley snapped.

"Of course not." She stepped further into the studio and flung out her arms, palms up, as if the room were welcoming her home. "I've come to work for you."

"Over my dead body," Adrian growled.

Who *was* this woman?

She didn't just know who *Adrian* was. She'd known to find him *here*. A terrible sign that called into doubt all Adrian's plans to escape Snowley's stronghold before gossip of Adrian's connection to a heartless criminal could taint his innocent sister.

And then there was the question of this woman's involvement. Something was off. Was she a spy of some sort? Or was she the wide-eyed waif she appeared to be, simply in over her head, oblivious to how truly dangerous a man like Snowley could be?

"I'll bite," said Snowley. "What's wrong with that shilling?"

"Not much." Mary held it up to show him. "Just these three aspects here, and two additional instances of..."

Adrian's jaw dropped open as she pointed out every one of his subtle, please-let-Snowley-lose-his-power imperfections...and three more minuscule mistakes he hadn't even realized he was making.

Had she spent the past fortnight staring at this shilling with a jeweler's magnifying glass in one hand, and the Crown's official mold in the other?

Adrian straightened his spine before the situation spiraled further out of hand. "I suppose you think *you* can do better?"

She smiled. "I know I can."

9

⚜

Marjorie beamed at the room full of dangerous men. She did her best to project a careful mix of confidence and cluelessness. Excitement rushed through her veins, making her almost too giddy to stand still.

She was here. She was *doing it*. Marjorie "Never-Leaves-Her-Art-Studio" Wynchester had infiltrated a criminal enterprise!

Which, admittedly, looked remarkably like...an art studio.

The stations set up were for molding, not painting, but the *feel* of the room was the same. She could smell art, taste it, see its colors bursting forth in wiggles and spriggles, brightening every corner of what otherwise would be a rather uninspiring, cramped little room.

Lord Adrian looked embattled. *Humph.* As if a man that attractive had ever battled anything in his life. The pampered lordling had been handed everything at birth. Status, wealth, privilege, a face more handsome than any blackguard had a right to possess.

Just look at those cheekbones. Wasted on a man. She itched to paint them. The glossy brown curls. The strong, tapered jaw. The hard lips. The soft, curling eyelashes over flashing green eyes. Marjorie remembered their exact hue from that day at the museum. The color bewitched her. She had always loved green eyes.

Marjorie would not fall for his false charms.

"I'm sure *your* presence is superfluous," she told Lord Adrian innocently.

"Superfluous!" he choked out.

"At a minimum, vastly overrated. Just like..." She allowed herself to rake her eyes down his tall, lanky form, taking in the stiff shoulders and firm muscles dressed to perfection in a tailored olive green coat that he *knew* complemented his beautiful eyes. "Well, I'm sure you know your...shortcomings."

Webb spluttered incoherently.

Snowley's men howled with laughter.

Marjorie recalled Graham's notes. The one with the scarred ear and the badly healed broken nose was called Joey Box o' Crumpets. The baby-faced one whose fingertips never left his pistol was Grinders.

And the calm white-haired gentleman whose unimpressed expression had not wavered from the moment Marjorie crossed the threshold...that was Snowley. Prince of this palace. Ruler of this rookery.

Decider of Marjorie's fate.

"So you've discovered a few false coins floating around," Snowley drawled. He smelled faintly of rosewater. "What makes you think I have anything to do with it?"

"Two things," she answered. "First, multiple individuals distinctly recalled receiving the coins here in your establishment."

"Coins come and go at all hours of every day," Snowley said mildly. "When you stumble across a new penny, do you presume the shopkeeper personally minted it?"

"I might if the shopkeeper was you," she replied. "Forging coins as good as these—"

"Ha!" interrupted Lord Adrian. "I told you!"

"—requires talent," Marjorie continued, "and disseminating them requires means. In this neighborhood, or perhaps in all of London, only one man has the required brains and the boldness to forge coins at quantity without fear of the law taking notice."

"Then how did you take notice, my girl?"

"I told you. This is my wheelhouse. The bumbling green bucks of Bow Street wouldn't know a forgery if it fell on their heads. Not only can I tell the difference, I can actually replicate coins so well *no one* would believe they were false."

Snowley arched his brows. "*You* are an expert forger?"

"I never said I was an expert," she demurred. Then she tipped her head in Lord Adrian Webb's direction. "But I'm unquestionably better than *him*."

Webb huffed in outrage at this renewed insult.

Snowley sent him a considering look.

Marjorie did her best to look fawning and eager. This *had* to work. It was more than just proving herself *to* herself—and to her family. Their client, Mrs. Lachlan, had three weeks to pay her rent, and possibly less time than that to recover her wedding ring... which, with luck, was somewhere on this property. Somewhere Marjorie could find it.

Her gambit also needed to succeed because they couldn't keep sending new Wynchesters until one of them stuck. One and done. Marjorie was it. A second stranger would be met with far too much suspicion to make any headway.

Everyone was depending on Marjorie to make the deal. Her family, their client, all the other defrauded customers...

"I'll tell you what," Marjorie said to Snowley.

Amusement flickered on his face. "*You'll* tell *me*?"

"I'll phrase it as a question if it makes it easier to answer," she promised. "Would you rather have the *second*-best forger in this room on your payroll? Or do you prefer to employ the best of the best?"

"Oh, he's not on my payroll." Snowley's smile was sweet and indulgent. Just a kindly old man having a little chat. "He gives *me* money. What makes you think I'd want to pay *you*?"

"Because you are also the best of the best," she answered without hesitation. "You did not become who you are today by letting others poach the most promising talent whilst you made do with subpar approximations." She fluttered her eyelashes at Webb. "Present company excepted."

Snowley's lips quirked. "Go on."

"A trial month," Marjorie said.

His eyebrows rose. "A ... trial month?"

"Four weeks of labor at half pay. I'll work for you ten hours a day, six days a week. After that time, once you've seen my work, I shall expect to be rewarded handsomely with increased wages. If, for any reason, you prefer to part ways instead ... then we do so, free and clear on both sides. Neither owes the other a thing."

Snowley was silent.

Grinders and Joey exchanged a matching gesture Marjorie hadn't seen before, and snickered. It must be a secret sign of some sort. She was determined to puzzle out its meaning ... *if* Snowley let her stay.

Marjorie tried to look as though she weren't holding her breath. Chloe and Faircliffe had helped her prepare this argument. A proposal no crime lord would reasonably refuse. Cheap labor, from a supposed expert? Sure, given Snowley's reputation, he might arrange an untimely disappearance for Marjorie once her month was through. Unfortunately for him, she wouldn't need that long to do her job. Marjorie would be in and out within a fortnight. Perhaps within a matter of days, if she was lucky—and if Snowley agreed to her offer.

He had not yet assented.

She tried not to fidget under Snowley's discerning gaze.

This was not his first negotiation. If she had come on too strong or not strong enough—despite following Tommy's role-playing instructions to the letter—Snowley might correctly suspect the offer was too good to be true, and the wise move would be to send "Mary" packing before she disrupted any more of his day.

"Working here," Lord Adrian bit out, his green eyes full of portent, "is an extraordinarily foolish idea, Mary."

Marjorie smiled and made a pointed gesture right back at Webb. Who was working here, in this very room, for Snowley.

"Exactly," Lord Adrian said dryly. "You see how it's turned out for me. I should hate for fortune to turn its back on you, too."

To be honest... so would Marjorie.

She felt oddly exposed before his frank gaze. As if she were stripped bare, rather than outfitted in the patched brown muslin Tommy had assured Marjorie would not raise a single eyebrow.

How she missed her sister! The Wynchesters were usually a team effort, not a solo act. Part of Marjorie longed to have all five of her siblings and all three of their spouses in formation beside her.

An even more seductive fantasy whispered, *But this is your first stab at independence. Are you going to run home now, and preemptively declare yourself a failure? Or will you prove yourself every bit as capable and courageous as your siblings?*

"Every bit," Marjorie mumbled.

All four men gave her puzzled looks. All right, perhaps she hadn't mumbled.

It wasn't her fault. It was Lord Adrian's. How was anyone supposed to *think* with him standing there all casually dashing and handsome like that? His striking good looks were vexingly distracting. No doubt his rakish beauty was how he got away with... everything he'd ever done.

If even a quarter of the gossip was true, he was every inch the cad they made him out to be. His presence here as one of Snowley's men only cemented his well-earned reputation as a thoughtless, selfish bounder. Who apparently paid Snowley for the privilege of destroying lives.

Never had Marjorie been more pleased for *spoil his lordship's plans* to be one of her primary directives.

But first, she needed to be welcomed into the crew.

Lord Adrian shot a sharp look to his left. Marjorie turned her head as well.

Joey and Grinders were laughing, their gazes skeptical and self-satisfied. One of them must have made an unflattering comment beneath his breath. She could not show weakness.

Marjorie struck a defiant pose. "What did you just say?"

"I *said*," Joey began with a smirk, "ain't never seen a woman who..." He batted at his nose while finishing the insult, leaving Marjorie just as clueless the second time around.

How was she supposed to craft a cutting, pithy response when she had no idea what was being said?

She clenched her jaw and held her ground. "What did you say?"

"What?" Grinders gaped at her. "He's said it twice now. Are you *deaf*?"

Here they went.

"Yes," Marjorie said blandly. "Mostly."

Lord Adrian covered his face with his hand. Was his secondhand embarrassment because of Grinders's thoughtless comment...or because of Marjorie's deafness?

She smiled as though whatever had been said was a compliment.

Joey and Grinders shifted awkwardly.

Good. Marjorie could use their discomfort to her advantage. *She* didn't mind that she was hard of hearing. It was other people who made a five-act tragedy out of it.

To the devil with Joey and Grinders, and Lord Adrian with his handsome face hidden behind his hand. Marjorie did not hide. She was proud of who and how she was.

And she hadn't lied about being the better artist.

"Well," said Grinders, removing the hatpin from beneath his teeth in order to move his mouth in outsized contortions. "If *that* doesn't prove you don't belong..."

Marjorie fought the urge to roll her eyes, then went ahead and gave in. Their ignorant assumptions could only aid her. After all, people heard "deaf" or "hard of hearing" and assumed "helpless."

Not "ulterior agent on a clandestine mission to destroy our operation from within."

"Perhaps what doesn't belong," she said sweetly, "is your—"

"Enough," Snowley cut in at last. "If indeed I am in the presence of the two best forgers in all of England, only a fool would give either one of them up."

Both Marjorie and Lord Adrian snapped to attention.

"After the trial month, your starting salary will be seven guineas."

Laughably low. A laundry maid could make more.

Marjorie named a sum more in line with what an upper servant might earn in an aristocratic household.

Snowley countered with a more modest salary.

"Agreed. How *wonderful*," Marjorie gushed. "You shan't regret this."

"I know I shan't. And no. I will not dismiss Lord Adrian ahead of schedule, even if he indeed proves to be the lesser artist. I have known him for years. I do not know you at all. Webb reports to me, and you report...to *him*. As his apprentice. You are not to leave his side until further notice."

"Absolutely not," she and Lord Adrian sputtered in tandem.

The guards sniggered.

"I'm nobody's apprentice," she told Snowley hotly.

"You're his," Snowley replied, unmoved. "For the next month."

You're his.

Snowley hadn't meant the words to sound... *lewd*. But when Lord Adrian's eyes locked on Marjorie's, electricity sparked between them, lighting the room with whites and blacks and reds. Lustful colors. Impossible colors. The faint scent of musk and spice.

Lord Adrian gave her a cocky grin. "Mine, eh? Perhaps I was hasty."

"Perhaps you'll find my half boot landing between your legs," she shot back.

"Well then." Snowley brushed off his hands. "It sounds like you two have things worked out. I'll authorize supper and sleeping quarters for you and check on your minting progress in the morning."

Marjorie whirled to face him, panic ricocheting in her chest. "I agreed to work for you during the day, not become part of your household." She was desperate to contact her siblings and ask for advice. Marjorie suddenly felt unbearably, horribly alone. "I will report at eight and leave at six."

Snowley chuckled. "You think *you* dictate your hours?"

"I do when I give them away at half price. You are not my master. I already have one," she added in a fit of inspiration. "I'm to prepare his breakfast every morning and his supper every night, and wash and clean besides."

"You plan to do all that *and* spend ten hours a day forging coins?" Grinders asked.

"I'd rather work here," Marjorie answered. "For more money. But until I earn the wages I deserve, I must balance both worlds."

Snowley narrowed his eyes. "You report three hours after sunrise and stay until sunset. Ten hours, no excuses. Then we'll see if I decide to keep you when your trial month concludes."

"I already know you will," Marjorie answered confidently, locking her legs to keep her knees from buckling in relief at having dodged involuntary confinement.

"I, for one," Lord Adrian said with a wicked smile, "am looking forward to the competition."

Marjorie clenched her teeth and gave a tight-lipped smile. She was part of the forgery ring, just as she wanted.

Even if it meant she was saddled with *him*.

10

*D*espite his bravado for Snowley's sake, Adrian could not allow this naïve young woman to remain under this roof. Not with the way the guards were watching her. Or Snowley's propensity to seek vengeance. The man regarded her right now with the wheels of his evil mind whirring behind his grandfatherly blue gaze. It was enough to freeze one's blood.

This was no place for a woman. Or anyone who wished to keep their head attached to their neck. Adrian was stuck in this room, committing treason on the hour. It was too late for him. But it was not yet too late for Mary.

"You won't be sorry you chose me," she assured Snowley.

Of course not. *Mary* was the one who would be sorry.

He had to get her out of here at any cost. There was no doubt she was in over her fetching blond head. Hell, *Adrian* was in over his head. Blackguard though he might be, he could not permit an innocent party to get tangled up in his mess.

Blackguard though he might be. That was the answer!

For once in Adrian's life, his reputation as an unapologetically roguish, self-serving, debauched libertine would work to his advantage. The fastest way to save Mary would be by proving himself beyond salvation.

Adrian would own his bad reputation, *be* his bad reputation, play the most rude-and-randy role possible, until any young lady with any sense of self-preservation whatsoever would have no choice but to run off screaming.

He waggled his eyebrows. "Who cares about forgery? With a delectable morsel like you in arm's reach, there are much more pleasurable ways to tutor an apprentice."

She stared back at him coolly. "I doubt you're any better at pleasuring than you are at counterfeiting coins."

He felt a muscle twitch in his jaw. "If you think you can do better—"

"Oh, did I forget to *prove* it?" She tugged open the string to her reticule and dumped its contents atop his worktable.

One might presume the items a beautiful young lady like Mary might carry about would be things like rouge or smelling salts or tuppence to purchase some frippery.

One would be wrong.

Out from Mary's reticule tumbled a pair of . . . chalk molds. As she opened them, he saw that one was for creating shillings, and the other for sixpence.

"You brought your own molds?" he said in disbelief.

"Someone had to provide a quality product." She lowered her eyes humbly and gave a self-effacing little shrug.

Adrian wasn't fooled for a second. What kind of young lady flounced about the city streets with counterfeiting molds in her reticule? Who *was* this woman?

"Well?" asked Snowley. "Are her molds any good?"

"No," Adrian said flatly.

Mary's blue eyes flashed. "You didn't even look at them."

With a heaving sigh and a roll of his eyes, he snatched up the closest mold and made a big production of inspecting every crevice and angle with a magnifying glass.

It was good, damn it.

Adrian wouldn't go so far as to call it perfect...only because he didn't want to admit it. Mary's molds were essentially identical to Adrian's molds, minus the purposeful imperfections he'd included and she had not. He would have to try much harder to frighten her off.

"Garbage," he proclaimed. "The first attempt of a talented but inexperienced neophyte."

"Make a coin," Snowley ordered her.

Bloody hell.

Adrian had made Snowley believe the coin-making process was complicated and time-consuming. If Mary waltzed over to the molten metal boiling over the fire and dashed off a shilling or two before Snowley's eyes, there was no telling how the vindictive criminal might take his revenge.

"She can't just *make a coin*," Adrian informed him, imbuing his voice with all the grating impudence of an arrogant *artiste*.

Mary bristled. "*I* certainly have no problem—"

"Even *you* brutes know that it takes hours to properly produce a masterpiece, rather than a poor imitation," Adrian continued, talking over her without taking his sardonic gaze from Snowley. "Come back in two hours. We'll have four new shillings completed then, and you can decide for yourself."

Snowley lifted his pocket watch from his breast pocket. "Two hours, Webb. I'll be back for my money."

Adrian nodded dutifully. "Two hours."

Mary should be long gone by then.

"Go on, then." Snowley motioned to Joey and Grinders. "Haven't you got posts to guard?"

"Sorry."

"Right away, m'lord."

Joey and Grinders bowed and scraped obsequiously as they bumbled their way out the door. As the three men swept from the room, Snowley closed the door behind them.

And locked it. With Mary inside.

Adrian gazed at her in dismay.

She folded her arms beneath her bosom and narrowed her eyes at him. "Are you really as incompetent a forger as you seem?"

"Are you really in as dire need of a good tup and an even better spanking as *you* seem?" he countered.

"I suppose you'd take two hours at that, too," she snapped.

He gave a wolfish smile. "Only when done right."

Her blond eyelashes fluttered as she rolled her blue eyes in disdain, but a hint of wariness had crept into her pale, pretty face.

It was about bloody time.

Adrian picked up one of her molds and began tossing it into the air and catching it. Maybe he should toss both of them into the air and juggle them. He hadn't the least notion how to juggle. The molds would crash to the scarred wooden floor and shatter into a million pieces, breaking Mary's tender heart—and preventing her from stumbling headlong into Snowley's web.

Matter of fact, he could chuck the molds directly at the brick of the fireplace just as had been done to his art so many times. Mary could accuse him of immaturity or professional jealousy or anything else she liked, but without her molds to show him up, what advantage would she have?

He caught the shilling mold on its next arc down and curled his fingers into a fist around it.

Throw, he ordered himself.

His arm stayed resolutely stiff.

It was a damn good mold, was the devil of it. An honest-to-God work of art. She was categorically daft to have walked into a cutthroat criminal's secret den on purpose, but she wasn't wrong about her talent.

"Are you planning to destroy the evidence?" she asked archly.

"The evidence of your inferiority as an artist? Even pulverizing these molds into dust can't cover *that* up. Take off your dress if you want to spend the next two hours in an activity worth my time."

"I didn't think heartless rakes such as you bothered with niceties like removing a lady's dress."

"It's not for your benefit. This is a dirty floor and I'm wearing a nice coat. I should hate to muss the fabric by writhing on it."

A frown creased Mary's brow. "Isn't the woman usually on the bottom?"

"Oh, *darling*," he drawled. "There is *so* much I can teach you."

She glanced over her shoulder at the locked door.

Good. They were making progress.

"A true gentleman would not abuse a lady's garments in such a selfish manner," she informed him. "An honorable lord would lay his coat over mud puddles to spare his lady's hems, and should not hesitate to perform the same etiquette when faced with the lesser foe of a dusty floor."

"I am neither a gentleman nor honorable," he reminded her. "And if you think your current gown is fine enough to be worth—"

Wait. *What* were they arguing about? Whose clothing would serve best as a bed for lovemaking?

"If you promise to cease this silly forgery nonsense," he said silkily, "I promise to sacrifice my favorite coat in the name of teaching you to ride astride."

"Oh dear." She made a pitying moue. "Is *that* your favorite coat? Perhaps you oughtn't be teaching anything to anyone."

Adrian's spine straightened in affront. "I've just arrived from the Continent. It is hardly *my* fault if Parisian fashions take longer to penetrate British skulls. By this time next season, all your dandies will be dressed just like this, and Paris will be off already to something else."

"You're just skipping the middle step and going straight to passé?" She arched her brows. "An interesting stratagem."

"What do you call that...unfortunate...*thing* draped over your petite frame?" he demanded. "Besides drab and lifeless and boring."

"I call it comfortable." She ran her hands over her slender curves and tossed him a knowing smirk. "I shan't be the one leaning over a pot of boiling metal wearing a tailcoat and a cravat with more fabric than the canopy of a four-poster bed. You're right, my lord. One of us was *not* thinking when they dressed for today's activities."

He gasped and pressed a hand to his sharply creased lapel. "No self-respecting gentleman would *ever* commit high treason without a competently tied cravat. Fashion is not a costume, my dear. It's a way of life."

She snorted. "Someone else's life, maybe."

He returned his attention to her chalk molds to hide his begrudging amusement. In any other setting, he would be tickled to meet someone capable of parrying his every comment with an equally adept thrust of her own.

In their current circumstance, however, such alchemy was worse than vexing.

It was dangerous.

"Well?" She sidled close enough for her arm to brush his. "Now that no one can overhear us, you can tell the truth. My molds aren't half bad for an unfashionable orphan who's deaf in one ear, eh?"

He stared at her in bafflement. "What the devil has your *ear* to do with counterfeiting? It doesn't seem to affect your *mouth* at all," he pointed out, then remembered himself. "A pretty mouth that I should be happy to assign an entirely different task to accomplish."

"I shan't kiss you," she said flatly. "I only kiss men that I *like*."

"I wasn't talking about kissing," he assured her.

Unfortunately, he was now plagued by visions of the sort of gentlemen Mary voluntarily pressed her lips to. Not gentlemen, he thought darkly. No gentleman would steal kisses without the intent of pursuing a lady honorably.

Not that Mary was a lady, Adrian was forced to acknowledge. Very much a woman—those attributes spoke for themselves—but a lady? Why did he keep thinking the rules of her world should mirror the rules of his? Even *he* did not play by them.

Ask anyone. The gossips would *love* to regale you with stories of Lord Adrian, Heartless Rogue.

"Let me see your chalk molds," Mary said. "There must be something stuck in the sixpence bowl to deform the circumference in that manner."

He tried to grab it out of her hand before she saw the truth.

By the look on her face, it was too late.

11

*Y*ou made the mold off balance on purpose?" Mary frowned up at Adrian. "No decent artist is so ham-handed as to believe *this* shape a true circle. You *meant* for it to be askew. But why should you—"

His heart thumped an alarm. She was far too perceptive. If she told her suspicions to Snowley...

"Let's try your molds, if they're so wonderful." He snatched his from her fingers before she could stop him and opened one of hers instead.

She tried to grab it from him, but he tapped her aside with his hip and poured a dollop of metal into the shilling chalk mold. There wasn't much metal left, which meant it was almost time to ask for more source material.

Adrian hated asking for more material.

"Hold this." He handed her the full mold. "Keep it closed tight."

"I know how to use my own mold," she grumbled.

He retrieved her other one from atop the worktable and tipped in just enough metal to fill the sixpence cavity, then closed it tight so it would begin to set.

"Well, that took sixty seconds." She arched a brow. "However shall we fill the other hour and fifty-nine minutes?"

"That's my line," he muttered. "Let me know when you're ready to do the gentlemanly thing with your hideous dress."

She handed him her mold, then reached around him to retrieve his shilling chalk mold. "In the absence of an interesting alternative, let's compare the quality of our work side-by-side, shall we?"

Before he could argue, she expertly tipped the molten metal into the purposefully flawed mold.

Adrian glared at her. Most men would find her bossy brazenness off-putting, not provocative. He wasn't supposed to *actually* long to kiss that smirk off her lips. He was supposed to be pretending.

She handed him the full shilling mold as soon as it set, then frowned at his sixpence chalk mold.

"What now?" he asked, his voice dripping with sarcasm. "Should I recalibrate the circumference of the circle with my sea captain's compass, Your Highness?"

She held up the mold. "I can't decide if you're a subtle genius or buffoonishly incompetent. This one is also asymmetrical, with barely detectable chipping about the edges. It would produce a coin that looks as though it was run over by a carriage, then trimmed for silver by some unscrupulous trickster."

Adrian shuddered theatrically. "Some people's morals."

"It will look like a coin that's been in circulation for years."

"So...better than yours, then?" he asked with exaggerated politeness.

"It would be," she admitted, "if this were the only such coin. But if *all* your counterfeits are worn and damaged in exactly the same way, a clever mind could recognize the impossibility and realize your coins are false."

This was true. It had also been done on purpose. Adrian had meant to make the coins good enough to fool Snowley, but wrong enough to get Snowley caught.

But everything had gone backward. The false coins had put the victims in harm's way, not Snowley. Adrian needed a new plan. A better plan. One that implicated Snowley without catching innocent victims in the crossfire.

It was impossible to think of anything brilliant with Mary standing by his side. Her simple muslin dress *did* look comfortable. And soft. And improbably fetching. This close to the fire, all he should be able to smell was the molten metal, but Adrian could swear Mary's hair gave off a faint scent of something flowery and sweet.

Adrian's fingers twitched with his urge to edge closer.

The uncomfortable heat warming his skin was one hundred percent due to the proximity to the fire and had nothing at all to do with the curves she'd accentuated when she'd passed her palms down her body.

He stepped away quickly. From the fire. It had nothing to do with the woman. After all, there was no sense looming over an open flame while wearing three layers and a mainsail's worth of linen at his throat, as Mary had pointed out.

Maybe *that's* what he could take off to use as a makeshift blanket...

"How much longer?" she asked.

"Twenty minutes," he answered hoarsely, then cleared his throat. "We didn't fill the crown mold."

"I didn't bring one. We can compare our craftsmanship with these."

"Snowley will want to make the most of his investment. He'll care a lot more about crown pieces than he will a pair of sixpence."

She yawned. "I don't care what Snowley wants."

He set down his molds and grabbed her elbow. "You'd *better* care what Snowley wants. What Snowley wants, Snowley gets. At this moment, he has both of us. If you're wise, the moment that door unlocks, you'll hie straight home."

The look she sent him was withering. "A key in the door isn't what's keeping me here."

"Was it the offer of a leisurely tup and a good spanking?" he asked hopefully. "Because I had the splendid idea to use my cravat for a blanket—"

She snorted. "You are impossible."

"And also very much in earnest," he promised. "Really, all we need to protect are my coat and your knees."

Not entirely true. He also had to protect his sister—and Snowley's victims. The longer Mary stuck around, the greater the chances that Snowley would discover Adrian's treachery before he could stop Snowley from defrauding the poor. And the scandal might make its way back to Iris.

While he worried at the problem, Adrian continued his work in silence. Then he cast a sidelong look at Mary. "Where did you really come from?"

She tilted her hand toward the window. "The neighborhood."

"But why come *here*?"

"Have you seen the neighborhood?" she asked wryly, jabbing her hand toward the window. "I don't know what sorts of fancy, well-paid posts you're used to, but there aren't any of those here."

"Snowley is a criminal."

She arched her brows. "Did he force you to become one, too? Or did you come to him *because* his line of business could give you the life—and the gold—you dreamt of?"

Adrian snapped his teeth together. Mary was right. He was in no position to judge her.

"Twenty minutes are up." She pointed at the scuffed clock on the worktable. "Pop out those coins whilst you recalibrate your seduction methods, and we can begin another round."

They tipped the coins onto the worktable, then cleaned and refilled each of the molds with fresh metal. As soon as all four chalk molds were closed and set, they picked up the first coins and rubbed them with rags before sanding and polishing each surface.

It wasn't until they'd been working together in companionable silence for several minutes that Adrian realized *they'd been working together in companionable silence for several minutes.* This was the opposite of chasing her away.

This was a disaster.

Adrian's heart pounded. She was good, was the problem. She was sweet and sassy and pretty and talented. If this had been his art studio back in Paris, rather than a dingy workroom in the middle of a rookery, he would have been eager for the company of a woman like this.

He'd never been more disgruntled by someone in his life.

Whatever happened, he could *not* allow a personal connection to form between them. She was a stranger and must remain one. This was destined to be their sole encounter. For her sake, *and* for his.

No matter how easy she was to work with.

12

They were on their fifth round when the key turned in the lock and Snowley opened the workroom door.

Adrian had never been happier to see his captor.

"Well?" Snowley said.

Adrian reached for the pile of coins.

"Just a minute." Mary pulled a *second* reticule from a hidden pocket and dumped their newly minted coins inside the pouch.

"What's in there?" Adrian whispered. "Can I search you for more hidden pockets?"

"Wheatmeal and bits of Cheshire cheese," she answered at full volume.

Snowley strode forward. "What did you say?"

Mary fished out the coins and dusted them with a rag before dropping them into Snowley's outstretched hand. "It's an aging technique. They can't look *too* new."

With the index finger of his other hand, Snowley poked through them. "Some of these are yours, and some of them are hers?"

Mary nodded. "Mine are the ones that are better."

Adrian shot his gaze at her. "But you said my coins were—"

"And I meant it. But I never said I played fair."

He chuckled despite himself. It didn't matter which mold produced the superior coins. Mary intended to claim the winners as her own.

Snowley glanced up. "I can't tell the difference. All of these look like any number of coins that have crossed my palm a dozen times today."

"We need to make them worse," said Mary.

Snowley frowned. "Worse?"

"We're using too much true silver in the mixture. It will be cheaper and just as fast to dilute the silver with inferior metals. As long as the materials we use have the right color and weight, no one will notice."

Snowley's eyes glittered. "An excellent point."

Blast. This was not the way to get Mary dismissed from service.

In fact... Adrian made a face at a sudden realization. He *couldn't* get her dismissed. If Snowley perceived wrongdoing or incompetence, he would retaliate with every ounce of his ingenuity and vindictiveness. Adrian couldn't put Mary at risk. He *had* to force her to abandon her post of her own free will.

"All right." Snowley curled his fingers around the coins and slid them into his pocket. "Double the labor means double the product. Your trial month begins tomorrow morning at eight. I expect you to be on time."

Triumph flooded Mary's face, giving her ethereal beauty even more energy and power.

"I'll be here at seven fifty-nine," she promised. "You can show your appreciation for my punctuality when you present my overdue wages in a month."

Snowley raised his brows and slanted a speaking glance at Adrian. "Was she this cheeky whilst I was gone?"

"Worse," Adrian said morosely. "I respectfully request permission to gag her at eight oh one tomorrow morning."

"That's between the two of you." Snowley motioned Mary toward the door.

Adrian followed close behind. His list of tasks was quickly

becoming overwhelming. He had to look out for Mary and Iris, save himself, stop Snowley, and avenge the victims—or at least prevent any more harm from being done.

Snowley swung out an arm to block Adrian before he could step into the corridor. "And where do you think you're going?"

"If she can return home for the evening, why can't I?"

"Because I don't trust you."

"You trusted me once."

Snowley's blue eyes were hard as sapphires. "I won't make that mistake again."

Adrian tried a different tack. "People know I'm in town. I was here, and then I disappeared. What if my father goes to the Bow Street Runners with a complaint that his son has gone missing?"

"Your father is the reason you went missing the first time," Snowley pointed out dryly. "The marquess is more likely to complain if you're still here in London. If anything, he'll send me flowers for keeping you out of his sight."

"Bad example," Adrian allowed. "My sister—"

"Won't be summoning any Runners, either," Snowley finished. "Not that it would aid you if she did. If they burst through this door, *you're* the one they'll catch in the act of forgery, not me. Besides," he added casually, "if you're caught in a scandal that outrageous, the person who will be hurt the most..."

"Leave Iris alone," Adrian warned.

"I'm keeping your sister at a respectful distance," Snowley promised lightly. "For now."

"Forever," Adrian growled. "Better yet, leave her out of it. You have me. I'll pay off my debt in full. You have my word."

"I had your word before," Snowley reminded him. "It was worth about..." He held up a counterfeit sixpence. "Therefore, I shall keep you here by any means I deem necessary. You're mine, Webb. No heroes are coming to save you. Not the Bow Street Runners, and not the do-good Wynchesters."

"What on earth," Adrian asked, "is a Wynchester?"

"Pains in the arse," Snowley answered. "As are you. But until your debt is paid, you live here."

"A holiday doesn't frighten me," Adrian muttered. "Even one spent with you."

"Then you're a bigger fool than I thought." Snowley smiled. "I should terrify you."

"Your sad excuse for a cravat is the only thing that scares me," Adrian assured him. "Fire your valet. You might as well wear a dirty handkerchief at your throat as *that* mess. Honestly, it's embarrassing to be in the same studio as—"

Snowley jingled the freshly minted coins in his pocket. "If you want out, then work faster."

"We haven't enough metal." Adrian stepped aside and gestured for Snowley to peer into the pot.

"I've just the thing." Snowley reached into his pocket and pulled out a beautiful engraved locket on a long silver chain. "This was just entrusted to me in exchange for a few of your special coins."

"Let's not use pure silver," Adrian said quickly. "Like Mary said, we can mix in a bit of—"

Snowley flicked open the locket. Inside was a miniature of a chubby-cheeked infant. Before Adrian could stop him, Snowley dug the portrait out with his fingernail and flicked it into the fire.

"You can't just—" Adrian spluttered.

"You want out, don't you?" Snowley tossed the necklace and locket into the pot of molten metal. "Joey will bring you more from the storage chamber tomorrow."

Adrian stared at what was left of the necklace as it sank into the melted silver murk. At last, he ripped his gaze from the crucible.

"Can Joey also bring a bit of tin and lead?" he asked quietly. "The silver will last longer, and you'll have more coins to spend."

"It'll be here within the week." Snowley left, the new coins jangling in his pocket.

Adrian rubbed his face with his hands, unable to step away from the bubbling pot. His gut churned. Thanks to his devil's bargain with Snowley, Adrian was becoming precisely the conscienceless reprobate he'd always pretended to be.

Whoever's necklace that was *loved* the baby inside. Planned to return soon for their memento. Had walked away with a handful of Adrian's coins. Forgeries that might or might not work to rescue her from whatever scrape she was in. Leaving her in the same trouble as before, but with less money and no heirloom.

Because of him.

13

One of the dusty, unadorned carriages the Wynchester family drove to pass for a hackney paused a few yards away from Snowley's fortress. From the seat beside her, Marjorie picked up a heavy basket. She wasn't going to wait on Snowley to provide inferior metals.

Marjorie stepped out of the carriage with care, keeping her hems free from the muck covering the cobblestones.

Instead of spending a typical day alone in her art studio, Marjorie would spend the next several hours alone...with Lord Adrian Webb. Her mission felt like an adventure.

She clutched her basket to her abdomen and hurried down the street, as if she could outrun the image of her nemesis in her mind. She wished she could wipe her thoughts clean. Surely the quickness to her pulse had nothing to do with overbearing, cocksure, entirely-too-handsome-for-his-own-good Lord Adrian.

Marjorie did not *like* rakehells, and she despised men who exploited others' desperation for personal profit. She especially did not appreciate the moments when Webb had managed to surprise a smile from her lips out of pure, unapologetic outrageousness. Marjorie did not want to be charmed. She wanted Lord Adrian and the rest of Snowley's crew rotting in Newgate for their crimes.

Before Marjorie could knock, the same weary-looking maid she'd glimpsed the day before swung open the door. According to Graham's notes, this was Ruby.

"Using the front door today, are we?" Ruby dipped her eyes, giving Marjorie a perfunctory appraisal before stepping aside.

As Marjorie crossed the threshold, she glimpsed two guards in the shadows, each with their hands in easy reach of their pistols.

"I'll take you up," said the one called Angel.

"I remember the way."

"Snowley's orders."

Oh, very well. It was an asset if they thought of her as helpless.

She fell into position between them. They walked past the kitchens and traipsed up two flights of narrow wooden stairs. Grinders escorted her from there. Joey stepped up to meet them. He paused at the workroom to push open the door, which had been left ajar.

Dim light spilled into the corridor, along with the smell of molten metal.

"Didn't think twice about this terrible plan, I see," Lord Adrian drawled as Marjorie stepped into the room.

She ignored him and crossed briskly to the fireplace to attend to the crucible and its contents.

From the corner of her eye, she could see Lord Adrian watching her. His vivid green eyes were bright with undisguised interest. Spirals of spiced blue-green and orange-pink rose from him like fragrant steam from a hot cup of chocolate. As much as he claimed not to want her about, it seemed anticipation sizzled through his veins as much as Marjorie's.

Er, except her excitement was due to being a lone Wynchester on an important, dangerous mission. Not to being forced to interact with a scoundrel like Webb for twelve hours.

"You know what to do," Joey said.

Without waiting for further comment, he and Grinders strode away from the workroom. Unlike yesterday, they left the door unlocked.

Marjorie was not fooled. She didn't need to poke her head into the corridor to know that one or both of them were stationed by the door. She turned away from the bubbling pot.

"Everything to your liking?" Lord Adrian asked sarcastically.

At least Marjorie assumed the question was sarcastic. His voice was pitched just a touch too low for her to distinguish tone. His expression was guileless and open, as if he'd been waiting all morning with genuine curiosity in anticipation of the moment when she'd stride through the door and pass judgment upon his work area... and by extension on Lord Adrian as an artist.

"Dreadful," she informed him.

This was a lie. Everything was impeccable, and he knew it. If she hadn't brought along her own supply of scrap metal, there'd be nothing for her to stir up or adjust. As much as she longed to put this heartless forger in his place, the truth was Marjorie couldn't have set things up better herself. Carefully, she added bits of tin and pewter to the crucible.

Lord Adrian beamed at her, correctly interpreting that her disgruntlement was not because she'd found fault, but because she had not. He gestured at the basket. "Did you bring a blanket?"

"Are we having a picnic?" she said sourly.

His smile grew wider. "I could eat."

She turned away from him and inspected his chalk molds. Both actions were pointless. The molds wouldn't be any different today than they were yesterday, and as for Lord Adrian... his image had imprinted on Marjorie's brain the first time she'd glimpsed him.

Today a gorgeous, touchably soft purple coat fit for a prince stretched across his shoulders and tapered to his narrow hips. His buckskins were scandalously formfitting—or perhaps it was Marjorie's reaction that was scandalous.

Webb's shiny black Hessians were probably the cleanest surface in the entire rookery, save for the intricately folded cravat flowing from his neck. The expensive linen was somehow still crisply starched and snowy white, despite leaning precariously over a pot of molten metal all morning.

Unless he hadn't. Perhaps Lord Adrian had waited until moments before Marjorie was due to arrive, and *then* tied on his cravat, so that he would be dandy-perfect when she walked through the door.

Ridiculous. He didn't care *that* much for her opinion of him.

Did he?

She risked a glance over her shoulder at him.

He was watching her, green eyes heavy-lidded, as though lost in a fantasy world of his own. When his gaze met hers, he did not turn away in embarrassment at having been caught staring. His eyebrows lifted in blatant invitation, and he took a deliberate step forward.

Marjorie clutched a pair of molds like pistols. As far as weapons went, these were worthless. She could maybe toss one at his head and further muss his carefully disordered bronze curls. Which would likely only serve to make the blackguard even handsomer.

Augh, when had she decided his hair was *bronze* and not an ordinary brown? Perhaps because nothing about Lord Adrian Webb was ordinary.

Even *if* the chalk mold stems clutched defensively in Marjorie's fists had actually been the grips of pistols, it was unlikely to be the first time the rake had faced down the threat of a bullet. Danger probably hadn't stopped him then, either. He likely had a preferred locale in the park for dueling an endless queue of outraged fathers and angry husbands.

"Has anyone ever told you—" he began.

"Yes," she interrupted. "Many times. You are neither original nor interesting. I'm here to work, not flirt with you. Come and take your chalk molds so that we can get started."

He tossed his coat over a wooden stool, revealing a white linen shirt with billowing sleeves. The softness of the material could not hide the hardness of the muscles beneath. Marjorie tried not to notice. Lord Adrian stepped closer, palms outstretched.

She slapped the molds into his hands.

He closed his fingers about her wrists, capturing her hands with his, with the molds caught in between their palms.

"Interesting," he purred. "I didn't say anything about flirting."

Normally, seductive murmurs were wasted on Marjorie. Whispers were too low, too subtle. She couldn't hear them. She *shouldn't* be able to hear his, either. But with both her smaller hands trapped in his larger ones, she could *feel* the sensual sound vibrating between them. Each syllable exited his mouth in a curl of pink and red and burgundy, traveling up the bare flesh of her arms—oh, *why* hadn't she worn long sleeves and woolen gloves?—and leaving a telltale trail of goose bumps in its wake.

She could not wrench her hands from his without risking damage to the fragile molds. That was the only reason she was standing still, her heart beating erratically. Fingers curled lightly about the warmth of his wrists.

Lord Adrian's pulse was unsteady, too, belying the veneer he projected of calm, careless rake. Marjorie's breath caught. He *did* care. He *was* interested. And uncertain of his reception.

She despised him. And would tell him so in just a moment, as soon as she found the right words.

The tips of her fingers grazed the short hairs on the backs of his wrists. It made her wonder despite herself whether his arms and chest would also be covered in soft bronze hairs.

Brown. Mousy brown. Boring, ordinary, commonplace brown. Drab. Dun. And lips the color of puce. Oh, why was she looking at his lips?

He rubbed the pad of his thumb against her bare skin. As though to say, *I wonder if the rest of you is just as soft. Let me find out. One tender, trembling, hard-won inch at a time.*

It was extraordinarily difficult to compose a sharp, pithy set-down when one's lungs failed to take in oxygen.

This was part of the mission. She was here to play along as though her fondest wish was to forge coins for Snowley, all the while searching for her clients' swindled possessions and taking advantage of every possible opportunity to sabotage Snowley's operation from within.

Her siblings had trusted her enough to let her be the lone Wynchester deployed within these walls. If she wanted to be trusted a second time, and a third, and a fourth, then she had to prove herself a match for the role.

Starting here and now.

Marjorie rolled her eyes as if dashing rakehells clutched at her hands every day of the week. Gently but firmly, she extricated her fingers from his, leaving the chalk molds behind. She turned to the worktable and selected one of the other molds, then walked it over to the fire as though she could think of no task more enthralling than the repetitive boredom of pouring metal into a mold and waiting for it to set. Over and over again. All day long.

Normally, she adored the mindlessness of her art studio. The way creating was pure emotion, without thinking. Just opening up her soul and letting its colors flow out through her paintbrush.

Here, though ... Lord Adrian was a devil of complication indeed.

14

⚜

 $\mathcal{M}$ arjorie made it through two rounds of molds before her sanity started to fray. Nothing to do for twenty minutes but stare at each other awkwardly and wait for the metal to set.

Lord Adrian's eyes sparkled. "Are you thinking what I'm thinking?"

"No," Marjorie said flatly.

She did not want confirmation that their minds were working in tandem.

"I was thinking," the rakehell continued casually, "of no less than twenty-three different ways one could pleasurably pass the time between rounds of coin-making."

She arched a brow and did her best to affect a bored expression. "I suppose you're alluding to lovemaking?"

"Good God, no." Lord Adrian stumbled backward, aghast, his hands clutching theatrically at his heart. "What on earth has *love* to do with anything? I've never experienced such a dreadful condition, and I certainly wouldn't let it impede a mutually enjoyable tup."

Marjorie smiled at him sweetly. "And I wouldn't find a quick 'tup' enjoyable with a man who takes less than fifteen minutes from beginning to end."

"You're missing out on variety," he protested. "Sometimes you want the whole pie, and sometimes a single bite can be satisfying."

"Never trust a man who doesn't want to eat the whole pie." She glanced at the clock. Only five minutes gone. "This would go much faster and be far more profitable for Snowley if we had more molds."

Webb's teasing indolence vanished. "We doubled the molds with your arrival. He's now becoming richer twice as fast."

"And yet here we are, sparring with each other instead of making more coins."

"I like sparring." He put on a playful face again. "Never trust a woman who cannot handle a sword."

Marjorie narrowed her eyes. It was almost as if... but no, Webb not *wanting* to make more coins made no sense at all. Counterfeiting was Webb's vocation. If he happened to be shockingly incompetent at it, well... that was just as well for Marjorie.

"I will make another mold," she announced.

He made an expansive gesture. "All that you see before you is yours to do with as you wish." He paused. "With the minor caveat that there is no more chalk with which to create a mold."

"When I see Snowley, I'll ask to visit the supply room."

"They'll laugh in your face. There's no exploring allowed. Which means no more molds."

"Then I'll ask Snowley for more chalk," Marjorie said with a shrug.

"Don't expect to see His Majesty often. It's Joey and Grinders who are our assigned doorkeepers. Other than our nannies, I've mostly been left to my own devices."

This wasn't going to plan at all. She didn't care about making coins. She needed to find where the stolen objects were kept.

"What about nuncheon?" she asked.

"You'll have to provide your own. Snowley feels that two meals a day are more than sufficient for— What are you doing?"

Marjorie crossed to the door. "I'm going to summon a snack."

"A snack? Did you hear what I just said? Besides, you've scarcely been here half an hour, and I—"

"I'm peckish," she informed him, and opened the door.

Joey and Grinders were at opposite ends of the corridor. Both snapped their gazes toward her at once.

"I'm feeling weak." Marjorie stumbled out into the hallway, closing the workroom door behind her. She let out a hearty sigh and pressed her arm to her forehead for good measure. "It's the heat."

Grinders lowered his hand from his pistol and exaggerated his words, making grotesque contortions with his mouth as he spoke. "It's hot in July."

"It's that room," Marjorie countered, fluttering her hand at her throat. "Lord Adrian says we aren't allowed to open the window..."

Joey sighed. "Open the bloody window. But don't stick your pretty head out, or our colleague on the roof will put a bullet in it."

Even Marjorie could tell he was using an overloud voice, exaggerating his lips just as his partner had. As if that was helping. She took a breath and concentrated harder.

"I'll do as you command," she promised. "You're so clever and wise. But I fear I require a refreshing remedy straight away, lest I swoon into the fire."

"A remedy like what?" Grinders asked.

"Like grapes," she suggested. "Or an apple."

Joey and Grinders exchanged aggrieved glances.

"I could visit the kitchens," Marjorie suggested.

"No visiting," said Joey.

"Blast," said Marjorie with a slump of her shoulders. "The scullery is probably too far away to find any fruit."

"The scullery is around that corner." Grinders pointed. "Not that you're allowed near it."

New plan: lure the guards away from the corridor, so that Marjorie could do some reconnaissance. "If one of you big, burly men could pass by the pantry, you would become my hero for your efforts."

"*We're* allowed in the kitchens," Grinders admitted.

"I'm not leaving my post," said Joey.

Marjorie batted her eyelashes at them both. "Please?"

Another look between Joey and Grinders, followed by a mutual shrug.

"Just this once," Grinders said gruffly. "Don't think I'll make a habit of it, because I won't."

She pressed her hands to her heart in overwrought appreciation.

Grinders shuffled off toward the scullery.

Joey's bored gaze strayed from hers. He hadn't left her alone, but his hands were nowhere near his pistol. He was maintaining his position out of duty, not because he perceived her as a threat.

A few moments later, Grinders stepped back into the corridor with a green apple in his hand.

He tossed it to her, underhand.

She carefully almost-fumbled the catch and pressed the fruit to her bosom. "Thank you ever so much."

"Thank us by minting some coins," Joey said, doing the exaggerated-lips thing again.

Grinders jerked his chin toward the door. "Back to work, pet. Crack your window and stay out of the corridor until we release you at the end of your shift."

Marjorie nodded. "Thank you again. You are princes amongst men."

With a final, swoon-adjacent sigh, she swept back into the workroom and closed the door behind her.

"Well?" Lord Adrian leaned against the worktable. "Did you find out that those overgrown bulldogs have no more heart than—"

She took a bite of her apple.

His jaw fell open. "Is that..."

She took another bite, then threw the apple at him as though pitching for a cricket match. He barely caught it before it nailed him in the solar plexus.

He lowered the apple and stared at it in stupefaction, as though he'd never seen such a fruit before in all his life. Then he shrugged and took a large bite, exactly over the spot where Marjorie had taken hers.

"I found out," she answered, "that Joey and Grinders hold no regard for my intellect. Also, we can open the window."

"Thank God." Webb circled around the worktable to do just that.

When he reached the windowsill, he took one last bite out of the apple before tossing it over his shoulder. Marjorie had to dash forward to catch it. Its smell was sweet and crisp, and full of reds and yellows.

While he wasn't looking, she took another bite. Not where he had bitten, but in the middle of the remaining clear section.

"Stick your head out," she said with her mouth full. "Let's see if the man on the roof really will shoot."

Lord Adrian jerked away from the window before anything more than a light breeze could ruffle his bronze curls. "There's a rifle aimed at this specific spot?"

"Allegedly." She took another bite, forgetting which was his part and which was hers. "It's all rumor and hypothesis until proven."

"Why don't you stick *your* head through to find out?"

"I'm busy eating this apple." She pulled a wooden stool away from the worktable. After positioning it within the welcome draft from the open window, she sat down to finish the apple and reconsider the situation.

Snowley's men were the sort to underestimate women—or any subordinate—in general. They didn't think Marjorie had the brains for a double cross. She hadn't tricked them into fully abandoning the corridor yet, but it was only her first day.

And then there was Lord Adrian Webb.

He did not treat her with self-congratulatory condescension. He didn't act as though she were different or inferior at all. Even when she was quiet or asked him to repeat himself. Even when she'd admitted her loss of hearing, he did not see her as lesser. He saw her as...someone attractive enough to tup. Someone capable and talented. Maybe even more so than him.

"Can you ask Punch and Judy for a newspaper?" he inquired as she finished the apple.

She shook her head. "I'm under strict orders to keep my pretty head inside this room until they come to let me out. You ask."

He made a shocked face. "And risk *my* pretty head?"

She shrugged. "Worth it."

Webb did not waste time considering the wisdom—or lack thereof—of bothering their guards so soon after Marjorie had done so. He flung open the door and called out, "Ho, there!" in his cheeriest, most ingratiatingly charming voice.

"Get back in the workroom!" Joey shouted from down the corridor.

"Oh yes," Webb said. "I certainly will. But first, could you bring me a copy of the *Times*?"

"You're not here for diversion and current events," Joey snapped. "The only thing you need to worry about is making Snowley more gold."

"Silver," Lord Adrian said apologetically. "Our molds are for shillings and sixpence, which anyone with eyes ought to know is actually made of—"

He flew into the room backward, as though tossed bodily. Seconds later, the door slammed behind him.

Marjorie threw her apple core out the window. "Was that a no?"

"I don't believe in no. I took it as more of a 'Not at this precise moment. Try again later.'"

"Give it five minutes," she suggested. "Make certain you step into the line of fire."

Marjorie turned to knock the coins from the chalk molds before he could glimpse any hint of amusement. She had to keep her wits about her.

"Are you going to help with these coins?" she asked.

"Is it too much to ask for you to be a wee bit less competent?" he muttered, grudgingly joining her at the worktable as if she'd interrupted a winning hand of high-stakes whist, rather than an idle rake doing absolutely nothing.

Quickly, they polished the coins, emptied and cleaned the casts, then refilled the molds with diluted metal. Next time the crucible emptied, only worthless scraps would find their way back in.

There. Work was finished for another twenty minutes.

She leaned back against the table.

Lord Adrian did the same.

The minute hand slowly ticked onward.

"What did you want a newspaper for?" she asked to fill the silence.

It didn't work. The silence grew longer. Deeper.

More intriguing.

She glanced up at Lord Adrian in time to glimpse what could only be his furiously thinking face.

"I have reasons," he said defensively. "I needn't share them with you."

Even *more* interesting. If it had truly been nothing, he would have made some lewd comment about finding his next mistress in the personal advertisements, or some other such balderdash.

Lord Adrian was up to something that he didn't want getting back to Snowley. Marjorie couldn't imagine what it might be, but any plot against Snowley automatically earned her full support.

"I know someone with newspapers," she mentioned casually.

Graham kept copies of them all, new and old. "You said you want the *Times*?"

"I need a copy from twenty days ago." His gaze held hers in challenge. He knew she was dying to ask what this ruse was all about, and he just as certainly would refuse to explain if she did so. The scoundrel looked forward to bickering about it.

Unfortunately for him, Marjorie lived in a house where every request was a strange one, and the explanations were often so convoluted and confusing that it wasn't worth inquiring the reasons. Webb wanted a specific newspaper? Done. She hoped he made a bomb out of it.

"I'll bring it tomorrow."

The tension ebbed from his shoulders. "Thank you."

Marjorie tilted her head and considered him. What if...

What if Webb wasn't a cad, after all? He was working here, yes, but so was she. What if the dashing—er, that was, *dissolute*—artist was forging under duress?

A sick feeling settled in her stomach. She'd allowed her horror at his past crimes to prejudice her against the possibility that he was blameless in the current situation.

There was no "what if." The evidence had been staring her in the eyes. Lord Adrian was working for Snowley, yes, but under the watchful eye of armed guards. He wasn't allowed to leave, or apparently even have access to newspapers. A prisoner held at gunpoint was the very definition of duress.

Her siblings were right. She *wasn't* ready for an assignment like this. Not if she ignored the evidence in front of her face. His flippant attitude made it seem like everything was fine, when it patently was not.

That he'd refrained from confiding in her was unsurprising. She'd judged him before she'd walked through the door and never questioned those assumptions. Until now.

"Do you *want* to make these coins?" she asked carefully. It was her understanding that they could not be overheard when the door was closed and the guards at their posts, but she kept her voice as low as possible all the same.

"Who wouldn't want to make money from nothing?" he said lightly.

She tilted her head. "Mayhap the workers who don't get to spend it?"

"Are you suggesting we *steal* these coins?" Webb looked down at the growing pile, then back up at Marjorie. "If you get caught spending counterfeit coins, you risk prison, or worse."

"'Worse' as in... what will happen to you if Snowley learns you created bad molds on purpose?"

"I never said..."

"I have eyes."

He looked away, presumably weighing the words he would say next.

"I didn't intend to involve myself in a counterfeiting scheme at all," he said at last. "I tried to sever all ties with Snowley and got pulled in deeper instead."

"And you can't escape because of the guards."

"I owe Snowley a debt. If I found a way to leave England, I could never return, which is not a trade I'm willing to make." His gaze softened and his eyes took on a faraway focus. "Not when I finally reconnected with someone my heart was certain I'd never see again."

Marjorie pressed her lips together. All that flirting he'd done with her, and he'd been in love with someone else the whole time?

"Is she your mistress or your wife?"

"What?" He goggled at her in befuddlement. "Oh no, it's not like...I told you. Romantic love is not something I'm capable of."

"And yet, if I'm interpreting your half explanation correctly...you're also not the heartless, selfish, greedy rogue you've made yourself out to be?"

"Oh, I'm doubtlessly *that*," he assured her. "It's just this specific instance in which I'm not out for myself. Snowley has leverage that I'd rather he not have. And until I find a way around it..."

"Tell me what the problem is." Marjorie stepped closer. "Maybe I can help."

"No," he said flatly. "I don't want you or anyone else involved."

She crossed her arms. "You don't think I'm capable of helping?"

"So far, *I've* not been capable of it. So, yes. Pardon me if I'd rather you not worsen the mess I already made for myself. It's horrific enough how many items from Snowley's treasure chamber have melted down to nothing in that pot."

Marjorie swung her gaze to the fireplace in horror. She hoped Mrs. Lachlan's lost jewelry hadn't become part of the soup. But how many other cherished mementos had been boiled down to make Snowley richer?

She closed the open window so they wouldn't be overheard. "Tell me all about this treasure chamber."

15

⚜

The next morning, Marjorie was nervously slathering honey onto her bread when the rest of her siblings joined her at the breakfast table. With their arrival, the dining room filled with life and color.

Eating en famille was common practice for the Wynchester siblings, but Marjorie's new post with Snowley meant they all had to rise earlier to break their fast together. As usual, Graham was paying more attention to the morning paper than he was to his plate. Jacob was feeding half a raspberry to a small hedgehog.

"Pass me the marmalade?" Elizabeth asked Kuni, her voice still groggy with sleep.

Tommy slid into the chair across the table, serving herself and Philippa plates piled high with rashers and eggs.

"Working in that rookery must be horrid," Philippa said with sympathy.

The neighborhood's poverty was not the problem. Marjorie chomped down on her sticky toast to give herself time to compose the right response.

"Horrid because it's a rookery?" Tommy asked Philippa pointedly. "Or horrid because she has to put up with that insufferable Lord Adrian Webb?"

Marjorie took a second bite of toast. Who cared if she hadn't finished chewing the first?

"Both," Philippa answered honestly. "I can't imagine Snowley provides good working conditions, and as for Webb..." She shuddered, then gave Tommy a playful look. "The only man I ever could abide was the dashing heir to Baron Vanderbean."

Tommy straightened, smoothing a hand over her linen gentleman's shirt and casting Philippa a rakish gaze from beneath short-cropped hair.

Marjorie had *just* begun to think the original question had been forgotten when Elizabeth picked up the slack.

"I can loan you a sword," Elizabeth offered. "Men are fifty percent more tolerable after they've been run through with a sharp blade."

Graham and Jacob protested in unison.

"Present company exempted," she acknowledged.

The shameful truth was that Marjorie was the first Wynchester into the dining room this morning not because she feared retaliation for a tardy arrival, but because the thought of seeing Lord Adrian again filled her with anticipation rather than revulsion. He was a rogue, but he was also...more complicated than she would have guessed. He liked to pretend the only thing in his head was the next conquest, but yesterday had given her a tantalizing glimpse behind the façade. She licked the honey from her finger.

Surely her interest would wane once she'd figured him out. No other man had turned her head for long. Not that there had been many chasing after her. She might as well enjoy the novelty while it lasted.

"The mission is going well," she informed her siblings, sidestepping the topic of Lord Adrian altogether. "I've learnt the most likely place to find Mrs. Lachlan's ring."

Graham lowered his newspaper in surprise. "Where?"

Usually he was the first to have that sort of intelligence, and Tommy the one to map it out.

"Snowley has a secret vault," Marjorie said in satisfaction. "A treasure chamber."

Tommy leaned over her rashers of bacon. "Where?"

"I don't know yet," Marjorie admitted. "But I'll find out. How are the rest of you progressing?"

"My spies are collecting as many samples of Snowley's past letters and contracts as they can," Graham said.

Jacob glanced up from his hedgehog. "To what end?"

"I don't know yet," Graham said in echo of Marjorie, giving her a conspiratorial grin. "First I collect information, then I see what use I can wring out of it."

"Can I see a sample?" Philippa asked.

"Of course." Graham fished in his breast pocket and pulled out a folded sheet of parchment. "This one was delivered this morning."

Kuni shook her head with affection. "Only a taskmaster like Graham would force his poor informants to work before dawn."

"Under cover of darkness is often the safest time," he protested.

"This is his seal?" Philippa held up the parchment. At the bottom, next to Snowley's signature, was a circle of wax with a unique design.

"From what I gather," Marjorie explained, "that mark comes from a special ring he keeps hidden on a necklace beneath his clothing at all times. No one else has ever so much as touched it."

"Clever," Elizabeth admitted. "*He* can't be forged without duplicating both his signature and the mark."

Philippa sniffed the parchment. "Why does it smell like roses? Was this kept in a perfume drawer?"

"Snowley smelled like rosewater when I met him," Marjorie said.

Graham nodded. "It's idle gossip until I confirm it, but sources claim Snowley is as particular about his toilette as he is about the operations of his criminal empire. Rumor has it, he takes a perfumed plunge bath every night, in a heavily guarded boudoir filled with either voluptuous prostitutes, racks of smuggled brandy, or miniature angel cakes topped with sliced elderberries."

"Elderberries on angel cakes?" Tommy repeated doubtfully. "Is he opening an underground pâtisserie for the discerning peckish forger?"

"I said it was unconfirmed," Graham muttered. "I'm working on it."

"One thing I have heard more than once," Marjorie said, "is that Snowley's primary asset is his word. His promise is his bond."

Jacob nuzzled his hedgehog. "Unfortunately, the things he typically says are variations on 'You will pay dearly for this.' Followed by someone paying dearly."

Voices sounded in the corridor.

All the siblings swiveled their heads at once as two newcomers entered the dining room.

"Faircliffe and Chloe!" Tommy said in delight. "To what do we owe this marvelous surprise?"

Chloe's gaze flicked toward Marjorie. The happy colors that had emanated from her sister before were even more pronounced now. She smelled like morning dew and sunshine.

Even Faircliffe looked like a maypole swirling in a cloud of confetti. He had heard the glad tidings and was overjoyed to be a father. Marjorie could not hide her grin.

"I wanted to catch you all together." As Chloe slid into an empty seat, her hand briefly caressed her belly.

"Is it about the other case?" Tommy asked. "I intended to stop by this afternoon with meat pies to fill you in on the Rappeneau situation."

"Wait, there's another case?" Marjorie dropped her bread back onto her plate. "When did you intend to fill *me* in on the Rappeneau situation?"

"You're *on* a case," Elizabeth pointed out. "Whilst you're single-handedly taking down a den of forgers, I'm fairly certain the rest of us can manage a simple matter of—"

Chloe's eyes shone. "We're going to have a baby."

"Congratulations!" Jacob pulled her up from her chair and swung her in a circle. "Oh, I'm sorry! Can you still...I didn't mean to cause..."

"I'm not breakable," she said, laughing. "I'm *with child*. Don't you start being as bad as Lawrence."

All the other siblings gasped and jumped up to embrace Chloe and Faircliffe.

Having already heard the news, Marjorie hung back slightly to give the others a chance to gush their felicitations.

Jacob noticed at once.

"You knew," he accused, jabbing a finger in her direction. "Graham is the one with the network of spies all throughout London, and *you* somehow outperformed him at his own game—"

"It's her colors," Chloe interrupted with a smile. "She just looked at me and knew."

"*I* suspected you were," Faircliffe said.

His wife elbowed him. "You did not."

"I did," he insisted. "The first clue was..." He cupped his hand to Chloe's ear to hide his whisper.

Her cheeks burned bright red. "All right, that was a good sign."

"Tell the rest of us the sign," Elizabeth called out.

Philippa hushed her with a scandalized face. "We can't talk about changes in bosom size and sensitivity at the breakfast table. I'll loan you a book I found instructive."

Faircliffe's brow furrowed. "You bought a book on the subject? Are either you or Tommy...somehow..."

"No," they both said with feeling.

"But the rest of us will be the best aunts for our new niece or nephew," Philippa promised.

"Perhaps you will," Elizabeth said. "I have dedicated my life to carefully avoiding the presence of children."

"Pah," said Jacob. "You'll change your mind once you hold the baby."

"I will never hold a baby," Elizabeth said firmly. "If you value my sanity—and the baby—you will never put either of us in that situation."

"Well, *I* can't wait," said Graham. He and Kuni exchanged secret smiles.

Chloe gasped. "Are you..."

"Not yet," Kuni said hastily. "But someday."

Someday. While the rest of the siblings bubbled around Chloe and Faircliffe, Marjorie worried her hands underneath the table. For Chloe, it was already here, or would be soon enough. In just a few months, the baby would arrive.

And Chloe would come around less...and less...and less.

It was a happy time, Marjorie told herself. A *joyful* time. And yet she could not shake the sensation that while she stayed the same, all of her siblings were moving on without her.

"I don't ever want a baby," Elizabeth said dreamily, "but I wouldn't turn down finding love. Man...woman...or someone who's both or neither." She waggled her eyebrows at Tommy and Philippa, then lifted Jacob's hedgehog. "I suppose I shall have to make do with Tickletums."

"Sorry." Jacob plucked the tiny brown creature from his sister's hands. "Tickletums is a *working* hedgehog and much too busy for entanglements of any kind."

Marjorie watched her siblings in horror. Good Lord, even

Elizabeth, the most outrageous misanthrope of them all, was thinking about getting married and leaving Marjorie behind?

What if it happened while she was off on her mission? What if these were the last few weeks she and her sister had left to share, and Marjorie missed every moment because she'd insisted on proving she could be useful outside of the home?

She'd known better than to leave her studio. Now everything would not only change…it would do so without her. She would complete this mission and come straight back home, and never leave it again.

Jacob frowned in Marjorie's direction. "Are you feeling all right?"

"I'm fine," she said quickly.

Marjorie couldn't stop the rest of the world from spinning, but *she* could stay the same forever. Artist. Spinster. Recluse. She would live vicariously through her siblings, and that would be enough. The more they changed, the less Marjorie would have to.

"It's almost time for me to go, that's all."

"Off to rub shoulders with Webb, are you?" Faircliffe shook his head in commiseration. "As far as I know, the Marquess of Meadowbrook has no idea his son is back from the Continent."

"He doesn't?" Kuni said with surprise. "I would visit my father straightaway."

"Meadowbrook is a hard man. He snubbed me when my father's debts became known and has stopped speaking to others for much less. Cutting off his son did not seem to bother him at all."

Chloe frowned in distaste. "No Wynchester ever turns his back on another Wynchester. No matter the circumstances."

"I'm sure Lord Adrian wishes his father shared the sentiment," Faircliffe replied. "Unfortunately, it shocked no one when Meadowbrook banished his own child. The only surprise is that the prodigal has bothered to return, knowing the lack of reception that awaited him."

"Maybe he didn't return," said Elizabeth. "Not really. He could be here on holiday, intending to spend the rest of his life on the Continent."

The hollow spot in Marjorie's gut deepened at the thought of Lord Adrian leaving London behind. "It's growing late. I need to summon a carriage."

"Tickletums and I will be coming with you." Jacob cradled the hedgehog to his chest.

"To Snowley's?" she said dubiously.

"Near enough. I'll be your hackney driver this morning, and Tickletums here will be your companion."

"What does he do?" Elizabeth asked. "I hope it's something dangerous. Or adorable. Is he a dancing hedgehog?"

"Tickletums is a homing hedgehog. In training."

"A homing...*hedgehog*?" Marjorie repeated. "What happened to Tiglet?"

"Nothing," Jacob assured her. "He's our best homing cat, and he's needed for the Rappeneau situation. I'm testing to see whether any of our other animals can perform a similar function. Tickletums can't be trusted to travel long distances—he gets sleepy and takes frequent naps—but I'll be right around the corner in the carriage."

Marjorie accepted the hedgehog. He relaxed in her hands, his white-tipped black quills lying flat against her palms. The quills felt rough and a little ticklish, but not sharp. Four pink paws protruded from the soft white fur of his upturned belly. His little black nose twitched as if sniffing her, and his eyes regarded her with interest.

"Let Tickletums go within the first hour, if you can. After that, I need to feed the raptors and trim the claws of the Highland tiger."

"Wait!" Tommy rushed over to Marjorie. "I almost forgot to ask. Can you duplicate these keys, please?"

She pressed a heavy key ring into Marjorie's free hand.

"Duplicate fourteen keys? In the five minutes before I leave?"

"I won't need them until tonight. Graham's right about some operations being best performed under cover of darkness. You said your post was mostly standing about, so I thought…" Tommy shrugged. "You can leave it until you return home, I suppose."

Marjorie cupped the hedgehog to her chest. Her siblings were so used to her being home all the time, they didn't all fully comprehend that she was no longer at their beck and call. But if they needed her, Marjorie would find a way.

She closed her fingers around the keys. "No problem. Idle hands, and all that."

"Here." Chloe slid Marjorie's basket onto her arm. "I packed you some treats for the long day. I pray Tickletums doesn't consume them all before you have a chance to try them."

"He's always well behaved," Jacob said, then added, "unless there are berries in that basket."

"Not for long," Chloe murmured.

Marjorie lifted the lid to see a collection of breads and fruits and cheeses next to her burlap bag of scrap metal. And folded to one side…a small gingham blanket. A flush rose unbidden to her cheeks at the memory of how Lord Adrian had suggested they share a blanket. Quickly, she spread a flap of the blanket to separate the repast from the hedgehog. She hid Tickletums and the ring of keys on the other side.

"Whilst I'm arranging this…" She turned to Graham. "Have you got a spare copy of the *Times* from twenty-one days ago?"

He brightened. "I do! I always keep a spare. No one has ever asked me for a copy." He shot a glance at Kuni. "I knew it wasn't a waste of space."

"One paper out of thousands," his wife replied.

His gaze softened. "The advertisements that led me to you are worth millions."

Kuni rewarded him with a kiss.

"What's the newspaper for?" Philippa asked as Graham hurried off to find his spare copy.

"I don't know," Marjorie admitted.

With Webb, it was so difficult to tell. He was a villain. A victim. A sinner. A saint. A heartless scoundrel. A loving brother. A liar. Probably a good kisser. Er . . . that was . . .

"Here it is!" Graham handed her a rolled newspaper with a flourish. "Let me know if you need anything else."

"I need something, all right," Marjorie muttered.

Whether she would get what she needed, however—that remained to be seen.

16

⬚

There you are!" Lord Adrian all but pounced when Marjorie walked through the door. "I've been waiting forever."

She glanced at the clock. "I'm five minutes early."

"I've been waiting since the moment you walked out the door last night."

Marjorie's heart fluttered. What was she supposed to do with an admission like *that*? Certainly not admit that she, too, had been counting down the hours until she would see him again.

"How adorable that you missed me." She shut the door and sashayed past him. "You didn't cross my mind once."

He watched as she pulled new and old molds from her basket and placed them on the worktable. They were almost identical to the molds she'd taken home.

Almost, but not quite.

Lord Adrian scooped them up and inspected them closely. "These appear to have an added—"

"I brought your newspaper."

"You did?" He set the chalk molds back onto the worktable and gave them a light pat. "Definitely the same molds. Nothing suspicious here. I could kiss you."

"To distract me from whatever you don't want me to notice?" she asked dryly.

"No," he said softly. "I just want to kiss you."

She turned away so he would not see the heat rising to her cheeks. Even though her back was to him, she suspected she wasn't hiding anything at all.

"I won't destroy other people's belongings to enrich Snowley's pockets," Marjorie said. "I'm no longer altering the ratio, like I told him we'd do. I'm substituting different material altogether. The new molds should also lower the risk."

She carried the burlap bag over to the crucible and upended its contents into the reservoir. A river of odds, ends, and shavings tumbled into the bubbling metal.

Marjorie gave the pot a stir, then passed the long handle to Lord Adrian, so she could tuck the jewelry they were supposed to be melting down into the safety of hidden crevices sewn into her skirts.

"Enriching your pockets instead of Snowley's?" Lord Adrian asked sarcastically.

"Mind the pot and your own business," Marjorie snapped. But the truth was, she'd have to tell him *something*. "I intend to return these objects to their rightful owners."

He snorted. "Sure you do. And just how will you determine who those rightful owners are?"

"I'll figure something out."

He gazed at her for a long moment, then seemed to take her at her word. "I told you that you weren't cut out for a life of crime. But this is no place for honor, Mary. If Snowley finds out that you—"

"He won't. Nobody searched me yesterday. They all think I'm harmless."

"Do they?"

"Perhaps they cannot imagine that anyone with half a brain or an ounce of self-preservation would be foolhardy enough to cross Snowley." Or they did not believe such treachery would occur to

Marjorie in particular, due to her sex or her appearance or her perceived defects.

He seemed to consider this. "We also produce a prodigious amount of coins, compared with my output before you arrived on the scene. If anything, they all believe you to be an unlikely but competent taskmaster, and an important part of the team."

That was true. Lately, the guards spoke to her as if it were a foregone conclusion that she would serve Snowley for life, just as Joey and Grinders intended to do themselves.

Marjorie shushed Adrian all the same. "Stop talking about my duplicity before someone overhears you."

"The guards can't hear a thing whilst the door is shut. Not from all the way down the corridor. And they won't open the door until eight o'clock this evening." He sent her a lecherous look. "Which means we have plenty of time to make good use of your blanket."

"First let me see if Tickletums chewed a hole through it to get to the blackberries." She carefully retrieved the softly snoring animal from inside.

"What the devil," Lord Adrian asked, "are you doing with that?"

"This is Tickletums," Marjorie answered brightly. "He's a homing hedgehog. In training. Which makes him sleepy. *Shh.* You'll wake him."

Marjorie tickled beneath Tickletums's chin. He yawned and batted her finger away with one soft little paw.

"How exactly does a homing hedgehog work?" Lord Adrian asked.

"I'm not certain it does," she admitted. "This is an experiment for my brother."

"Has anyone told you that you have a strange brother?"

She lifted her head—and one eyebrow. "Pot, kettle."

"Oh, very well, I suppose I'm the strange brother to my own siblings. But I've never trained a homing hedgehog."

"Today is your lucky day." Marjorie crossed over to the open window, then hesitated.

Lord Adrian was at her side in seconds, his expression on guard and his stance protective. "What is it?"

"I've just recalled the guard on the roof. He might shoot you or me, but surely no one with a heart would kill an innocent hedgehog."

"There's one way to find out." Lord Adrian reached for Tickletums.

Marjorie cradled the tiny creature to her bosom. "No hedgehogs will be harmed on my watch. My brother wouldn't hurt a fly, but he'll murder *me* if anything happens to Tickletums."

"Does your brother know there's an armed guard on the roof?"

"He's been informed, yes."

"Then perhaps this is…a rare, homing, bullet-evading, defensive hedgehog."

Marjorie looked at Tickletums. He licked the pad of her thumb.

"And maybe it's just a hedgehog," Lord Adrian added. "Have you considered the possibility that you'll set him outside and he won't go anywhere?"

"I think Tickletums is considering that possibility at this exact moment."

They both looked at the drowsy hedgehog.

"Kittens manage the homing without issues," Marjorie muttered.

Lord Adrian's eyes lit up. "They do?"

"But hedgehogs…Oh, I suppose we must try it. My brother is around the corner, waiting for Tickletums's safe return." She edged closer to the window.

At the first hint of the sooty Seven Dials breeze, the hedgehog perked up and rolled to his feet. His little black nose sniffed the air.

"He smells adventure," Marjorie said.

"Or old rubbish," Lord Adrian added.

"Mr. Tickletums, you are to go straight back to Jacob," she told the hedgehog firmly. "No pausing to eat berries or be riddled by bullets. Fast as a hummingbird, straight as an arrow. Do you understand?"

Tickletums made a snuffling sound.

"Was that a yes?" Lord Adrian whispered.

"I hope so," Marjorie said grimly. She took a deep breath and lowered the hedgehog over the sill onto the soil below.

Tickletums sneezed, then sniffed the air again.

Marjorie tensed as she waited. No gunshots rang out. Hedgehogs were apparently exempt from offensive fire.

Suddenly, Tickletums stiffened, then took off as quickly as his short little legs and tiny little paws could carry him.

It was not, admittedly, *fast*—but his movements were speedier than Marjorie would have anticipated. With a subtle sway to his fluffy backside, Tickletums waddled away from Snowley's fortress and down the street toward the exact corner Jacob was waiting in a Wynchester hackney with a bowl of fresh berries.

"I'll be damned," said Lord Adrian.

He was right by her side. Her skirts fluttered against his leg. The sides of their arms were pressed together.

Lord Adrian was warm. Hot, even. Marjorie could feel the heat of his skin through the layers of his shirtsleeve and coat. He was like a forge himself, melting anything that dared come into contact with him.

Heaven knew Marjorie was close to melting.

His fingers brushed hers. "Shall we counterfeit some substandard coins?"

"Yes," she gasped. Said. Gasped. Said-gasped. Dear God, why was she talking in this raspy, breathless voice? "Let's . . . let's work."

He lifted her hand in his.

She let him.

In this position, they looked more likely to break into a waltz than to mold false coins. All he had to do was place his other hand on her back...but no. Waltzing was not his intent. *Please, God, don't let him touch me anywhere else or I will melt into a puddle*, she prayed.

He lifted her hand to his mouth instead. His lips grazed the knuckles of her fingers.

"I smell like hedgehog."

"You smell like...fresh honey."

Breakfast. *Blast.*

He lifted her hand to the side of his face. It was smooth-shaven. It had been yesterday, as well as at the museum...but not her first day at Snowley's, when Lord Adrian hadn't known to expect her. He was shaving his face for her. The painstaking cravat she'd noted yesterday. The impossibly shiny boots. The glitter of gold and turquoise shimmering from him every time he looked her way.

It was all for her.

He lowered her hand back to her side carefully, then gave her fingers a gentle squeeze before letting go.

His eyes met hers. "Your move."

She fled to the fireplace.

Marjorie's hand stirred the melted metal as if her life depended upon it, but her head was spinning with memories of every second of the moment they'd just shared. His warm kiss against her fingers. The texture of his face. The soft squeeze of her hand.

Your move, he'd said.

There was no need to ask him what his choice would be. He'd already told her. *I just want to kiss you.* He could have stolen a kiss, right then and there. Marjorie shamelessly would have let him.

And then she would have promptly stuck her head out of the open window in the hope that the guard on the roof would put her out of her misery.

She didn't gad about kissing *libertines*, for heaven's sake. And if Lord Adrian proved less of a degenerate than advertised, well, a Wynchester didn't go about kissing *clients*, either.

Not that Lord Adrian was a proper client, if one wished to get technical about it. He hadn't engaged her services. He didn't even know she was a Wynchester. He thought she was Mary, Random Girl From Seven Dials.

And he wanted to kiss her.

She drew in a shaky breath at the implication. He wanted to kiss *her*. Who she really was, despite the pseudonym. He didn't look at her and see *infamous Wynchester sibling*, just like he didn't look at her and see weakness. He looked at her and saw a woman he wanted in his arms.

That was all. That was everything. That was more than Marjorie had dreamed.

She frowned as she stirred the pot. Damnable man. What kind of rake said "your move"?

The flirting was different this time. It had been a jest before, but it seemed real now. The kiss hung there between them, untaken but still present, filling the room with possibility like the morning fog over a peaty moor.

Maybe she could dive into the crucible. The bubbling liquid certainly couldn't be any hotter than the blush searing her face. Flushed not because he had embarrassed her with his unspoken question.

But because she was seriously considering the possibility.

She turned away from the pot, away from him, and scurried over to the worktable, where she busied herself with her basket for far longer than was truly necessary. When she had herself under control, she turned to face him.

"I have another project." Her voice trembled only slightly. "I...I need to create copies of these keys." She lifted the key ring. "These."

His eyebrows shot up. "Who do they belong to?"

She shrugged. "I've no idea."

"And when do you need copies?"

"Tonight."

"Did you bring your tools?"

Blast.

Marjorie glared at Lord Adrian in consternation. She'd been so busy thinking about *him*, she hadn't given her siblings' mission her full attention.

"We can use mine," he offered. "If you don't mind sharing."

"I don't mind," she said quickly.

"Should we break in the new molds first? I think the metal is ready."

"Oh. Yes."

She took the chalk molds to the bubbling pot and filled each one. Then she set them aside to harden and turned back to Lord Adrian.

He held up the keys. "You're thinking molds for these, too?"

She nodded. "That's the usual method."

"Can you describe your usual method?"

She did, keeping a sharp eye on his expression. "All right, I'll bite. I presume you have a better idea?"

"Your way will work," he said quickly.

"I know it will. I do this all the time." She realized she sounded defensive, but couldn't help herself.

He regarded her with uncharacteristic hesitation.

She sighed. "Oh, go ahead and tell me."

"I copy things all the time, too. There are functional substitutes, and then there are facsimiles so identical, even the original owner would not be able to tell the difference, side-by-side."

Was that what Tommy needed? Probably not. Then again, why take the risk of creating anything less than the best? Marjorie was a competent forger, though primarily with paint and ink. What if

Adrian's method was somehow better than her own? "You consider yourself an expert?"

"It's what I've spent the past seven years doing. Usually not keys. Artifacts. Greek, Roman, anything." He gave a sardonic chuckle. "It's how I got into this scrape."

Realization dawned. "Snowley sold your...duplicates?"

"Unbeknownst to him, yes. He thought they were originals."

"For seven years?"

"For seven years."

"And the buyers believed it?"

"Happy customers, every last one."

"Until?"

He made an aggrieved expression. "Until the war ended, and travel could resume. Some lord sent his lordling on Grand Tour, only for the lad to stumble across the very treasure allegedly on display in his father's parlor."

"That's the hold Snowley has over you?"

"It's the debt," he hedged. "The way he sees it, every transaction we ever had was fraudulent."

"Every transaction you undertook *was* fraudulent."

"Well, yes, there's that." He gave a roguish grin. "But he needn't be so medieval about it. All but one of the clients are delighted with their purchases. So really, *is* there a debt to be repaid?"

"I'm guessing this logic held no sway with Snowley."

"It did not." Lord Adrian sighed. "He has no imagination. Or heart. Or sense of irony. So here I am, counterfeiting coins to make up for my counterfeit antiquities. Or I would be, if I wasn't busy making keys instead."

"We can take shifts. I'll create the base copies whilst you continue on with the coins."

"When those are ready, I'll age the material and copy every nick and scratch until there's no material difference between the two sets."

"It's a deal."

Marjorie set to work at once. She had made hundreds of copies of keys for her siblings. Perhaps a thousand. But they'd always been just that—rough copies capable of opening the same doors and drawers.

Objects and sculpture weren't her medium. Marjorie was most at home in front of paper or a canvas. Her best tools were brushes, pencils, pen and ink. She could forge a copy of the Regent's signature with enough precision to fool Prinny himself. And paint a preemptive portrait of the moment, besides.

But this...Lord Adrian was talented in a different way. A complementary way. By working together as a team, Marjorie would be able to provide her siblings with a tool perhaps even better than they needed.

And what else? a tiny voice whispered. *As soon as the mission is over, will you kiss him then?*

She might have no choice in the matter. As soon as she sprang Webb from his prison, why should he wait around where Snowley could find him again? Why not be on the next boat to Paris, or Rome, or Greece?

If you were a handsome rakehell who had the whole world to choose from, why wander around Islington looking for Marjorie?

"You're making a terrifying expression," Lord Adrian informed her. "What are you thinking about so vehemently?"

She couldn't tell him the truth. Not *that* truth. So she gave him a different one instead.

"I'm thinking about those keys," she said. "My family assigned the project to me, and here you are, helping with it."

"Does your family not help each other?"

"They do. Always. But we each have our talents. Forging is supposed to be mine."

"You're afraid they'll think less of you if you accept the freely given labor of an experienced counterfeiter on a project that requires counterfeiting?"

"I'm afraid they'll..."

Love me less. Believe in me less.

Ridiculous, all of it. She *knew* her family loved her unconditionally. She knew it from her heart to her toes. But if the one thing they came to her for was a thing they could find elsewhere...

No, not just that. If it was a thing someone else could do even *better*...

"I want to be worthy of them," she said, the words raw. "I want them to admire me, to be proud of me, to think I'm..."

"You are." He turned and grabbed her shoulders, his green eyes molten. "Whatever it is you worry you aren't, *you are.*"

She stared up at him. "I'm just a—"

"You're not 'just' anything," he said roughly. "You assume other people believe you limited, and yes, that's what many will do. But I saw you handle Snowley. I saw you handle his guards. Hell, I see you handle *me.* Let the doubters think what they want. Theirs isn't the opinion that matters." He cupped her face and stroked her cheek with his thumb. "Don't you *ever* be the person who limits you."

She drew in a shuddering breath, unable to speak.

It was as though he had stripped her bare. As though he had seen beyond the protective varnish and the careful layer upon layer of paint, to the jagged, uneven sketch beneath...and did not find it wanting.

He saw all her layers and thought them a work of art. Not just "enough." More than enough. He thought she was already everything she had ever wanted to be.

Could there exist a better compliment than that?

"How did you get so wise?" she asked shakily.

He made an aggrieved expression and dropped his hands. "A clever man would not be in this pickle. I certainly would not have dragged my sister into Snowley's sights. If it weren't for protecting her, I'd..." He shrugged and attempted his usual leer. "Didn't you say you were carrying around a blanket that was just begging to be tupped upon?"

"Your sister?" She shoved at his chest. "*Your sister? *Why have you been going out of your way to impress upon me what a selfish nodcock you are, looking out for no one but yourself, when this whole time you've been trying to protect your *sister*?"

"Er..." He shifted his feet in embarrassment. "It would tarnish my image?"

17

~~~

*W*hat image?" Mary sputtered. "Your carefully crafted reputation as a bacon-brained ne'er-do-well?"

"Ne'er-do-well rakehell, if you please," Adrian corrected her, offended. "No one has ever called me bacon-brained."

"*I* did," Mary said. "Just now. That was the nicest thing I could think to say. If you had led with the extremely pertinent detail about having a sister who needs protecting, my family would have treated your sibling as one of our own. But no, you're determined to be a crusty old bear who's secretly all soft inside, determined to do everything himself, even if it's the hard way."

Adrian pointedly glanced down at the copied keys in her hands but didn't say a word.

Mary threw the keys onto the worktable and shoved her fists to her hips.

"I never claimed not to be just as stubborn," she admitted. "But sisters are special. There's nothing I respect more than the bond I share with my siblings. I understand putting family first. And yes, to help them best, sometimes what you need is . . . *actual help.*"

"How was I to know you *could* help?" he protested. "I'm still not convinced of it. What will you do, surround my father's town house with a wobbly miniature army of adorable attack hedgehogs?"

"That's only one possibility." Mary's gaze softened. "I forgot.

You still don't know." She hurried to close the window, then turned back around and took a deep breath. "I'm not Mary. I'm Marjorie Wynchester."

Adrian blinked. She closed the window for *that* big reveal? He nodded encouragingly to show he was listening, and waited for the rest.

She gazed back at him expectantly.

"You're a Wynchester?" Adrian repeated politely. "I don't see how that's...Oh! A *Wynchester.* Snowley mentioned your family!"

Mary—er, *Marjorie*—straightened with pride and delight. "He did?"

"He warned me, with great portent, that no Wynchester could save me now. Yet here you are!"

"Wynchesters do impossible things all the time. Though to be fair..." Marjorie lifted her dainty shoulders apologetically. "It's just me this time, and I'm not here to save *you.*"

"Someone else?" Adrian crossed his arms and leaned back against the worktable. "Ah. Your stratagem to use alternative metals instead of melting pawned mementos. I *knew* you were too good for the likes of Snowley. You're here to stop him from counterfeiting coins?"

"I'm here to stop everything he does," Marjorie said, her eyes fierce. "No more defrauding the poverty-stricken out of their prized possessions. No more forging coins to deepen his own pockets. No more *Snowley.*"

"I fully support abolishing Snowley. It's a worthy goal. One you have no hope of achieving, but what is life if not an unending series of disappointments? You concern yourself with your aims, and I'll worry about mine."

She stared at him. "You still don't want my help?"

"I'm certain you are more than capable of sabotaging Snowley from within," he assured her. "You've already proved as much. But my sister is..." *The only thing I've got.*

Except he didn't have her back yet. And if he didn't get himself out of this mess, he never would. It was a future Adrian could not accept.

During his exile, he had missed his sister more as time went on. With each passing year, he felt their once-close bond fading. But Adrian could not give up hope. For family, for redemption. For a second chance.

Iris was too important to leave her fate in an unknown party's hands. If Adrian involved a family of total strangers only for some harebrained—or hedgehog-brained—plan of theirs to backfire, Snowley would retaliate by ruining Iris's social standing or much worse. At which point, Adrian would never be able to forgive himself *or* the Wynchesters.

After Adrian settled his debt, Snowley would call off his dogs. Once Iris was no longer at risk, Adrian could spend the rest of his life making amends. There was a lot to make up for.

God willing, Iris would never know about his criminal past or his current disreputable employment. Nonetheless, Iris still remembered how her beloved brother had abandoned her to their father's complete control. He would not add "causing her total ruin" to the long list of his crimes.

Marjorie lifted her hand to touch his upper arm. "Please think about it. If you're in trouble, don't be afraid to depend upon other people."

He made a humorless chuckle. "Relying on others has never worked before."

Her gaze held his. "It will always work with me."

Adrian yearned to believe her. But if life had taught him anything, it was that in his lowest moments...he was always alone.

He shook his head.

Miffed, Marjorie snatched her hand from his arm. She stalked back to the worktable, flung open the lid to her basket, and pulled out a rolled newspaper. She slapped it into his chest as though killing a fly.

Or squashing a scoundrel.

"Your delivery, as promised." Her eyes were full of challenge, but she made no further comment. Nor asked any questions about the paper's intended use.

"I could kiss you," he said lightly as he accepted the gift.

Marjorie snorted and turned away, apparently uninterested in Adrian or his kisses. For Adrian the rebuffed kisses weren't the worst part. This past week, his list of women to protect had *doubled*.

Now there was Marjorie, too.

Since her arrival, Adrian had let himself become too complacent. He needed to get Marjorie out of here without risking either of their hearts—or their lives.

And since *he* couldn't leave . . . he would have to convince *her* to.

"As soon as my debt is paid, I'm leaving and taking my molds with me. There won't be any more forging. It'll end on its own." Hogwash, but if it convinced her to save herself . . .

"You think Snowley will let you walk away?"

"He'll have to. The thing he values most is his word. He even signed a contract to that effect. Not naming specific duties, of course."

Her eyes glowed. "Where is this contract?"

"In his private quarters. I have my own copy as well, not that carrying around his seal and signature helps me any. The important thing is, if Snowley says I can leave once I've repaid my debt, then he'll let me go. You should leave, too."

"Neither you nor Snowley is the master of my actions. I have a client, and it is her I am fighting for. Her, and all the women like her, who were defrauded out of their keepsakes and left holding a heap of worthless tin."

"It was real silver," Adrian muttered.

"Does using melted heirlooms make you feel better?" Marjorie snapped.

No. Every coin he'd counterfeited was forged with Adrian's guilt. No gentleman would ever choose to protect one woman by means of destroying the hopes of countless others.

He forced himself to shrug. "I'm a criminal, remember? I falsify things for a living. What does it matter to me if my molds make statues or sixpence? As long as I can pay my tailor, I'm happy."

"You don't mean that."

"You don't know me."

"Perhaps I don't wish to."

"Perhaps that's best. You should leave. If you insist on meddling with Snowley, at least have the manners to come back after I've gone, so as not to bother me."

"Manners! Of all the gall and arrogance…" Teeth clenched, she glared at him for a long minute. "You really expect me to walk away. You *want* me to go."

"Yes," Adrian said with feeling. "I have not been subtle about this. Go home. I can look after myself. If you want to tangle with Snowley after the counterfeiting has ceased, I suppose I cannot stop you. But someone ought. This is no place for…"

"No place for what? A woman? A person like me?" She tapped her ear. "Poor weak, timid, useless little Marjorie. Always someone more capable. Not just the last to be picked, but the one never chosen at all. Pity her, protect her, forget about her, leave her."

He tried to reconcile her words with what he knew of her, and could not. Any claims of Marjorie being weak and useless were clearly unfounded.

She spun away from him stiffly to center her attention on the duplicate keys.

He sighed. "Give them here. You've done your bit. Let me do mine."

"Are you sure?" She slapped them into his palm, her voice dripping with sarcasm. "If you do this, it will *help* someone."

He dropped the keys as though they had scalded him. "We're counterfeiting for a *good* cause?"

"Those are the only causes I care about." Her blue eyes lost some of their fire as she visibly calmed herself. "It is not forgery I object to. It's the ruining of lives. If you want to break laws, be my guest. But do it for the right reasons. Not for yourself."

"I'm falling in line for my sister's sake. Besides, you said yourself you're not here for *me*. Pardon me for being the one person who *is*."

She curled her lip and turned her back on him. After donning leather gloves, she stalked the chalk molds over to the fire.

He busied himself with the keys.

After a moment, she returned with the filled shilling molds. She placed them on the far side of the worktable to set, then carried the empty sixpence molds to the crucible to fill them as well.

Not speaking to him, then. Well, it wouldn't be the first time.

Historically, even those who were meant to love Adrian most preferred to have entire countries between them.

He pretended it did not bother him at all to work side-by-side in growing silence. That he did not miss their flirtations and their banter, and even their arguments. He liked the sound of Marjorie's voice. It was loud and sharp and *present* in a way so few things in his life ever were. It filled up little holes inside of him he hadn't even realized were there.

Worse, the more they bickered, the more he liked her. If Adrian hadn't needed her to give up on him and Snowley both, and go away for her own good... he'd be foolish not to pursue her.

Even her silent treatment was something special. She was still here, at his side. Despite what he'd first claimed, he could not think of her as an apprentice. She was his colleague. His equal. Working *with* her on the coins, on the keys, was nothing short of wondrous. He could get used to this. Get used to *her*.

No. That was a lie. Adrian would never be used to Marjorie no matter how much time they spent together. Every day, he would be reminded of how lucky he was all over again.

"There," he said gruffly, and shoved the finished keys across the worktable.

She scooped them up without a word and crossed over to the window to examine them next to the originals in the sunlight.

Adrian always kept a pencil in his pocket. One never knew when one might need to sketch a pretty face or pen a heartfelt letter of regret. He unrolled the newspaper and ripped off half of the top broadsheet.

He was just replacing his pencil in his pocket when Marjorie turned away from the window.

"Well?" he asked.

"They're good," she admitted grudgingly.

He affected an expression of offended hauteur. "Merely 'good,' madam?"

She lifted up both key rings. "They're flawless, and you know it."

A warm rush of pride washed through him. Not at a job well done—that had never been in doubt. But he had provided something Marjorie needed. He had helped her. She was pleased with him, if only for a moment.

She returned to the worktable to slip both sets of keys into her basket, then turned to face him. "Please. Is there nothing more I can do to help?"

He pressed his lips together as he weighed his limited options. "There is one more thing. But doing a favor does not mean I am open to further meddling. There's to be no charging about in my name, assuming you know best. If I ask you to let me manage my own affairs, can you please respect my wishes?"

She nodded. "Occasional favors, only when asked. Understood."

He hesitated for another long moment, then held out a folded square of broadsheet, sealed with a dollop of candle wax. "I need this delivered to my sister. You can tell her I meant to give it to her when I saw her last. If anyone asks, that's when she received it."

Marjorie slid the square into her basket. "Tomorrow is Sunday. I'll deliver it then."

"Tell her not to open it under any circumstances without my authorization," he added. "It must remain sealed at all costs."

A dozen questions filled her eyes, but to her credit, she did not ask them.

"You needn't play the blackguard," she said softly. "You have the potential to be whatever you choose. Good or bad is a decision we all make every morning."

His heart gave a painful lurch.

If only it were so simple. Marjorie was giving him another chance, the benefit of the doubt. The one thing his own family refused to give him.

Adrian wasn't the one who had debauched that young lady years ago. His brother Herbert—the heir, the important one—had let Adrian take the fall.

And no one had questioned his elder brother's version of events.

Adrian's wish to be an art instructor, to work like a commoner for a monthly pittance, had horrified his sire. Father relentlessly accused Adrian of choosing that mortifying path explicitly to bring shame upon the family. Father was ashamed of *Adrian*.

He did not know how to react to the opposite reception. To Marjorie's faith in him, and her conviction in his (possibly untapped) goodness.

"Why do you insist on believing me a better man than I am?" Adrian rasped, the words scratching his throat.

"It doesn't matter what I think." She spread her fingers over his lapel, above the too-rapid beating of his heart. "What matters is what's in here. The person you need to believe in most is yourself."

"I did once," he admitted. "It didn't work out."

She lifted her hand to the side of his face. "Belief isn't something you do once. Belief is every minute of every day. Give yourself a little bit of grace. Maybe then you can accept it from someone else."

He closed his eyes and leaned into her hand. It was soft and warm and gentle. Her touch did not quite feel like absolution...but it did feel like a second chance. A chance worth taking. The possibility of a new life. Of a new *him*. Of a different future.

If he couldn't get there on his own, he would need to accept help...and give it.

"All right," he said roughly and opened his eyes. She was watching him. He could gaze into her sweet face forever. "Stay, if you insist. Tell me what you need. I'll help."

A smile flickered at the edge of her lips. "You'll be an apprentice Wynchester?"

He would be anything she wanted, as long as she kept touching him. Believing in him. Standing next to him.

"I'll be good," he promised. "To the best of my ability."

If he managed that feat, maybe then he would deserve her trust.

18

⟨⟩

$\mathcal{T}$ he next day, Marjorie took the elegant Wynchester coach-and-four with the family crest to Mayfair, but she wasn't sure for whose sake she'd done so. Was she expecting to impress the infamously impossible-to-please Marquess of Meadowbrook with the coat of arms of a mere baron? Laughable.

Was she simply hoping to fit in? To belong in this beautiful neighborhood of austere homes filled with buttoned-up aristocrats?

Also unlikely. Anyone who recognized Baron Vanderbean's crest would know her for a Wynchester, and her family name was synonymous with scandal. She smoothed her new ivory spencer trimmed with ribbons of expensive Balcovian amaranth and wished she could look half as fine for Lord Adrian. But nothing Marjorie wore, nothing she ever did, would make her deserve an address in a neighborhood so refined. To these people, Marjorie was born lesser and unworthy. She would always just be an orphan taken in by an eccentric foreign baron on the fringe of society.

This was where Lord Adrian had grown up.

His roots were here. This was where he had been happiest, and angriest, and saddest. His family home. A closed-off world of privilege and excess unwelcoming to the likes of Marjorie Wynchester.

And now she was here to call upon his sister.

After sucking in a fortifying breath, Marjorie rapped the knocker with significantly more confidence than she felt. Was this what it had been like for Chloe when she first approached the Duke of Faircliffe? Had the row of connected houses felt too wide, the brick too hard and imposing?

"You've no need to belong here," she muttered to herself as she rang the knocker. "You already *have* a place you belong. Besides, even Lord Adrian doesn't belong here anymore."

But he wished he did.

The butler swung open the door. From his bemused expression, perhaps Marjorie hadn't been muttering as quietly as she'd thought.

"Good afternoon," she said brightly, then remembered that the ton still considered three o'clock in the afternoon to be *morning calls.* "Is Lady Iris at home?"

"I'll ascertain her presence." The butler paused.

Marjorie waited.

The butler tried again. "Who might I say is calling?"

"Oh! Right." She fished inside her reticule. Tommy had offered a plethora of stolen calling cards to choose from—and matching costumes besides—but Marjorie preferred direct simplicity whenever possible. "Here you are. Miss Marjorie Wynchester, friend of Lord Adrian Webb."

The card contained Adrian's (forged) pencil scrawl: *Iris, this is a friend of mine. Let her in.*

The butler did not blink. He merely inclined his head and shut the door in Marjorie's face, leaving her out on the front step to wait and wonder what would happen next.

At least she knew Lord Adrian's father and older brother were not in residence. The marquess would have been equally unimpressed by the Wynchester name and his son's signature beneath it. At best, his lordship would toss her out on her ear. At worst, he would attempt to banish her from Mayfair—or London—completely.

Lady Iris, on the other hand…She had welcomed her brother before and kept the secret from their father. But would that allegiance extend to a stranger?

The door swung back open.

"If you'll follow me, miss."

As Marjorie hurried to keep up with the butler, she craned her head to look at every corner of the fine interior. The painted ceiling, the gold-colored ormolu door furniture, the sash windows, the smooth oak floors. It was technically beautiful, yet devoid of the chaos and color of the Wynchester residence. The walls were closer, the rooms much smaller, the air beige and gray and flat and flavorless.

When they reached a mint-and-white parlor, a slender young woman with wavy brown hair leapt up from a chaise longue to greet her. Here, at last, was color. Lady Iris sparkled so bright, the bland elegance around her blurred into nothing.

"How do you do?" said Lady Iris, taking Marjorie in the way Marjorie had taken in the house. "It is an honor to meet you."

"Is it?" Marjorie said dubiously. She was fairly certain she was supposed to be curtseying to Lady Iris, who significantly outranked her, but the young woman was already motioning Marjorie over to a half circle of chairs facing a small table.

"Of course it is. I've not met a friend of Adrian's in years. Then again, I was too young to be *allowed* to speak to adults the last time he was home. Living here, I mean. Shall you stay for a few minutes? I took the liberty of ordering tea."

"I like tea," Marjorie managed.

Lady Iris was a whirlwind of pastels and fresh spring rain, as bright and cheery as her voice and manner. She seemed like exactly the sort of sister Marjorie would hope for Adrian to have. A man hiding such a deep well of sadness badly needed some happiness and light to balance out the darkness.

"I was just reading the latest Sir Gareth Jallow." Lady Iris held up a thick volume. "Have you read these? Jallow is superb. His sublime, wrenching poetry is the key that opens every fluttering heart in Mayfair."

"I'm not from Mayfair," Marjorie said inanely. "My brother says Jallow's poems are horrid."

Good God, was *that* her best sally? She wasn't here to insult the poor woman's reading choices. Philippa would have Marjorie's head. Any book a reader chose to invest time in was by definition a worthy book.

"Does he?" Lady Iris said in delight. "How contrarian! Is he the sort who loves to disagree with whatever everyone else is currently enjoying?"

"No, he's..." *Jealous. And a fellow poet.* Neither answer was appropriate to share, and both made Marjorie feel disloyal for considering them. "He's the sweetest man I've ever met," she said instead. "To my knowledge, Jallow is the second-most thing he despises."

Lady Iris leaned forward with interest. "What is the first thing?"

"People who mistreat animals," Marjorie answered without hesitation. This was no secret. Rescuing animals from ugly situations was Jacob's essence. "He could coax a lion to eat out of his hand like a kitten."

"He sounds like a sweetheart. Nothing like my brother," Lady Iris added with a laugh. "Although gossips used to claim Adrian had that effect on young ladies." Her eyebrows snapped together and her eyes narrowed. "You and he aren't..."

"No," Marjorie said quickly. Possibly too quickly.

The fact that there had been a moment where Lord Adrian would have kissed her if she'd given him the slightest encouragement did not signify. The moment had passed. It was over. The kiss had vanished.

Mostly vanished. It still hung heavily in the corners of the workroom like the thick scent of fresh jasmine after a hard summer's rain.

"I should have supposed not," said Lady Iris. "Even Adrian would be unlikely to form an attachment with a Wynchester."

Marjorie flinched. "Because we're so far beneath his station?"

"Because you lot are too unpredictable to follow such an obvious path. I've no doubt that he has met his match with you, which tickles me to no end. Besides, Adrian gave up on his 'station' years ago when he set out for France."

"*Did* he give it up?" Marjorie said with a surge of loyalty. "Or was it taken from him? Are you certain your brother left of his own volition, or did his own father cast his child out from the only home he'd ever known?"

Lady Iris reared back, shocked at such candor.

Marjorie immediately regretted her leap to Lord Adrian's defense. "I'm sorry. I didn't mean—"

"You did mean," said Lady Iris. "And it's a good thing you did, because I think I needed to hear it."

"He loves you. He said his heart feared he would never see you again."

"So did mine," Lady Iris admitted. "All this time, I've felt abandoned by him, when the truth is, he was abandoned, too. Not by me— I was in the schoolroom. But by our father, certainly, and our brother Herbert."

"And the rest of 'polite' society," Marjorie added.

"You're right," Lady Iris said in dawning realization. "I was so young when he left. No, as you said—when he was banished. I wasn't part of society yet myself, so I had no notion of what it might be like to be expelled from it. Now that it's as much a part of me as breathing, I can only imagine what it must have been like for Adrian."

Two young maids entered the room with trays of tea and refreshments. Marjorie leaned back while they set the table.

Lady Iris thanked the girls, then leaned forward to pour the tea.

"As interesting as you are, I cannot imagine Adrian sent you for a social call. Is there a reason he isn't joining us?"

"Er," said Marjorie. She hadn't prepared for that question.

Or rather, she *had* prepared various plausible answers, but now that she'd met Lady Iris and taken her measure, Marjorie had no wish to lie unnecessarily. Nor could she break Lord Adrian's confidence—or risk what was left of his reputation—by confessing the truth of the matter.

She decided to sidestep the question and barrel forth with the meat of her visit instead.

"I've come as a courier of sorts." She pulled the sealed square of newspaper from her reticule. It was large and lumpy and felt as though something hard was lodged within the folded paper. "I've no idea what this is, but he wanted me to tell you that he wished he could have given it to you on your last meeting…and that, if anyone were to ask, he should be grateful if you were to intimate that that is exactly what occurred."

Mystified, Lady Iris accepted the thick broadsheet square and slid her finger toward the seal.

"Oh! You mustn't open it," Marjorie said quickly. "That's the most important part. He said it must remain sealed, unless you receive clear and direct authorization from him to do otherwise."

Lady Iris lowered her finger from the seal and stared at the square in befuddlement. "But we don't know why, or what it is?"

Marjorie nodded. "That's the situation exactly."

Perhaps what it said inside was, *I knew you would break the seal and my confidence.* Or perhaps it said nothing at all, and was an article on fashionable mantua-makers a dandy like Lord Adrian had determined to send to his sister.

She could not help but suspect that Lord Adrian's nondisclosure of the newspaper's purpose was partly a test. Of either Marjorie's honor or Lady Iris's.

Marjorie toyed with her cup of tea. What did it mean to not even trust one's own sister? Did he trust anyone at all?

On the other hand, *should* he?

"I suppose it's just like my brother," said Lady Iris. She slipped the folded square of newspaper beneath the cover of Jallow's latest works. "He does have a flair for the dramatic. Wherever he is, I'm sure he's having a good laugh at my expense."

"I'm certain he is not," Marjorie replied hotly. "He's not nearly the rogue that people like to—"

She broke off. Not out of embarrassment for her continued defense of Lord Adrian, but because if Marjorie was being honest...the current situation did not speak well to his honor. After years of forging artifacts and lying about their provenance, he was actively counterfeiting coins, knowing full well the harm it caused for all the innocents involved.

As for being a rakehell...well. Marjorie had no doubt how the gingham blanket in her picnic basket would have been used if she had accepted Lord Adrian's offers for a mutually pleasurable tup.

No emotional attachment requested.

"All right, yes," Marjorie forced herself to admit. "He's a rogue and a cad and a libertine and a—"

"He's my *brother*," Lady Iris snapped, looking in great danger of throwing her steaming tea into Marjorie's face. "Despite being six years older than me, he never once hesitated to sit cross-legged on the nursery room floor to play dolls and dress my hair. I used to think he was a nighttime nanny, because whenever he was home, he would fold himself into my bed and read fantastical tales to me. It is to him that I owe my love of reading. I had no sibling my own age, but I never noticed the lack until he was gone. He single-handedly made my childhood bearable."

They stared at each other, then burst out laughing.

"Like I said." Marjorie gave a crooked smile. "A shameless rogue, yet not nearly the caitiff people make him out to be."

"He's not perfect," Lady Iris admitted, "though I believed him to be at the time. I looked up to him so much. Herbert had no time for me, and Father even less so. I was so *hurt* when Adrian left me behind. You can't imagine..."

"I might be able to," Marjorie said softly. Being left behind, or growing apart from her family, was one of her worst fears.

"Later, when I discovered my great and magnificent brother wasn't infallible... I was so disillusioned to hear those rumors. It's one thing for a heart to ache over the loss of someone splendid. To feel the same yearning, despite yourself, for someone who isn't nearly as wonderful as you'd always believed him to be..."

Marjorie stirred her tea. "The thing about being idealistic is that ideals are fantasies. People aren't good or bad. They're good *and* bad."

Lady Iris's chin rose. "You're suggesting we should all forgive him for the horrible things he did?"

"I cannot say what he did or didn't do. What I do know is that's not what forgiveness is. You forgive the person, not the deed. The act was bad. The person is your brother."

Lady Iris picked at her tea cake. "I don't know if I can do it. If I *should* do it."

"I can't answer that, either. Only you have the power to forgive or not. It's not up to me or even your brother. It's up to you. As everything that affects your life and your well-being ought to be."

Lady Iris gave an abashed smile. "You seem like an excellent sister."

Marjorie lifted a shoulder. "I'm good and bad, too. I just do my best to make my bad deeds cause good things."

Lady Iris winced. "Some of my bad deeds are just... bad things. Mayhap it's Adrian who would refuse to forgive *me* if he knew the hole that I've dug."

Marjorie waited, but no more information was forthcoming. "No matter what it is, your brother loves you."

"And you, too, I suspect," Lady Iris murmured.

"What?" Marjorie reared back in her armchair. "He doesn't love me. We cannot stand each other."

"That can't be true." Lady Iris lifted the folded square of newspaper. "He *trusts* you."

"If that bit of broadsheet is proof that he trusts me, then you must see that he trusts you, too."

"He shouldn't." Lady Iris's springtime scents and colors shimmered and seemed to fade.

Marjorie tilted her head in concern.

Lady Iris let out a heavy sigh. "Can you keep a secret?"

"From your brother?"

"From everyone."

Marjorie inclined her head. "I've spent a lifetime keeping secrets."

"I don't doubt that's true. Yet here I am, burdening you with mine." Despite this speech, Lady Iris picked the raisins out of her cake for several moments without speaking. When she finally glanced back up at Marjorie, her expression was bleak. "Dun territory."

Marjorie blinked. "Your father is living on credit?"

"Not him. *Me.* Father would kill me if he knew. He's cut off my pin money, but the people I play with allow IOUs. I've given vowels to more people than I can ever repay, and yet I cannot stay away from the gaming table. If it's that simple to lose, it must be that simple to gain. I've won before. I'll win again. It's just taking so blessed long, and the debts are piling up . . ." Lady Iris let out a quavering breath. "If word got out that I was gambling, that I've gambled away more than my dowry is even worth . . . I'll be ruined."

Dear Lord. Not a word of that was good news.

"You should tell your brother," Marjorie said automatically. But what would Lord Adrian do? Mold buckets full of tin shillings and start handing them around Mayfair?

Lady Iris shook her head. "Not yet. With luck, not ever. It's my muddle, and I want to solve it on my own. I've been the coddled baby for far too long. I've grown up and need to act like it. I want my brother to see me as an equal."

"I understand that sentiment more than you might think," Marjorie admitted. "It's how I got myself into my current situation. But every puzzle can be solved. If you'd let me tell my siblings—"

Lady Iris gasped. "They'll tell Adrian."

"They've never even met him. If you say they're not to breathe a word, not a syllable will be spoken."

Lady Iris considered this, then shook her head. "I've another game coming up. I'm feeling lucky. Perhaps this is the one that will get me out of this scrape once and for all."

A strained silence entered the parlor.

"And if it doesn't?" Marjorie ventured.

Lady Iris's shoulders stiffened. "If I fail to recoup my losses, I will take you up on your offer. But please, take no action until we know the results of the next game."

To say Marjorie had misgivings about this plan would be vastly understating the matter. But she would take no action against Lady Iris's express wishes.

"All right." Marjorie sighed. "You have my word."

19

By Monday morning, Marjorie was bursting to get back to Lord Adrian.

Er, Snowley's fortress, that was. The mission. Not specifically a certain rakehell. Despite the wanton activities in last night's dreams.

She had kept herself busy on her day away from the rookery.

For now, her girls and the Duke of Faircliffe were relegated to a single day of Marjorie's tutoring. Between all that and the visit to Lady Iris, there had barely been any time left to break for a meal or two.

Though she had somehow found plenty of time to think about Lord Adrian, Marjorie was certain she didn't *miss* him. How could anyone long for the presence of a self-admitted scoundrel? He was a heartache waiting to happen.

Lord Adrian must also be on tenterhooks to hear whether she had paid the call on Lady Iris, and whether Marjorie had been allowed in to pass along the message.

"You're not here for Lord Adrian," she muttered as she strode up the path to Snowley's front door. "You're here for Mrs. Lachlan, and all the women like her."

A pair of starlings on the roof startled and flew off with a flutter.

The front door opened before Marjorie could knock. It was the same exhausted maid as before, but this time Ruby didn't look surprised at Marjorie's appearance. With little more than a grunt of greeting, Ruby stepped aside and allowed Marjorie through the door.

Grinders and Joey Box o' Crumpets were deep in conversation. Their voices were low and their heads bent together at such an angle that Marjorie could not tell what they were talking about. She couldn't even see the omnipresent hatpin hanging from Grinders's mouth. Whatever it was smelled like soot and tasted like trouble.

She ground her teeth at her failure to eavesdrop. *She* was the principal on this mission. Only two-and-a-half weeks remained before Mrs. Lachlan was evicted. Everything was riding on Marjorie alone being just as effective as the entire team of Wynchester siblings and their spouses.

The guards were cagey enough not to disclose any confidential information, no matter how innocently Marjorie asked, but she was making headway with the maid who brought the daily repast to the workroom.

Marjorie doubted overworked Anna had been entrusted with a key to the treasure room, but even if the girl didn't know its precise location, she might be able to identify all of the other rooms, leaving Marjorie to find her target using the process of elimination.

Joey and Grinders led her down a corridor she knew by heart and took their respective posts. Marjorie waited until they were only visible from the corners of her eyes before she pushed open the workroom door.

After a full day and two long nights, she wanted nothing to spoil her first glimpse of Lord Adrian.

He was leaning against the windowsill, looking positively splendid. Clean and freshly shaved, with his brown—all right, *bronze*—hair in careful disarray.

Lord Adrian's face lit at the sight of her, and he leapt upright at once. His cravat was sharp and white, his Hessians spotless. The jade silk of his waistcoat matched the deep green of his eyes, which heated as he drank her in just as thirstily. The room throbbed with cinnamon and apricots.

Marjorie pulled off her bonnet. She wished she were wearing anything but a drab muslin. A pretty day dress, a fine evening gown, a rakish riding costume.

Lord Adrian did not seem to mind her plainness. If anything, he seemed to be imagining her without any garments at all.

"You're here." His voice was husky. "I've been waiting by the window since dawn."

"It faces the opposite direction. You wouldn't be able to see me arrive."

"But I could smell you."

"You cannot smell me!"

"Is that what you think?" Lord Adrian crossed the room in three strides. He cupped her small shoulders in his large hands and dipped the edge of his jaw to the top of her windswept hair. "This is my favorite part of every morning. When I finally breathe in the scent of your soap and the flowery sweetness of your hair. I don't have to see you to recognize you. You're part of the air inside my lungs."

She swallowed hard, her throat dry, her hands trembling. Did he really see through the drab exterior to the woman she was beneath, or was that just wishful thinking? Or was this the nonsense prattle of a practiced rake?

"I like how you smell, too," she mouthed into his cravat so that he could not see or hear.

She would recognize his scent anywhere. Up close, he smelled like hot sunshine streaking through cold shadows. Notes of summery gold and springtime green and winter blue with a hint of muted jewel tones like crisp autumn leaves floating to the last patch of green grass on the ground. An entire year's worth of colors, bundled inside one man with as many changing winds as the four seasons.

She didn't just want to kiss him. She wanted to paint her world with every shade of him. To step into the rainbow mist of Lord Adrian's essence and let his colors envelop her skin, her body, her soul. She wanted to lose herself in his pigment the way she gave herself over to the creamy richness of oil paints on canvas. Without fear, without hesitation. Dive straight to the bottom and see what magic they could create together.

He breathed deeply one last time and stepped back to see her face.

She did her best to ensure it revealed nothing.

The door was closed, the guards presumably back at their posts. The workroom was now a private haven in which anything could happen.

His eyes were intense. "Did you see Iris?"

Ah yes. He wasn't thinking about kissing. He was thinking about the mission he'd sent Marjorie on, the mission whose details she should be relaying to him rather than gazing at the striations of green in his eyes.

"I did." She stepped back and sat on a stool. She needed something firm and stable beneath her. "Your sister is charming. She took the paper, and agreed not to break the seal without a direct order from you."

His muscles visibly relaxed. He leaned his wide shoulders against the wall and kicked one shining black boot over the other in a languid pose she could imagine him taking at a ton ball, the better vantage point from which the wolf could peruse his sheep.

Assuming there was ever a spare moment without a willing tribute in his arms.

But Lord Adrian was not looking at Marjorie with the focus of a hunter. His eyelashes had lowered, giving the impression there was no object in this room more fascinating than the tip of his boot.

"Does she hate me?" he asked at last.

"She idolizes you."

"Maybe when she was a child." He raised his gaze to meet Marjorie's and gave a sardonic half smile. "Back then, she didn't know any better. Now she does."

"I'm sure it's complicated," Marjorie admitted. She suspected he was looking not for answers, but absolution. "Have you talked to her about it?"

"When would I have the chance?" He gestured at the workroom around them, then shook his head. "After the war ended, I did get my chance. I saw her briefly. Once. Right before I saw Snowley. And I *did* try, but now..."

He glanced toward the closed door.

Marjorie straightened. Lord Adrian was always listening for footsteps. "Is someone coming?"

He shook his head. "No one is coming."

By his defeated expression, he did not refer to the guards. He meant no one was coming to save him. That his conviction he'd find a path out of hell had been shaken. That even if Snowley let him go, there might not be a home to run to.

Lord Adrian's smile was bleak. "How can I convince Iris I'm not the ogre she thinks I am, when here I am, in the belly of the beast?"

"I declined to mention that detail," Marjorie promised.

"Thank you." He made a wry face. "That doesn't make it any less true."

"She needs her brother. And you need your sister."

"I don't need anyone. I've been on my own in one sense or another since long before my exile became literal."

"Feeling alone doesn't make you need people *less*."

He folded his arms over his chest with a harrumph.

"You needn't pretend to be hard and unfeeling. Lie to me if you want, but don't lie to yourself. Those are the most dangerous falsehoods."

His jaw tightened.

She tried to soften her voice. "It's all right to admit that your family's disapproval hurt you. That your banishment was unfair. That forcing *you* be the one to go away didn't make it any less an abandonment."

"*She* wasn't part of that," he gritted out. "Iris was as much a victim of our father's whims as myself. For as long as he controlled the purse strings and kept me penniless, I could not return. But when I finally became solvent, due to my deals with Snowley..."

Marjorie waited.

His tortured eyes met hers. "I could have come back sooner, yet I didn't. I *am* a wretched brother."

"You cannot undo what you did or didn't do, nor can your family rewrite their part of your shared past. You're here now—"

"Here," he repeated. "Not *there*."

"But you will be. When I take down Snowley—"

He laughed harshly. "Do you still think that will work?"

"I know it will."

"Do you, little mouse? Why would *you* succeed in taking down Snowley when the Home Office has failed, time and again?" His voice was mocking. "Because you're a Wynchester?"

"Yes," she answered simply. "Wynchesters do impossible things all the time."

He snorted and glanced away.

"Lord Adrian—"

"Oh, for God's sake, call me Adrian. We fight too well to waste time on forced politesse. It's just a courtesy title anyway. We both know I don't deserve..."

"Courtesy? Oh, Adrian." She rose to her feet and went to him.

He stared fixedly at the ceiling.

"Everyone deserves to be treated like a human being with thoughts and feelings and a heart. Even surly, rakish forgers." She touched his chest. "Don't let yourself be defined by what others think about you. Only you can choose the kind of man you'll be."

He let out a slow breath and covered her hand with his own. "How did you get so—"

Two sudden taps rattled the windowpanes.

They spun to look in time to see a large black bird tap its beak once more against the center pane, then lower itself to the windowsill beneath the open section of the window.

"Did that bird just...knock before entering?" Adrian murmured.

Marjorie felt, rather than heard his words. Her hand was still splayed to his chest, his own hand still pressed protectively over hers.

The bird let out a loud squawk, and a rolled-up strip of paper fell from its mouth.

Adrian stared. "Did that raven just say... 'Nevermore'?"

"It's a crow." Marjorie slipped her hand out from beneath his. "And he said, 'Letter for...'"

"Wait." He stared at her. "You *know* this bird?"

"It's Piffle. The message must be for me." She crossed over to the window and knelt down to retrieve the slender spool of paper from the floor. She unrolled the long, narrow scroll. "Oh, thank God."

"Good news?"

"Graham's handwriting. I love Jacob dearly, but I sometimes think the real reason no one will publish his poems is because they can't make out a single word he's written." She scanned the note, then glanced up with a smile. "Success!"

"You've taken down Snowley?" he said dubiously. "Standing around a workroom, whilst we're supposed to be counterfeiting coins?"

"Sorry," she apologized. "I meant the other case. The ring of keys you and I made worked splendidly, and today my siblings were able to resolve the last outstanding matters. I'm to convey how impressed they are, not just with your craftsmanship but with your willingness to jump in, even when it wasn't your fight."

"It doesn't say all of that."

She handed him the curling strip of paper.

He studied at it for a long moment. "This is the brother with the *good* handwriting?"

"Admit it," she chided him. "You loved being on the right side of the war."

"I don't even know what the battle was about. I was duped. I never meant to be one of the good soldiers."

"And yet you served the squadron with skill and honor." She plucked the paper from Adrian's hands and took it over to the worktable in order to dash a reply on the opposite side.

"What are you writing?"

"That you're an apprentice, not an ally. And that I'm patently the better artist."

"Give me that pencil." He bumped her out of the way and squinted at the paper. "This says, *A. W. thrilled to be part of the team.* I said no such thing!"

"You're a self-centered, pleasure-seeking scoundrel," she pointed out. "By definition, you wouldn't have joined in if it wasn't amusing to do so."

"I don't dispute that part," he said over his shoulder as he scribbled. "I'm just letting them know *I'm* the better artist."

She huffed and reached for the note.

Adrian rolled it up and held it high over his head. "I'd like to see you take it from me now!"

Piffle shot from the windowsill and snapped the paper from Adrian's fingers with his beak.

Adrian chased after him. "I wasn't done with that!"

But the crow was already out the window and gone.

"Rude." Marjorie crossed her arms beneath her bosom. "First you send secret messages to your family, then you send secret messages to mine. *I'm* the only person destined to remain in the dark about what exactly you're thinking—"

"When *you're* within sight, there's only one thing I'm thinking. If there's any doubt about what that might be..." He grabbed her wrists and pulled her to him. "I might show you."

She stared up at him in challenge, her heart fluttering in anticipation. "I'm waiting."

"I'm through waiting," Adrian growled. He dipped his head until his mouth brushed hers. "I tried to be good, but this is who I am. And you are the only thing I want."

His lips crushed hers. Marjorie lifted up on her toes, pressing every part of herself into him, as though blending two distinct colors into something wondrous and new.

He slid the fingers of his left hand into her hair, cupping the back of her head as he kissed her. His other arm wrapped possessively around her waist, holding her to him as though he could not bear for any portion of their bodies to remain apart.

This was what she had wanted. A brief, quenching indulgence to put out the threatening fire.

But instead of snuffing the spark, the feel of his muscled hardness ratcheted up the heat. And when he coaxed her mouth open to tangle his tongue with hers, Marjorie felt each stroke tingle throughout her entire body. As though she were molten metal being molded into something new.

Good Lord, this kiss was the last thing they needed. Passion could only cloud their judgment and make the stakes higher than ever. Kissing him was a terrible idea.

She wrapped her arms about his neck and held on tight.

20

*A*drian drank Marjorie in like the selfish, greedy blackguard he was.

He knew he shouldn't touch her. Shouldn't kiss her. Shouldn't savor every curve and breath and taste. She was so slender, he could scoop her into his arms and make love to her right here against the wall.

Not that he would. Even Adrian wasn't boorish enough for that.

Yet.

She was a star from the heavens. Tiny and full of light, and burning so much brighter than he could fully comprehend. She tasted faintly of tea and marmalade, and when he'd lowered his head to hers he'd caught a glimpse of violet paint smudged on the shell of one perfect ear.

Her small size gave the illusion of fragility. That the slightest breeze could lift her up and whisk her away like the seed of a dandelion. But her feet were planted firmly on the ground. She could face down a tempest and emerge the victor on the other side. Had probably done so today, ten times before breakfast.

She was not afraid of the likes of Adrian. Not his past, not his reputation. Not the things he was rumored to do, or those he admittedly had done. She looked at him not as though he were thrice as large as her and a hundred times as dangerous. She took in his height and his muscles, heard his growls and his snarls, and somehow saw a kitten at the heart of the beast.

He was no kitten, of course. He wasn't even the beast. He was the tempest. Wild, gray, violent, unruly, billowing out of control, faster and faster. She turned him into centrifugal motion, spinning with him faster and faster like a potter's wheel until they blended into each other's embrace.

Her specialty was to stand before a blank canvas and create something from nothing. She had done the same with him. Filling him where he had been empty, adding color where he had been gray. Revealing him not as he was, but as he could be.

If she was right about his potential. If he was the sort of man she believed he could be.

Her hands caressed his face, his shoulders, his arms. She was an artist in this, too, as much as with paint on paper. He had never felt so seen, so understood, so *well defined*, as when she poked at his soft spots and smoothed his rough edges.

His specialty was physical. Whittling away, destroying bit by bit, until all that was left was a shameless copy of the original. Sculpting someone else's art. Forging their talent.

But there was nothing fake about these kisses. No moment of his life had felt truer than when he'd pulled her into his arms and covered her mouth with his. It felt real and wonderful and well beyond his reach. She was Polaris, and he the dark star leaching away her light for his own selfish ends.

"Push me away," he said roughly between kisses.

"No," she replied, and kissed him.

God help him, he leapt right back in. Soaring in her light. Dipping, flying, dizzy with desire. Rattled by the loss of gravity, his feet no longer on terra firma where he'd left them. The center of his world had become the diminutive woman so soft and warm in his hands.

"This is wrong," he told her. "I'm taking advantage."

"I'm doing everything you are," she pointed out huskily. "Does that mean I am taking advantage of *you*?"

He wished she would. He'd swipe his arm across this worktable, knock every item to the floor, then throw his back atop the pitted wooden surface and bring her curves right along with him for the ride.

"I'm not a good man," he tried again.

She kissed him. "I know."

"I mean it. I am not good enough for you."

Her eyes sparkled. "*I know.*"

Good God, how could he *not* kiss her? His plan to scare her away by appearing the self-centered, morally corrupt libertine everyone believed him to be now seemed so foolish.

His kisses did not frighten her off. His kisses made her melt against him even more, taking each new kiss and building upon it until he no longer had any idea who was seducing whom.

All he knew was that he didn't want it to end. Not this morning, not today, not this month, not at the end of her mission, not when he left Snowley, not if Adrian was forced to flee England. Kisses like these weren't for the late-life remembrances of a lonely old bachelor drowning his sorrows in sherry.

Kisses like these were for *keeping*. For savoring and cherishing. Kisses like these were to be given and taken and shared at every possible moment, until they were as much a part of his life as breath.

What if this wasn't a meaningless flirtation? What if, instead of pushing her away, he did his best to bind her to him? What if Marjorie could believe Adrian was good enough to deserve a second chance at life? That he was also worthy of love?

Was he foolish to want such things? Probably. Would he ever deserve a real chance with her? Unlikely. Was he going to try anyway?

Without a doubt.

He wanted it all. Every part of her, every shade, every curve, every angle.

Of course, mutual desire was dangerous enough. But *feelings...* nothing made a man more vulnerable.

If Snowley were to catch wind of a budding romance, he'd use Marjorie as more leverage. But what if Adrian could get them both out from under Snowley's thumb and save his sister in the process?

He would unleash any storm necessary to keep Marjorie safe.

Even if it tore him apart in the process.

21

⚛

*D*ays later, as soon as Joey and Grinders melted back into their respective corners, Marjorie closed the workroom door and immediately fell into Adrian's arms.

This was the new routine, and Marjorie loved it.

Pour metal into a mold? Earn a kiss. Pop out a counterfeit coin? Earn a kiss. Clean the chalk mold and fill it all over again? Another kiss. They made just enough coins to give the impression that they were studiously at work as instructed.

Between the coins and the kissing, she had also begun to teach him sign language. He knew his numbers and the letters of the alphabet, and was slowly adding common nouns and verbs to his vocabulary. It would take years for him to reach her siblings' level, but for rudimentary conversations they could not risk being overheard, any level of competency would suffice.

Between lessons and passionate kisses, they managed to have several heartfelt conversations, ranging from Adrian's family to hers, and what kinds of art stirred their spirits the most. It was beyond sublime. Marjorie was fascinated by all of Adrian's experiences and views, many of which clashed delightfully with her own.

But there at the bottom of every kiss, behind every smile, in the blank spaces between each hip bump or signing lesson or spirited debate, was the knowledge that passion was not what she had come for. She was here to take Snowley down, not mash her mouth against Adrian's.

This wasn't a holiday. It was a mission. There was a client relying on Marjorie...who could not even guarantee that Mr. Lachlan's wedding ring was still on the premises.

The possibility that it had already found its way into a cauldron before Marjorie infiltrated Snowley's crooked family haunted her. Just over a fortnight remained before Mrs. Lachlan was evicted.

Marjorie had managed to gain the confidence of three different maids, who confirmed that Snowley's riches were somewhere on the premises. The maids helped identify many areas that did *not* contain a treasure room. Not the kitchen, obviously. Not the pawnshop. Not the dining room or many parlors.

Every day, Marjorie's reconnaissance was more complete than the last. She went home every night and helped Tommy update the siblings' maps. Unfortunately, the *right* location remained stubbornly undiscovered.

"We need to find that storage chamber," she said to Adrian.

"Can't just stroll about," he reminded her. "There's armed guards in the corridors."

They had this conversation at least ten times a day. But there *had* to be a way.

When Piffle arrived with another note, she caught Adrian staring at her pensively.

"What is it?" she asked as she rolled her reply and handed it back to the crow.

He lifted a shoulder and busied himself with the molds. "It must be nice to have a family like yours."

"It is," she agreed. "I would not trade my siblings for anything. But you are not an only child yourself. You have a sister, a brother, *and* a father."

He snorted. "Only one of which acknowledges my existence—and even *that* is provisional."

She looked over at him in surprise. "You think Lady Iris will shun you?"

"I don't think she'll have a choice. My father has instructed the staff to turn me away on sight and forbidden Iris from any contact with me."

"I have the impression," Marjorie said carefully, "that your sister might not cleave to his edicts as much as you think."

"Oh, I'm certain she doesn't *wish* to let him govern her every thought and action. But he who holds the purse strings, holds the power."

Was that why Lady Iris gambled to excess? Was it not a compulsion after all, but a frantic bid for freedom?

"What if she marries? Your father won't have any control over her then."

Adrian slanted her a look. "You think some high-in-the-instep, proper lord will allow his wife to welcome a devil-may-care scoundrel into their home?"

Marjorie arched her brows. "You think Lady Iris wants some high-in-the-instep, proper lord?"

"What one wants is not always what Fate delivers."

She plucked the mold from his hand and set it aside. "What is it you want and think you cannot have?"

"You, naked, atop this table."

She rolled her eyes. "Be serious."

"I am."

"You know what I meant."

He raked a hand through his hair. "I want a real relationship with my sister. I want to stroll through art galleries with Iris at my side. I want to ride in the park with her and whomever her future beau might be. I want to be an uncle to all of my siblings' children. Not in secret, but in fact. The sort of uncle who sinks to his knees and opens his arms wide, allowing his nieces and nephews to bowl him over onto the grass."

"It sounds splendid."

And...was yet another privilege Marjorie would have that Adrian did not. When Chloe's baby was born, Marjorie would have the freedom to be any kind of aunt she wished. There would be no objections to bedtime stories or plump little hands smearing paint around a canvas. The impossible life Adrian dreamed of was one she could take for granted.

"It *would* be splendid," he said with feeling. "If my father and brother wouldn't make her life hell for daring to consider letting me back in."

"How do you know they feel that way? It's been many years, has it not?"

"Too many," he confirmed, his expression haunted.

"Your father may be a difficult man, but surely by now your brother must have forgiven your transgressions."

He chuckled humorlessly. "What transgressions?"

Her cheeks heated. "I meant no disrespect. The rumors about why you left are common knowledge. I now suspect it was idle gossip and not factual at all."

He looked at her for a long moment, then sank onto a wooden stool. She did the same.

"I am tired of holding on to my anger," he said haltingly. "But I've never told anyone the truth about that summer."

"You needn't share with me, either, if you'd rather not. Your secrets are yours to do with as you wish."

"That's just it. They're not *my* secrets." He let out a frustrated breath. "Everything you've heard about that poor defiled girl who was forced to visit the country after a shameless seduction and was thereafter never heard from again...it's all true. Except for one small detail."

"She wasn't defiled?" Marjorie guessed. "She was a willing, eager partner?"

"You'd have to ask my brother for details," Adrian answered hollowly. "I wasn't there."

Marjorie pressed a hand to her chest as though she could push her involuntary gasp back into her lungs. "It wasn't *you*?"

"It was Herbert," he confirmed. "The holy, golden heir. He could not marry the girl, despite his promises to the contrary and her growing belly. Father had already betrothed him to another, and as I mentioned...the person holding the purse strings wields the power."

"But...if the young woman was with *child*..."

"Then Herbert was in want of a scapegoat. Who better to blame for such a shameful situation than the flirtatious little brother cutting a swath through London on his first season?"

"But how..."

"Herbert is clever. He came to me first. He told me he was in a bind, and I alone could save him. All I had to do was tell Father I had behaved in an ungentlemanly manner with the girl, if Father broached the topic. He implied his intended bride was jealous over an innocent flirtation. I asked no further questions."

"You just said yes?"

"I worshipped my elder brother. And I had in fact flirted with the young lady myself. Specifically *because* I had seen my elder brother looking at her and wanted to prove myself just as good as him. How's that for ungentlemanly? I even stole a kiss from her in a tea garden. But I had no notion until later how much further Herbert had gone."

"By the time you found out..."

Adrian nodded. "Herbert told his tale to Father before I had any knowledge there was scandal afoot. Father accepted without question Herbert's 'explanation' of having rescued me—and the family name—from yet another boorish scrape."

"So when your father asked you about the incident..." Marjorie stopped. Was impregnating, ruining, bribing, and abandoning a young girl an *incident*? "When he inquired, then you, with all guilelessness, answered honestly and said yes, you had indeed behaved dishonorably with the lady in question?"

"Father turned purple and threw me out of the house on the spot. I was banished and destitute before I fully comprehended just what it was I was alleged to have done. All the same, I *would* have offered to marry the girl, if I'd known how to reach her. She didn't deserve her fate. Of course, a sudden wedding would only have reinforced my guilt in my father's eyes."

"It was your brother who should have taken responsibility for his actions. You agreed to the earl's scheme without realizing the extent of his crimes. That's a horrible trick. He lied to everyone."

"For hours, the morning before my ship sailed, I tried to tell my father the truth. He wouldn't allow me across the threshold and had informed the servants not only to turn me away at the door but also to burn any incoming correspondence. After he sent footmen to have me forcibly removed from the front step, I left believing we would never speak again. I was right."

"Horrible. That poor young woman and her child were also exiled from everyone they knew and loved?"

"I did what I could. Sent money to her family anonymously every time I received a payment from Snowley, in the hope it would make it to the child. I may never meet my niece or nephew, but I want them to have a comfortable life."

"You would be a marvelous uncle. But it is the earl who should have been a good father. How despicable! I hate your brother. I ought to have my sister run him through with a sword."

"Don't. My father would be distraught if I were to inherit instead of the son he loves."

Marjorie's heart twisted in sympathy.

"Elizabeth wouldn't kill him," she assured Adrian. "She would just poke a few extra holes until he repented for such shameful lies. The earl defrauded you out of your own family. What's more, your disgraceful father deserves a few well-placed blade pricks, too, for accepting the absurd notion that one of his sons is an angel and the other a devil."

"I was a devil," Adrian said. "I made mistakes daily. I was rash and impulsive. Full of my own superiority and invincibility. I flirted because I *could*. Stole kisses because I should *not*. It didn't matter to me with whom. Such behavior was a lark."

"You were nineteen," Marjorie said firmly. "Your age doesn't excuse you for being a rakehell. But your brother took advantage of your youth and your desire to please him. To be *helpful*. To be needed."

Her voice shook. Many of those same emotions had driven Marjorie to step out of the safety of her studio and into Snowley's den.

The difference was, her siblings loved her. They were *here* for her. Never more than a crow or a hedgehog away. They saw her need to expand her role, and responded with acceptance and encouragement. They worked *together*, not against each other.

And Adrian...did not have the first clue what such support could feel like. His brother had manipulated him. His father had discarded him. And every day since had been spent on his own, struggling to overcome abrupt loss of fortune and a sudden dishonorable reputation thrust upon him by the very people who should have been there to lift him up, not leave him behind.

Marjorie cupped his face in her hands and coaxed his mouth down toward hers.

Her lips had just touched his when the handle turned at the workroom door.

They sprang apart at once. Marjorie grabbed the closest chalk mold wrong-side up, and Adrian flew to the fireplace to inspect the bubbling pot.

Snowley strode through the door with a self-satisfied smirk on his pale, grandfatherly face.

"What is it?" Adrian said as if bored. "We're busy."

"And you'll stay that way for a long time," Snowley said with satisfaction. "The next decade, at this rate."

"What the devil are you talking about?" Adrian turned his back to the fire. "We're producing coins faster than ever before—"

"You're working with an assistant, so you only get credit for half of them."

"What?"

"Regardless of our current contract terms, I don't think you'll be leaving my employ...ever."

"Why would I stay a minute longer than I have to? You gave your word that once I'd repaid the value of the forged antiquities—"

"—you'll have completed *your* debt. You're right. I gave my word, and I stand by it." Snowley held up some folded papers. "*This* woman's word, on the other hand..."

Adrian frowned in confusion. "What woman?"

Marjorie's stomach churned with trepidation. She had a very, very bad feeling about the contents of the notes in Snowley's fist.

"I have amassed a collection of IOUs from one..." Snowley made a production of opening one of the notes as if he'd forgotten the name inside. "Ah, yes. Lady Iris Webb, daughter of the Marquess of Meadowbrook. Isn't that *your* father? Why, these debts must belong to your little sister."

"Iris?" Adrian blurted out in astonishment. "Gambling?"

"Indeed. And for shockingly high stakes." Snowley clucked his tongue. "When I caught wind of her unladylike extravagances, I arranged for a private game between a few unsavory characters and our charming young woman."

Oh *no.* Marjorie closed her eyes. Lady Iris's big game meant to extricate her from her hole had been against *Snowley*?

"I promised the lady the opportunity to win back all of the stray IOUs, which I had conveniently purchased en masse. Had she won the game, I should be honor-bound to cancel her debt. Unfortunately for her, she not only lost, but kept losing. And I am the sole owner of...let's see here..." He made a show of counting the papers. "A debt of six thousand, three hundred, and forty-eight pounds."

Good Lord. Marjorie's stomach roiled. There were celebrated heiresses whose dowry didn't touch that number. And Lady Iris owed the sum to Snowley?

Adrian stalked across the room, hand outstretched. "Give those here."

"I don't think I will," Snowley said calmly, and tucked them into a hidden waistcoat pocket. As he did so, the chain bearing his ring glinted in the firelight before disappearing back beneath his lapel.

"I'll pay them," Adrian said quickly. "The money is in my account in Paris. I will have to visit a bank to make the withdrawal."

Marjorie's chest rose with hope.

"Once you're out of my sight, I don't trust you to return," Snowley said, as if bored. But wisps of blood red and dirty brown curled about him like smoke. "What I want is your *servitude*." Snowley patted his lapel. "Or I can take my little collection of letters to Marshalsea, and Lady Iris can spend the rest of her life rotting in irons in a debtors' prison."

"It's not actionable," Adrian said in desperation. "Those are debts of honor, not legal contracts. And she's underage. Iris is only..."

"Past her majority as of two years ago," Snowley finished smoothly. "You've been gone a long time. Your sister is all grown up. She's signed her notes quite prettily, making them actionable debts indeed."

"It won't work." Adrian straightened. "If you attempt to gaol her, my father will have her out by nightfall."

Snowley smiled as if he'd been waiting for this argument all along. "Will he? Or might your father do exactly what he did for you: absolutely nothing? Is your little sister's freedom a gamble you're willing to take?"

Adrian's face drained of color. His teeth clicked together loud enough even Marjorie could hear it.

"Ah," Snowley said. "I see we are of one mind about your father's honor. But even if some wealthy benefactor were to swoop in and pay your sister's debts to rescue her from prison..."

"The damage would be done." Adrian looked gutted. "Ruined beyond repair. And yes, likely tossed from my father's home."

Snowley shook his head with faux sympathy. "A terrible situation for a young lady to find herself in. Why, she could fall prey to *any* sort of mishap."

Snowley would see to it.

22

$\mathcal{M}$ arjorie's heart was heavy when she walked through the front door of the Wynchester residence. *She* could go home, but Adrian could not. Possibly not for months or years, unless Marjorie found a way to take Snowley down faster.

And now Lady Iris was caught in the net, too.

The Wynchester siblings would meet soon for supper, but Marjorie couldn't wait that long to assure herself that her entire family was safe, sound, and accounted for.

Or maybe she just missed them. A secondary effect to being the primary Wynchester out on adventure was that she was no longer home all day to run into this brother or that sister at regular intervals.

Marjorie hadn't realized how much peace she got from the knowledge that she was never alone. That there was always another Wynchester in the house. That if she needed help—or just a hug—all she had to do to be reunited with someone who loved her unconditionally was step out of her studio.

Snowley's lair suddenly seemed much too far away from home.

"Oh, there you are." Elizabeth was coming down the stairs bearing a baby bunny in one hand.

Elizabeth's top lip had a faint green tint...as did the bunny's. Marjorie suspected Elizabeth had once again been sharing her pistachio ices, despite Jacob's repeated scolding. Marjorie had never missed stained skin and brotherly scoldings more in her life.

Elizabeth's eyes sparkled. "Survive another boring day in someone else's studio?"

Marjorie threw her arms about her sister and hugged her tight.

Alarmed, Elizabeth patted Marjorie's back with her free hand. "Are you all right? What has Webb done? Say the word, and I shall behead him."

"It's not about Adrian," Marjorie said into her sister's shoulder.

Except it *was* about him. Even if Adrian had been granted the same freedom to leave Snowley's nest every night...he still couldn't go home to his family. He had a father who believed the worst of him, and a brother who had orchestrated it. And a sister who, now more than ever, could not risk the ire of their father.

"Can the family meet early?" Marjorie asked. "I have an auxiliary case."

Elizabeth moved the bunny to her shoulder. "Does your case involve me running blackguards through with my rapier?"

"I hope so," Marjorie said darkly.

Elizabeth clapped her hands in delight. "Tell the others. I'll pen a note to Chloe."

Marjorie hurried up the stairs. The doors to Tommy and Philippa's connected suites were open. They were both inside Tommy's boudoir, Philippa curled in an armchair with a book, and Tommy at her dressing table, squinting at her reflection as she added deep wrinkles to her young face.

"Aha! Just the genius I was praising." Tommy held up a collection of cosmetics set into a wooden case. "Your idea to organize my cosmetics into thematic palettes works phenomenally. All I have to do is grab Crotchety Old Man and voilà! I can't thank you enough."

Marjorie flushed. "It's my pleasure."

"Don't go anywhere!" Philippa set down her book and leapt to her feet. "I've something I think you will like. Wait here."

She dashed to her private chamber, which the siblings teased her was only used for storage. Philippa's mattress had been piled with books for months, because she spent all her nights in Tommy's bed.

"I'm not going anywhere," Marjorie said, although Philippa had disappeared before Marjorie could answer. "I have a new case, and I was hoping we could meet to discuss it."

"Of course." Tommy dropped Crotchety Old Man into a drawer and rose from her dressing table without question, one half of her face covered in deep sagging wrinkles.

Philippa sailed back into the room with a large stack of thick books. "Here they are! These took forever to collect, and I've been dying to give them to you."

"What are they?" Marjorie wasn't usually a reader, but she accepted the towering stack gamely all the same.

"Look and see!" Philippa bounced in excitement.

Marjorie shifted the books to view the titles. "Biographies of all my favorite artists!"

"Some contain illustrations of the most famous pieces. You'll love it. You should consider making a book of *your* work."

"*My* work?" Marjorie repeated doubtfully. "I'm nobody's favorite artist."

"You're mine," Tommy said with good cheer. "Every Wynchester would pick you first."

"No one outside the family thinks I'm special," Marjorie amended.

"There are a dozen little girls being tutored who would disagree with that assessment," said Philippa. "Over a hundred more if we count even a fraction of your former pupils."

"Speaking of wagering," Marjorie said, "I have a case. Whilst I

"Hmm." Tommy handed the note to Chloe. "I'm not sure that's the full explanation."

Chloe's eyebrows shot up. "After that, it says: *You must all realize how lucky you are to have her.*"

Yes. Yes, that sounded exactly like a contentious working arrangement between two mortal enemies who were definitely not wrapped in each other's embrace at every opportunity.

"The case," she blurted. "Shall we concentrate on our client? Wynchesters can do anything, given enough time and opportunity, but neither Mrs. Lachlan nor Lady Iris has a moment to lose. Is this a case where we ought to involve the Bow Street Runners?"

"To do what?" Kuni asked. "If there's nothing we can use as blackmail, then there's nothing the courts can use against Snowley, either."

"Are you trying to avoid talking about Lord Adrian?" Tommy asked.

"Interesting," Elizabeth drawled with glee. She rested her chin on the backs of her fingers and batted her eyelashes at Marjorie. "I can live vicariously through you. Tell me everything. Was it a single stolen kiss? Multiple passionate kisses? Does he drool?"

"All right, all right." Graham settled the room. "We've got two linked clients and one puppet master. Let's spend the rest of the evening ruminating on how best to use our talents to bring down Snowley, and we'll reconvene as soon as any of us has a workable plan. Shall we adjourn until supper?"

The siblings nodded and rose to their feet, talking among themselves as they exited the Planning Parlor.

Marjorie hung back. Her sister's colors were off today. Bruised purples instead of fluffy pinks. She must be worried about something.

Chloe waited until everyone else had gone before closing the door. Because the room was fortified against sound, not a single word spoken would be audible outside the Planning Parlor's walls.

"Is the baby all right?" Marjorie whispered, alarmed.

Chloe placed a hand over the growing bulge beneath her gown. "The baby is doing splendidly. How are *you*?"

"Fine, thank you," Marjorie answered automatically.

Chloe sent her a look. Ah. Her sister was worried about *Marjorie*.

"Oh, very well," she grumbled. "Yes, he's a rake, and yes, a few tiny liberties may have been taken. By both of us. Mutually."

"I see."

"It's not serious," Marjorie said quickly. "He's never serious, for one. And for two, I like my life just as it is. The last thing I'd want to do is marry and move away. Er, I mean no offense. I know you fell in love. That's just not something I'm looking for."

"No offense taken," Chloe said. "For the record, I wasn't looking for love, either. It just found me."

"It won't find me," Marjorie said firmly. "I'm an almost thirty-year-old spinster who hates change."

"Do you? I've been gone from the house for so long...remind me where your art studio is located. Is it on the third floor, or is it in the back of a criminal's secret stronghold in the middle of a rookery?"

Marjorie closed her lips and said nothing.

"It's all right." Chloe touched Marjorie's arm. "Whatever it is that you want is a perfectly acceptable thing to desire. You don't have to be a wife or a mother. Though I'm afraid you're burdened with being an aunt."

Marjorie gazed at the curve of her sister's belly.

Aunt, yes. That went without saying. But the truth was...

Marjorie wanted all the things, no matter how contradictory. How could she not want to find love, with so many joyful examples all around her? Yet how could she possibly leave her family, if even a few hours apart from them left her a maudlin, quivering mess?

"Nothing of note will develop between me and Lord Adrian."

"Because he's no gentleman?"

"Because he's a client."

"Oh, darling, of all the flimsy excuses... *Philippa* was a client, and Tommy essentially married her. She's one of us now, and Tommy couldn't be happier. When something is meant to be—"

"It's not meant to be," Marjorie interrupted.

She did not want to admit that Chloe's argument held merit. Adrian wasn't an actual client. Keeping him at a distance because of the case was an absurd justification for Marjorie's fear of change... or the risk to her heart.

"Like you said," Chloe said softly. "Examples of how it *could* be are all around you."

Yes, they were. Marjorie nodded. That was the other reason it would never be her.

If seeing her siblings pair up had taught her anything, it was that one's partner was the one person who fully and thoroughly saw one's unvarnished true self, flaws and weaknesses and mistakes and all.

What could be more terrifying than that?

23

$\mathcal{A}$drian was in the workroom long before dawn.

He'd spent the first half of the night staring up at the cracked ceiling, worrying about his sister and doing his best to be grateful that at least Snowley could be taken at his word—even if his words were nothing Adrian wanted to hear.

Not only might it be years until Adrian was his own man again, but over that much time, someone would discover Adrian's illegal activities. Any chance of reconciliation with Iris would be gone forever.

The one bright spot in his life was Marjorie. She was the shining light that made his incarceration bearable. The powerful sun, capable of shooting its brightest rays through the darkest of shadows.

Missing her this way only made him feel like more of a cad. What kind of man longed for the presence of an honorable woman, instead of wishing her to remain as far from Snowley's reach as possible?

The door to the workroom swung open.

Marjorie. There at the threshold. A basket on her arm, a smile at her lips, and a thousand shooting stars exploding in Adrian's chest.

He scarcely allowed her to shut the door behind her before swinging her into his arms and covering her eager mouth with his. As he kissed her, he slid the basket from her arm and up onto the table in order to pull her more fully into his embrace.

She melted against him. "I missed you, too."

"I never said I missed you."

"You didn't have to."

"If I could stop missing you, I would. You shouldn't be here. Snowley cannot be negotiated with."

"Neither can I."

His muscles hardened. "You stubborn, foolish angel. Is there nothing to convince you to safeguard yourself first and foremost?"

"It's not what Wynchesters do. Which is why we're going to—"

He pulled his mouth from hers and jerked out of her embrace. "I told you. Leave it alone. There's a way out written into my new contract. Meddling will cause more harm than good. I'm not one of your clients."

"No," she agreed, unperturbed by his outburst. "But Lady Iris is."

"My sister?" He felt his voice rise and carefully brought it back under his control. "She came to you for help rather than me?"

"She has no way to reach you," Marjorie pointed out.

"Did she bother to try?" Heart sinking, he rephrased his question. "Would she have come to me, even if she could?"

"It's moot," Marjorie said. "I know that doesn't make you feel better, but it's true. She asked for my help because I was there, right in front of her—"

"When I sent the packet? You've known about this for *days*?"

"—and you're doing everything you can from in here. You're rescuing her as best you can, in the *only* way that you can."

"I will ask you again," he ground out. "When did you learn Iris was in this trouble?"

"She asked me not to tell."

"You tell *me*. That's who you tell. *I'm* her brother. You are no one to her at all. I'm the one with every right to—"

"You hold no dominion over Lady Iris whatsoever. You're her brother, not her keeper. Nor do you own *me*. You have my kisses, not my unconditional allegiance." Marjorie crossed her arms and scowled at him. "Should you continue in this vein..."

He stepped back. "Are you threatening me?"

"With common sense! If you think I or any woman *owes* you anything, you are incredibly mistaken."

He stalked over to the worktable and took the chalk molds over to the fire, filling them with molten metal one by one until it was the molds that ran hot and dangerous, not the fury in his veins.

Damn it all, neither woman owed him anything. Not her time, not her trust, not the benefit of the doubt. He *wanted* to be the one they chose, but his protectiveness and his pride did not make their will his to command.

The whole point of choosing him was that it had to be their *choice*. Not something he demanded.

Once the molds were full, he carefully pushed them into parallel lines. He turned back toward Marjorie, his hip leaning against the worktable. Before he spoke, he rubbed his face with his hands.

"You're right," he said at last. "I apologize for being jealous."

"You have the right to your feelings. I would be distraught if my siblings came to you with a private problem, rather than to me. But you or me feeling sad or hurt does not mean that others should not have free will over their lives."

"So tell me." He kicked out one of the stools and sat down heavily on it. "What has my sister been doing with her free will?"

"Employing the Wynchesters. There's no charge," Marjorie added. "We never take money from our clients."

"I'm not sure you understand the meaning of 'employ' and 'client,'" Adrian muttered under his breath.

"Maybe it's you who are choosing not to understand," she answered.

He closed his mouth into a thin line. He'd forgotten she could read lips. Besides, his anger wasn't with her—or even Iris. Adrian was angry at himself.

"All right," he said. "Now that my sister has summoned the Wynchester team, what will you and your siblings do about her predicament? If there's anything that *can* be done."

She gazed at him for a long moment, then pulled the other stool right in front of his knees and sat down to face him.

"My sister Elizabeth and my sister-in-law Kuni are giving Lady Iris defense lessons," Marjorie began.

Adrian's spine snapped up straight.

"You anticipate *violence*?" he asked in horror.

"No plan without a contingency," she hedged. "We don't expect a skirmish, but Lady Iris might as well be able to defend herself against any attack."

He blanched. "Defense lessons. Excellent. I shall have the most 'accomplished' sister in England."

"My other siblings are lending their talents as well. We don't just want to pull Lady Iris out from under Snowley's shadow. No more reckless gambling. We want to leave her in a position where she need never take risks like that again."

The full Wynchester crew was treating Iris as one of their own? Adrian was flabbergasted that a family could be like this. Completely, fully, unquestionably on Iris's side. Rallying behind her not because she was perfect or innocent, but because she was *im*perfect and in trouble and needed their help. To the Wynchesters, seeing someone floundering meant offering a hand, not withdrawing their support.

Marjorie was fortunate to be part of such an admirable, incredible, dependable team. This was what family *meant*. He was lucky Iris had found them.

"Well?" Marjorie prompted. "What do you think?"

"I want to do my part."

Which was what? Continue counterfeiting?

The treasure chamber was full of empty promises and broken dreams. The artifacts of people who turned to a man like Snowley out of utter desperation.

Artifacts.

Antiquities.

Forgeries.

Excitement coursed through his veins. He leaned forward and grabbed Marjorie's hands. "We've got to get into that treasure chamber."

"I know. That's been the plan from the beginning."

He shook his head. "Not just to find your client's wedding ring. I mean to divest Snowley of every single item in that room."

She arched her brows. "You don't think he'll notice his best pieces turning up missing?"

"No, I don't think he will." Adrian smiled like a fox. "Not if we leave spares in their place."

24

❦

The next morning, Marjorie spent several extra minutes arranging her hair. To be fair, she did not normally spend *any* time before a looking glass, which was why she often ended up walking about with smudges of paint on her cheeks or her nose. But since she couldn't impress Adrian with one of the many colorful gowns in her wardrobe, the least she could do was invest a few moments on...uneven ringlets?

With a sigh, she gave up on mastering her sister's curling tongs and hurried downstairs. Adrian had already seen Marjorie in messy hair and a dull, patched dress every previous day. Why spoil the pattern now?

Within the hour, she was back in Snowley's den. As soon as the workroom door closed behind her, Marjorie launched herself into Adrian's arms.

He caught her, kissed her, completed her. Made her heart beat faster and caused time to slow all around them. A rainbow of sugary confetti exploded throughout all of her senses. When she was in his arms, nothing mattered but the current kiss, and the next one, and the next.

She had tried her hardest to avoid thinking about what this meant. To cleave to her identity of determined spinster, of being the woman who could fill any empty spaces in her life by painting an alternate world on canvas.

But how did one paint a kiss? The feel of freshly shaved jaw in the morning, or the pleasing roughness of a hint of stubble in the afternoon? The taste of a man's tongue? The sensation of his body pressed against yours, and the knowledge that every plane, every muscle, was now as familiar to you as your favorite palette?

How did one paint how it felt to be *wanted*? To be missed? To be desirable? What brush did she use to capture the scent of Adrian's skin as he wrapped his arms about her and held her so close it felt as though he'd rather die than let her go?

She was more obsessed with him than she had ever been with oils or acrylics or watercolors. He was a world of color and texture and expression. She didn't want it to end. But she knew it would.

And after their affair was over, when Adrian walked away... Marjorie would have to, too.

Unless.

Her heart beat faster. Keeping Adrian was impossible, but Wynchesters did impossible things every day. There could be a way. There *would* be a way.

If she were brave enough to take it.

"I suppose we ought to at least pretend to create a few coins," she murmured against his mouth.

His lips twisted. "Must we? I'm already indentured for decades. What damage can five minutes do?"

"We've been kissing for..." She glanced at the clock. "Half an hour."

"Half a day wouldn't be enough."

Marjorie suspected neither would half a lifetime.

Adrian scooped up a chalk mold and headed over to the crucible.

She joined him at the fire in silence at first. Words were Jacob's skill, not Marjorie's. Her talent lay in color and gesture and blending ordinary things in order for something extraordinary to emerge.

"Where would you be if you weren't beholden to Snowley?" she asked at last.

"With Iris," he replied without hesitation. "Begging for a second chance to be the big brother I always meant to be."

"And after she says of course, you've never stopped being her brother?"

"What makes you think she will?"

"What makes you think she won't?"

He stared at the floor for a long moment. When he spoke, she could not hear his words, so she could only assume he murmured them beneath his breath. "I want it too much."

"Maybe she does, too," Marjorie said softly.

Adrian's gaze flew to hers, tortured. "Do I deserve a second chance?"

"Doesn't everyone?" She touched his arm. "You *will* have one, Adrian. I know it. Sisters are special."

"Is that where you would be if you weren't in here? With your family?"

"Probably." Marjorie gazed off out the window. "Normally I would say *in my art studio*, but...I think I'm going to consciously enjoy more time with my family whilst I have them. How are you planning on enjoying your sister's company, once you've fully reunited?"

"I don't know," he admitted. "My imagination always got stuck on the reuniting part."

She turned her gaze back to him. "How long will you stay in London?"

He frowned as if the words held no meaning. "How long?"

"This visit. Was it meant to be a week, a month, the entire summer?"

"I don't know," he said again, his expression embarrassed. "My rooms in Paris are paid through the end of the year."

"Ah." A pit grew in Marjorie's stomach. "I assumed you'd return there."

"I don't know that I will," Adrian said, surprising her. "Rather, of course I must, if only to collect my things. But I've traveled too much these past seven years to think of any one place as home."

Of course he didn't. Marjorie swallowed her disappointment. What was worse, knowing where he was, off in Paris, someplace she would never be? Or *not* knowing where he was, in some corner of the globe or another, also someplace she would never be?

"I had hoped..." Adrian said, then trailed off.

"To take your sister to Paris?"

"She would like that," he agreed. "As would I. She said she's looking for adventure, and who better to deliver than her big brother?"

"But you had something else in mind?"

"Someone else in mind." He touched her cheek. "I had hoped *you* might like to visit."

"Me?" she squeaked.

"Have you ever been?"

She shook her head. "I've never even left London, save in the company of my siblings. None of us have ventured abroad. This Christmastide, we'll be visiting Balcovia with my sister-in-law, which is more adventure than any of us ever dreamt of having."

His eyes narrowed. "*None* of you have ever dreamt of adventure?"

"Oh, very well. Probably most of us have. For most of my siblings, their regular lives are an adventure. Throwing knives, scaling buildings, infiltrating Parliament, impersonating the Regent, training Highland tigers..."

Adrian blinked at her. "I have so many questions, I don't even know where to start."

She laughed. "I'll tell you stories as we work, if you listen for footsteps. I can't let on that I'm not from the rookery."

"Tell me stories about the Wynchesters as if they were a fairy tale," Adrian suggested. "There once was a family who..."

"That could work," Marjorie agreed. "There once was a family that came into being over the course of one summer. All of the *Before* portraits I painted are from that period."

"And the *After* portraits?"

"I've not made much progress on the Then-and-Now series lately," she admitted. "I only have Sundays free, which I'm sure to you sounds like—and *is*—a luxury. But first there's the private tutoring. Now that it's only once a week, my sessions with Faircliffe are longer than ever."

"He's making progress?"

"*So* much progress. From there I go to the studio in Charlotte Street, where I give lessons to over a dozen little girls every season. I feared I would lose some when we moved from Saturdays to Sundays, but they've all stayed with me."

"I imagine they worship you."

"And I, them. They are so talented and clever and fearless. They put paint on the paper to see what will happen, rather than wait for a muse to inspire them. They are their own muses and inspire one another."

"It sounds lovely," he said wistfully. "What I longed for when I dreamt of becoming an art instructor. I'm sure it doesn't pay well."

"I volunteer," she admitted.

He laughed. "That *is* the genteel way. Perhaps my father would have responded differently if I'd framed my ambitions as an extremely time-intensive hobby, rather than a profession I intended to pursue."

Marjorie set the finished molds on the worktable. "I should like to see some of *your* works."

He made a face and slumped onto a stool. "I haven't any."

"Did you sell them all?" A terrible thought occurred to her. "You weren't robbed, were you?"

"No, I mean..." He rubbed his face. "I'm not like you. I cannot create something from nothing. I can look at a thing someone else created and duplicate it down to the slightest detail. But that doesn't make it *my* work. It's just a copy."

"Oh, Adrian." Her heart twisted. "Do you want me to tell you what I tell my girls?"

"I don't know. Do I? Children are made of hardier stuff than adults."

"We begin every day with a blank canvas. What we put on it is up to each of us." She touched his arm. "The same is true for you. The fact that you can sculpt things with your hands is what makes you an artist. Just because you didn't invent ancient Etruscan pottery doesn't make you any less talented."

"I would argue that it's imagination, not skill, that makes an artist. I value creations invented from the air over any of the forgeries I made for Snowley."

"And yet which one earns money?" She shrugged. "That's the nature of art. The artist doesn't determine what a piece is worth. The person who falls in love with it does."

"So children's art is meaningless?"

"The opposite. It means everything." Her heart warmed just thinking of all the ways. She scooted her stool closer to his and pulled a chain from around her neck. "I've carried this with me every day for the past two years."

He nodded. "A pocket watch."

"This one used to be Bean's. Baron Vanderbean, that is. My adoptive father." She ran a loving finger over its surface. "He used it as a locket. There's a portrait inside."

"Of you?"

"The two of us. Sort of. If you squint as hard as you can, and use a healthy dollop of the imagination you value so much." She opened the lid to show him.

He couldn't stifle his chuckle.

"I *know*," she said dryly. "Believe me. I had gifted Bean several passable landscapes, but this was my first attempt at a portrait and it shows. I thought that my career was over before it ever began. That no one should take me seriously. That I had no talent. I was just a foolish, fumbling little girl who ought not to be allowed near a paint set."

"What did Baron Vanderbean say?"

"He adored the miniature. My protests that it was embarrassingly amateur didn't make the portrait not *art*. He admonished me to never, ever devalue myself or my work."

"That's beautiful."

Marjorie nodded. "I didn't believe it for a second. I told him if he liked terrible portraits so much, he could keep it. I never wanted to look at it again, because all I could see was my own failure."

"He didn't accept that?"

"He accepted the miniature, just as he accepted all my gifts. But this time, he forced me to accept a silver crown in exchange. Bean said every time he looked at me, he saw potential. And every time he looked at anything I created, he saw *art*. His personal chambers were filled with it. There's even a portrait of him hanging over our mantel."

"That's beautiful. The baron left you the pocket watch in his will?"

She nodded. "He'd carried it with him every day for the rest of his life. Whenever he checked the time, there was our portrait. Where I saw failure, he saw potential. And he made me see it in myself, too."

Marjorie handed him the watch.

He held it up. "The hands have stopped. Is it broken?"

"No." Her voice cracked. "I stopped winding it the day Bean died, so it would be forever frozen in a moment in time when he was still here, loving me. Accepting me. Encouraging me."

Adrian's gaze met hers. "Have you any idea how lucky you are?"

"I do, actually," she said softly. She would never forget. "What about you?"

He scoffed. "*Me?*"

"You're an artist, too," she prompted. "I imagine you have been, ever since you were a child."

"Is that what you imagine?" Darkness crossed his face. "Shall I tell you about the time I presented my father with original pottery, and he threw it against the brick fireplace? I never attempted to create something of my own again."

"I cannot imagine how much it hurt to have his censure rather than his support. No child deserves that." She placed her hand on his knee. "But Adrian, your father banished you seven years ago. Don't let his cruelty back then control you for the rest of your life."

He closed his eyes and let out a ragged breath.

She touched him gently. "Every day after you left, when you traveled the world making forgeries... what happened to those works of art?"

"I sold them," he said flatly. "To fund drunken nights of debauchery and a wardrobe full of the latest fashions."

"That's right," she said. "You *sold* them. Because you have talent. Because your work has value. And even if you hadn't sold them, art is worthy on its own merit. Because *you* have value." She held up the pocket watch. "Just because the thing you created isn't the thing you dreamt of creating, doesn't mean you won't get there if you try."

"Try." He folded his arms over his chest, hugging himself. "Do you think... Do you think I should take art lessons?"

"I think you should acknowledge that your father threw a piece of *pottery* into the fire. Not your potential. And not your career." She pulled the watch chain back over her neck. "Don't let him break *you*."

"All right, you win. A few decades from now when I get out of here, I promise to try my hand at something original again." His posture turned intimate, his gaze intense. "Make a note on your calendar. I plan to live in London, and I want to be tutored by the best."

"Decades from now? I'm going to be busy then."

"Oh." His cheeks flushed. "I see."

"And so will you, Adrian. Very busy. I'll get you out of here sooner than you think, I swear it."

He cupped her face. "I told you—"

"You're not my client," she finished. "I haven't forgotten. You are the most infuriatingly stubborn, swaggering, distractingly handsome—"

He slanted his mouth over hers.

When he pulled her into his lap, Marjorie did not resist. She twisted her spine to press her bosom against him. Dug her fingers into his hair. Met him kiss for kiss and returned for more. Her breasts felt heavy and swollen, the nipples taut with desire. The sensation of them straining against the thin muslin of her bodice, scraping up against the hard expanse of his chest, was almost too exquisite to bear.

As if he sensed her need for release from this delicious torture, Adrian cupped one of his strong hands over her breast. She gasped against his mouth and immediately pressed into his touch. He rewarded her with more kisses. His fingers toyed with her erect nipple, sending scarlet shock waves of desire throughout her body. The cleft between her legs pulsed and swelled with each new caress, as though he were touching her *there* as well as her breasts and nipples.

She shifted on his thighs, begging him wordlessly to attend to other areas of her body. He obediently lowered his other hand and began gathering up her skirts. Her inner muscles clenched in anticipation, growing slick at the promise of a decadent new sensation.

Which might explain why neither of them heard the workroom door open.

"Why, look what we have here," Snowley drawled. "Isn't this a cozy scene?"

Marjorie and Adrian scrambled apart. Or tried to. She was on his lap and her skirts were caught beneath his boots, which resulted in both of them tumbling from the stool in a tangle of limbs and muslin.

Snowley stalked closer. "Is this the reason you wanted an 'apprentice' about? So that you could waste my time behind closed doors?"

"I didn't know her then," Adrian said. "And you were the one to force an assistant on me against my will."

"Against your will," Snowley repeated. "I can see how repulsed you are."

Adrian hauled himself up and pulled Marjorie to her feet.

"Evidently, you want to keep this chit close. Very well. I shall grant your wish." Snowley's smile was cold enough to freeze the sea. "I no longer trust either one of you to leave. Enjoy all the kisses you want on your own time after hours. But from this moment until Mary's trial month is through, she remains under my roof."

"No," Marjorie blurted out. "No, I cannot possibly stay here. You cannot make me—"

"Watch me carefully." Snowley placed his hand at the small of her back and pointed her toward the door. "Allow me to show you to your new sleeping quarters. From now on, you will either be on your cot or in this workroom. I'll alert the guards. You shan't leave my property without my permission."

25

~~~

$\mathcal{A}$drian stared at the slamming door in horror. If the workroom had felt unbearably empty without Marjorie in it during the long nights before, the knowledge that his actions had caused her to be *stuck* within Snowley's lair filled him with guilt and rising panic.

Marjorie didn't belong here. She could barely survive twelve hours without her siblings, much less weeks on end.

Oh God, her siblings! They were going to kill him. And he would deserve their wrath. But Adrian would trade his life for rescuing Marjorie's. Was there some way the Wynchesters might help? Could he get a message to them?

He raced over to the worktable and flipped open the lid to Marjorie's basket.

Bread. Cheese. Fruit. A gingham blanket. The empty canvas bag she'd brought today's extra metal shavings in. A smear of lilac paint.

No hedgehog.

Not that Tickletums was much of a messenger anyway. He'd managed to return to his owner when Jacob was waiting right around the corner, but Adrian didn't know if the hedgehog could travel farther distances than that, or convey important messages.

What Adrian needed was Piffle.

He dashed to the open window and peered outside. Crows were

scattered throughout the rookery, perched atop this clothes wire or that broken wall. How was he to know which crow was *the* crow? Was Piffle even here? Could Adrian summon him?

He leaned against the windowsill and cupped his hands around his mouth. "Ca-*caw*, ca-*caw*!"

Nothing.

Well, not entirely nothing. At Adrian's noise, the visible crows flew away.

"Piffle!" he called. "Here, boy! Come at once!"

The workroom door opened.

Adrian spun around. "You're back!"

It wasn't Marjorie. It was Joey Box o' Crumpets, wearing a loaded pistol and an annoyed expression.

"What's the meaning of this racket, Webb? There's no screaming for help. None is coming. And if you don't shut your bone-box, I'm authorized to shut it *for* you."

Adrian ignored this and rushed into the corridor. "Where's Mary?"

Joey grabbed Adrian's arm, stopping him in his tracks. The cold tip of a pistol pressed into his side.

"No running, either," Joey snarled. He used his pistol to gesture at one of the doors. "Your skirt's in there, taking a talking-to from Snowley. I'm not interrupting the big man, and neither are you."

In any other circumstance, Adrian would have pointed out that "big man" was a bit of a stretch. Snowley was barely larger than Marjorie herself. Adrian had *boots* that were almost as tall as each of them. But this was not the moment to let his mouth cause worse trouble.

"When is she coming back?" Did he sound desperate? He tried to hide it. But how *else* was he supposed to feel with Marjorie alone in a room with Snowley?

Joey shrugged. "S'pose she'll be back when he's done with her."

Yes. Yes, that made Adrian feel not one whit better. This was a disaster.

"Best not be dangling about when Snowley opens the door, lest he think you prying into his affairs, Webb," Grinders called out.

"It would give me a good excuse to shoot him," Joey said.

"Boss repeated himself three times," Grinders replied, the hatpin between his teeth bobbing. "'Shoot to maim, not to kill. This one's worth money.'"

Joey swung his pistol toward Adrian's trousers. "I think I can find a body part he won't need."

Adrian lifted his palms. "You know what? I'll go counterfeit a few coins whilst I wait."

"That's a good idea."

Adrian backed into the workroom and shut the door. Alone, he sagged against the doorjamb and rubbed his hands over his face in the hope of inspiration.

None came.

He just wasn't creative, damn it. Not when it counted. He could make love in a hundred different positions, but he could not think of a single move to rescue Marjorie from this trouble.

His gaze fell on the open window. He could make a run for Bow Street, he supposed, but the guard on the roof would shoot to maim before Adrian reached the street.

He leaned his head back against the door. Perhaps he ought to be molding coins, but Adrian could not bring himself to act in service to Snowley. Not while the blackguard had Marjorie.

Long minutes later, muted voices sounded in the corridor. Adrian pressed his ear to the door. He couldn't make out the words, but the tones belonged to Joey, Grinders . . . and Snowley.

Silence fell again.

All right. Snowley was gone. Marjorie should be back at any moment.

Adrian edged over against the wall so that he wasn't blocking the entrance. He wanted nothing to delay her return.

No more voices. No sign of Marjorie.

He swung his gaze to the clock. The minute hand seemed to take an hour to *snick* forward. And then another hour for the next minute to pass. And the third.

By the time forty-five minutes had crawled by, Adrian was well and truly losing his mind. Where was Marjorie? What the devil had Snowley done to her? Was she locked in that chamber? Or left physically incapable of leaving it? His belly churned with bile.

This was all his fault. Making a hash of Adrian's own life was one thing. He had never meant to ruin hers along the way.

"I *knew* you being here was a bad idea," he mumbled.

Seventy-five minutes.

Ninety.

God help him, Adrian couldn't take it anymore. This was his debacle, and it was his responsibility to put it to rights.

If that was even possible.

He couldn't escape, which meant he had no idea how he was meant to get *Marjorie* to safety. But he had to try. No matter what.

"Let them shoot me," he muttered, and opened the door.

26

Adrian burst into the corridor.

He would stop at nothing to defend and protect the woman who not only saw him as he really was but believed in who he *could* be. He would be the hero. For her.

If they wanted Marjorie, the guards would have to go through him. Or bullets would go through him. Or both. So be it.

"Halt!" Joey barked.

Both he and Grinders swung their weapons toward Adrian.

This time, Adrian didn't put his hands up. He continued down the corridor as if he had every right.

"Where do you think you're going?" snarled Joey.

"Mary's room," Adrian answered.

"How do you expect to enter, when you haven't a key?" asked Grinders.

"I don't need a key," Adrian guessed. "My chamber isn't locked and I doubt hers is, either."

Grinders snorted. "She didn't request your company."

That stung, but didn't mean anything. Perhaps Marjorie *couldn't* ask for help. Joey had prevented Adrian from trying to summon Piffle. Marjorie was unlikely to fare any better.

But it did give Adrian an idea. After all, Snowley hadn't forbidden their romance. His exact words were, *Enjoy all the kisses you want on your own time.* There was no better time for a private moment than right now.

"I don't have to press my attentions on beautiful women," he informed the guards, and struck an obnoxiously rakish pose. "They beg for it. And I live to deliver."

"No fornication amongst the staff," Joey drawled. "Snowley's rules."

"We're not staff," Adrian assured him. "I'm not being paid. Mary and I are prisoners, not employees. And prisoners have the freedom to do as they please."

Joey frowned. "He's right. No such rule amongst prisoners."

Grinders lowered his weapon. "You and Mary…"

Adrian nodded and tossed each of the guards a new coin. "Snowley already knows about Mary and me. He's doing everything he can to ensure we spend more time under the same roof, not less. Which means, Mary is under his protection *and* mine."

Joey and Grinders pocketed their coins.

"What do you think?" Grinders said. "We let the poor bastard spend a moment with his little morsel?"

Joey motioned Adrian toward Marjorie's door. "Half an hour, Webb. Make it count. Mary's supposed to return to the workroom to keep making coins."

"Thirty minutes," Adrian repeated dutifully. "We'll be out in twenty-nine."

"All right, then. Go and tup your bit o' muslin. Then drag her arse back to work. After that, no leaving the workroom until you've met your quota. You owe us a little extra to make up for this largesse."

"With pleasure." Adrian swaggered forward, waggling his brows as lasciviously as possible. As soon as he reached Marjorie's room, he flung open the door, threw himself inside, and shut the door behind him.

Her room was just as low and confining as Adrian's piteous bed-chamber. Barely enough room for a cot, a stool, and a skinny table.

And yet, Marjorie was not alone.

She sat cross-legged atop the mattress, casually chatting with a plump white woman holding a drawn sword in one hand and a cup of tea in the other.

A dapper and unarmed Black man leaned one well-tailored hip against a narrow window.

At his feet, inexplicably, stood a fluffy white sheep.

Marjorie smiled. "Oh, Adrian. I was wondering when you'd get here."

He stared at her, gobsmacked.

She leaned over the cot toward the thin rickety table and produced a cup and saucer. "Would you like some tea?"

Adrian was still trying to process the information that Marjorie was not in danger, and all appeared to be well. "Did you just say...would I like some *tea*?"

"No one thought to bring coffee," she said apologetically. "The kettle is fresh from the fireplace. But if you want milk, you'll have to get it from Miss Ophelia yourself."

The sheep gave a faint *baa*.

Adrian eyed Ophelia warily. He would not be adding milk to his tea. "How in all that is holy...?"

"We're Wynchesters," the handsome Black man said, as if that explained it.

Maybe it did.

"Introductions, please," said the woman with the sword.

"Of course, how rude of me." Marjorie set down her cup and saucer. "Adrian, this is my brother Jacob and my sister Elizabeth. Family, this is Lord Adrian. Oh, and you've met Ophelia."

There was no possibility that three such different-looking people were full-blooded siblings...but then again, a few seconds ago, Adrian would have sworn there was no possibility of someone being on the other side of the wall taking tea with a sheep.

"Wynchesters," he repeated. "How did you know to come?"

Jacob pulled the tip of a tiny scroll out of his breast pocket. "Marjorie sent for us."

Piffle, that traitor. Adrian had *tried* to summon him.

"I was going to rescue her," he informed Marjorie's siblings. "I was...regrettably delayed."

Elizabeth stared at Adrian blankly. "*Rescue* her?"

"Oh, that's so sweet," Marjorie assured him with an indulgent smile.

Adrian didn't feel sweet. He felt superfluous. The crew of actual heroes was here on the case.

He was just...Adrian.

"I think you have it backward," Elizabeth informed him. "Marjorie is here to rescue *you*."

Ophelia sneezed. It sounded like judgment, too.

Marjorie cleared her throat. "He's asked me not to. He doesn't want to be a client. In any case, I call this meeting to order."

"Meeting?" Adrian repeated. "Meeting for what?" He sat on a wooden stool Jacob passed his way.

"For stratagems," Marjorie explained. She leaned over the edge of the cot to fiddle with the tea, then handed Adrian a cup and saucer.

"Thank you." He settled as far as possible from the sheep and tried to pretend this wasn't the most peculiar moment of his entire life.

"For now," said Marjorie, "all that we have is..."

She immediately set off into a mind-boggling recitation of facts. There were documents, letters, contracts. Maps and sketches. Even an interview with a rare prior servant who left Snowley's employ and managed not to disappear immediately after.

"The first wrinkle," she continued, "is that for as long as I'm stuck here, I cannot smuggle jewelry home every night."

"Not a problem," Jacob assured her. "I'll send Hippogriff."

"The hawk?" Elizabeth asked.

Jacob nodded. "She can carry more contraband than Piffle."

"If you can just pop in wherever you please," Adrian interrupted, "then why not pick up the pieces yourselves?"

"We were almost caught," Elizabeth admitted. "We made it in, but I'm not sure how we'll get out undetected. We can't risk human intervention a second time."

"I'm not certain the sheep is helping this time," Adrian murmured.

"Plus," Marjorie continued, "there's the matter of my art lessons. Faircliffe might forgive me if I disappear for a fortnight, but my students are counting on their Sunday-afternoon creative respite."

Jacob glanced up from the sheep. "Perhaps Faircliffe could tutor them in your absence."

Elizabeth made a face. "That's no substitute. Anything Faircliffe can paint, Marjorie can paint better."

"But is our sister a duke?" Jacob countered. "Marjorie will have provided not only professional instruction, but also an introduction to a potential future noble patron. The girls' families will be overjoyed."

"True," Marjorie mused. "Ask him if he minds."

But she didn't look happy.

"You don't think it will work?" Adrian asked.

"It'll work," she said with a sigh. "I'll just miss the girls so much. I adore our lessons. Oh, who am I bamming? I shall miss *everything* more than words can say. Meals with my family. Nights in my own bed."

Adrian's stomach twisted in sympathy. Marjorie hadn't *said* her current situation was his fault... but none of them would be taking tea with a sheep if Adrian hadn't forged his way into this mess.

"Then let's get you out of here." He set his cup and saucer on the floor.

Ophelia immediately ducked her head to lick from the cup.

Adrian gave up on tea and nudged the saucer over to the sheep.

"The problem isn't Marjorie being confined to Snowley's residence," said Jacob. "The problem is Snowley. How do we stop him?"

"Well..." Elizabeth toyed with her sword.

"No poking holes," Marjorie said quickly.

"I wasn't going to!" her sister protested with too much innocence. "I was thinking, why not use Marjorie's long and storied experience with forgery?"

Adrian glanced at her with interest. "Vases? Tiaras? Statues?"

"My skill is with paper, not sculpture," she reminded him. "Which means I can reproduce virtually any drawn or painted art, including handwriting."

"Then forgery is what we'll do," said Jacob. "Once we have a plan to extricate Lady Iris from danger, we shall mount a mission to take the rest of the treasures all at once. All Wynchesters on deck, no holds barred."

"They'll see you coming," Adrian pointed out.

"I'm depending on it," she answered with a smile. "Every good escapade needs a suitable distraction in order to succeed."

"One problem," Jacob said. "We need the ring to replicate his mark."

Marjorie's smile fell. "You're right."

"The ring Snowley wears about his neck?" Adrian asked with misgiving.

Jacob nodded. "His signature alone isn't enough. We need the exact ring and the special wax, so that even Snowley himself wouldn't be able to prove a forgery has taken place."

"Then we get the ring." Adrian turned to Marjorie. "Have you got a plan?"

"This stronghold is crawling with guards." She pondered the options. "The fewer people are involved, the better the chance of success. You and I must do it ourselves."

Elizabeth bristled and sat upright, clearly on the precipice of rejecting this solution.

Jacob jumped in. "If she says she can, then she can." He turned to Marjorie. "You know how to contact us if anything goes wrong."

Marjorie nodded, then looked at Adrian. "Are you in?"

"More than in. I'm your apprentice from this moment forward. Tell me what you need, and consider it done."

She smiled at him. "That is noble of you."

He gave a lopsided smile back. "Slander! You'll ruin my reputation."

She reached over and ruffled his hair. "Whatever will the gossips say?"

Elizabeth and Jacob exchanged glances.

"Shite!" Adrian scrambled to his feet, startling the sheep. "What time is it?"

Jacob pulled out a pocket watch and showed him the hour.

"We have to go." Adrian held his hand out to Marjorie. "We need to be back in the workroom in the next two minutes or the men guarding the corridor will barge in with questions."

Marjorie scrambled off the bed and over to the door.

"I'll see you as soon as I can," she said to her siblings.

All three Wynchesters touched their fingers to their chests and lifted their palms toward the sky. It looked like a secret sign of some sort. Perhaps symbolizing love or unity.

"We must hurry," Adrian told Marjorie, eaten up with jealousy at her easy, loving relationship with her family.

She nodded and slipped out into the corridor.

Before Adrian could follow Marjorie, Elizabeth's sword rose in front of him, nearly slicing the buttons off the fall of his trousers.

"Er," he stammered.

"Hurt her and I'll kill you," she whispered into his ear, then shoved him into the corridor.

The door swung shut behind him.

27

'm sorry you're stuck in this hell because of me," Adrian told Marjorie as they filled their chalk molds with cheap tin and pewter.

"I was an eager and willing part of the activities that led to my confinement," she replied. "And I'm not stuck. My siblings could smuggle me out."

"*Once*," he reminded her. "If you leave for any reason, Snowley won't allow you back. If you did manage to sneak out, he'd redouble security to the point where a gnat couldn't enter without his knowledge, much less a Wynchester. You'd never abandon a client or a mission. Which means...*stuck*. And I'm sorry."

"I suppose that's all true. For the record, I'm sorry you're stuck here, too. That wasn't the case at first, when I thought you were complicit in Snowley's schemes—"

"I *was* complicit at first. There didn't seem to be any harm in duplicating artifacts rather than smuggling them." He rubbed his face. "I compounded his avarice with my own."

"But that's not why you're here now. You're trying to save your sister from ruin. That's a selfless and noble aim."

"Possibly the first selfless and noble thing I've done all decade."

"When I first met you, I might have believed that. But I no longer do." She poked his chest. "Despite your best efforts, my lord, you have given yourself away. I'd wager your dissolute, checkered past is altogether *riddled* with selfless and noble acts."

"A mortifying hypothesis." He shuddered. "You must not mention it to anyone."

"You should mention it to Lady Iris."

"To manipulate her into forgiving me?"

"To show her a complete picture of who you are. You're a whole person, not a caricature. Reintroduce her to the brother she longed for all those years."

"The first step is *seeing* my sister again." His heart ached from missing her. "I was willing to wait a month or two, but I can't devote my life to serving Snowley."

His initial thought to replace the stolen artifacts with forgeries no longer had merit. There was no need to create duplicates when Snowley believed the originals had gone into the pot, rather than a secret pocket of Marjorie's skirts. As long as she and her siblings kept trading contraband for scraps of inferior metal, no more treasures would be destroyed.

But they also weren't solving the problem. New victims were being swindled every day, leaving their valuables behind and going home with counterfeit coins. He and Marjorie were treading water. They needed to stop the rising tide.

"When does your client lose her house?"

"She *won't* lose her home," Marjorie said firmly. Only after Adrian nodded in understanding did she add under her breath, "Two weeks from today."

He tightened his jaw. "We need a plan."

"I have a plan."

"And it's a good thought. Steal Snowley's ring. Steal his sealing wax. I am on board. But how? Snowley may not have guards watching him every second, but he'll certainly bar any doors when he's alone.

I can copy a key, but I cannot pick a lock. And unless you know how to render a man unconscious—" Adrian closed his mouth and cocked his head to one side in concentration.

"What is it?" Marjorie signed.

"Footsteps," he fingerspelled back.

When the door swung open seconds later, Adrian was studiously stirring the contents of the crucible above the fire.

Marjorie, on the other hand, bounded up to Grinders like an over-excited puppy.

"There you are," she admonished him. "I rang an hour ago."

He stared at her, the hatpin in his mouth working. "There's no bell pull in the workroom."

"I thought about you very hard, and now you're here!" She wrapped her arms about him for some unfathomable reason, hugging him as though he were her favorite doll and not one of Snowley's armed guards.

Grinders peeled Marjorie off him with effort. "What do you want?"

"A sandwich," she answered brightly. "One for Lord Adrian, too, please."

"No sandwiches." Grinders flicked his gaze over her shoulder toward Adrian. "Boss says work faster."

Adrian set down the wooden spoon and folded his arms over his leather apron. "I can't work at all with you in the same room. I can feel you breathing."

"I wish you weren't," Grinders muttered as he shut the door behind him.

Adrian held up a finger until the guard's footsteps faded.

"What did he say at the end?" Marjorie asked. "I didn't catch it."

"That he wishes I weren't breathing." Adrian rubbed his face. "Who cares what Grinders wants. What the devil were *you* about?"

"Working." She returned to the chalk molds. "No plan without a contingency."

He hurried after her. "We can't make contingencies until we've finalized the first plan. We—"

Before he could continue, she reached into a hidden pocket of her skirts and pulled out...Grinders's key ring.

"That's why you were hugging him," Adrian whispered.

She grinned at him. "My sister Chloe can nick anything from anyone without them noticing her presence. I haven't mastered invisibility, but misdirection is a good trick."

She slid the keys onto the worktable. One of Grinders's hatpins was stuck between the ring and the keys. She tucked the pin out of the way in her pocket.

"Now then. Shall we set a record for how fast we can duplicate a set of keys?"

This time, there was no need for artistry. The new keys didn't need to be visibly identical to the old ones. They needed to open doors.

They worked together, dividing the keys between them and making quick work of the duplicates. Marjorie clearly had much more experience and was twice as swift as Adrian. In no time at all, they had the new keys hidden behind a loose brick in the fireplace.

"What do we do with Grinders's keys?" Adrian asked. "If we're caught with them before we have a chance to act..."

"We do nothing." Marjorie piled a handful of rags next to the door and placed the keys on top. "He'll think he didn't hear them fall because they landed on dirty linen."

Adrian was less convinced. "That's awfully convenient. These men are dangerous, Marjorie. We don't have swords or pistols. This is when we need the contingencies. If you ever have to throw me to the wolves to save yourself, I want you to do it."

She fluttered her eyelashes at him. "Don't worry, I will."

"I'm serious. If Snowley ever—"

"Footsteps." He made the sign to Marjorie.

She sprinted to the worktable and picked up a chalk mold right as Grinders swung open the door.

"I disagree," she said loudly. "My molds are still superior to yours. Your coins may be technically perfect, but my chalk texture and chromatic essence when combined with sulfuric heat density—"

Sulfuric heat density? Marjorie was babbling random words that made no sense. Not that Grinders understood the transitive properties of metal.

Although Adrian's and Marjorie's backs were to the door, Adrian was able to tilt his eyes from the worktable just in time to glimpse Grinders catching sight of the keys next to the door. His hulking muscles relaxed visibly. As Grinders bent over the rags to snatch up his keys, he darted a furtive glance toward the worktable.

Adrian pretended to be wholly consumed by the argument over whose molds were superior, and tossed out a few nonsense phrases of his own to refute Marjorie's claims.

Too relieved by his charges' apparent obliviousness to the fallen keys to ask questions, Grinders slipped back into the corridor without announcing his presence. He closed the door softly behind him.

As soon as the corridor was silent, Adrian pulled Marjorie into his arms and kissed her.

* * *

"I can't believe you think this is the best plan," Adrian mouthed several hours later as they put away their chalk molds. "Instead of stealing the ring whilst Snowley is asleep, we'll rob him whilst he's *naked* in the bath?"

"He won't know it happened," Marjorie said. "You have the satchel?"

"I have the satchel."

The small canvas bag strapped beneath Adrian's waistcoat contained the tools he would need to cast a mold of Snowley's ring. As for the scented wax, they only needed to slice off enough for a single seal.

Presuming they could reach the chamber where Snowley took his evening plunge baths undetected.

"You're certain you know when he bathes?" Adrian asked.

"Graham memorized the schedule. As of five minutes ago, Snowley entered a large private bathing chamber that shares a wall with the kitchens. In the absence of a natural hot spring, one must use the heat from one's fires to warm the water."

"How dreadful for him," Adrian said. "Plunging into a pristine pool like a king...next to the scullery, like a servant. How he must suffer."

"The private dressing room is adjacent to the pool. That's where his clothes and personal items will be. No one disturbs Snowley's bath, so we won't be bothered—or detected. We also can't linger too long, in the event our absence from our rooms *is* noted, and a guard raises the alarms."

"About that," Adrian said. "How *do* we sneak out of this workroom with two armed sentinels on either side of the corridor?"

"We wait for the sign." She pressed her right ear to the door, then stepped aside and motioned for him to listen instead. "Do you hear anything?"

"No. It's silent as a tomb. There's not even—" Adrian jerked his ear from the door in surprise. "Two pairs of footsteps just ran past. Joey and Grinders must have left in a hurry."

Marjorie grinned. "Then our distraction is under way. Strangers have come to call on every door. All hands will be downstairs to guard the entrances and stairways. Which means it's time."

And she opened the door.

28

$\overline{}$

*M*arjorie crept up to Snowley's dressing room door with a hedgehog in her bodice. Adrian followed close behind.

Her heart pounded in her ears. Each beat landed with a shocking new splash, like a piece of onyx tossed into a puddle of rainbow-hued paints. Being the Wynchester leading the charge was heady. Exciting, exhilarating, *terrifying.*

She placed her trembling fingers on the door handle. Locked. Adrian was right behind her. This was it. The final threshold. On the other side of this door was the dressing chamber. On the other side of *that*, was Snowley.

Hopefully. If all went to plan.

With trembling fingers, she pulled the duplicate keys from her pocket and tried each one until she found the key that fit. Carefully, she turned the key to unlock the door and swiftly returned the duplicate keys to her pocket.

There was no time to dawdle. All the guards should be arriving back at their posts within seconds. It was now or never.

She twisted the handle and eased open the door.

Darkness.

Adrian's breath tickled the ear that could hear. "What in the—"

She clapped a hand over his mouth and yanked him into the room with the other. She pulled the door shut behind them.

Blackness surrounded them.

Her heart thudded ominously. Marjorie could not see anything. Just pure, disorienting darkness.

Nor could she and Adrian speak. Not with Snowley on the other side of the dressing room door. She and Adrian must continue in silence.

The thought of not being able to communicate at all filled Marjorie with panic. Her hearing might not be acute, but her sight was second to none. It was the sense she relied upon for everything. Understanding her environment, parsing spoken words, gesturing with signs. Her near-perfect visual recall was her greatest gift. Without her eyes, she was lost.

Fingers unsteady, she slipped a hand into a hidden pocket. Inside was the nub of a candle, and a tinderbox for lighting it. But she could not risk the sound of steel and flint without knowing for certain Snowley was too far away or too busy to overhear.

She removed her fingers from her pocket, leaving the tinderbox and candle where they were. She reached for Adrian's hands instead, and placed them on her hips, with her backside nestled against his thighs. She pressed hard, indicating he should keep his fingers where she held them, so that they did not knock into each other or otherwise create unintended havoc.

He lowered his head until the side of his cheek touched hers, and nodded his understanding. The slight stubble at his jaw scratched against her soft skin and sent luxurious shivers down her spine, each whisker all the more noticeable in the darkness. She did her best to ignore the decadent sensation.

Slowly, she raised her hands, feeling about the dressing room one methodical inch at a time until her fingers brushed the wooden edge of a sideboard or a large dressing table.

Her hands made careful progress along the surface, lest she knock over a bottle of perfume or other object. Her fingers brushed lawn fabric. She froze. If this was Snowley's clothing, then she was close.

Here! Her fingertips padded against the unmistakable line of a long, thin chain. *This was it!*

She lifted the necklace and hefted the ring, then quickly undid the clasp. The ring tumbled into her palm. Marjorie replaced the chain on the table for safekeeping. She took one of Adrian's hands from her hip, then placed the ring in his palm and closed his fingers about it.

He set about making the mold at once.

She pressed urgent hand signs against his abdomen. "Make two molds. Just in case."

He spelled his response against her arm. "Don't worry. I'll create as many as I can."

She returned her own hands to the table and continued to explore, memorizing the folds of each garment as she went in order to replace them exactly as they were. She just had to find the pocket with the wax. It must be...

Here! She lifted the thick stick of wax to her nose and inhaled deeply. It smelled of fire and brimstone and honeysuckle and red roses. It was unquestionably the right wax.

Quickly, she removed a small knife and set about slicing a thumb's-width from the bottom of the wax, mirroring the precise angle. Just enough for a few seals. Once the dagger returned to its hidden scabbard and the wax coin was safely nestled in the tinderbox, Marjorie held herself as still as she could and waited for Adrian to finish his part.

Despite the fact that she couldn't see him, his warmth and scent and color filled the darkened room. She was glad to be together. He might be a light only she could see, but his staunch loyalty and artistic essence only made him glow all the brighter.

Being expected to execute a complicated, delicate maneuver in an unfamiliar, pitch black closet was akin to being asked to perform a miracle. He was not used to missions like these. To taking orders from a woman, to fumbling around for a contingency when plans inevitably went awry.

Yet he did so without complaint, and with impressive speed. After he formed each mold, he handed it to Marjorie to safe-keep while it hardened. Two molds...three...four. A rush of affection and pride rushed through her. He was practically a Wynchester. No plan without a contingency. *One* of these molds was bound to work.

And if not, Adrian was talented enough to combine the best parts of each in order to sculpt something that *did*.

At last, he lifted her palm to his cheek. He pressed a kiss to her wrist, then placed the ring back inside her hand.

As much as she longed to throw her arms about his neck and show him what kind of kiss she'd been waiting for, Marjorie wasted no time in returning the ring to its chain and spreading the necklace back out exactly how she'd found it. Then the shirtsleeve on top, and...done.

She returned Adrian's hands to her hips and began the slow, careful waddle back toward the dressing room door, taking care not to bump into anything unexpected along the way.

Her fingers curled about the door handle. Marjorie did not know what to expect on the other side. Nothing for it. They'd made it this far. All they could do was press on.

Marjorie turned the handle.

29

Adrian squinted into the unexpected brightness of a dimly lit corridor. Muted candlelight emanated from several sconces. After the utter blackness of Snowley's dressing room, the weak flicker felt like spears of light shooting from the sun.

Marjorie relaxed visibly.

As elated as Adrian was to see again, he was not entirely certain it was cause for celebration. There was no protective cover of darkness to keep him and Marjorie out of view... and out of the line of fire.

Up ahead, the hallway took a sharp left. Halfway down that corridor was their workroom—and the two armed guards who believed Adrian and Marjorie to be in their workroom.

"Tell me you have a plan," he whispered into her working ear.

She held up a hand and wiggled the fingers. "I have five different plans."

"Which is the one most likely to succeed?"

She glanced down the hall.

"No sign of Grinders yet," Marjorie whispered. "Which means we have somewhere between five minutes and five seconds before he appears in the corridor and starts shooting."

"Marvelous. Do something Wynchester-y to save us from certain doom." He waved her forward.

"All right." She lowered the material of her bodice.

The befuddled face of a sleepy hedgehog poked out.

"That cannot be our secret weapon." He clasped his hands together in supplication. "Please tell me there's more to the plan than Tickletums."

"First, we need to..." She dashed to a window, hauled up the glass, and tossed a handful of seashells out into the street.

"Are you summoning Poseidon?" he mouthed.

"A force even more powerful," she whispered back. "From the roof, the shells look like normal detritus, but the operatives stationed in the street below will know—"

Two dozen well-dressed ladies bearing candles and little baskets appeared out of nowhere. They began singing "God Rest Ye Merry, Gentlemen" at the top of their lungs.

"It's July," Adrian said in wonder. "What's in the baskets? Bombs? Mistletoe?"

"Blackberries." Marjorie slid the window shut and closed the curtains. "Those berries are Tickletums's favorite."

"What does that have to do with—"

She darted away from him down the corridor, heading straight to the turn where Grinders stood just around the corner with a loaded pistol at his side.

Adrian cursed under his breath and sprinted after her.

Marjorie stopped so suddenly three feet from the end of the corridor that he almost hurtled into her like a lawn ball barreling down a bowling green.

She held up three fingers, then lowered one, then lowered the second.

An ear-piercing shriek rent the air.

Footsteps sounded just on the other side of the corridor. Footsteps *leaving*. Grinders had been close enough to the corner that they almost could have heard him breathe.

Marjorie removed Tickletums from her bodice.

"What are you doing?" Adrian whispered.

"That was Elizabeth throwing her voice. It *might* have been enough to clear the corridor of both guards, but just in case..." She lifted the hedgehog. "No plan without a contingency."

"What will Tickletums do? Dodge bullets?"

"Chase after blackberries." Marjorie set the hedgehog down on the hardwood floor. She placed Grinders's silver hatpin into the creature's mouth and gave his prickly bottom a little pat. "Go get those berries, sir. Show those pompous guards what a homing hedgehog can do."

Tickletums took off around the corner, heading toward the stairs—and all those baskets of blackberries—with surprising alacrity.

"What the *devil*?" came Grinders's distant voice. "He's got my hatpin! Get back here, you little—"

His voice faded.

Marjorie grinned at Adrian. "Shall we make a dash for it whilst the corridor is clear?"

"Let's." He hooked his arm around hers and raced toward the workroom.

They made it inside and closed the door seconds before Joey's and Grinders's shouts filled the hallway. Adrian lowered his ear to the keyhole.

"Fat little bastard shot between Ruby's legs like a greased pig," Joey said in astonishment and admiration.

"That's the second oddity today. You don't think someone's trying to distract us from..."

"We'd better make sure."

Adrian grabbed Marjorie's hand and yanked her over to the worktable. They were both studiously polishing counterfeit coins when the door swung open to reveal the mean, suspicious gazes of Joey and Grinders.

"Lost, lads?" Adrian gestured toward the window with a chalk mold. "Best pub in the neighborhood is in that direction."

The guards exchanged relieved glances.

"I've had about enough of your humor, Webb," Joey snapped. "Mind your mouth when you talk to me, or I'll have Ruby sew it shut."

"If he can't eat, he can't counterfeit," Marjorie pointed out. "And then Snowley will be vexed with *you*."

Adrian smirked. "If your wit isn't sharp enough for light banter, you'd best keep to your post rather than interrupt us at our task."

Joey made a sound like a raging bull and charged forward.

Grinders blocked his path and shoved his confederate back out into the corridor. "Leave him. He's not worth it. You know Webb is nothing but a…"

The insult was lost as the door closed behind them.

Adrian and Marjorie tossed the chalk molds onto the table and threw themselves into each other's embrace in relief and exultation. This kiss was different from the others. It was more than pent-up passion. It was elation, vindication, and triumph all in one. It was a kiss that recognized how much stronger they were together as a team. A kiss that promised there was even better yet to come.

"You," Adrian said when they paused for air, "were magnificent."

Marjorie sent him an impish grin. "Wait until you see what's next."

30

By nine of the clock the next morning, Marjorie's faux IOU signed by what appeared to be Snowley himself was ready and waiting for Adrian to supply the coup de grâce.

He had spent all night creating a perfect replica of Snowley's ring. Well, not *visual* perfection. The seal on Snowley's ring was made of hand-carved stone, whereas Adrian's duplicate was made of the same tin-and-pewter mix he and Marjorie were using to forge coins.

But it was otherwise identical, down to the last detail. Every flourish, every flaw, would be represented in the wax exactly as if it had been placed there by Snowley's own hand.

He lifted a corner of the letter. "With luck, one copy will suffice."

"We don't need luck." She tapped the side of her head. "We have my memory and your talent."

"*Our* talents," he replied.

Marjorie had sifted through an entire stack of Snowley's contracts, amassed by her brother Graham.

She was the one who noticed it wasn't just the special mark and the scented wax, but also a certain pressure and angle when applying the stone seal to the melted wax. Even if they'd had Snowley's actual ring, if they didn't wield it just so, it wouldn't look right at the end.

Marjorie was in charge of that step. Adrian had duplicated the ring, but only she could tilt it into an angle of total perfection.

"Once we do this," he said, "Snowley will know the truth."

"He was always going to know he never drafted any such vowels."

"I don't mean the IOU. He could suspect we worked together to forge this. I will claim I worked alone, but only a fool would still trust you. And Snowley is no fool."

"He's no fool," Marjorie agreed, "but he is limited to his world. You have never shown interest in joining his crew, which is why he had to force you into it to begin with."

"You don't think he'll paint you with the same brush?"

"Like the rest of his staff, I came here willingly to be part of his criminal family. Snowley believes all I care about is earning a piece of the Grandfather of St. Giles's money."

"The power*ful* lording over the power*less* is the only kind of relationship he understands."

She nodded. "It's what he knows and what he expects. You might have the money and means to get on without him, but Mary-from-the-rookery does not. Snowley doesn't think he *has* to manipulate me. Life has done the difficult part for him."

"He saw me . . . kissing you."

"He saw more than that." Her cheeks flushed. "Which also works to my benefit. You're a conscienceless rake. I'm a naïve, simple girl. Of course you would take advantage. Of course I'm not clever enough to know better. I could even pretend to betray some confidence of yours in a blatant attempt to curry favor with Snowley. He'll trust me, inasmuch as he trusts anyone."

"And he has no such confidence in me," Adrian finished dryly. "I began our acquaintance by lying and cheating, and am only here under duress. This latest treachery won't come as a surprise. The part I most dislike about the plan is your involvement. Once my sister is out from under his thumb, I'll be free to go—and you'll still be stuck here."

She shook her head. "Once your sister's IOUs are in your possession and Lady Iris is no longer at risk, we immediately launch into step two."

He paused. "Everything that's happened up until now...was step one?"

She nodded as she pressed the counterfeit seal into the hardening wax.

"Good God. What's step two? Outright war?"

"The law," she answered. "My family is sending a team of Bow Street Runners over later today."

"I thought there wasn't enough direct evidence to arrest him."

"There is in the treasure chamber," Marjorie said. "We'll have the Runners search the stronghold as a personal favor to the esteemed Duke of Faircliffe himself."

"Where there's treasure, there's evidence? You're assuming something in that room will tip Snowley's hand."

"We'll tip it for him. My family has been collecting affidavits from the men and women Snowley swindled with counterfeit coins. Singly, not one of the victims is willing to speak out against him, but together as a group, their voices will be heard. He could retaliate against one person without consequences, but he cannot take revenge on dozens of people throughout London at once."

Excitement filled Adrian's chest. "The treasure chamber won't just prove their stories are true. It's also likely to reveal other crimes you and I don't even have knowledge of."

She held up a chalk mold. "We have knowledge of *this* fraud."

"You can't implicate yourself! Counterfeiting is a capital crime."

"It won't come to that." Marjorie lifted up the letter in triumph. "All dry and ready for trouble."

Adrian looked at Marjorie instead of at the seal. He couldn't tear his gaze away from her shining face. She was so bloody competent.

And quickly becoming one of the most important things in his life. The more she elbowed her way into his heart, the more entrenched Marjorie became in the short list of people Adrian would defend to the death.

He plucked the letter from her hand. Rather than inspect the contents, he pushed the paper onto the worktable and pulled Marjorie into his arms instead. At this moment, he wasn't looking for a way out. He was looking for a way in. He wanted her to feel even half as ardently toward him as he did every time he looked at her.

As Adrian's eyes fluttered closed, his lips lowered to hers. Had he thought gazing at her was dangerous? Her taste was a thousand times more so. The warmth of her soft body nestled against his should have made him tread with caution and tenderness. Instead, he crushed her to him, possessively, demandingly, clinging tight as though she were the one solid boulder amid a maelstrom.

Perhaps she was. She'd certainly grounded him when he'd believed himself lost to the wind. What would he do once she was gone? What could he do to make her stay?

Not under this roof, of course. But what else could he offer? He had no home, no land. A rented studio in Paris, but even a secret romantic like Adrian wasn't fool enough to believe the Continent would tempt her. She was a Wynchester.

Wynchesters lived in London. Wynchesters were *good*.

Whereas Adrian...was everything a good man would never wish for Marjorie to find. A liar, a scoundrel, a restless, shiftless vagabond with more charm than morals. She deserved someone who matched her in intellect, in optimism, in philanthropy. She deserved a hero, not a villain.

And yet Adrian could not bring himself to let her go. To unwrap his strong arms from her slight frame. To lift his unyielding mouth from her inviting lips.

To accept that this was as good as goodbye.

At that wrenching thought, he broke his lips from hers. Not to pull away, but to haul her close. To press her to his chest, right there against the heart she made thunder so violently. He held her as tight as he dared without hurting her, and settled his cheek against the softness of her hair to breathe in her essence.

She was so sweet, it pained him. So mischievous, it charmed him. So unpredictable, it dazed him. So *Marjorie*, that just being near her made him feel as though he were welcome in the heavens.

She tilted her face back and placed a kiss on the underside of his jaw. "What was that for?"

"I was seducing you," he said automatically. "Take off your clothes."

"You were snuggling me," she corrected, and cuddled him back. "I liked it."

So did Adrian. Far, far too much.

31

It was midafternoon before the guards responded to Adrian's request to have audience with Snowley somewhere other than the stifling workroom.

Joey ushered Adrian and Marjorie into the same suffocating, windowless parlor Snowley had forced Adrian to wait in on his first day, back when he'd still believed Snowley would be an easy mark to trick, and that there would be no problem walking away.

Now Adrian knew better.

He motioned for Marjorie to take the comfortable armchair and settled himself in the closest one to her side. They were about to enact Marjorie's extraction plan for Iris. *Her* plan, *her* extraction. She would finally get to be the hero of her family.

And at long last, so would Adrian.

The Grandfather of St. Giles did not bother to hide his annoyance as he strode into the waiting room.

"You do not summon me," Snowley enunciated. "Under this roof, you are not lord. *I* am."

"About that," Adrian said. "I'm leaving."

Surprise flickered across Snowley's face. "Are you, now? How interesting. There are two lads in the corridor and others posted elsewhere who don't believe you're going anywhere."

"They don't have to believe it," Adrian said. Nervous excitement rushed through him. "They'll watch it happen."

"We have a contract," Snowley drawled, bored again. "If this posturing is for Mary's sake, save us the charade. She's already willing to let you have your way with her. And with me, you'll get nowhere."

Marjorie inspected her fingernails as though she had no idea what trick was up Adrian's sleeve, but her alert gaze kept flicking up toward Snowley in concentration.

Adrian stretched out his legs and crossed one over the other. "Any contract with you was signed under duress."

"Your word, my word." Snowley gave a little shrug. "You and I both know I don't need a contract." He patted his lapel. "I carry your sister's vowels."

"For now," Adrian agreed. "You're about to hand them over."

"Am I?" Snowley chuckled. "And why should I do that?"

"Because I have *this*." Adrian pulled the forged IOU from inside his waistcoat.

Snowley's smile disappeared. "What is that?"

Adrian unrolled the parchment and held it up for Snowley to view.

"I never signed that!" he sputtered. "That's not even my... You forged my handwriting? *And* my insignia?"

"*Is* it a forgery?" Marjorie asked innocently. "It looks exactly the same as the one on Lord Adrian's contracts."

Snowley snatched the foolscap from Adrian's hands and stalked over to the fireplace to examine it in the light. "It does look identical. And it's in my hands, you fool. All I need to do is rip this up and toss it into these flames—"

"Oh dear." Marjorie stepped closer. "Would it be *very* bad if there was another copy?"

"Another...another copy? Yes, it would be bad, you daft— Hand the duplicate over to me at once."

Marjorie made an expression of pure misery, as though unable to lift her eyes to meet Snowley's. "I'm afraid I can't. He had me give it to a boy to post."

"What boy? When?"

"The night before you said I couldn't leave anymore."

"Of all the...I should never have let you leave! I won't make that mistake again, I can assure you." Snowley's face flushed with color. "Where did this letter get posted to?"

Marjorie gave him a bewildered look. "How should I remember?"

He would never imagine that she remembered everything she saw.

Snowley whirled on Adrian. "You sent it to your sister's house, didn't you?"

"If I did, that's where my father lives as well. You cannot breach the home of the Marquess of Meadowbrook. And if I sent the document to a solicitor, I'd especially recommend against going after it."

Snowley ripped the letter into long, thin pieces, then turned the strips sideways to rip them asunder. When he finished, he carried the fistful of scraps over to the fire and hurled it into the flames. The seal stank as it burned.

A draft from the open doorway and the light weight of the paper caused the torn bits to float up in a cloud of white like oversized dust mites. One by one, the pieces settled down, swirling back toward the flames to be gobbled by the hungry fire and consumed into tiny wisps of smoke.

Snowley visibly collected himself before turning back toward Adrian with his usual calm, cold demeanor. "I noticed the sum on that paper matches the total of your sister's vowels."

Adrian inclined his head. "Indeed, it does."

"You did not think to include the debt you owe me?"

This was the one point of contention between Marjorie and Adrian about the scheme to free Iris. There was no commensurate extraction planned for Adrian, because he had refused her meddling. The only foolproof way out from under Snowley's thumb was for Adrian to keep his word and repay the debt. No shortcuts. No involving the Wynchester siblings.

Rescue Iris, and Adrian would handle himself.

"My debt is between you and me. Iris has nothing to do with it, and shall have nothing to do with *you*. She is an innocent and will stay that way."

"I could kill you," Snowley offered. "And then collect on my IOUs."

"You could try," Adrian agreed. "But you'd be out England's best forger, and I doubt even *you* are reckless enough to murder the son of a powerful peer of the realm. My father might not care about me, but the law certainly cares about the murder of lords."

"What about your little flame?"

Marjorie stiffened visibly.

"What about her?" Adrian asked, as if bored.

"If you're not concerned about your own well-being, perhaps you'll respond better to the loss of hers."

"Hurt *any* woman in an attempt to control me, and you will lose my cooperation altogether. Without your forgers, you have nothing. Our business is a private gentlemen's agreement between you and me. No one else."

Snowley glared at him in silence.

Adrian gave him a sunny smile. "Just toss Iris's vowels in the fire. Then we'll be back where we started. You and me, and no one else. Just as it should be."

Snowley's bloodless lips pressed together in a thin line. He nodded, slowly, as if in deep conversation with himself. Then he reached beneath his lapel and pulled out the folded stack of Iris's IOUs.

Relief swept through Adrian. He nearly drowned in the welcome balm.

"I won't forgive this," Snowley warned. "The moment your debt is repaid, you can either sign a new, lifetime contract of your own volition, or you can leave England forever and never again lay eyes on your darling little sister."

"I understand your terms." Adrian stepped back grandly and made a sweeping gesture toward the fireplace. "Off to make ashes, then."

Snowley looked as though he'd rather stuff each page down Adrian's throat, but he stalked heavily toward the fireplace behind him.

The first of the IOUs was inches from the licking flames when the door swung open and two men in clean, tidy clothes strode inside... flanked by a pair of guards he had not yet managed to charm—Barnacle Bill and Angel.

Adrian straightened. Neither guard was visibly wearing his pistol.

Snowley turned away from the orange fire. "What's this? You know I'm not to be interrupted."

The guards began to talk over each other.

"I wasn't—"

"We weren't—"

"They didn't—"

"It's not—"

"Basil Newbury," said the first gentleman. He held out a card. "Bow Street Runner."

His compatriot did the same. "John Yarrow, Bow Street Runner."

Marjorie straightened, her blue eyes bright and shining in obvious delight. Adrian could practically hear her shouting, *They came!*

Yes, he could see that. He could also see that the interruption had stopped Snowley from destroying Iris's IOUs.

Newbury glanced at Adrian. "Lord Adrian Webb, if I may be so bold?"

There was no sense denying it. Adrian inclined his head. "Were you looking for me?"

"Yes, although I didn't expect to find you here. Your father once had an order for us to alert him if you were ever spotted again in England."

Once. The marquess had long since ceased caring, if he ever truly had. More likely, Adrian's father would've had shackles and a boat ready to ship his son off for good. The Continent would be too close for comfort.

But with or without the aid of the Runners, Adrian assumed at least one of the neighbors had noted Adrian's visit to Iris and informed the marquess. The problem wasn't that Father didn't know his son had returned. The marquess simply didn't *care*. Why renew his request to the Runners when he was happier without Adrian in his life?

"If you're not here for Lord Adrian..." Marjorie prompted the Runners.

Newbury turned toward Snowley. "There's been a credible complaint about improperly acquired goods under a Mr. Leander Snowley's roof. We've come to investigate. If any such evidence should be found, I'm afraid you'll be coming with me."

"Boss—" Angel began.

"Should we—" Barnacle Bill added.

Snowley held up a hand to silence them. "Illegal property," he drawled. "In *my* home?"

Marjorie glanced toward the ceiling. In a room just above, four chalk molds lay beside a pile of tin shillings. Adrian nodded. The nature of their work might not be clear to the Runners at this distance, but they could point them in the right direction.

"I warrant you would not search an upstanding citizen's home without probable cause," Snowley said casually.

All eyes were on him at once.

"Of course not, sir," Yarrow said fawningly. "I said as much to Newbury. A fool's mission, this is. No matter what nob ordered it. We won't take much of your time."

It had long been rumored that Snowley kept several corrupt Runners under his thumb, either through extortion or illicit payments. Yarrow was apparently one of them.

Snowley gave a grandfatherly smile. "What if I also had the word of a peer that no nefarious transgressions have occurred?"

"What peer?" asked Yarrow, eyes artificially wide, as though this escape hatch had been practiced in advance.

"Why, my dear friend and confidant Lord Adrian Webb, of course."

Adrian's blood ran cold.

Snowley gave an indulgent smile. "Whatever he says about my character, you can rest assured it is one hundred percent true. I give you my word."

Marjorie made meaningful eyes at Adrian. *Tell the Runners*, she seemed to say. *This is our chance. Snowley gave his word!*

Skeptical Newbury was clearly one of the good ones, who wanted nothing more than to see Snowley behind bars.

But Adrian had received the warning.

The IOUs that Snowley had held so close to the waiting fire were now tucked safely again in the breast pocket behind his lapel.

And there they would stay, was the message.

Stalemate.

If Adrian spoke out against Snowley, Snowley would do the same against Iris, leverage be damned. There was no way for Adrian to take down Snowley without taking his own sister down with him.

"Actually," ventured Marjorie.

"Not you, sweetheart," hushed Snowley, his glittering blue gaze on Adrian. "What will it be, Webb, my boy? Is there anything you'd like to say to this fine gentleman before he continues on his way?"

Yes. There was plenty Adrian wanted to say. He clenched his teeth closed to tide the flood of curses and epithets threatening to rush free. He couldn't let down Marjorie and hundreds of swindled customers.

Nor could he risk Iris.

"Well?" Yarrow brushed his hands as if the matter was already solved. "Have we been sent on a wild goose chase?"

Newbury kept his hand above his truncheon.

Adrian could feel Marjorie's gaze boring into the side of his head.

If he disappointed her now, he would break more than the tender bond that had grown between them. He would shatter her staunch idealism. Adrian's palms went clammy.

He could do the right thing and turn in Snowley, at the cost of Adrian's sister. Or he could do the wrong thing and defend Snowley, at the cost of his soul...

And Marjorie.

32

⚜

$\mathcal{F}$ive minutes ago, Marjorie had felt as though she were flying. All her hopes and plans to save the day were working. When the first Runner had walked into the room, it had been a wrinkle—the timing was off—but Basil Newbury's colors indicated he was a friend, not a foe.

Then there was Yarrow. From the moment he spoke, the room filled with blood red and sickly green and tendrils of bilious yellow. The air stank of rotten fruit.

The careful stratagem Marjorie had constructed with such pride...the painstaking forgery...the harrowing, risk-filled trip to Snowley's pitch black dressing room...It didn't work. And it was all Marjorie's fault.

She'd sworn to Adrian and to her family that the bit with the IOUs would not only go to plan, but happen quickly. The debts should have been burned hours ago, long before the Runners arrived.

She'd believed herself ready. She'd insisted she could do it on her own. She'd promised Adrian that if he just went along with her plan, Iris would soon be free. And then it all started unraveling before her eyes.

It was a pity the Bow Street Runners had come across them in this sterile parlor instead of in their usual workroom abovestairs. She wondered if Graham had felt like *this* the first time he launched himself across a high rope without a net.

Yarrow might be on Snowley's payroll, but Newbury clearly was not. He would leap at any opportunity to lock Snowley behind bars for the rest of eternity. All he needed was a single shred of hard evidence.

Evidence Marjorie and Adrian could hand him on a silver platter. Or one forged of pewter, lead, and tin.

God only knew what else the Runners might find if they performed a thorough search. Counterfeiting coins and fleecing customers were a minuscule part of Snowley's sprawling enterprise. But even that much would be more than enough for Snowley to be in prison for life—or worse.

"No response, Webb? Ah, well," said Yarrow. "It seems we've indeed been sent on a wild goose chase. Shall we be on our way, Basil?"

Newbury raised his brows. "Are you certain there's nothing we can do here, Lord Adrian?"

Marjorie swung her gaze toward Adrian. His colors were upside down, his scent backward, the texture of the air around him curdling like rancid milk.

This was their chance to lock the Grandfather of St. Giles away for good. All Adrian had to say was—

"Would I be here if Snowley were some sort of criminal?" he asked smoothly, his face the picture of peer-of-the-realm innocence. "I'm afraid you've come all this way for nothing."

"You're saying...*no* crimes have ever or are currently being committed beneath this roof?" Newbury said with incredulity.

"I'm saying: none to my knowledge," Adrian replied with a gregarious grin. "Snowley and I are just two gentlemen caught in the act of discussing the weather. If commenting upon gray skies is probable cause for barging in and threatening his liberty, then I'm afraid you'll have to add a hundred thousand other names to your list as well. Such as my father, the Marquess of Meadowbrook."

Marjorie closed her eyes to block out the fireworks of elation springing from Snowley and his men, and the sludge of disappointment and resignation dripping from Newbury.

The same sludge that was probably sloughing from her own skin.

"That's settled, then," said Yarrow briskly. He held out his hand to Snowley.

All six men in the room ignored Marjorie. Snowley, because he believed her under his thumb. Joey and Grinders, because they saw her as simple and harmless. The Runners, because the son of a marquess had already spoken. The word of a woman carried no weight compared with these men.

And Adrian, because he... had trusted Marjorie, and she had let him down.

Yarrow bowed. "As I said, we're very sorry to have interrupted innocent talk of rain and fog."

Newbury kept a careful eye on Adrian. "If you're positively certain there's nothing else, I shall beg your pardon and take my leave."

"Nothing at all," Adrian replied with false joviality. "Have a splendid day. Goodbye."

Snowley gestured the Runners to the door. "Please allow my associates here to escort you to the exit."

In seconds, the Bow Street Runners—and the Wynchesters' sole chance to take Snowley down—were gone.

Marjorie felt her spirit crumble.

"Well done, lad," said Snowley.

"Now then," said Adrian. "Where were we? Ah, yes. The destruction of debts."

Snowley gave an affable smile. "You must be mad if you really believed I'd destroy your sister's IOUs on your say-so alone."

"But..." Adrian straightened. "You said—"

"We came to an agreement," Snowley interrupted smoothly.

"Which is the following: you agreed to assume all debts incurred by your sister, payable to me, via your labor, abiding by the terms I set. You will not leave this building until every penny is paid."

Marjorie gave Adrian a slight shake of her head. This was still a terrible deal. If he would just give her the opportunity to—

"I'll do it," Adrian said without hesitation, his shoulders bowing in defeat.

Marjorie wrapped her arms around her roiling stomach. He had seen her shake of the head. He didn't trust her anymore. Not her judgment, not her plans, and certainly not her ability to save him...or Lady Iris.

Worse, she was just as guilty for standing there speechless while it happened. At least partial success had been right there, in the palms of their hands, only for everything to fall apart—and keep falling.

"Then I own you, Webb. Body and soul. You belong to me. I'll call off the watch on your sister and put my men to more important tasks. Remember, you've promised me your full and willing cooperation. I know where to find Lady Iris if you should dare break your word."

"I shall not forget."

Marjorie moaned. Things could not be going worse.

Snowley mistook her anguish as concern over her continued employment with him. "Don't worry, pet. Our arrangement continues on as planned. After defending me to the Runners, Webb is now a known associate. He cannot tattle on us without implicating himself. Which, as we've both seen, is not a sacrifice this 'gentleman' would ever make." He patted Adrian's back. "We'll have a long and profitable career together."

Wonderful. Exactly what she'd hoped would never happen.

Snowley's smile disappeared. "Now get to work. Both of you."

He strode from the parlor without awaiting a response.

As soon as the door shut, Marjorie crumpled into an armchair. Her plan had been worse than ineffectual. She had caused *harm*. Adrian was more embroiled than ever, and after his enthusiastic defense of Snowley, the Runners wouldn't return. They were back to the beginning: nowhere.

Snowley had won.

Marjorie had lost.

"Please don't be angry with me." Adrian dropped to his knees at her feet. "I had no choice. Not with my sister in peril. Choosing Iris will always be the right thing."

"Angry at you?" she choked out. "I'm angry at *me*. I'm the one who didn't keep my word. I insisted to my siblings...I swore to you...I *promised...*"

The parlor door swung open.

Grinders poked his head inside, a hatpin protruding from his mouth. "Come on, then. Back to the workroom for you. Stay at it an extra two hours tonight to make up for lost time."

Marjorie could barely lug her bones out of the chair and up the stairs to the room where they would continue to enrich Snowley's pockets by melting his victims' broken dreams.

This was what happened when the Wynchester family let an inexperienced, less talented disappointment like Marjorie take the lead. She let down not only their clients and all the other victims, but also every single one of her siblings.

The next time she saw her family, she'd have to tell them they'd been right not to believe in her.

She'd failed them all.

33

❦

When tensions ran hot...Marjorie Wynchester froze.

Palms clammy, she sagged against the wall next to the closed workroom door. The door was unlocked, not that it mattered. The Runners wouldn't return anytime soon. Yarrow clearly hadn't wished to come at all, and as for Newbury...*Damn* it.

Today had been their chance, and she'd made a hash of every step of it!

It was worse than being a wallflower. Wallflowers were overlooked while hoping to stand out. It wasn't that the Runners had ignored Marjorie's impassioned outburst decrying Snowley as a demonstrably conscienceless villain. It was that she hadn't *made* one.

She had grown flustered, which led to panic, which led to even more fluster, which led to her mouth shutting down altogether. Silence was her signature move. Understandable, when alone in her studio. Untenable, when justice had literally been standing within arm's reach.

Marjorie's skin flushed hot with shame.

Adrian was now even *more* of a prisoner than he was to begin with.

For the first time in her life, Marjorie was grateful to have an excuse not to go home and face her family. She did not know what to say or how to explain herself. They had done their part, all of them. But when it was Marjorie's turn to take the helm, all their hard work had fallen apart.

She was here instead of any one of her talented, capable siblings because she had insisted she was the right person for the role, and could handle the assignment. She had been wrong.

She should have stayed home in her art studio where she belonged, and let the real heroes handle the action.

"I'm sorry," she said bleakly, unable to meet Adrian's eyes. "I said I could help, and I couldn't. I said the plan would work, and it didn't. I'm the reason—"

"*No.*" Adrian cupped her face and forced her to look at him. "Snowley is the reason. He's the one pulling the strings."

"I thought I could be a puppet master, too," she mumbled. "I was too dense to notice I was a doll made of wood."

"Stop it. You're brilliant. Just because Snowley is stronger does not make him smarter. I know you'll find a way."

"A way to make things worse?" she said wryly.

A Wynchester always did *something*. A Wynchester was useful.

Unlike Marjorie.

He held her gaze. "Blaming yourself isn't helping. Let's think of something that does."

"Nothing I've thought of has helped."

"Your new molds are helping. Substituting inferior metals for the jewelry is helping." His thumb rubbed her cheek. "You're Marjorie Wynchester. I will always have faith in you. You should, too."

That was part of the problem. With Snowley's renewed victory, Marjorie had lost all faith in herself. But... she *did* have faith in the process.

Adrian was right: Wynchesters never stopped trying to right wrongs, no matter the odds. And what was the one thing all their adventures had in common? No Wynchester without a plan, and no plan without a contingency.

"I need a contingency," she muttered.

"Good," Adrian said. "Do you have one in mind?"

She rubbed her face. "Not yet."

"If it helps," he offered, "don't forget you can always throw me to the wolves."

She stared at him. His words gave her an idea.

"Adrian," she said slowly, as hope filled the room with color once again. "I believe we might have a contingency."

He kissed her until she was breathless. "Tell me."

She sketched it out, nervous that she might once again be overestimating her planning prowess. Not for the first time, she wished she had the power of all her siblings' minds in the room with them.

"Will it work?" she asked nervously.

He kissed her cheek. "One way to find out."

Marjorie nodded and squared her shoulders. Then she flung open the door and burst out into the corridor.

"Snowley!" she yelled. "Snowley!"

"No shouting," Grinders said, hatpin between his lips. Marjorie wondered briefly if it was the same hatpin Tickletums had had in *his* mouth. "What do you need Snowley for?"

"Private business. Take me to him at once."

"Snowley dislikes interruptions." Grinders gave her a considering look. "But I'll let him know you've requested an audience."

"Straightaway."

"Go back to work. If he wants to meet with you, he will."

Marjorie returned to the workroom and left the door open. She tried to busy herself with the chalk molds. When Adrian lifted his head sharply, his body pulsing with pinks and toasted barley, she knew there were footsteps in the corridor. She turned just as Snowley appeared in the doorway.

"What is it?" he asked impatiently.

"Not here," she said, and tipped her head toward Adrian.

Snowley's white eyebrows rose and he considered her for a long moment. At last, he inclined his head. "All right. Come with me."

She hurried to Snowley's side. "Thank you for granting my petition to meet with you."

"Follow me." He led her down the corridor and motioned her into an empty room several doors down from the workroom. "I don't have long. I'm very busy interviewing what's left of my staff."

She frowned. "Did something happen?"

His sweet smile was chilling. "Webb happened. He must have sneaked into my bedchamber whilst I slept unawares. The only way to gain access would be if one or more of my employees were complicit. I have sacked everyone guarding my bedchamber. When I learn which one of them betrayed me...let's just say, he won't have a second opportunity to do so."

Marjorie swallowed. "You're interviewing the rest of your staff in case there's another traitor?"

"We shall see. I'll keep a close eye on all my guards, not just the replacements. Now tell me, what did you want to talk about? If you're worried about the Runners, they won't be back."

She took a deep breath. "I wanted to talk to you about Adrian."

Snowley's blue eyes glittered with interest. "Do you know who helped him?"

Marjorie shook her head. "I'm not sure anyone did. I saw him hiding this."

She pulled a duplicate copy of a certain silver hatpin from her pocket.

Snowley took it from her. "Does this belong to Grinders?"

She nodded. "Yesterday, I saw Adrian using that hatpin to pick the lock. I asked him to teach me, but he wouldn't. He said he needed the hatpin for something important."

"I'll bet he did." Snowley curled his fingers around the silver pin. "I'll keep a closer eye on Webb, and have a little chat with Grinders about his personal belongings. In fact, I'll have a discussion with both guards about how carefully they're searching the prisoners. Next time, come to me posthaste. Is there anything else I should know?"

She nodded. "He's dallying."

"Who is? Webb?"

"Yes. He's been playing you from the beginning. That woman discovered the coins were counterfeits because we're releasing similar coins too quickly. We should be working slower, not faster. And with new molds. I don't know what Adrian's game is, but he is not loyal to you."

Not like me, was the unspoken promise. Marjorie didn't want to lay the subservience on too thickly. Snowley was clever enough to follow along without her spelling it out for him. Besides, he had no reason to believe otherwise. She had come to him of her own free will, begged to work for him, returned repeatedly of her own volition, bragged about being the superior employee.

And now, by throwing Adrian to the wolves, she was proving that her allegiance lay with Snowley, not her fellow counterfeiter. If he believed Marjorie was angling for an increase in salary or other such boon, so much the better. It could only sell the fiction that Marjorie was on Snowley's side and worthy of his trust.

He seemed to reach a decision, and turned toward the door. "Come with me."

Marjorie trailed after him in silence. In part because she had never been chatty, particularly with dangerous underworld criminals.

But mostly because a tiny wisp of bright green hope had risen from the mire of her fury and self-flagellation. Something *different* meant something *new*, and something new meant information. If the new development was significant enough, her siblings would know how to exploit it. They'd rescue more than their clients' possessions.

They'd save Adrian, too.

She followed Snowley in the opposite direction of the kitchen and his private plunge bath, to...the unused water closet at the end of the corridor. A sign indicating it was out of repair had hung from the handle since the first time Marjorie had glimpsed it.

Snowley unlocked the door.

What in the world? Even if the water closet was usable again, Snowley certainly couldn't expect her to watch him perform his ablutions. Could he?

The water closet did not appear to be refurbished. Inside was a wooden seat speckled with the most disgusting residue Marjorie had ever seen in her life. If Snowley placed his bare buttocks upon that lid, she would have to push him out of the way in order to vomit into the basin herself.

Or, she supposed, she could vomit anywhere she pleased in the tight, windowless chamber. It looked as though the last dozen people who came before her certainly had. The floor was stained with God-only-knew-what, and the walls...the walls...

Did not smell like vomit. Or bodily functions of any kind.

It was *paint*, not flecks of intestinal residue. Her lips parted in surprise. The water closet had been painted to *look* like a slice of hell even the hardiest of characters should hesitate to enter.

Snowley put his hands on the disgusting wooden seat and gave a tug. The entire tall, wooden block of furniture gave way from the wall as though the commode weighed nothing. A gaping hole stood in its place. Narrow stairs led down into murky darkness.

Without waiting for Marjorie's reaction, Snowley ducked under the low transom and into the shadows. "Follow me, and pull the door shut behind you."

By "door," he apparently meant the commode. Marjorie ducked in after him and did as requested.

Even though she knew it was paint, afterward she could not help but wipe her sweaty palms on her muslin skirt in a futile attempt to clean them.

Candlelight flickered ahead.

They were now in a cellar below street level. Sconces dotted the walls instead of windows.

No wonder it had been so difficult for Graham to ascertain the location of the treasure room. Snowley had filled the building with rooms that weren't visible from any of the exterior windows, from the top floor to the bottom. This lower level ran the entire length of the back half of Snowley's property.

Below, a lone guard stood sentinel beside a solid mahogany door, a pistol at each hip.

"Pretty Percy, this is Mary." Snowley pushed her forward. "She's the one melting down the pieces we need to get rid of."

Marjorie flashed a tight smile.

Pretty Percy's appreciative leer made her shiver in distaste.

Snowley's voice hardened. "She's not to be bothered, understand?"

Percy nodded in alarm, his expression serious. "I will protect her as I protect all your possessions, m'lord."

"Good. Remind the others." Snowley opened the door to the treasure room and lighted the sconces before ushering Marjorie inside.

The well-lit chamber was as large as the Wynchesters' front parlor. As far as riches, the room didn't *quite* resemble the stories of King Midas, but it came closer than anything Marjorie had ever witnessed with her own eyes.

"Is this your office?" she asked innocently.

"No. I conduct my personal business in my private chambers. This is where I store valuables."

Other people's valuables. Snowley's were in his bedchamber. No wonder he had sacked all the men supposed to be guarding the door after he'd thought it had been breached.

"What a lot of things," Marjorie said fawningly, in the hope of spurring Snowley to spill some helpful confidence.

He remained silent.

She looked around the room, memorizing everything. The treasure chamber was outfitted in floor-to-ceiling shelves above tall sideboards. The interior was stuffed with little tables. Every single surface overflowed with necklaces, pocket watches, rings, musical instruments, fine china, canisters of tea—even the odd pineapple, an exotic fruit so expensive that hostesses frequently rented them by the hour, just to grace the centerpiece of a table and impress aristocratic guests.

"All of this is yours?" she tried again, in what she hoped was naïve wonder.

"Some I purchased outright. My temporary arrangements include an expiration date, after which the pawned items belong to me." He waved a careless hand toward the overflowing surfaces. "Most of what you see will be used by myself or my household. Expensive items will be resold to a third party."

"And the objects I'm to use?"

"Over here."

He led her to a sideboard. The drawers on the left-hand side were filled with pieces of jewelry like the ones the guards had been bringing to the workroom to be melted down.

"These are the items acquired with counterfeit coins. Anything that could be easily unloaded has been sold. Everything else is to be repurposed."

She poked through a tin mug spilling over with what appeared to be wedding rings. The one belonging to Mrs. Lachlan's husband might be inside.

Snowley tapped a silver tray containing tools and a ceramic bowl. "Any jewels go in here. You're only to take plain silver from this room. Pretty Percy will inspect each item you've collected before allowing you back upstairs. *You* are not the daughter of a marquess. Any disloyalty will be your last. Understood?"

Marjorie jerked her hand back from the rings and nodded. "Is that why you didn't bring Adrian here? Because his father gives him impunity?"

Snowley's smirk was chilling. "He *thinks* his father's name has that power. And perhaps it would, if his father were remotely interested in his youngest son's life. No, Webb is not to have access to this room for a far more mundane reason."

Marjorie watched his lips carefully.

"Do not trust him," Snowley said, his expression dark. "Mind yourself. He's a snake."

"Believe me," she assured him. "I know."

Yet the irony of a criminal lord fussing over her protectively was not lost on her.

Snowley showed her where the logbook was kept and opened it to the first page. "When you remove each item, draw a line through its corresponding record."

Marjorie's eyes widened as she flipped through the book. The first line was a description in intelligible English: *heart-shaped locket on silver chain*, et cetera. The rest was in some sort of code. She imagined the cipher detailed the origin of the item—and the price, if Snowley had paid for it—but there was no way to know for certain until the code was deciphered.

Luckily, Miss Damaris Urqhart, a dear friend of Marjorie's

sister-in-law Philippa and a member of the reading circle, was famed for her skill in cryptography.

Unfortunately, Damaris had no access to the logbook. It wasn't as though Marjorie could invite the reading circle to Snowley's lair for tea. Nor could she smuggle out the book without Snowley noting its absence and easily determining the most likely source of deception. Marjorie could memorize its contents, but she couldn't leave, either. She pressed her lips together in frustration.

Snowley continued his instructions. "Only take pieces from this collection over here. This rubbish only held value to its owners and will be much better off as coins."

Marjorie's heart clenched at the brimming drawers of treasures referred to so callously as rubbish. Just because a wedding ring was more brass than gold did not make it worthless. Melting down these items was the equivalent of rending the owners' hopes and dreams with her bare hands.

"I thought customers could return for their pawned objects," she ventured.

"They have a fortnight to do so, after which ownership reverts to me. I can count on one hand those who have retrieved their objects within that window. Now I don't even bother to wait."

Didn't even bother to wait! Marjorie gazed at the drawers in renewed horror. That was illegal and unethical and—

"Every time you leave this room," Snowley continued, "Percy will check your selection against the register. Remove any paste or stones and other non-metallic elements with these tools prior to taking the silver abovestairs. Any questions?"

She shook her head. "Draw a line, those drawers only, no jewels, Percy searches me before I leave."

He handed her a metal pail. "Go on, then. Take what you need for today."

Marjorie wanted to begin with the rings, in the hope of coming across Mrs. Lachlan's, but she did not want to be forced to dismantle it just because Snowley was watching.

Instead, she collected necklaces and bracelets without any jewels or custom identifiers, in order to maximize the possibility of returning the unique pieces to their owners in as good a condition as possible. The plain pieces, she and Adrian would be able to re-create later—but that was a contingency.

"One last thing," Snowley said as Marjorie filled the bucket. "You shall not be allowed to leave my roof without protection."

Her heart leapt. "I can leave?"

"Not yet," he amended. "After you complete your month and we sign the official contract. From then on, you'll have monthly half days to do with as you please, but you'll need to take a guard with you everywhere you go. Understood?"

She nodded her comprehension.

The guard would be for Snowley's protection, not hers. He believed Mary to be loyal—to his coin, at least. But her presumed ignorance could cause trouble.

Marjorie stared at him vacantly, as if nothing she had seen or heard was cause for concern, and lifted the bucket. "I have enough for today."

"Good." Snowley gave her a grandfatherly pinch of the cheek. "No more shillings and sixpence. Let's counterfeit crowns from now on, shall we? And when we're finished with the silver, we can move on to gold sovereigns."

34

❀

$\mathcal{W}$hen sunset fell, Marjorie returned to her assigned chamber. She shut the door and threw herself face-first onto the mattress.

A slight brush of cool air and a vibration against the floorboard indicated her brother Graham had come in through the window. Or rather, it indicated that his wife, Kuni, had joined him on tonight's visit. Graham's footfalls were undetectable, but Kuni was still learning to scale walls and pop up where least expected.

Marjorie wasn't ready to have the conversation she knew was coming.

"Go away," Marjorie said into her pillow. "No one's home."

The bed creaked as an extra weight distorted its balance. Kuni knew what it was like to spend her life being told she wasn't good enough, not capable enough. The difference was, Kuni had set out to prove the doubters wrong—and succeeded.

Graham lit a candle and set it on the small wooden table.

Marjorie groaned. She rolled up into a sitting position to face her sister-in-law and her brother. Kuni and Graham's gazes were not angry but concerned. Their empathy and understanding made disappointing them all the more difficult.

"Newbury told us he left empty-handed," Graham signed.

"Adrian chose to save his sister. How can any of us be angry with him for a motive such as that? He wouldn't have been in that position if my plan hadn't fallen apart. If *I* hadn't fallen apart."

Kuni's brow furrowed. "What did you do?"

"Nothing," Marjorie signed bitterly. "I stood there watching my plan disintegrate without saying a bloody word. I'm a disappointment to myself and to all of you."

"You're new to being the lead and mishandled the situation."

"'Mishandled'?"

"You panicked and went quiet. It wasn't the first time. It won't be the last. It was a mistake, but mistakes are not the end of the world. That's why we have contingencies."

"I didn't have one," she signed. "I was so certain my art skills would save the day, I didn't even question the hundred other variables that could go wrong. Until they all went wrong. It hadn't even occurred to me to search Snowley's pockets for Lady Iris's IOUs. The documents might have been *right there...*"

"Or they might not have been," Kuni pointed out, fingers flying. "Didn't you tell us there was a long delay between Webb 'summoning' Snowley, and Snowley actually appearing? Isn't it possible that he used that time to fetch the letters, specifically to flaunt them to Webb as retaliation for presuming to command Snowley's presence?"

"Maybe. We'll never know, because I didn't look."

"You made mistakes, yes. But even if the vowels *were* there, Snowley would have noticed the conspicuous absence of a pile of papers. Mistakes are an opportunity for creativity. The key is to remain flexible. Once we locate the treasure chamber—"

"Oh. I know where it is. I was in there earlier. Hold on a moment." She yanked up her overskirt. "I have dozens of necklaces and bracelets to be returned to their owners."

Kuni and Graham exchanged astonished glances.

"Marjorie, *schatje*." Kuni fingerspelled the Balcovian endearment. "You and I appear to use two different definitions of 'failure.'"

"How on earth did you sneak in?" Graham demanded with sharp gestures.

"I can't sneak," Marjorie reminded him. "Adrian helped me come up with a contingency plan, and it worked. Snowley let me into the storage room himself. There's an access hole behind the commode in a water closet that leads to a secret cellar. I'll sketch a map, but I warn you there are no windows and no path in except past armed guards."

Kuni silently clapped her hands. "You have free rein?"

"For now. He is short of staff and someone may soon take over in my place."

"But you have a place right now," Kuni signed. "That's what matters."

"When did Snowley tell you this?" Graham asked.

"When he showed me the storage room. After the Runners left. I summoned him to a private meeting."

Graham touched her arm. "Marjorie, do you hear yourself? You found your voice! You stayed flexible and creative, and developed a contingency plan from thin air. You're a true Wynchester."

Marjorie gave a shy smile. "I couldn't have done it without Adrian."

Kuni nodded. "If it weren't for him presenting that IOU and then spoiling our plans with the Runners, Snowley would never have shown you the treasure."

"That's right," signed Graham. "So what's the next step?"

Marjorie bit her lip. "I'm not sure. Snowley has doubled up guards at his private quarters and outside our workroom, but he doesn't know we have another ring."

"Which means we can use it again." Kuni's black eyes shone. "But on what?"

"The logbook!" Marjorie exclaimed.

Graham stared at her. "What logbook?"

"Snowley keeps detailed journals of all his transactions, including the ones where he defrauded women for counterfeit coins. Can you smuggle me a blank journal? I'll tell you exactly what type."

"You want to forge a logbook?"

"It's in code. I can re-create the bits I saw, but I didn't have time to scan every page. If I make a copy, Damaris can decipher it." Marjorie rolled back her shoulders and straightened her spine, attempting to project newfound confidence. This time, her plan had to work. "And if we can't find enough evidence... I'll create it myself."

35

✾

*A*drian lay on his back in his cot, trying to get through the night without Marjorie.

It wasn't going well.

Despite the fact that he had never actually shared a night with her, his entire soul rebelled against the idea of missing out on so much as a minute of her company. Yet he'd signed away the rest of his life to Snowley. Did he really expect a woman as magnificent as Marjorie to wait around for decades for someone like him?

Assuming she could leave at all. By aligning herself with Snowley and wading into his inner sanctum, Marjorie had taken on even more risk.

"Should've stayed at the museum," he mumbled.

Adrian wasn't a catch. He was a mistake to dodge.

"You're a peculiar man, Webb," came an unfamiliar masculine voice.

Adrian bolted out of his bed. "Who's there?"

A man stood between Adrian and the sole candle, the backlit orange glow casting his trim frame into silhouette.

"I'm Graham Wynchester," said the low voice.

Adrian wished he weren't standing before Marjorie's brother in stockinged feet and an ankle-length nightshirt. "Have you come to kill me?"

"For God's sake. Are you always this dramatic? If I'd wanted you dead, I would've sent my wife."

Was that good news? Adrian decided to take it as such. "Then what *do* you want?"

The man turned to crouch before the flames, then rose to light the bedchamber's wall sconce with a spill. Even with the sconce, enough shadows danced about the small room that Adrian could just make out a well-dressed man with curly black hair and light brown skin and absolutely no smile on his face whatsoever.

"What I want," said Graham Wynchester, "is to know your intentions."

"With...Marjorie?"

"No, with Tickletums. Yes, of course with Marjorie. Tickletums can look after himself."

Adrian straightened. "So can Marjorie. She's strong and clever and capable."

"Ah. It's like that, is it?" Graham settled on the wooden stool, his voice taking on a considering tone. "Got her measure, do you?"

"It doesn't take a genius to see how extraordinary she is."

"And you're a good judge of genius?"

"I'm not a good anything, I'm afraid."

"Marjorie thinks that's untrue. Something about being a natural mimic with sculpture and other objets d'art. She says you're particularly brilliant at working with your hands."

"She's probably referring to—" Adrian coughed into his fist. Now was not the time for rakish humor. "I don't know if you know this, but your sister is astonishingly brilliant herself."

"I do know that. I came to see if you did."

"Have I passed the test?"

"You've started a new one. It begins with the same question. What, precisely, are your intentions?"

"You expect me to declare myself to you, at this precise moment? Or are you warning me that staying away from your sister is the only way to ensure her happiness?"

"Only you can decide which path is the right one."

"Then what do you *want*?"

"For you to choose."

Adrian raked a hand over his face. "I've been lying there for an hour, trying my best to...think...about..."

His hand had blocked his eyes scarcely a second. Yet Graham had disappeared into the ether as soundlessly as he had arrived.

Adrian peered out the window. He was alone once again. Huh. He began to pull his head back into the bedchamber.

A throwing knife sailed past his cheek with the buzz of a hummingbird, riffling the hair on his head and nearly taking off an ear. If he hadn't just shaved that cheek, the knife would have done the favor for him.

He leapt away from the window, swearing under his breath at the close call. Whoever had thrown that blade had almost killed him!

A second knife flew toward the window, impaling itself in the center of the windowsill just inches from where the crotch of Adrian's trousers had been moments before.

A folded piece of parchment was tied to the handle.

He counted to fifty before edging forward and yanking the dagger out of the soft wood in order to retrieve the missive.

If I wanted to kill you, you'd be dead.

End of message. Cute. Charming.

He reached forward and slammed the window shut, sweltering July heat be damned.

Adrian supposed there were two ways to take the meaning. As a threat, for one. The thrower was more than capable of killing him. Or it could indicate that there *was* no threat. Not yet, at least. The thrower had spared his life in order to see what Adrian intended to do with it.

He turned to the wall behind him to pull the first dagger from where it hung, two feet above the bed.

This hilt also bore a folded missive:

Protect her with your life.

It did not add *or forfeit yours*, but the message was clear. It was also unnecessary. He did not need her siblings' prompting. Life without Marjorie was no life at all. Blankness, where there had once been color. If the occasion arose, Adrian would trade his own life to save Marjorie's without hesitation.

36

The next morning, Adrian woke before dawn—if, indeed, one could say that he had slept. He'd lain awake most of the night thinking about Marjorie, his entire body tense and on alert for sharp blades.

He remembered how Marjorie had told him Sundays were her favorite days of the week. She spoke of her habitual activities fondly, with an enthusiastic sparkle in her blue eyes. There was the tutoring with the Duke of Faircliffe, then the volunteer work teaching art classes to the dozen little girls Adrian had glimpsed that day at the museum. Between those diversions, meals with her siblings—charmers, all of them, to be sure—followed by a long, lazy evening in her studio, putting the final touches on the portrait project for her family.

People were looking forward to seeing her. Relying on her. And instead, she was trapped here just like Adrian.

Because he'd ruined the Runners' chance to arrest Snowley.

Noises sounded in the alleyway outside Adrian's window. He glanced up from his shaving bowl in time to glimpse the most elderly couple he'd ever seen clutching each other for balance as they hobbled through the alley at a snail's pace. No, not a snail's pace. Snails were positively *swift* compared with this couple's progress. Every inch forward was punctuated by a finger-jab at this brick or that crop of weeds, followed by a long-winded discussion or heated argument.

Adrian could not hide his smile as he watched them. These two were the embodiment of his most secret dream. Not a one-night dalliance, not a summerlong *affaire*, but a love that lasted.

The elderly man caught Adrian watching and pointed his stick in Adrian's direction. "Eh! You, there! Green buck!"

Adrian could have sworn three birthdays passed him by as the ancient couple doddered ever-so-excruciatingly slowly up to his open window. He hoped the exertion of crossing the alley did not cause them to expire on the spot. In the pink light of the rising dawn, he could see that even their wrinkles had wrinkles.

"Youngster," barked the old man when he and his wife at last reached a spot below Adrian's window.

He gave a welcoming smile as they drew closer.

"Move along!" came a shout from overhead.

Adrian flinched. The guard on the roof wouldn't shoot at innocent passersby, would he?

"Eh, what's that you say, lad?" The old man cupped a hand to his ear. A prodigious quantity of white hairs protruded from it.

"I said move along!"

"We live here," the old man shouted back. "Our rooms are just ahead."

"Then hurry up and—"

"Can't you see they're old?" called out a voice. A nondescript young woman all but hidden beneath a loose tea-colored cape jogged up to the old couple. "I'll help them get where they're going, but they need a moment to catch their breath."

"Rest quickly," the guard called back. "They have two minutes to leave the alley."

The young woman curtsied, but she did not herd the elderly couple away from Adrian's window. Instead, she joined them, peering up at Adrian from beneath the oversized hood of her cloak.

The old man lowered his spotted hand from his hairy ear. "Now, where was I?"

"Resting, dear," said his wife. Their voices were no longer shouts, but rather pitched at a volume that barely reached Adrian, much less the guard far above.

"Good morning," Adrian called down, unsure they'd hear his voice at such low levels. "How are you this fine day?"

"Bah." The old man shook his fist. "I'd be better if my free-spirited sister Marjorie wasn't being tied down by a . . . How do the gossips put it? A no-good, two-faced, shameless, dissolute, capricious, dishonorable drifter."

Adrian's brain sputtered like water droplets falling in hot oil. This ancient eccentric was somehow . . . one of Marjorie's siblings?

The old man's wife nuzzled his shoulder. "A wee bit harsh, love."

"But true," cackled the old man.

"Who *are* you?" Adrian managed.

"Tommy and Philippa," said the old woman.

"And Chloe," said the young woman in the cloak. "But that's 'Your Grace' to you, Webb."

The Duchess of Faircliffe?

She smiled prettily, and he realized she wasn't nondescript after all. She was just deuced good at blending into her surroundings.

"The real question you need to answer," said the old man—er, Tommy—"is who are *you*?"

"I know who I am," Adrian replied in confusion.

"Do you?" Tommy's bushy white eyebrows shot up mockingly. "Or are you still figuring it out?"

"Be better. This could help." Philippa reached a gnarled hand into a wicker basket.

A flying projectile sailed through the window and slammed into Adrian's chest before fluttering to the floor.

"Oof." He smoothed his lapels as best he could before crouching to pick up the object. "A book?"

"Poetry by Jallow. If his verses on love don't inspire you, nothing will."

"Jallow?" Adrian repeated.

"Can you read?" barked Tommy.

Adrian nodded. "First marks at Eton."

"Then stop asking questions you can see the answers to. What are your intentions toward my sister?"

"Er..." Adrian set the book on the windowsill. The answer to that question had changed over the past four weeks, since he'd first glimpsed Marjorie at the museum. Adrian was barely ready to admit the truth of his feelings to himself, much less to her siblings.

"Not fast enough." Tommy turned to Philippa. "I told you he was a no-good, two-faced, shameless, worthless, capricious, dishonorable drifter. You know what happens to those?"

"What?" Adrian asked with apprehension.

Tommy pulled an oblong brown object from his trouser pocket and hurled it at Adrian's chest.

A potato. He'd thrown a potato.

"What is *with* you Wynchesters?" Adrian sputtered, rubbing what was sure to be a humdinger of a sword-book-potato bruise.

"Oy!" the guard shouted. "What did you just throw at the building?"

"He's got a rifle," Philippa whispered behind her liver-spotted hand.

"They killed a rat," the duchess called up. "There's an infestation in this alley."

"Then get out of the alley," the guard yelled back. "You have one minute before I start shooting."

"Now, now," Philippa chided Tommy, hooking her arm onto his

and doddering down the alley. "What have I told you about throwing vegetables at strangers?"

The Duchess of Faircliffe held her ground. She glared up at Adrian from beneath the beige hood of her cape.

He stepped back. "Are you going to throw a potato at me, too?"

She smiled. "I just wanted you to know that you cause my sister the slightest twinge of pain..."

"I've got the idea," he assured her, his head still spinning at all these Wynchester visits.

This was what unconditional love looked like, Adrian realized. It was not blood that made a family, but the bond they formed together.

He could not prevent a twist of envy that they all had each other.

"I've never been more enamored of anyone than I am by your sister," Adrian admitted. He'd happily consign himself to any fate if it meant more years to spend in Marjorie's company. "But is what I can offer her enough?"

He tried to strike a casual pose and failed miserably. He probably looked as lost and lovelorn as the poet who'd written the verses in the book of poetry on the windowsill.

Chloe gave a commiserating half smile. "Only she can answer that."

She had understood the question behind the question. It was not a matter of what possessions and privileges Adrian could offer, but whether *he* would be enough.

Regardless of his feelings for her, if the answer was no...he would lose Marjorie forever. Was it any wonder a large part of him preferred not to find out?

"What if," he said haltingly, "once Marjorie and I get out of here and our temporary partnership dissolves, she realizes she can do much better?"

"Then she'll walk away without looking back."

"I don't want her to walk away," he said quietly.

"Then be the better choice." Chloe's eyes held his. "Or break it off before she gets hurt."

Before Adrian could answer—and before the guard began shooting—she hurried off down the alley after Tommy and Philippa.

Adrian leaned against the wall beside the window, his shoulders sagging. The room was littered with a potato, two daggers, and a book of poetry.

Slowly, he realized the Wynchesters were not trying to scare him off. They merely wanted him to make up his mind. Either go for it or get out. None of this rakish rubbish of passing time with fleeting pleasures only to hurt their sister with his inevitable goodbye.

The Wynchesters were saying there needn't *be* a goodbye. Not if he and Marjorie chose to stay together.

Despite knowing what sort of man he was, they trusted their sister. If she thought he was worth giving her heart to, they would support her, no holds barred.

They didn't see Adrian as good or bad, or the world as black and white...or even gray. Like Marjorie, the Wynchester siblings likely lived in a world of pink-and-blue checks and green-and-yellow stripes. To them, there was room for everything and everyone. All the colors could mix together or stand out as they pleased, in eternal harmony. If Adrian fought for what he desired most.

And what he wanted was Marjorie.

37

Adrian wrapped the book and the daggers in a spare cravat. He tucked them in the small of his back beneath his coat, then stepped out of his bedchamber. It was past dawn now.

If Marjorie wanted company, he was here for her. He would *always* be there for her. Of course, the first step was to get past the guards.

He beamed at the armed men crowding the hallway. There were two at each end of the corridor—twice as many as before.

"Where do you think you're going?" asked one of the new ones.

Adrian allowed the old role of rakish wastrel to drape about his shoulders like a cloak of dissipated arrogance.

"To Mary's bed," he answered with a pointed waggle of his eyebrows. "Sunday *is* the day of rest."

He kept his conspiratorial gaze not on the new guards, but on Grinders, who had helped convince Joey Box o' Crumpets to allow Adrian half an hour of privacy with Marjorie the last time.

"Again?" Grinders said with a laugh, just as Adrian had hoped—and feared.

What did it say about him that this role was so easily convincing? That the more exaggerated his performance, the more people took him as he appeared, never looking beneath the overblown exterior for more?

"You know how it is," he answered carelessly. "Just popping next door for some light ravishing. Do ignore any screams. I assure you, they will be of pleasure."

"Half an hour, and not a minute more," Joey said firmly.

"Aw, let him have a bit of diversion," Grinders cut in. "It's Sunday. If the man wants to spend it buried in his mistress's skirts, let him have his spot of fun. It's not like he can have any other pastimes."

Joey drummed his fingers on his pistol as he considered the proposition. "Oh, get on with you." Joey gestured Adrian forward with his pistol. "The less I have to see your face, the better."

Adrian bowed, then made a production of strutting lasciviously down the corridor. By the time he slipped into Marjorie's room, he felt slimy, as though he'd waded through an oil slick and could not scrub the greasy residue from his body.

She was sitting cross-legged on her bed with a leather book.

"Is that the latest Jallow?" he asked with interest.

She made a face. "I wish."

He stepped forward and handed her the book Philippa had thrown at him. "Your wish, granted."

She hugged it to her chest. "My brother Jacob would disown me if he knew I read his poetic rival."

Adrian doubted there was anything Marjorie could do to make any of her family members disown her.

The question was whether she would wish to keep *him* after all he'd done.

Adrian dropped down on his knees next to her bed. "I've been sick with worry about the risks Snowley poses to you. I will do everything I can to protect you."

She wrapped her arms about his neck. "I haven't been thinking about Snowley at all. The only man on my mind is you. Is it bad if I'd hoped your thoughts about me were a little more...rakish?"

"It's a happy coincidence. I will die to protect you from other men, but when it comes to me . . ." He covered her body with his and joined his mouth to hers. He was ravenous for her kisses. Desperate for her touch. But it was more than physical. He wanted to connect with her in every way. Not just skin-to-skin, but heart-to-heart.

He was in love, blast it all. Hers, utterly and completely.

Adrian yearned to prove himself the man she believed he could be. Choose? He wanted it all. Not just a friend, not just a lover. He wanted to be her husband, and for her to be his wife. To hold tight to each other and never let go.

He wanted forever.

38

⟨⟨⟩⟩

*B*y late evening, the new plan was coming together.

Marjorie sat at the head of her bed, her back and shoulders propped up with a limp pillow. Adrian sat cross-legged at the opposite end, with Marjorie's stockinged feet in his lap. He had spent the past half hour massaging each foot in turn, making lovely relaxing circles with each deep, slow stroke of his thumbs. Each rub, a cascade of soft pastels with golden highlights.

It was difficult to plan an escapade while practically purring in pleasure.

"How do you think your brother is getting on investigating the fraudulent acquisitions?"

"Knowing Graham, he's done by now and is twiddling his thumbs in impatience for the next step."

"Done! But you scarcely gave him the duplicate copy ten hours ago. There were hundreds of names in those pages."

"And Graham has hundreds of informants throughout the city. Hunting down addresses for each of Snowley's victims would be impossible for you or me, but it's child's play for him."

The copy Marjorie made wasn't an exact duplicate. On the first page, she'd added a fictitious open contract from Snowley, indicating that every "client" listed in the book could purchase their item back for a shilling. Marjorie had signed the statement in Snowley's hand,

and then affixed the special wax insignia using the forged ring Adrian had made.

Would this hold up in court? Probably not. But the Wynchesters didn't need it to pass legal scrutiny. They only needed to give the Runners a plausible excuse to raid Snowley's lair and send his operation crashing to the ground.

On each of the interior pages was the name of a client, the description of their stolen possessions, and a reiteration of the supposed terms: immediate return upon request, if made along with the prompt payment of a shilling. Beneath this was a line labeled RETURN TO OWNER bearing tomorrow's date. Then TRANSACTION APPROVED BY, filled in with Snowley's name and forged signature, followed by extra lines for each client to print and sign their name as well.

Once each of the victims had signed the receipt for their item, Chloe and Faircliffe would pay a visit to the Bank of England and deposit a grand total of eleven pounds in Snowley's account to cover all two hundred and nineteen items in the log book.

After commissioning a letter from the bank manager indicating that the sums had been provided in accordance with the signed contracts, Faircliffe would entrust all of the documents to his solicitor— who was the younger brother of a magistrate.

As a contingency plan, the Wynchesters would steal the stolen goods back and deliver the items to the rightful owners themselves.

"The paperwork is the easy part," Marjorie said. "The tricky bit will be emptying the treasure chamber."

"No windows in the cellar," Adrian said as he rubbed Marjorie's feet. "The only way into that room is through a single corridor."

She nodded.

"Heavily monitored by armed guards," he added. "Surly attitudes and pistols with bullets."

She nodded again.

"*Loads* of treasure. More treasure than anyone can carry." They had argued about this more than once.

"Just the items fraudulently acquired," she reminded Adrian. "Everything else in that room remains where it is."

"Bah," Adrian muttered. "If Snowley doesn't care about ethics, why should we?"

"If we only steal *stolen* items, Snowley cannot publicly claim he was robbed."

They both glanced out the window at the darkening sky. The plan was for them and all the Wynchesters to spring into action just before dawn.

Chloe and Faircliffe would be ready and waiting as soon as the bank opened. The Bow Street Runner, the treasure room robbery, and the destruction of Adrian's indenture contract were up to the rest of the Wynchesters.

Marjorie shook her head in wonder. "A simultaneous triple caper. That will be a first for my family."

"I don't like the sound of that," Adrian said. "If anything were to happen to you..."

Her throat grew tight. "If anything were to happen to *you*..."

They stared at each other. Then Adrian lifted her feet from his lap and climbed up her body to capture her mouth with a kiss. He cradled her in his arms. She held on tight. His warmth and color enveloped her as they kissed. As did her worries.

The problem with a triple caper—besides all of the many and obvious complications inherent in any caper—was that Marjorie and Adrian would have to split up.

They wouldn't know until it was all over and the entire crew reconvened a safe distance from Snowley's residence whether each team had in fact successfully and safely completed their portion of tomorrow's mission.

"If all goes to plan," she murmured against his lips, "this is our last night beneath this roof."

For a moment, his eyes looked bleak rather than relieved.

"Yes," he said roughly. "After tomorrow morning, it's all over one way or the other."

Before she could respond, he kissed her even harder than before. His muscles flexed beneath her fingers. His body burned hot as a forge.

No matter what happened on the morrow, she and Adrian had scant hours left together.

Marjorie might never again have his undivided attention. The thought could have been depressing, but instead it was liberating. It meant there was no reason to hold back, to keep her desire to herself. If she wanted to know passion, this was her chance to experience it with the one and only man she wanted.

"If it's our last night together..." She wrapped her arms about his neck and fluttered her eyelashes up at him in faux innocence. "However shall we while away the long hours?"

His voice was hoarse. "You don't know what you're asking."

"I know exactly what I'm asking," she said hotly. "If *you* don't know how to deliver..."

His mouth crashed back to hers with renewed need.

Marjorie gloried in his hunger, in his desire, in every demanding kiss. She felt the same. And she knew what she wanted: *Adrian*. That she had never made love before only enhanced the experience. Who better than an accomplished rake to give her one perfect night in his arms?

"I hope you weren't planning on sleeping tonight," he growled into her right ear.

A breath-stealing tingle spread out through her entire body at the wicked promise in that warning. "I hope you weren't planning to waste time talking about it. Has your mouth nothing better to do?"

A wolfish grin graced his lips. "Your wish is my command."

She'd meant to goad him into kissing her again. Instead, he tugged down her bodice and closed his mouth around one of her breasts.

Her own mouth fell open in surprise...and pleasure. Her nipple hardened and rose to meet his tongue. Her spine arched from the mattress of its own accord as she smashed her bosom into his face.

Adrian slid his arms beneath her back and rolled her on top of him, allowing her to control the angle and the pressure. He coaxed her knees to straddle him, causing the full length of his hard shaft to press against the slick heat at her core.

His hands slid down her waist and past her hips to cup her buttocks. He gave them a light squeeze.

Elation and power ricocheted through her body as she felt him harden against her belly. *She* had done that to him!

He dragged his mouth to the opposite breast and her thoughts scattered. Her focus was so concentrated on his tongue teasing her nipple and all the sensations spiraling out from that sumptuous point of contact that she did not notice him hiking up the hems to her skirts until warm air skated across her bare bottom.

A heady frisson feathered across her skin. Not just the breeze, but a delightful sensation of naughtiness, of impending pleasure and previously unknown freedom. Nakedness was not something to hide, but to revel in. Her body pulsed with need and anticipation. Wanton wasn't something she *was*, but a joyful act to be performed together in harmony.

Adrian reached between them to unbutton his fall. *I can teach you to ride astride*, he had taunted her the day she became his apprentice.

Marjorie did not want to wait to be taught. She wanted to find out for herself.

Experimentally, she rocked her hips to rub herself against him. Pleasure shot through her. The cleft between her legs seemed to pulse and swell, as if all of her nerve endings had rushed to gather in the same place so as not to miss a single stroke of heady friction.

She rubbed herself against him again and again, whipping the currents of desire building inside her into a barely constrained maelstrom of pressure just begging to be released.

Adrian mumbled something that tasted like warm butter sprinkled with sugar and cinnamon.

"What?" she gasped. "I couldn't hear you."

"It's not words," he said, and returned to her nipples.

The humming sensation spread out in delirious patterns of ivy and pumpkin. At first she thought that he had told the truth, that the vibrations coursing through her were the unintelligible moans of a man gripped in the throes of passion.

Then she realized that these *were* words he was whispering against her skin between kisses. Words he wasn't ready for her to hear. Vulnerable words. Love words. She did not have to make out their syllables to hear what was in his heart. The pulsing between her legs quickened even more.

He slid one of his fingers into her wetness. Shock shot through her, and her muscles clenched around him in pleasure. Her legs began to shake. He drove his finger within her until she fractured against him. Colors exploded all around her in a deluge of gold and purple and red.

She dug her fingers into his shoulders for strength, her climax filling the night with fireworks of color.

39

Adrian gloried in the sensation of Marjorie coming apart around his finger, her slickness coating him. He loved this woman so damn much. Watching her reach orgasm was almost enough to send him over the edge as well. The flutter of her eyelashes, the little noises in her throat, the strength of her spasms...

He couldn't wait any longer. He slid his hands up her smooth hips to hold her steady. Then he sheathed himself fully in her wet heat with a grunt of transcendental satisfaction.

The shocked gasp of pain that came from her mouth...was significantly more tortured than transcendental. His skin went cold.

He yanked himself free and reared up on his elbows, aghast. "You're a *virgin*?"

"*Was*," she managed. "Until a few seconds ago."

"You said you knew what you were asking for!"

"I knew in *theory*. My sister-in-law loaned me several informative books on the subject of human procreation, and I—"

"The full extent of your knowledge of lovemaking comes from a *book*?"

"And several illustrations. I realize pen and ink cannot convey the entire experience, but I didn't think you would care."

"Didn't think I would care..." Adrian dropped his head back onto the pillow and covered his face with his hands. Unbelievable. This couldn't be happening.

After years of stubbornly refusing to become the depraved debaucher of virgins all the gossips and his own family believed him to be, Adrian had accidentally become exactly the dishonorable rogue they all thought he was.

And he'd done it to Marjorie.

The woman he loved.

Ruined. Because of him. Adrian had thoughtlessly taken her virginity and her innocence and...God, he'd even taken her *freedom*. They were trapped in this terrible room because of Adrian. She was far from her family and her art studio and her pupils because of Adrian. And now she was no longer a virgin because of Adrian.

"Are you going to continue?" she asked in a small voice.

"Continue *debauching* you?" he burst out in horror. "No, I shan't continue debauching you! If there were any way to reverse this calamity, I would not hesitate to undo every second of—"

"You would undo lovemaking with me?"

His anguished eyes snapped to hers.

"No, don't answer. I can't bear to hear it a second time." Without meeting his gaze, she disengaged their bodies, her legs trembling this time for an entirely different reason. "I just wanted...one perfect night, that's all. And I wanted it to be with you."

"Marjorie—"

She yanked down her skirts to cover her sex. Her cheeks flushed with embarrassment, where before there had been no awkwardness between them. She rolled away from him, her face to the wall, her eyes shut tight.

Emptiness spiraled out from deep within Adrian's bones.

He had hurt her. More profoundly than he'd realized. And not by the act of lovemaking. His cock piercing her maidenhead had not wounded her, but rather his callous rejection of her seconds afterward.

She wanted one perfect night. With him. And instead, he'd given her...

This.

"Marjorie," he said again, softer, coaxingly. Could she hear him? The last thing he wanted to do was shout at her. He was the one who deserved to be yelled at. He turned her toward him and tipped her head to face him.

Her eyes glimmered with unshed tears. Each one a blow to his hollow gut.

She had given him a chance he didn't deserve, and he had turned a sweet moment sour. Instead of giving her a night to remember, he'd turned it into a moment she would spend her life trying to forget.

"I'm so sorry, love," he said tenderly.

She shook her head, blinking rapidly to keep the tears at bay. "Please do not apologize for making love to me. As though it was a mistake you will always regret. That will only make it worse."

"I'm not apologizing for that. Yes, I thought I would. I thought I *should*."

His whole life, things had seemed so clearly defined. Black and white, right and wrong, good and bad. But hadn't Marjorie helped him realize that the world wasn't black and white? That it was filled with colors, and textures, and shades of meaning.

What could be more colorful and meaningful than making love to the woman who held his heart in his hands? Lovemaking was an act done together, not *to* her. Regardless of the state of her maidenhead, she had chosen to be here, in this bed, with him. They had chosen each other.

He hoped they kept choosing each other, again and again.

"I was wrong, love. And so are you." He pulled her into his arms. "Come here."

She fell forward limply, neither resisting him nor embracing him in return. "I was wrong about what?"

"That wasn't lovemaking." He kissed her forehead, the tip of her nose, each corner of her mouth. "It could have been, had I not ruined it, believing I had ruined *you*. But you're not ruined, are you? You're magnificent. Perfect just as you were, and just as you are."

Adrian had choices. So did Marjorie. No one would be ruined as long as they decided their future together.

Marjorie wanted one perfect night. Why not give it to them both?

He caressed her cheek. "Would you please let me try again?"

Her lowered eyelashes lifted as her startled gaze met his. "You do want to make love to me?"

"I have wanted nothing else since the moment I met you. That ardor has increased exponentially ever since. I wake every morning with a stiff cock, eager to be inside of you. I close my hand around it every night, imagining you're in my arms."

These were not the words a gentleman used to woo a bashful wallflower. But Adrian was no gentleman. And Marjorie bloomed brighter than all the fields of flowers together.

Her eyes cleared of tears as she searched his own. "Is that true?"

"More than true." He stroked her hair. "I'm not only the best forger in England, but also do some of my best work at half-mast. Trying desperately not to give away that the sight of you melts me hotter than a vat of silver."

"No silver," she mumbled. "Thirty percent tin-and-copper shavings and seventy percent lead."

He kissed her. Tentatively, she kissed him back.

"Only *half*-mast?" she murmured against his lips.

He took her hand and wrapped it around his erect cock. "Perhaps

I misspoke. How would your informative books describe this steel rod?"

"'Passable,'" she replied primly. "'Middling' to 'somewhat satisfactory,' if all other options have been exhausted, and the only choice that remains is to accept—"

"I'll show you *satisfactory*," he growled, and flipped her onto her back. "Tell me what your books have to say about *this*."

He tossed her skirts up to her waist and spread her legs wide. Rather than bury his shaft inside her, he knelt between her calves and pressed a kiss to the inside of her knee.

"That's not lovemaking," she informed him. "That's a kiss to the knee."

"I knew your books were woefully inadequate. *All* kisses are lovemaking, when done right."

He gave her another slow, lingering kiss, just above the previous one.

Then another, just above that.

He grinned at her sudden intake of breath when she realized this game would lead him up the inside of her leg to the juncture of her thighs.

"Adrian," she gasped.

"Shh," he said. "I'm busy."

A tenth kiss. A twelfth. He made it take forever, stretching out the anticipation as the aroma of her musk reached his nose and her legs trembled with want.

Only then did he give in and kiss her deeply at her cleft.

Her fingers gripped his hair. Twisting, pulling, holding him in place. But there was nowhere else he'd rather be. He adored her taste. Her scent. Her heat. He loved the way she gripped him with her legs, claiming possession of him even as his mouth was claiming her. He loved *Marjorie*.

"Adrian, I'm going to—"

Her climax was already here, rewarding him for his attentions. His cock had never been so stiff. But this time, he would take it slow.

When the last of her spasms eased, he lifted his mouth to give her an arrogant smile. "How would you rate that? 'Passable'? Or 'middling'?"

"Shh," she mumbled, her eyes fluttering closed in satisfaction. "I'm sleeping."

"What a shame," he said sadly. "I suppose you'll have to miss what happens next."

Her eyes flew open and she tugged him to her. "Show me."

"With pleasure." He positioned himself between her thighs. "Are you ready?"

"Will it hurt like last time?"

"I don't know," he answered honestly. "Contrary to what you may have heard, I don't make a habit of performing this act with virgins."

"Luckily..." Her eyes twinkled up at him. "I'm no longer a virgin."

He made an exaggeratedly pained face.

Her grin widened. "Debauch away, my lord." She wiggled her hips beneath him. "Your apprentice awaits her lesson."

"Then let me teach it to you." Carefully, gently, as slowly as he could withstand, Adrian eased forward with his cock until he was once again nestled deep inside.

"It doesn't hurt," she said in wonder.

"Thank God," he muttered.

She squeezed him with her inner muscles. "Do it again."

He tried to take it slow, really he did. But she lifted her hips to meet him thrust for thrust, sending his good intentions and every thought in his head right out the window.

They surged together again and again. Panting, gasping, kissing, until the tremors of orgasm took her once more and nearly brought Adrian along with it.

He barely managed to withdraw his cock in time before spending in his hand. He wiped his palm clean with his discarded cravat, then rolled onto his back, cuddling her to him.

"Thank you," she murmured sleepily into his chest. "It was perfect after all."

He pressed a kiss to the top of her head.

One perfect night would never be enough.

40

◦◦◦

*M*arjorie did not mean to fall asleep. She wanted to spend the night memorizing every rise and fall of Adrian's chest. To bask in the possessive way he curled his arms about her protectively as he slept.

But her wishes were no match for his warmth and the comfort of his arms. She slept deeper than she could ever remember doing before, and startled awake with a gasp of surprise at the first tap at her windowsill.

"Letter for!" announced Piffle.

"Wha?" Adrian mumbled into Marjorie's hair.

Regretfully, she rolled out of his arms and off the bed, bending quickly to retrieve the thin scroll the crow had dropped onto the wood floor.

Jacob's handwriting greeted her:

> *Siblings evenly divided. Need deciding vote.*
> *Should Team B deploy a False Lamkin or a*
> *Black-Eyed Susan?*
> *Standing by for immediate response.*

"What was that?" Adrian asked groggily.

"Reveille," she replied.

He rubbed his eyes. "It's not even light yet."

"We launch at dawn," she reminded him.

His face brightened. "So there's time to make love again?"

"First I need to answer my brother. Since this is about your team, you should have a vote. Do you prefer False Lamkin or Black-Eyed Susan?"

"What do you recommend?"

"Sally In Our Alley."

He pulled the shirt over his head. "Which one was that, again?"

"Contingency three."

He rubbed his eyes, then nodded. "I remember."

Did he? Her lips twisted in concern. Before meeting her, he had never executed a caper. What they had planned was dangerous.

She touched his cheek. "*Do* you remember?"

"Every step. I was just sleepy." He kissed her palm. "Someone kept me up late, as I recall."

Her cheeks flushed in remembered pleasure. "Stay alive, so that we can try it again."

"I have never heard a better incentive." He nodded at the note. "Two votes for Sally."

She grinned to herself as she scratched their response onto the back of the scroll and sent it back with Piffle. When the crow flew off, Marjorie grinned at Adrian. "There might be time for a kiss or two."

They had barely begun when wings fluttered behind her. "Letter for!"

"Or not." Marjorie sighed and turned toward the crow. The new note was on the floor.

Sally In Our Alley in twenty minutes.
Counting down now.

"No more kisses." She tossed him his shirt and waistcoat with regret. "Your team launches Sally In Our Alley in twenty minutes."

"There are definitely more kisses in your future." He forced his legs into his pantaloons and buttoned the fall. "Oh, before I forget. Since you'll be with your sisters, you can return these."

He unwrapped a cravat on the floor to reveal twin daggers.

"Kuni loaned you her throwing knives?" Marjorie said in surprise.

"'Loaned me,'" he repeated. "What an interesting interpretation of her assassination attempt."

Marjorie snorted and took the knives. "If she wanted you dead, you'd be dead."

"That's what she said," he admitted. "I'm glad she'll be with you."

"You'll have Tommy and Graham. They're not as effective in combat as Elizabeth and Kuni, but in theory you won't be in danger."

"Because we're to steal pieces of paper, whilst you're off breaking into a heavily guarded treasure chamber."

"It has to be me," she reminded him. "I have permission to be there."

"I know," he said with a sigh. "I just hate letting you out of my sight. If this is the last time…"

"It won't be," she promised him.

"It had better not." He pulled her to him and kissed her deeply. "My apprentice still owes me a ride."

She grinned up at him cheekily. "You can collect that ride in two hours."

"I said half-mast," he groaned. "Now I have to Sally In Our Alley with an erection taller than the Tower of London."

She gave him one last kiss. "I'll reward you later."

"No, darling. I'll reward *you*."

They linked hands, then turned toward the door.

Adrian took a deep breath and counted backward from ten.

A crash sounded on the other side of the wall, followed by what sounded like a drove of wild pigs and a stampede of footsteps.

Marjorie grinned at him. "That's our cue."

"One hell of a distraction," he muttered.

He gave her hand one last squeeze before they burst into the corridor and hurried in opposite directions.

Two new "maids"—otherwise known as Elizabeth and Kuni Wynchester—entered through the hallway window. They escorted Marjorie to the treasure chamber under the watchful eye of her new personal guard, the gentleman formerly known as Mr. Jacob Wynchester.

Normally, such unexpected changes to the routine would be challenged. However, two critical details were on the Wynchesters' side.

First, ever since Adrian counterfeited the IOU, Snowley had set about on a spree of enlisting new guards to replace the old ones. Most of the men on the overnight posts barely recognized each other, and would not think to question another man's claim that he was a new hire, just like them. Especially since Marjorie had taught her siblings the secret gestures the guards used as codes. The hand signals were just like sign language.

Second, and perhaps most important, Snowley was not at home. He had been jarred awake by a messenger boy with an urgent summons to another property. Snowley had set out across town, bleary-eyed and in a foul humor. His absence should buy the Wynchesters an hour to an hour-and-a-half of time. The emergency was false, of course, though the impending trouble was real.

Adrian was flanked by two new guards as well: Tommy and

Graham fell into step beside him the moment he reached the corridor. Tommy looked nothing like the old man he'd been just a few days earlier. If anything, the lad looked younger than Adrian himself.

"Webb, you've met my sister Tommy?" Graham murmured in greeting.

Adrian blinked at Tommy.

She grinned and handed him a meat pie.

His stomach growled in response. He'd been longing for one of these for years. "What's this for?"

"Marjorie said to treat you like family." Tommy shrugged. "Family gets pie."

Adrian's heart made a strange little flip.

Like family.

He wasn't even certain he knew what those words meant. One could argue that his own family had not treated him like family. But one request from Marjorie, and the entire Wynchester clan welcomed him among them. Even though this family wasn't his to keep, Adrian would savor every moment with them, because this might be the only time he ever experienced such a thing. To feel valued, trusted, worthy.

"Eat quickly," Graham warned. "We're almost there. If ever there's a moment when they'll shoot to stop us..."

True. Adrian shoved the pie into his mouth. At least he wouldn't die with an empty stomach. "Ready."

"Good." Graham gestured up ahead. "Snowley's private chambers are around that corner. We're used to these maneuvers, but you...try not to get shot."

"How *do* I avoid being shot?" Adrian whispered to Tommy.

"Well," said Tommy. "That involves a wee bit of luck."

"Luck?" Adrian sputtered. "What kind of contingency plan is *luck*?"

"You're the one who picked Sally In Our Alley," Graham reminded him. "You can't complain if you end up with a few romantic scars."

"Or dead," Tommy added. She pushed Adrian forward. "Let's find out which."

41

*N*ew maids?" Pretty Percy said doubtfully outside the treasure room door.

Jacob's hand signal to Percy had confirmed Jacob a member of Snowley's crew, but Percy still looked askance at Kuni and Elizabeth, both of whom would have happily launched a knife or a sword in his direction had Jacob not extracted a promise for violence to be a last resort. They would start with a classic stratagem: misdirection and bribery.

Marjorie rose on her toes, ostensibly to murmur into Pretty Percy's ear, but mostly to give the guard a distraction he'd appreciate: an unhindered view straight down her bodice.

"They're my assistants, not maids," she whispered into the guard's ear. At least, she hoped she was whispering. Sometimes it was difficult to find the sweet spot between too loud and inaudible. "They're here because Snowley doesn't trust Lord Adrian. But of course *you* know what's going on. You guard the treasure, after all."

Percy's chest swelled. He flicked an arrogant smirk over Marjorie's shoulder at Jacob, who had his hands above his pistols and his suspicious gaze trained on Kuni and Elizabeth.

"I know everything," Percy whispered back. "You're the expert forger."

Definitely a whisper. Marjorie couldn't hear him at all. She concentrated on his mouth. If he took it as sexual interest, well...the more distracted he was, the better.

She kept her voice at the same pitch as before. "Have you seen the product?"

He shook his head.

"Can I trust you not to share with the others?"

Percy's gaze glittered with greed. "I won't breathe a word."

Marjorie glanced over her shoulder.

As planned, Jacob had conveniently backed the two new "maids" against a wall for an interrogation. Elizabeth gripped her cane with visibly trembling hands. None of the three was looking this way.

Marjorie dipped her hand into her basket and pulled out a pouch of shiny silver crowns. Well, pewter and tin, but who could tell in this lighting? The coins would be more than a fashionable Mayfair butler earned in a year...if they were real.

Percy's eyes widened. It was probably more than *he* earned in five years.

Rather than offer him a couple of the coins, Marjorie dropped the entire bag of crowns into the guard's trouser pocket.

Jacob spun about. "What was that noise? Is that chit up to something?"

Marjorie turned her head so that Jacob couldn't see her face. She affected a panicked expression for Percy's sake and brought a hurried finger to her lips.

"Nah," Percy said loudly. "Just jangling my extra bullets. Are you going to let these girls get to work or not? If they lag behind on their schedule, I'll tell Snowley it was *your* fault. He'll give you the sack...if you're lucky."

Jacob's face flashed a credible impression of terror. He motioned the three women forward. "Go on, then. We haven't got all day. Five minutes to gather what you need, and then it's back to work with you."

"On our way, sir." Marjorie winked at Percy and disappeared into the treasure room.

As soon as Kuni and Elizabeth joined her, Marjorie shut the door behind them, leaving Jacob to do his best to bond with his criminal colleague.

Kuni's lips rounded, indicating she was whistling under her breath.

"This really *is* a treasure chamber," Elizabeth signed. "Look, he's got a Scottish claymore like mine! I want to see—"

Marjorie grabbed her sister's arm before she lost herself among the weaponry. "In and out, and only what we came for."

Elizabeth's expression was of comical disappointment. She pouted, but followed Marjorie to the sideboard containing the fraudulently obtained jewelry.

All three women set their empty baskets on the floor and began filling them with the contents of the drawers. The loose jewels from the porcelain bowls disappeared safely into hidden pockets.

"So many people swindled like Mrs. Lachlan," Kuni signed.

"All their beloved mementos will soon be back where they belong," Marjorie signed back.

Between she and Adrian, they would repair every piece of jewelry that still existed, and re-create anything that did not. The replicas would be visually identical to the originals, but also bearing the original jewels.

"Now we waltz out of here?" signed Kuni.

"Think that guard was entranced enough by Marjorie's bosom?" Elizabeth signed back. "Should have shown mine. It's five times bigger."

Marjorie elbowed her sister in the ribs.

"He *was* more interested in the coins than in Marjorie's charms," Kuni agreed.

Marjorie elbowed her in the ribs, too.

"Ouch!" Kuni glared at her. "You got me right in the dagger."

"Be serious," Marjorie scolded them. "You have to cower fearfully behind me until we're safely back upstairs."

Elizabeth nodded. "Then we dive through the closest open window..."

"...and run like the devil," Kuni finished.

Marjorie took a deep breath and opened the door.

Kuni and Elizabeth followed meekly behind.

"All right, you three." Jacob motioned them forward with his pistol. "No dallying."

"*Wait*," Percy commanded.

All four Wynchesters froze.

Pretty Percy made an apologetic face toward Marjorie. "Rules are rules, pet. I must inspect the merchandise. Snowley would have my head if one of the new girls tried to sneak off with a jewel."

Elizabeth and Kuni exchanged grins and set down their heavy baskets.

"*Finally*," Elizabeth said with feeling. "I thought I'd never get to use my sword."

Startled, Percy sent her a quizzical glance. "Your what?"

The words were barely out of his mouth when the handle of her sword stick crashed against the side of his head.

Percy's eyes fluttered closed and he dropped at once. Jacob caught him just before he hit the floor and eased the guard to the ground without a clatter.

"I said no violence," he chided Elizabeth.

"We agreed violence was a contingency plan." A mischievous smile spread across her face and she kissed the handle of her sword. "It was time for the contingency."

CHAPTER 42

U nder the watchful eye of a guard called Barnacle Bill, Graham tackled Adrian to the floor, right outside Snowley's private quarters.

"I *swear*," Adrian fake-sobbed. Mostly fake-sobbed. He very much wished to avoid a bullet hole in his second-favorite waistcoat. "I couldn't enter Snowley's chambers if I tried. I haven't a key."

Tommy, on the other hand, did have the duplicate keys. Their possession made her appear to have even more authority over the other men. It was also how she was currently inside, covertly pilfering Snowley's copy of Adrian's contract and Iris's IOUs.

Graham finished "searching" Adrian and turned to the guard called Barnacle Bill. "Seems he's telling the truth. Couldn't even find pocket lint on him. Want to have a look yourself, mate?"

Bill looked from Adrian to Graham and back again with transparent indecision. On the one hand, he markedly did not trust Adrian. On the other, there was no way for Bill to check Adrian efficiently himself without holstering his pistol—leaving it within grabbing distance of the prisoner.

Tommy swaggered out of Snowley's quarters looking bored with the whole proceedings. "Nothing out of place in there. How goes it out here?"

Relieved, Barnacle Bill motioned her toward Adrian. "Check him good, will ye? This one says he couldn't find nothing, but Webb's a wily one. I don't trust his smug face."

Graham and Tommy exchanged the briefest of glances.

Adrian couldn't begin to fathom what information they'd just communicated between them, but he could practically see a sign flipping over to reveal: AND NOW, FOR CONTINGENCY PLAN FOUR.

It probably had a code name like Greensleeves or Old Maid In The Garret.

Tommy dragged her thumbs out of her waistband with an audible sigh, as if touching Adrian was tantamount to licking a slug. "Get up and put your hands on the wall."

He scrambled up from the hallway floor and placed his palms above the wainscoting. Exquisite wall coverings in this corridor. Nothing at all like the peeling paint outside the workroom. Adrian hoped his sweaty palms left lasting prints in the fine silk.

Tommy started at his neck, checking beneath his collar and inside the knot of Adrian's cravat. She moved down, inch by inch, with the precision of a clockmaker. Because of her careful and thorough search, Tommy indeed stumbled across both objects Adrian had hidden on his person. She continued on smoothly, leaving the items unremarked.

When she reached his ankles, she tapped one of his shins. "Boots off."

"What?" He glanced over his shoulder at her.

"Your boots. Take them off."

She had to be jesting. "I just champagne-shined these this morning. I can't remove them without a valet, and—"

"He ain't *got* a valet!" Barnacle Bill crowed in glee at having caught Adrian in an obvious lie.

Graham held Adrian's arms behind his back as Tommy pulled off the first boot and shook it upside down.

Empty.

She tossed the boot into the air. Graham caught it behind his back.

Tommy pulled off Adrian's second boot and turned it upside down. Only from his angle could he see her release a handful of coins from her fist, rather than shake them loose from the toe of Adrian's boot.

"Ha!" Barnacle Bill puffed out his chest. "I knew it!"

"I made those crowns myself," Adrian protested.

"And if Snowley wanted you to have them," Bill snapped, "he'd have *gave* them to you himself."

Graham slapped the boots into Adrian's chest. "Put these on. No more trips out of the workroom for you."

With ennui, Tommy gestured at the coins littering the floor and sighed in Barnacle Bill's direction. "Whilst we return the prisoner to his cell, can you collect those crowns and give 'em back to the boss? You can say you're the one who found them."

Barnacle Bill holstered his pistol and sank to his knees at once. "Perhaps Snowley'll be so pleased, he'll give me—"

Fast as quicksilver, Tommy slapped a pair of handcuffs on the kneeling guard and snatched his pistols from their holsters.

"Oy! Wot do you think you're—"

Graham whipped his cravat from his neck and stuffed the starchy linen into Barnacle Bill's gaping mouth.

"*Run*," he ordered Adrian and Tommy.

"But—" Adrian fumbled with the boots still clutched to his chest. "My Hessians—"

"No time!" Tommy looped her arm through his and yanked him toward the closest window. The boots clattered to the wood floor as Adrian scrambled to keep pace with her in his stockinged feet.

She climbed out through the window and tugged Adrian through after her.

The guard on the roof fired without warning, his bullet coming dangerously close to Adrian's bare feet.

Graham dove through the open window headfirst, flipping through the air as Tommy called out, "Philippa! Now!"

The street instantly filled with two dozen carolers in fancy walking dresses, the fine ladies belting out a Sunday hymn at the top of their lungs.

Tommy, Adrian, and Graham ran straight at the crowd of women.

The gunmen swore audibly but held their fire. Shooting an indentured forger was one thing, but murdering half of polite society on a public street was a step too far. At least, not without the boss's direct command.

A carriage swerved around the corner, slowing just enough for the side door to fling open and allow the fugitives to leap inside. The coach tore off down the cobblestone road at top speed.

Tommy and Graham looked at each other, then burst out laughing, congratulating each other on a job well done.

Adrian's stomach, however, filled with nerves. He and two of the wild Wynchesters might have made a safe getaway...

But what about Marjorie?

43

∾

*M*arjorie stood at the front windows of the Puss & Goose inn her family often used as a rendezvous point. Her team had finished first and left through the scullery disguised as maids, leaving her to await Adrian with growing anxiety.

When a Wynchester hackney carriage slowed in front of the window, Marjorie ran out of the inn to meet it. Before the carriage could come to a complete stop, the door flung open. Adrian tumbled out with his cravat askew and no boots upon his feet.

"You're safe!" Though his handsome face was visibly relieved to see her alive, his pace did not slow. He raced across the lawn in ripped stockings, swung Marjorie off her feet, and kissed her hard, in full view of all of her siblings.

She allowed herself to be twirled in jubilation as she returned Adrian's kiss just as passionately.

Vaguely, she sensed Tommy and Graham alighting from the carriage and joining the others at the entrance to the inn.

Adrian did not stop crushing her to him in relief and happiness until a third coach appeared at the front of the property. Graham and Tommy rushed forward to hand down their respective women and give much the same welcome Adrian had shown Marjorie.

He laced his fingers with hers and gave a somewhat sheepish smile at her siblings.

They grinned back. The Wynchester family believed wholeheartedly in love and affection, and didn't give a tossed teapot about the rules of propriety.

Adrian's gaze shot to Marjorie. "Were those carolers the same bluestockings who loaned you the books about..."

Cheeks flushing, she nodded.

Impressed, he shot up his eyebrows. "That's one hell of a reading circle."

She pointed at the tattered stockings clinging to his muscled calves. "What happened to your shoes?"

"Tommy happened to them," he said wryly.

Tommy did not look abashed at all. "I'll find you a new pair of boots." She looked him up and down to take his measure. "And some fashionable clothing in better condition."

He gave a wounded expression. "You try being held prisoner in a criminal's rookery headquarters for a month with no valet, and see how fashionable you end up on the other side."

"Shush," teased Philippa. "Tommy will have nightmares about the horrors of being kept away from her eight wardrobes of costumes."

"I hope you can survive our upcoming holiday in Balcovia," Kuni said.

"More than survive," Tommy promised her. "I plan to add to my wardrobes."

"You'll love Balcovia," Adrian told her. "It's beautiful there. As to my attire..." He glanced at Tommy's slender frame with skepticism. "Are you certain your clothes will fit me?"

She gave him a withering look. "I know how to select garments."

"Trust her," Marjorie said. "She could tailor Brummell himself from a single glance out of the corner of her eye."

A messenger boy arrived with a note for Graham.

Meanwhile, Adrian glanced about the street. "Where are the duke and duchess?"

"At the bank," Marjorie answered with satisfaction. "They were the first appointment of the day. By now, the transaction has been made and the stolen objects legally no longer belong to Snowley."

"Legally according to a forged contract and logbook," Philippa amended.

"Pah." Marjorie waved a hand. "Minor details. The victims' signatures are real, and they're all looking forward to their belongings' safe return."

Graham, sans cravat, looked up from his missive. "Breakfast is ready for us at home. As soon as we arrive, the footmen will spread out the lost treasures the ladies collected onto the parlor table. Once we get the items sorted by owner, our staff will make the deliveries."

Adrian glanced at Tommy. "The meat pies weren't breakfast?"

"Pies are pies." She patted her stomach. "They're for the space between meals."

"Cease your dawdling," called Elizabeth from the inside of a coach. "There's champagne with our eggs and kippers today!"

Marjorie cupped her hand to Adrian's ear and whispered, "And a bed upstairs once the deliveries are done."

Adrian's eyes filled with hunger. Without a moment's hesitation, he scooped her into his arms and carried her to the closest carriage.

44

𐙪

*A*drian relaxed hip-to-hip with Marjorie on a comfortable sofa in the Wynchesters' parlor. It had taken hours after breakfast, but with everyone working together, all of the confiscated heirlooms had been paired with the names of their rightful owners.

The Wynchesters' footmen were ferrying packages all over London at this exact moment, reuniting defrauded victims with their belongings. Mrs. Lachlan had been the first to receive her lost wedding ring. She cried to be reunited with such a cherished part of her husband.

In celebration, Adrian hurled his contract and Iris's IOUs into a fire. Within seconds, his sister's markers were consumed by orange flames.

With joy, he clinked his glass of champagne against Marjorie's and toasted the Wynchester siblings—who immediately toasted him back. As the bubbles from the champagne tickled Adrian's nose, a strange new warmth spread throughout his body.

This was what it felt like to be part of a team. To be good. To have effected meaningful change.

Before embarking on the final step of the restoration plan, Adrian sent a note to his sister, letting Iris know they were both safe and that Adrian would come to see her as soon as he tied up the last of the loose ends. He and Marjorie planned to return the loose jewels that once belonged to rings and necklaces, and give the owners the option to have Adrian and Marjorie re-create any missing pieces. They would take their sketchbooks with them to ensure they captured every last detail.

Tommy approached the sofa with a pair of boots and a pile of folded clothing in her arms. "Here you are, as promised."

"Thank you." Adrian set down his glass of champagne and rose to his feet. "Is there somewhere I could use as a dressing room?"

"Of course!" Marjorie jumped up. "You can use my...er..."

Tommy gave her a knowing smile. "The guest chamber next to your bedroom?"

"Yes," Marjorie said quickly. "For no reason except for pure convenience and expediency, and not at all because of the connecting door. Also, I might have had the presumption to order a bath to our rooms."

Adrian's heart warmed. He pressed a kiss to her temple. "You are a gem."

He followed her up a grand marble staircase to the next floor. A pretty corridor led to a well-appointed bedchamber, complete with a large four-poster bed and dressing room. A team of footmen followed each of them into their chambers with hot water for their baths.

As soon as the servants left, Adrian threw his ruined stockings into the grate and sank into the steaming water. It might not be a rose-petal-strewn plunge pool like Snowley preferred, but it felt like heaven on Adrian's tight muscles.

In no time, he was clean and dry. Adrian made short work of donning the articles of clothing Tommy had given him. True to her word, everything was of the first stare, and fit as though sewn by London's finest tailor.

Rather than emerge through the main door the way he'd entered the guest chamber, he knocked instead on the connecting door that led to Marjorie's bedroom.

She answered looking stunning in a day dress of celestial blue jaconet muslin with delicate frills about the wrists and bodice. Her beauty stole his breath. The only remedy he could find was to pull her into his arms and kiss her until his heart threatened to thunder out of his chest.

"My hair is not yet dry," she said apologetically when they paused for air.

He pressed her fingers to his lips. "Come over to my bed and allow me to make the rest of you just as wet."

Her eyes sparkled. "I shall consider your scandalous offer after supper. But first, we have a list of names to visit."

"Then let us do so as expeditiously as possible."

After one last kiss, she took his arm and allowed him to lead her back down the stairs to join the others.

The siblings were still in the parlor, and not alone.

Adrian's neck flushed with mortification when he recognized one of the visitors as Basil Newbury, the Bow Street Runner he'd deflected from Snowley's trail. Now that Iris was safe, Adrian wanted nothing more than to cooperate to the fullest.

"Lord Adrian," the Runner said politely.

"Newbury," Adrian responded.

"We've informed the Runners of Snowley's successful plot to defraud the unfortunate using counterfeit coins," Philippa told Adrian and Marjorie, sending them a quelling look. "I've explained Their Graces' role in aiding the victims to recover their lost items, as per the legal contract signed by Snowley himself—"

Adrian squeezed Marjorie's hand.

"—and reiterated our request for Snowley to be formally charged and arrested for his illegal dealings with his fellow citizens and his treasonous acts against the Crown."

"The problem is," said Newbury with a sideways glance at Adrian, "we attempted to search the premises once, but were thwarted by a sudden and unforeseen alibi."

Awkwardly, Adrian cleared his throat into his fist.

"If the illegally acquired items and counterfeit goods are no longer in Snowley's possession..." the Runner continued.

"There's evidence," Adrian said quickly. "Inside a workroom on the second floor. There are two chalk molds for creating counterfeit sixpence, two molds for making shillings, and another two for crowns. And...a witness."

The Runner's eyes lit with clear interest.

"We've never had anyone willing to testify before," said Newbury.

Marjorie squeezed Adrian's arm in warning. *Beware. Here be sharks.*

But here also were redemption and absolution. An opportunity to do the right thing. Make the right choice. To be the *good* one instead of the bad apple.

This was Adrian's opportunity to confess his own part in the proceedings and act as the prosecution's principal witness in the case to lock Snowley up for good...Or he could say nothing and allow Snowley to walk free. Free to exact revenge on Iris or Marjorie.

He swallowed hard and glanced down at Marjorie's soft hand on his arm. What would the Wynchesters do? Simple. Any act necessary to right a wrong or protect the disadvantaged. Adrian could do no less. Not if he wanted to be worthy of Marjorie.

This was his chance to prove what kind of man he was, once and for all.

"I will testify," he said at last. "I will be the witness of your dreams."

Marjorie squeezed Adrian's arm tighter, hard enough to bruise, but she did not interrupt.

"For the record," said the Runner. "You personally witnessed Snowley counterfeiting coins?"

"I personally counterfeited the coins at Snowley's request."

Adrian's voice rang out loud and clear in the preternaturally silent parlor.

The Runners exchanged glances.

"You're confessing...to treason?" Newbury asked carefully.

"I'm admitting to having been forced to commit crimes at gunpoint, as orchestrated by Leander Snowley." Adrian's breath shook. "Is that enough to send him to gaol?"

"Snowley? Yes." The Runner pulled a pair of handcuffs from his pocket. "But since you also committed crimes, until your trial I'm afraid you must call Newgate your home, as well."

45

〰

"Don't cause any trouble," warned the guard, fingering his truncheon. "Full moon tonight, and the gaol's already so full, we have to stuff men in the women's wing. None of us are in the mood for your mouth or your machinations. Step out of line, and you'll live to regret it."

Adrian nodded his understanding.

Satisfied, the guard tapped his truncheon against the iron bars, then strode off to collect the next prisoner.

Adrian slumped onto the low, uneven wooden bench in his cell, his knees pointing up at awkward angles. He tried to keep the back of his new coat clear of the dusty stone wall, but to what end? Why bother if it was to become his bed tonight as well as his attire for tomorrow and every day forth?

He crossed his arms atop his jutting knees and dropped his forehead atop them with a frustrated sigh.

Do the right thing, he had told himself. *Be the hero for once.*

This was where it had led him. The trial wouldn't be for months, and it was unlikely freedom was on the other side. The Runners had assured him that cooperating with the Crown's long-sought-after prosecution of Snowley would at least let Adrian avoid the death penalty for treason.

But which was worse? The loss of his head, or the loss of his freedom forevermore?

"Marjorie," he mumbled into the shadows between his knees.

He'd left so much undone and unsaid. He should have kissed her one more time. Found the courage to say *I love you.* There might never be another chance to look into her eyes and express how he felt inside.

On the other hand, perhaps it was best for her that he'd guarded his tongue. What did he expect her to do, *wait* for a prisoner with a life sentence? Visit him biweekly and pat his hand through the bars?

It would be better not to see her at all than for her to see him like this. At least her final memory of him would be of a clean, well-dressed gentleman, sacrificing himself in the name of justice, and to save others.

Adrian supposed word of his latest scandal should be out soon enough. Like caged animals in the Royal Menagerie, the prisoners were on display to any onlookers who visited the cells. Once the court proceedings became public record, it wouldn't even be gossip, but actual fact.

Poor Iris. Adrian's past scandal was just that—*in the past.* This would dredge up all that old gossip and cause a new wave to come crashing down over the family. Just when he and Iris were starting to become close again, Adrian had managed to turn her life upside down once more.

A guard rapped his truncheon against the bars. "Stay back and stay silent, Webb."

Adrian nodded. He watched with envy as the gray-haired woman opposite was released from custody. While Adrian was being ushered into his cell, the woman's husband had arrived to post bail.

He wished he could do the same. The amount had been set at an astronomical sum. Treason did not come cheap.

A commotion sounded down the hall.

Adrian sprang to his feet and ran to the front of his cell. He gripped the bars as he strained to see what was happening.

No less than four guards were leading an unwilling prisoner in his direction.

Snowley.

Elation bubbled throughout Adrian's body as though his veins had filled with champagne.

They'd done it. Ha! Adrian might be stuck here in this hellhole, but so was the criminal long considered untouchable.

Snowley struggled against the guards to spit at Adrian as they dragged him past.

"I'm not done with you," Snowley called. "I shall have my vengeance. You will soon rue the day you dared to cross me. Wait and see!"

Adrian had, in fact, been ruing quite a few of the decisions that had led to his indefinite incarceration, but taking Snowley down with him was a silver lining richer than all the coins in England.

"Do your worst," he said under his breath.

There was no greater punishment than being separated from Marjorie for the rest of Adrian's natural life. What could Snowley possibly do to top that?

He found out the answer a heartbeat later when new voices sounded down the hall.

"*No,*" he whispered in horror.

This time, a single guard led a lone prisoner toward the empty cell across from Adrian. A woman with flyaway blond hair and terrified blue eyes and a lavender smudge on the pretty cheek Adrian had kissed mere hours earlier.

The guard tossed Marjorie into the cell without care or ceremony, then locked the door and strode on by, the keys to her freedom jangling at his hip next to his loaded pistol.

Adrian's knuckles were white as he gripped the iron bars. He wished he were strong enough to rend them asunder and release Marjorie from her cell.

"What happened?" he asked hoarsely.

"Snowley." Marjorie's voice was softer than Adrian had ever heard it before. A rustle of silk over tiny shards of glass. "He correctly determined that your cohorts in your grand escape were the Wynchesters. He couldn't name the others, but he could describe your apprentice in astonishing detail. If he's to be hung for his crimes...so am I."

"*No*," Adrian croaked, his throat too raw to make a single sound.

The dirt floor seemed to spiral out from under him.

Marjorie wouldn't be in gaol, wouldn't have met Snowley at all, if she hadn't been trying to put a stop to Adrian and his damnable forgeries. He'd turned himself in to the Runners with dreams of being the hero...and instead mired them both into an even worse nightmare.

He'd destroyed Marjorie's life as utterly as his own.

46

Marjorie stared bleakly through the iron bars. Adrian did the same from the gaol cell opposite.

This was not how she'd imagined they'd spend the night together.

Her expectations had been more in line with a celebration. A big meal with her entire family, more champagne, then off to the glories of a full-sized bed in which there would be plenty of room to pass the hours any way she and Adrian pleased.

Her insides felt cavernous. Being thrown in gaol was terrible for herself and so many others. There would be no more tutoring Faircliffe, and no more art classes with little girls.

There would also be several dozen defrauded women who would not have the opportunity to receive a replacement of their stolen jewelry because the two people capable of forging them were trapped rabbits awaiting a foxhunt.

"I'll get you out of here," Adrian mouthed from across the divide.

No, he wouldn't. How could he? If they both reached their arms through the gaps and stretched as far as they could, they wouldn't even be able to touch fingertips—much less save each other.

"How are your boots?" she asked. "They're not pinching your feet?"

He stared at her. "I will eat this boot, if it would help you—"

A guard strolled by, rattling his truncheon against each cell's iron bars as he approached. He paused outside Adrian's locked door.

"You got a lawyer, Webb?"

"That's Lord Adrian to you," Marjorie called out.

The guard ignored her.

"I have not," Adrian answered evenly. "Will I be afforded an opportunity to acquire one?"

"Most trials don't bother with representation for the defendants. Depends what you can afford."

Which, with all Adrian's finances still in France, was nothing.

The guard turned to Marjorie. "What about you, Wynchester? Got a lawyer?"

Marjorie shook her head. But her family had money. And contacts.

"She doesn't need a lawyer," Adrian called out. "She's innocent."

"Eh? Not what I heard."

"From whom? Snowley? You'd trust the word of a known criminal over the son of a marquess?"

"Ain't you in here because you're a known criminal, too?"

"I know my crimes and my accomplices," Adrian said firmly, not meeting Marjorie's eyes. "This woman was never engaged in illegal activity on Snowley's premises."

"Is that right," said the guard. "You'd swear to this?"

"I would." Adrian's eyes met Marjorie's. "Tell the magistrate."

The guard narrowed his eyes. "Humph. We'll see. Till then…" He ran his truncheon over Marjorie's bars. "You're here for the foreseeable future, duck."

She jumped backward before his truncheon could bang across her knuckles.

The guard chuckled and sauntered on down the row.

"Son of a…" Adrian growled. "The first thing I'll do when I get out of here—"

He broke off mid-sentence, the pallor on his cheeks growing deeper as he realized yet again that there would be no getting out of there.

"If they would let me pop over to the bank for a minute," Adrian jested weakly, "I could clear out my London savings account. There's not enough for either of our bail, but...I could buy you a nice prison frock?"

She frowned and tilted her head. "You've no money at all?"

"Not even a tin shilling. I had to take everything I owned with me." Adrian's eyes were hollow. "No term limit on a banishment."

Marjorie's heart twisted.

It wasn't that Adrian had wished to leave. It was that he hadn't believed any of the people he loved would have wanted him to stay.

He'd braved the return trip anyway, fully expecting to be shut out, not welcomed in. And now he was stuck here, far from family and far from home.

"I made something," he said. "I wasn't going to show you, but... you inspire me."

He reached into his pocket and tossed something small and gray across the divide.

Marjorie trapped the projectile in her palms.

It was a locket. A faithful replica of Bean's pocket watch case, if it had been made of lead and tin shavings instead of gold.

She undid the clasp. A choking laugh scratched her throat.

Rather than the hands of a watch, each side bore a miniature portrait of a face with pursed lips. The one on the left was presumably her, and the one on the right was meant to be Adrian. With the locket closed, their lips would meet, pressing them together in a kiss.

They were the worst portraits she'd ever seen in her life.

"I'm a sculptor, not a painter," Adrian said, as though reading her mind.

"I adore it." Her voice cracked. She pulled a guinea from her pocket. A real one, made of solid gold. "I'll pay you for it."

He shook his head. "Keep it. For free."

"Never undervalue yourself," she said fiercely, and threw the guinea to him. "You are worth far more than your family sees. Than the world believes. You always have been, Adrian. *I* see you. *I* believe in you. I..."

Love you.

She choked on the words, unable to squeeze them free from her tight throat. She closed the portraits to lock her and Adrian in an eternal kiss, and added it to the chain about her neck.

Did he realize he held her heart in his hand, as well as the guinea?

"Marjorie," he said, visibly gathering strength. "No matter what happens, I want you to know—"

Guards spilled into the passageway. Two new ones she didn't recognize.

One unlocked Marjorie's cell while the other tapped his truncheon against his palm.

She stepped back, alarmed.

"That's enough chatting, love." The one with the keys went in and dragged her forward by the elbow. "You want to come with me."

"Wait!" Adrian banged on his iron bars in panic. "Where are you taking her? On what authority? I'll give you a guinea to give us another moment together. If you so much as disturb a hair on her gorgeous head—"

The guard slammed his truncheon against the iron bars of Adrian's cell, cutting his words off mid-sentence.

As they led Marjorie away, she twisted backward in order to touch her chest and lift her hand skyward, trying her best to make the Wynchester salute, a gesture she and her siblings made when they felt something deeply or wished to make a solemn vow.

Distantly, she could see Adrian's arm rise through the bars, as if he had reciprocated the sentiment.

Barely slowing, the guards herded Marjorie through the connecting hall and into a private room.

Inside, the Duke of Faircliffe paced before a window. His posture melted in unconcealed relief at the sight of her.

"Marjorie, thank God." He held on to her shoulders and looked her up and down. "Are you all right?"

"I don't know," she said honestly.

"I'll leave you to it," said the guard, shutting the door behind him and leaving Marjorie and Faircliffe in privacy.

"What's happening?" she said in bafflement. "Did you bring papers that will allow me to spend my inheritance on bail?"

"You won't have to." He gave her a crooked grin. "Tommy came up with a plan."

"Tommy would," she said with pride. "She's been detained on countless occasions, each time under a different name."

"Exactly. *Different names.*" Faircliffe's eyes twinkled. "Snowley's complaint is against a *Mary* Wynchester. Who, in case you are wondering, is your twin. She has run off to parts unknown, confounding her beloved family, and causing nothing but strife for poor *Marjorie* Wynchester, who bears a superficial resemblance."

"Mary," she breathed. "That little minx."

"We have plenty of proof that you are not the same individual. Not only my word as a duke, and your siblings' word as your family members, but also the book club Mary attends on Thursdays, and the matron of an orphanage we might have recently helped to solve a problem. She *clearly* remembers how naughty your twin was." He winked. "You, my dear, are sweet Marjorie. Not at all the alleged miscreant the law is looking for."

"You mean... I can leave?"

"And never return." Faircliffe held out his elbow.

Marjorie hesitated before taking it.

As thrilled as she was not to spend another moment trapped in that cell, she had been with Adrian—who was currently out of his mind with panic and fear for her safety. This turn of events was as terrible as it was wonderful.

Marjorie would have to leave Adrian behind.

47

Long after the guards had taken Marjorie away, Adrian still gripped the bars of his cell, straining for any sight of her, for the sound of her voice. He rested his forehead against the cold iron and sucked in an uneven breath.

There was no way to know what was happening to her at the moment. And nothing Adrian could do about it even if he did. How he hated feeling this powerless! He'd meant to be the *hero*. And instead all he could do was press himself against the solid locked gate and pray.

A new sensation, that. It had been a long time since Adrian had held faith in anything.

Not until Marjorie.

She filled him with emotions he hadn't felt in years. Purpose. Happiness. Hope. She gave him a reason to keep trying, no matter what the odds. If the current road led back to Marjorie, Adrian would crawl through fire to get there.

If he wasn't locked in a gaol cell, that was.

Defeated, he let go of the bars and slumped back onto the low wooden bench. There was nothing to do but wait. For news of Marjorie. For his trial and sentencing. For decades of confinement.

There was no doubt the judge would find him guilty. Even though he'd been coerced into this particular felony, he had no expectation of leniency. People had believed the worst of him his entire life, whether it was deserved or not. His black soul was common knowledge, regardless of the truth. There would be no mercy.

A door swung open at the end of the walkway, followed by footsteps. Adrian sprang up from the bench and flew back to the bars.

Two guards approached. Alone. One had thick red side whiskers, and the other a long gray mustache.

"Where's Marjorie?" he called out.

"Far away from the likes of you," responded Side Whiskers.

Panic seeped into Adrian's bones.

"Please," he begged. "Where is she? What have you done to her?"

Side Whiskers rolled his eyes. "Ain't touched her. Went off with a duke."

"With a duke." Adrian sagged against the iron bars in boneless relief, doing his best to ignore the pang in his chest that said he might have already seen Marjorie for the last time.

He wished he'd savored the moment.

Side Whiskers smirked at Adrian. "Don't suppose you've got a duke coming to collect *you*?"

No, Adrian supposed he didn't. Not a duke, not a marquess, not a big brother . . . no one.

But he did have one card left to play.

"I can prove my innocence," he blurted out.

Side Whiskers's gray eyebrows shot up. "Hear that, Murphy? Our mate here is innocent."

"I have *never* heard that before," Murphy answered, deadpan. "Should we let him go, Craig?"

"My sister is holding evidence that proves it," Adrian insisted. "Send a man to speak to Lady Iris at the Marquess of Meadowbrook's residence. Tell her Lord Adrian personally requests she cooperate by surrendering the document in question."

"What's your little note say? *Wasn't me*?" Craig asked sarcastically.

"Tell Basil Newbury of the Bow Street Runners," Adrian commanded. "They'll send someone. I'm the—"

"Aye, we know who you are, mate. Don't mean you'll get special favors from *us*." Craig pantomimed a yawn.

Murphy lowered his voice. "But if there *is* such evidence...ain't it better if *we* find it, rather than the Runners?"

Craig brightened. "Might be a bonus in it, you think?"

Murphy tipped his head. "From this one's father."

If anything, the marquess would slip these gentlemen ten quid to put Adrian on the next boat to Australia.

But this wasn't the moment to argue.

"All right," said Craig. "We'll send a lad 'round to retrieve it. But if this paper doesn't prove what you claim it does..."

Adrian held up his hands, palms out. "It does. I swear it."

Murphy harrumphed. The guards continued down the walkway, inspecting one side of the cells before turning about and peering into the other side. It took ages for them to finally disappear whence they came.

Who knew if they would honor Adrian's request?

An hour ticked by, excruciatingly slow. Then two hours. He supposed the clock wasn't supposed to matter, once you were a prisoner. You had nothing *but* time. And yet it became the single most precious resource you had ever wasted.

When the door at the end of the walkway opened again, Murphy entered with an unarmed, well-dressed stranger. The men paused in front of Adrian's cell.

"Your lawyer," Murphy said as if bored.

Adrian had a lawyer?

"Did Iris send you?" he asked in equal parts surprise and gratitude before he remembered that Iris did not have the means to save herself, much less her brother. This was not the moment the old fantasy of familial reconciliation finally came true.

The lawyer's eyes were sympathetic. "Miss Wynchester sent me."

Of course Adrian's family had not come to his aid. The foolish hope was reminiscent of the gullible young buck he had once been, when he'd believed the elder brother he so looked up to would never cause him harm. That a father's love was unconditional.

Marjorie sending a lawyer was…so very Marjorie. Thoughtful, caring, helpful, stalwart. *She* was the family Adrian had always wanted and never believed he could have.

He still couldn't have one. Unless the Wynchester lawyer could perform miracles.

"Might my lawyer and I meet in a private room?" he asked the guard.

"No." Murphy chuckled. "You're *in* your private room. And that's only because we won't round up the drunks and whores until nightfall. Then you'll have plenty of company. If there's something you need to say, talk now. I'll be back within the hour, and you'd better be done by then."

Adrian gave a jerky nod.

The lawyer waited until Murphy was out of both eyesight and earshot before introducing himself. "How do you do, Lord Adrian? I am Noah Vick. I understand it has not been a good afternoon for you thus far, but I am here to change that."

"Have you much experience in these matters?"

"I recently obtained the release of a Miss Marjorie Wynchester, who had the misfortune of finding herself the victim of a case of mistaken identity. It appears a certain Leander Snowley mistook the diminutive blonde for her sister Mary, who shares similar coloring…and has fled to parts unknown."

Adrian's grin stretched across his face. So *that* was how they'd done it. Joy spread throughout his entire body.

"Your insistence Marjorie had nothing to do with you or Snowley will be instrumental testimony as well," Mr. Vick added. "She sends her deepest gratitude."

"And she sent you."

"And me," the lawyer agreed with a smile. "Miss Wynchester said you were family."

"You mean she said to *treat* me like family."

"No," Vick said softly. "She and two of her sisters informed me you *are* family."

Adrian's throat prickled and grew tight. The Wynchesters had vouched for him.

He was family.

"Well, my lord," said Vick. "How may I be of service?"

"Get me out of here," Adrian pleaded. "If you can."

"I've arranged for Tommy's release on a hundred and one different occasions," the lawyer assured him. "And under one hundred and one different names and guises."

That sounded like Tommy.

"I don't suppose any of those arrests were due to treason, high or otherwise?"

"Not as of yet," the lawyer admitted.

Adrian's spine slumped.

"Why don't you tell me about your case," Vick suggested.

"Marjorie didn't brief you?"

"She told me her side. I'm here to fight for yours. Start at the beginning."

The beginning. Very well.

Adrian went back seven years. He summarized the story of a young man so eager to please, he'd taken the fall for his elder brother without hesitation—or any idea how catastrophic that single decision would prove. How he'd been cut off and banished to the Continent. How he'd been forced to survive by his wits alone...and his art. That he'd lied to Snowley for years, but Adrian hadn't committed a capital crime until forced to do so at gunpoint.

Vick considered him. "Have you any witnesses we can call to the stand to speak to your character?"

Hundreds. Thousands. But few who would say *good* things.

As for the Wynchesters, Adrian had met most of them only in the past few days—and all under legally dubious circumstances. He would not beg them to embroil themselves in a web of lies on top of everything else they had done.

"There is *one* person who would defend me."

The lawyer looked pleasantly surprised. "Who is that?"

"Me."

Adrian was just finishing explaining about the parcel he'd sent Iris when the doors opened at the end of the walkway.

A bustle of activity spilled into the corridor. Murphy, leading Snowley in handcuffs. Craig, holding the sealed square of broadsheet aloft. Minutes later, a familiar Bow Street Runner entered the corridor.

"You called for us?" Newbury asked Craig.

"Thank God," Adrian said to the Runners. "This is evidence you need to see."

Adrian's lawyer, Mr. Vick, took the sealed paper from Murphy. "Where did your man find this?"

"In the home of Lady Iris, daughter of the Marquess of Meadowbrook."

"And how long has it been in her possession?"

"Since earlier this month. Her brother came to visit her the morning after he arrived on shore, and entrusted it to her for safekeeping before attending to a summons by Leander Snowley."

Vick turned to Adrian. "And why did you do that, my lord?"

"Because I didn't trust Snowley," Adrian answered. "I was afraid of being tricked into a situation I could not control, which is exactly what happened."

"My word is my bond," Snowley growled. "You're the knave who—"

"No questions for you at this time," Vick interrupted smoothly, then handed the square to Newbury. "Would you unseal this missive in full view of all the witnesses here?"

"It looks like a piece of newspaper." The Runner showed the square to his colleague and then carefully broke the seal.

A trio of coins and a few slips of paper fell into his palm as he unfolded the broadsheet.

"What date is the newspaper?" asked the lawyer.

Newbury checked. "July eleven."

"And the pieces of paper inside?"

"Receipts of passage for Lord Adrian Webb, from Paris to London, with a scheduled arrival the day the newspaper was printed."

"The same day her ladyship took possession of the items in question, as stated previously. Very well. Now that the seal is broken, can you tell us what is written on the broadsheet inside?"

"*My darling Iris,*" Newbury read aloud. "*I have been commissioned by a notorious criminal to create a custom work of art. I know that I should not keep such company, but the challenge of this particular project has proved too tempting to resist.*"

Snowley's face lined with confusion. "That cannot possibly be what—"

Vick shushed him and motioned for Newbury to continue reading.

"*Snowley has summoned me to create replicas of English coins. He assures me the resulting artistic representation will only be on display in his private chambers and not used for counterfeit purposes or otherwise leave his possession. I cannot trust him and fear he will hold me against my will if I rebel. I enclose a sample of the art to prove my words."*

"'Art'?" Craig said disbelievingly. "It looks like a counterfeit coin to me. You've just admitted in writing—"

"*Art*," Vick repeated firmly. "Each is marked with the symbol of the man who commissioned the work of art."

Snowley spluttered in fury. "They *what*?"

"There, in the coat of arms on the back," Adrian said helpfully. "You might need a magnifying glass to make it out properly, but every single re-creation bears Snowley's identifying seal."

Vick withdrew an object from his pocket. "I happen to have a glass."

The Runners took turns inspecting the tail of each coin.

Adrian held his breath. The letter had been written—and the coins minted—long before he and Marjorie had duplicated Snowley's ring. The result might not be precise... but it *was* uniquely identifiable.

Whether the gambit worked or not...

"It *is* your seal," Newbury exclaimed. "We've seen this exact symbol on every one of your contracts."

Snowley launched himself at the bars of Adrian's cell. "You Janus-faced, self-righteous son of a bitch!"

"So you *do* admit to hiring Webb to make counterfeit coins," Vick said smoothly.

"I admit to nothing!" Snowley spat.

"Fortunately, you don't have to. Not when you've already done so." The lawyer produced a folded piece of foolscap from his waistcoat pocket and handed it to the Runner.

Newbury unfolded the paper. "It's a contract, bearing Snowley's signature and seal—and Lord Adrian's signature as well."

It was? Adrian pressed his face to the bars.

The Runner scanned the contents. "This contract is dated the day after the packet to Webb's sister. It says in exchange for room and board, Lord Adrian Webb shall be employed indefinitely in the pursuit of an undisclosed project. He is not to leave the premises nor have access to a valet or other servants, but will be provided laundry services to include ironed cravats." He sniffed the seal. "This wax smells like rosewater."

God bless Marjorie and her forgeries. Delighted laughter threatened to spill at her ingenuity. She'd had the same idea, and left her "evidence" vague enough to cover any story Adrian might concoct. *And* she had the duplicate ring and the special wax to make it official.

"Your word is your bond," Murphy said to Snowley. "You said so yourself."

Snowley's face empurpled with rage.

Vick returned his glass to his pocket. "Well, that clears my client's name. Lord Adrian was hired to make artistic reproductions, which is exactly what he did. That Snowley then used my client's art to circulate counterfeit coins and defraud others... well. *That* is an act of treason."

Snowley looked apoplectic. Craig and the Runners dragged him down the walkway to his cell in a torrent of screamed insults.

48

Murphy and Craig looked at each other, then at the Runners.

Basil Newbury gestured toward Adrian's cell. "Unlock it."

The key had just released the locking mechanism when the doors at the end of the walkway burst open.

A guard led Iris into the passage.

"Adrian!" She raced toward his cell, her face streaked with tears. "I've been demanding to see you for the past hour!"

"It's all right, miss." Vick motioned her away from Adrian's iron bars. "If you would please step aside?"

Iris gasped. "Are they... Are you..."

Murphy swung open the door and allowed Adrian out into the walkway.

"I'm free," he said with joy and dizziness.

Iris fell into his arms. He held her tight.

"Thank you," he murmured into her bonnet. "Thank you for coming. Thank you for believing in me. Thank you for keeping the letter. Thank you for everything."

"I would never abandon you," she said into his cravat. "*Never*, Adrian."

"Nor I you." He patted her back. "I'm sorry I left you when you were a child."

"You didn't leave me. You were tossed out like rubbish. I'm sorry you were treated so shabbily." She pulled back to gaze up at him tear-fully. "I'm sorry I didn't fight harder."

"What could a thirteen-year-old girl have done against our elder brother and our all-powerful father?"

"Slapped them," Iris said without hesitation. "Bit them. Whatever it took to make them see that you're *family*. A human being that matters more than any stodgy old reputation."

They talked over each other joyfully, each promising to be a better sibling than before.

"Come." Vick ushered them down the walkway toward the doors. "This is a conversation that deserves to take place in the light."

When they were finally out of the prison, Adrian turned to his sister. "Thank you for giving me another chance."

"You gave *me* one when I needed it most." Iris wrapped her arms around him. "Thank you for being my brother."

He held her tight. "Always."

49

As happy as she was to be home, Marjorie could not stop worrying about Adrian. They'd commissioned the best lawyer in London, but high treason was not a crime taken lightly. She'd sent one last little forgery along, in case it could assist Adrian's case in any way. All that was left to do was wait for news.

Waiting for news was Marjorie's least favorite activity.

Fortunately, she needn't wait alone. She was in the sitting room the siblings relaxed in after meals and between cases. Tommy, Philippa, and Graham were at the big table working on their various projects.

Elizabeth and Kuni were just outside the open windows, in the rear garden, fencing to and fro across the grass. Good-natured teasing and goading insults punctuated their clashing swords.

Chloe and Faircliffe were snuggled up before the unlit fire, on one of the sofas. Chloe's back was to her husband's chest as he wrapped his arms about her. His soft embrace stretched the silk of Chloe's walking dress, making the ever-growing roundness of her belly all the more noticeable.

Marjorie wished above all things that Adrian were here with her. She was by herself on the sofa opposite her sister. Although she hadn't completed the current Then-and-Now project, Marjorie realized that soon she would have to paint another *After* portrait of Chloe and Faircliffe . . . and baby.

Not long ago, the thought of so much change would have filled her with anxiety and dread. But after the month she'd just had, Marjorie had discovered she was able to handle anything Fate decided to send her way. Infiltrate a criminal stronghold? Join a forgery ring? Evade gaol? Fall in love with a rakish scoundrel who secretly carried about a locket containing miniatures of the two of them kissing?

She had done all that and more.

Marjorie no longer feared life. It turned out, she was as resourceful and clever as any Wynchester, and stronger than she'd ever suspected.

"What are you thinking about?" Chloe asked.

"Adrian," Marjorie answered honestly. "And how I wanted to be the lead Wynchester on this case to prove myself as capable as all the rest of you."

"But you *are* just as capable," Faircliffe said in surprise. "All of you are the best at what you do."

Chloe smiled in agreement. "No job is smaller or less important than another."

The duke nodded. "It's like paints on a palette. They're all important. Sometimes you need to use certain colors more than others to paint a specific thing, but on the next canvas, it's the other way around."

Marjorie considered this idea. "We're like parts of a rainbow?"

"You *are* a rainbow," he said. "Every color is present in every refraction, even when invisible to the naked eye. This family wouldn't be a rainbow without every one of its hues, no matter how bright it shines that day."

Tommy and Graham came to sit at Marjorie's feet.

"You didn't have to prove yourself, you silly goose," Graham chided her. "You've been equally as important as the rest of us all along."

Tommy rested her elbow on Marjorie's knee. "I've donned thousands of disguises and never stop being me. You can only be true to *you*."

"Exactly." Philippa knelt on the floor beside Tommy and kissed her partner's cheek. "Because your you is the exact you that someone else has spent their life searching for."

Jacob ran into the room wearing a leather apron. "Has anyone seen Lord Fluffinghop?"

The siblings burst out laughing.

"I cannot wait to see the person Jacob has been searching for," Chloe said fondly.

Philippa touched Marjorie's shoulder. "You didn't do too badly."

Marjorie slanted her a sharp gaze. "He's in gaol."

"Bah." Chloe waved a hand. "Not for long. He's practically a Wynchester."

Mr. Randall, the butler, suddenly appeared in the doorway. "Right this way, then."

The siblings looked at each other in surprise. Mr. Randall rarely ushered guests into private areas without announcing them first and inquiring whether the family was receiving.

The butler stepped aside, revealing Adrian.

With a squeal of delight, Marjorie leapt up from the sofa, knocking her siblings asunder like so many dominoes. Or perhaps Tommy had been looking for a pretext to toss herself into Philippa's embrace.

Adrian sprinted across the room and swung Marjorie up into his arms. The rest of the siblings rose to their feet and clapped.

"You made it home," she said into Adrian's warm chest, squeezing him as though he could be whisked away on the wind like an autumn leaf.

"Thanks to you," he murmured into her right ear.

She tilted her head up to look into his face. Before she could do more than blink, he slanted his mouth over hers and sealed their reunion with a kiss she would remember for all time.

When she was flushed and breathless, he set her down and sank to one knee before her.

"Marjorie Wynchester," he began.

"Yes, I will!" she answered, pressing his hands to her bosom in joy.

"Let him ask," called Graham. "This part is nerve-racking. If he wants to do it in front of an audience, at least let us see him suffer."

Marjorie affected a serious expression and nodded. "I rescind my premature acquiescence."

Adrian began anew. "Although a small part of me will always miss the view of the fetid alley outside the glorified linen closet where we spent our last night together—"

"You're right," Tommy said, pitching her voice loud enough to ensure Marjorie could hear. "Ye gads, this is awful. I'm so glad we get to hear it."

"Taking notes as he speaks." Jacob's pencil whipped across one of the pages in his poetry notebook. "'Things Not To Say During A Proposal.'"

"—I would go anywhere, fight anyone, endure anything, if it gave me the chance to spend one more second with you."

"Give him credit," Philippa said. "He managed to turn that horrid opening into something romantic."

"I love you as you are and I'll love the woman you'll become through every phase of our lives. I only beg to be right there with you, at your side." He pressed her fingers to his lips and then took a deep breath. "Will you please make me the happiest of scoundrels by consenting to be my bride?"

"Can I answer now?" Marjorie signed with her free hand.

"Answer!" Kuni shouted through the open window.

Marjorie threw her arms around Adrian's neck. She sank down until she was seated on his knee, then leaned forward to whisper into his ear, "Only if you take me upstairs at this very moment and teach me to ride you during lovemaking, just like you promised."

"You...might not have whispered quite as whispery as you think you did," Jacob said.

Marjorie didn't care. She was already in Adrian's arms. He dashed out of the room and up the stairs to coax a yes or three or twelve out of his future bride.

All night long.

50

~~~

One month later

It took all of Marjorie's willpower not to jostle Iris out of the way and barrel past Adrian into the gorgeous apartment the moment he unlocked the door.

"Your view from this height is amazing!" she exclaimed in delight, dashing from window to window to take it all in. Paris stretched on in all directions, roof after roof and park after park and—oh!—the Seine, with its glittering ripples and glorious boats.

"Only you would judge an apartment by the sight of what's *not* in it," Adrian teased.

"The trimmings aren't half bad, either," Iris assured him. "You're certain you don't want them to go on the boat with the rest of your belongings?"

"The landlord has already agreed to purchase the complete set, in order to rent these rooms as furnished in the future," Adrian assured her. "Which means it's ours for the next fortnight, and then *yours* for months, if you like. The apartment is paid through the end of the year."

Iris had heard this promise no less than a hundred times on the voyage to France, yet looked as awestruck now as she had when Adrian first proposed the plan. Everything about her was fizzy and sparkly, as if sunshine were springing out of her in bright yellow coils.

"I'll be home before Christmastide," Iris said, as though she still couldn't quite believe it. "I promised Father."

Adrian had made no such promise, in large part because his sire had not thought to invite him. Nonetheless, things were not quite as frosty as they had once been. Iris had managed to convince their father that Adrian was not the monster he'd been made out to be, which had gained Adrian an audience with the marquess. He'd taken Marjorie with him.

The homecoming hadn't exactly been a whirlwind of tears and heartfelt fatherly embraces, but the two men were now on speaking terms again. The marquess had even attended Adrian and Marjorie's wedding.

Adrian's brother Herbert had not been invited.

It pained Marjorie to know that the rift in Adrian's family would likely always exist, but she also knew that true family was where one found it. Adrian had his sister, and he had the Wynchesters, and he had *Marjorie*, which, after seven years of drought, was a very large family indeed.

"All that Marjorie and I are taking with us," Adrian was telling his sister, "are my personal effects and the art supplies. Do you want to see my studio?"

Both women very much did.

Marjorie clapped her hands when she entered the large, sunny room. There were pottery wheels and worktables and a kiln and any number of tools of the trade, but what most caught her eye were the floor-to-ceiling shelves covering every one of the walls with row after row of artifacts from all over Europe.

"You *collected* these?" Iris said in awe.

"No," Marjorie corrected her as she turned in a slow circle. "He *created* these."

Adrian's face flushed red, but his body sparked with sprigs of peppermint. "Guilty as charged."

"Can I please keep one?" Iris begged.

"Pick anything you want." Adrian's tone turned teasing. "Just don't gamble it away for pin money."

"I no longer have to," Iris said primly, her cheeks blushing. She hurried to the wall of vases to make her selection.

Marjorie elbowed Adrian in the ribs. "She hasn't gambled since she lost to Snowley."

"I know," he answered. "But that's my sister. If I don't tease her about her sordid past, who will?"

Marjorie rolled her eyes good-naturedly. He was right. Siblings teased. It was part of the package. She supposed he'd missed that just as much as breakfasts and horse rides.

"You're certain your pin money will be enough?" Adrian asked more seriously.

Iris nodded. "Father has been surprisingly generous."

Once the marquess understood that he had effectively estranged the one child still living under his roof, he created a trust in her name. The money would not only provide stable income every quarter, but also allow Iris the independence she'd sought for so long.

When he'd learned Adrian had been sending money to the unwed mother Herbert had ruined, the marquess had also created a small trust in his grandchild's name, and instructed Herbert to do right by his daughter, no matter what scandal it might bring. Adrian had paid for crimes he did not commit for seven long years. It was past time for Herbert to be a man and prove himself worthy of inheriting his father's title.

The best part was that Adrian could now be an uncle, just like he'd always wanted. Twofold! He now had a niece on the Webb side, and Chloe's impending baby on the Wynchester side.

Marjorie turned to Adrian. "We needn't pack everything up on the very first day. Now that we're in Paris, I'd like to enjoy it. What should I experience first?"

His green eyes glittered wickedly. "Have you heard of the Moulin Rouge?"

* * *

Two weeks later

Now that Adrian, his funds, and the belongings he most cared about were back in England, he could afford to purchase Marjorie the house of her dreams—but they were already living inside it.

So he bought her a three-story art studio instead.

Thrice weekly, the duo taught public classes together. They also provided private tutoring, as well as monthly showings for other emerging artists. Between teaching and helping the Wynchester family with their cases, Adrian's life was full of purpose and meaning.

And romance. On the top floor of their art studio, Marjorie had painted Adrian a trompe l'oeil view of the alley he so missed behind Snowley's residence, as seen from the tiny window in the room where they'd first made love. There were flourishes of inside jests in the painting as well, such as Hippogriff soaring in the sky, and Piffle perched on the sill.

In the corner of the studio was a very real gingham blanket...and no sign of a picnic. It turned out that a large square of thick cotton indeed did an exemplary job of protecting Adrian's backside from floor dust.

One day, Marjorie would paint herself an *After* portrait, but she couldn't say when. Her adventures were still unfolding.

She'd shocked and delighted her husband by painting him a fantasy portrait of Marjorie performing nearly nude dances, like they'd seen at the Moulin Rouge.

Adrian had done one better by superimposing their faces on a traditional Etruscan pottery scene depicting graphic sexual acts.

When not teasing each other with words and kisses and scandalous art projects, the two divided their time among the bedroom, the studio, their volunteer work, their growing family, and the many cases the Wynchester family took on.

For a woman who had once hated the thought of change, Marjorie considered her new life to be very blessed indeed.

EPILOGUE

Early December

The Wynchester residence was abuzz with activity.

Iris stepped up to Adrian's side.

"Thank you again for lending me your apartment," she murmured. "The past three months were positively glorious. You are the best brother in the world."

"Stop thanking me," he admonished her. "I told you not to mention it."

"If it weren't for your help when I thought all was lost, I wouldn't now have my own apartment and financial independence. As well as a better relationship with Father than I ever dreamt possible. For all that and more, I will be grateful to you every minute of every day."

Iris was honored to be the newest member of Philippa's reading circle. Especially once she learned their meetings always included cakes and wine, scandalous topics, and the occasional questionably legal caper.

"Oh, there's Philippa," Iris said now. "I wanted to talk to her about setting up a children's reading circle. I don't suppose you'd want to be a patron?"

"A patron? I want to be a member!"

She widened her eyes in faux horror. "No boys allowed."

"Then I shall settle for patron. As long as it includes an outing with you afterward, where I can hear all about everything I missed."

She beamed at him. "Done. I'll be right back, after I talk with Philippa."

He watched her edge through the crowded, chaotic room.

Servants bustled about, loading up the carriages with valises. The family would be leaving just after dawn tomorrow to spend a six-week holiday in Balcovia, as the personal guests of Kuni's dear friend Princess Mechtilda.

Most of the family, that was. Chloe and Faircliffe would be staying behind because of the new baby. Which was the other reason for the send-off soirée currently filling the large salon.

"Dorian is so sweet," Adrian signed to Marjorie. At least, that's what he hoped he'd signed. He was still learning, and occasionally accidentally said things like "My orangutan is melting" when he meant to ask for a cube of sugar.

Marjorie leaned her head against Adrian's shoulder and smiled dreamily at the baby. "Is it too early to start a *Before* portrait?"

"Any excuse to create art is a good reason."

"I knew you would encourage me," she said happily.

What he wanted to do was enable her right upstairs to their connecting bedchambers, where they spent every night—and most mornings, and frequent afternoons—locked in each other's arms.

Faircliffe glanced up from his baby and met Adrian's eyes with a smile. "Still meeting me in the studio tomorrow afternoon during Dorian's naptime?"

"Wouldn't miss it," Adrian replied.

Jacob turned around from the conversation he'd been having. "Are you and Faircliffe planning another joint exhibit?"

Adrian shook his head. "We get together to paint a few times a week just for fun."

"It would be a shame to keep your finished canvases to yourself," Jacob said. "You're very talented. The world should know about it."

Adrian flushed with pleasure. He still wasn't used to receiving compliments about art of his own creation. "Thank you."

Elizabeth turned around and tapped her brother on the shoulder with the crook of her cane. "And it's past time for the world to see *your* poetry, don't you think?"

"What's that?" Jacob tilted his head as though in deep concentration. "I think Hippogriff is calling me."

As he slipped off toward the refreshment table, Elizabeth sent Adrian a disgruntled look. "The worst part is, he probably *can* sense the emotional state of his attack raptors from a hundred yards away."

Marjorie hooked her arm through Adrian's. "We each have our talents."

Elizabeth brightened. "Is my talent murder?"

Elizabeth always blustered like that, but Marjorie knew the truth. Her brilliant sister was more than fierce. Elizabeth longed to help people and yearned for adventure. Marjorie often thought Elizabeth could have run rings around the rest of them.

Softhearted, sword-wielding Elizabeth was amazing with Jacob's animals, could mimic with her voice the way Tommy could with cosmetics, could quote laws with Faircliffe or books with Philippa. Elizabeth was as brave as Kuni, as clever as Chloe, and, on days when Elizabeth's body cooperated, as limber as Graham.

The only thing holding her back, Marjorie suspected, was Elizabeth's unfounded fear that it still wasn't enough. She didn't see that by constantly trying to be bigger and braver and more belligerent, she was closing herself off from everyone outside the family.

Or maybe she *did* see that. And what she needed was someone just as big and brave and belligerent to knock down those walls and sweep her off onto a mutual adventure.

"Your talent is tenacity," Marjorie said firmly. "You learn things faster than anyone I've ever known. If you *wanted* to discern the inner feelings of attack hawks, you wouldn't rest until you figured out how to do it."

Elizabeth wiggled her eyebrows. "And now that you're married, you won't rest at all."

Marjorie's face went bright red. Adrian kissed her temple.

"I cannot wait to sail to Balcovia," Elizabeth said with a sigh. "I've always wanted to storm a castle."

"We're not *storming* the castle," Jacob reminded her, holding out a plate piled with cakes. "We're *visiting* it."

"Don't you dare spoil my fun," she grumbled as she accepted a cake.

Adrian grinned at her. "Wynchesters do impossible things every day. If your life's dream is to storm a castle, perhaps it will happen."

"Don't say that," Marjorie begged. "Now her wish will come true."

Elizabeth's eyes shone with mischief. "I vow to make certain it does."

Don't miss Elizabeth's story, Coming Late 2024

ACKNOWLEDGMENTS

As always, this book would not exist without the support of many wonderful people. My fabulous editor, Leah Hultenschmidt, who is always willing to hop on a call and chat things out. The team at Forever, including Dana Cuadrado. My brilliant agent, Lauren Abramo, for your wisdom, encouragement, and friendship.

My utmost gratitude to Rose Lerner, who makes every book better. Erica Monroe and my early reader crew—thank you so much for your feedback and enthusiasm. Enormous thanks also go to intrepid assistant Laura Stout, for being my right hand in the United States, handling everything I cannot from Costa Rica. All the co-writing dates with Alyssa, Mary, and Coven—you guys keep me grounded, and I love you for it. Thanks go to Darc, Lace, Shauna, Susan, and Team #1k1hr for the texts from the trenches and all the mutual support.

Muchísimas gracias to Roy Prendas, who makes every single day happy ever after. *Te adoro, mi poporico.*

Huge hugs also go to all the fans who suggested names for various characters! The delightfully dastardly thugs wouldn't be half so colorful without Christa Chilton, Diana Aden, Jan Watling, and Santa O'Byrne. And the baby's name is courtesy of Tina Hairston and Reinelle Barrett. My heartfelt thanks to all of you!

And my biggest, most sincere thanks go to my amazing, wonderful readers. You're all so fun and funny and smart. I love your reviews and TikToks and Bookstagrams, and adore chatting together in the Ridley.vip newsletter list, on social media and Patreon, and in our Historical Romance Book Club group on Facebook. Your enthusiasm makes the romance happen.

Thank you for everything!

ABOUT THE AUTHOR

Erica Ridley is a *New York Times* and *USA Today* bestselling author of historical romance novels. When not reading or writing romances, Erica can be found eating couscous in Africa, zip-lining through rain forests in Costa Rica, or getting hopelessly lost in the middle of Budapest.

You can learn more at:

EricaRidley.com
Twitter @EricaRidley
Facebook.com/EricaRidley
Instagram @EricaRidley